Meet Me at the
Seaside Cottages

JENNY COLGAN

Meet Me at the Seaside Cottages

HODDER &
STOUGHTON

First published in Great Britain in 2025 by Hodder & Stoughton Limited
An Hachette UK company

The authorised representative in the EEA is Hachette Ireland,
8 Castlecourt Centre, Dublin 15, D15 XTP3, Ireland (email: info@hbgi.ie)

1

Chapter opener images © Shutterstock

Extract from *Sandwich* by Catherine Newman published by Doubleday.
Copyright © Catherine Newman 2024. Reprinted by permission of Penguin Books Limited.

Lyrics from 'Tyrannic Man's Dominion' by Karine Polwart used with permission of
the author.

A CIP catalogue record for this title is available from the British Library

Hardback ISBN 9781399734226
Trade Paperback ISBN 9781399734233
ebook ISBN 9781399734240

Typeset in Plantin Std Light by Manipal Technologies Limited

Printed and bound in Great Britain by Clays Ltd, Elcograf S.p.A.

Hodder & Stoughton policy is to use papers that are natural, renewable
and recyclable products and made from wood grown in sustainable forests.
The logging and manufacturing processes are expected to conform to the
environmental regulations of the country of origin.

Hodder & Stoughton Limited
Carmelite House
50 Victoria Embankment
London EC4Y 0DZ

www.hodder.co.uk

Where my heart has room to grow
Where I can open up my hand
This space to be
In which to love and be loved
What's that worth to me?
What's that worth to us?
'Tyrannic Man's Dominion', lyrics by Karine Polwart

'I made your whole body from scratch – the least you can do is put some lip balm on it.'
Sandwich by Catherine Newman

I

'*B*erne?'

    The dark locks cascading down Essie Munroe's back retain just a bit of the expensive styling they'd had the day before, to tame them before the Burns Night charity ball, and she tries not to fiddle with them as she stands in front of her boss. He hasn't even asked her to sit down.

'So,' she says, keeping her voice absolutely level, which is difficult, because the party only finished at three a.m., and she vaguely remembers drinking something that might have been on fire. 'So . . . I'm moving to Berne?'

Essie's suave boss, Hari Mendip, looks at her with a hint of sad affection in his eyes. As finance bros go, he certainly isn't the worst. Her boyfriend Connor's colleagues are much worse. But even so . . .

They are in the smart boutique office in the West End of Edinburgh where Essie works. Nobody has changed the expensive lilies in a couple of days, and they are starting to smell weird. Belatedly, Essie wonders if this might have been a sign.

Even to Scottish people, coming from as far north as Carso, as Essie does, is pretty extreme, and Hari calls her Teuchteress (first having checked with her that she won't report him to HR, which is frankly very progressive behaviour for the industry).

'Teuchteress, where do you think Berne is?'

1

Essie bites her lip. She isn't from the kind of family that went on fancy foreign holidays, so the question makes her prickle. She doesn't have the faintest idea.

'Uh . . . Europe?'

'It's okay,' says Hari. 'There's no good way of saying this, Teuchs: you won't need to know. The news is right: I'm afraid we're relocating. The mother ship is calling us back home. And . . . we're going to have to do it without you.'

Essie is so stunned that it takes a moment or two for her eyes to start pricking with tears. She'd read the news alert first thing this morning, but she hadn't believed it until she'd got the text summons to come in on her day off.

It had taken her so long to get this job. Unpaid internships – where other people got their parents to pay their rent, she was working long shifts in bars and living off purloined peanuts, desperately networking and burnishing her CV and cosying up to posh people she had nothing in common with. Plus some begging.

'You can't . . .'

'Have you got French or German or Italian language skills?'

'I've got a phone with Google on it!' she says, defiantly.

She glances round the shiny glass office. It is incredibly quiet. People must be being summoned in one at a time. Starting with her. Bottom up, she realises. Get the bad news out of the way first. The ones coming in this afternoon will probably get a party. They'll go to the free-flowing champagne fridge Hari has in his back office and talk about mountains, tally ho.

She isn't going to cry. She isn't.

'When . . . when is this happening?'

'Beginning of March,' says Hari, trying to be hearty. 'Lovely for you! Take the spring off, plan your next move. There's a severance package.' Then he frowns suddenly and checks his laptop. 'If you've been here two years. Ach. Sorry.'

'But I'm . . . I'm good at my job.'

'You are!' says Hari. 'You'll find something else in five minutes!'

He is beaming at her in a way that suddenly makes her want to poke him with his poncy fountain pen.

'*Please* can I come to Berne?' she says, quietly, swallowing hard. It costs her a lot to say it.

'It's the other side of the Himalayas,' says Hari. 'You'd have to commute by elephant.'

Essie frowns. 'That's not funny,' she says.

'I know,' says Hari. He puts both hands down on the shiny boardroom table, lets his jolly face slip. 'Honestly, Essie. I have to spend today telling people with families, mortgages, kids, caring responsibilities that they're losing their job. I'm sorry. You're young, free, great head for figures, completely employable. I genuinely thought you would be the easiest.'

Essie nods. 'I'm glad you have faith in me,' she says.

'I do!' says Hari, surprised. 'I absolutely do!'

'Okay,' says Essie.

'You can look for another job using the resources here; we'll help as much as we can,' says Hari. 'Maybe not as a geography teacher?'

Essie tries to smile, but she doesn't make a very good fist of it.

'It's just losing your job,' says Hari. 'It's not the end of the world.'

Essie comes from the end of the world. She doesn't want to go back there.

2

At the end of the world, in Carso, Janey Munroe – her corkscrew curls just like her daughter's, if rather less glossy but instead tightly pinned back for work, her blue eyes shrewd, and certainly shorter in the eyelash department – is having a rather wonderful morning.

Her scrubs are turquoise with a navy trim, which she rather likes; they don't cling, but they do accentuate her softness and her large bosom. She knows her daughter Essie spends quite a lot of time in the gym trying to defeat this particular genetic quirk. Janey has decided to embrace it.

'Come on, then, let's be having you,' Janey signs with a grin to the tiny child she has in her clinic that afternoon. This is her very favourite part of her job, by miles.

As chief audiologist at the county hospital, she has her own consulting room, even if it is in a prefab shed. Most of her clients are either children or the elderly, so she has flowers and a big squishy bear called Frisko who wears hearing aids (in case you're feeling nervous and need something to cuddle). A surprising number of people, young and old, quite like clinging on to Frisko, it turns out. His nose is nearly worn away, and one of the women in Carso, where they are intense and competitive knitters, has knitted him a cheerful red hat with ear holes. He is quite a smart bear these days. In fact, she would quite like a

4

red hat for herself. She might mention it to the knitting circle. It would suit her dark curls, which, with a bit of cunning root-dyeing, still look pretty good. She knows they are a bit long for a woman of her age – Essie points it out quite often – but she is vain about her hair, if little else these days.

Janey spends a lot of time improving the lives of elderly people in particular; the small renewal of independence a better hearing aid brings is incredibly rewarding, giving people a huge fillip in wellbeing, even if the grumpy old codgers sometimes then complain that everyone is, in fact, too noisy and they're going to keep it switched off for the foreseeable. But that's alright too. After her dad died, ten years ago, her mum upped and moved to Spain and is living it up like nobody's business, which is great that she's happy, but Janey misses her.

Her very favourite times are days like today, when she joins the ENT clinic for babies who require aftercare for their cochlear implants. Implants aren't for everyone, and Janey entirely sympathises with people who do not think they are suitable for them or their deaf children and don't see being deaf as a handicap. Janey respects this a hundred per cent.

But for those who want them, it can be transformative, and this morning is one of those days.

Baby Ruaridh, the magnetic receiver on his head, looks around nervously, his large hazel eyes blinking anxiously as his mother strokes him reassuringly. His dad is filming the whole thing on his phone. The ENT consultant, Dr Joshi, a well-respected colleague of Janey's, nods at her as she hushes the room, and for the first time they turn the implant on.

The child's face is comically confused as his head shoots up, and his mother, her voice cracking a tiny bit, says, 'Hiya there, Ruaridh. Hello.'

The head twists as she moves him round to see her; his eyes go wider, if that were even possible. His mother kisses him.

'Hello, my beautiful baby boy. It's very nice to say hello.'

Janey has seen it a hundred times, and it gets her every time. Dad puts down his phone, eyes shining. 'Hey, wee man,' he says, clearing his throat. 'Hiya.'

The baby's head turns again, and he points a small chubby finger directly at his father.

'Oh, my God,' his mum says. Then, quickly, 'Sorry. That sounded like a swear. I don't mean it.' She turns bright red and buries her face in the neck of her goggling baby. 'Oh, my beautiful boy.'

Dr Joshi takes various notes prior to starting to run tests but glances up to say briefly, 'I believe everything seems to be working reasonably successfully at this stage,' in the quiet murmur Janey knows indicates he is delighted with the results.

So Janey is in buoyant mood heading off for lunch – until she remembers what's on the lunch agenda.

Her pace noticeably slows as she cuts through the hospital, which was put up shiny and new by one government, and left to lapse by another. The once-cheery wall paintings are looking a bit faded, particularly the mural of a group of children having a good time in a field, something everyone feels is a bit embarrassing anyway, as they can't imagine anyone, particularly children, wanting to be reminded that they aren't, currently, children having a good time in a field, rather than in hospital.

It is hard to talk about sex at the best of times, never mind when you're looking at a pallid omelette and a very wilted excuse for a salad. But her friends have decided it's time. After a rotten divorce, finally, it's time.

The nutshell version Janey has learned to spiel off – as if she doesn't care, it's all years ago, even though it can still wake her in the middle of the night as if it's happening that very day – is that Colin had an affair, they decided to stay together for Alasdair and Essie, their then teenage children, and then neither of them had been able to be the thoughtful, endlessly kind, unselfish outstanding citizens the counsellor and endless magazine articles had ordered them to be. Janey had been sad and snappy, then menopausal, which had taken sad and snappy and hurled in a touch of simmering rage; Colin had been unable to give up the other woman entirely, and they had bumped along for years trying to do the right thing, making everything worse day by day. Being a little older, Al was already one foot out of the door; Essie was right in the middle of enough teenage drama of her own without adding her parents to the mix, and, when Colin had filed for divorce the week after she'd moved to Edinburgh for college, it had cracked her world apart. Her dad had moved away, to a new build on a new estate with a new wife and, eventually, a new child, Logan, with whom he was utterly besotted.

Janey had had to give up the house and rebuild everything she had ever known, as well as taking the blame from Essie, who needed someone to use as a punching bag. What Essie thinks is more or less what Janey feels about herself – she should have been kinder, should have worked harder. It drives Al up the wall. And her friends, in fact, who are spending this lunchtime giving her an ultimatum: it is finally time to get back out there and date again.

Janey wonders what Essie will think about this, then discards the thought immediately. Essie will think it is gross, almost certainly. Her funny, contrary daughter. She hopes she's having a good day.

3

The real kicker is, Essie thinks, meandering very slowly back from the office, completely distraught, that the day had started so well.

She had woken up with a hangover, but a happy feeling when she realised where she was: her favourite place in the entire world, her boyfriend Connor's vast, beautiful apartment set high in Moray Place, in the heart of one of the world's most glorious cities: Edinburgh, Scotland.

Moray Place is the loveliest street – it isn't even a street; it is a circus, or circle, of huge grey stone houses laid out around a private garden. Cars aren't allowed all the way round, so it is a blissful haven of quiet in the noisy city, normally just busy with people recreating scenes from the many films and television shows shot here. Essie quite likes passing them, heading up to the shiny big black door as if she belongs there. It would be nice if she also had a key, but they aren't – she'd glanced at her blond boyfriend Connor, happily snoring next to her – they aren't at that stage yet.

She had nipped up to the huge bathroom with the vast claw-footed bath on the black and white tiles to make herself look nice before he woke up. They had both taken a day off, after the ball the night before, and thank goodness. She felt ropey but not too awful. The boys – Connor and his flatmates, Tris and Trumpet – had drunk a lot more. It was some finance-sponsored shindig, everyone in kilts. She'd worn a pretty red cocktail dress from Mulberry Walk – it had been far too much money, and she'd justified to herself that she'd wear it again but in the ceilidh it had got ripped and, well. That was what credit cards were for.

She had pulled the silk scarf out of her long dark curly hair and let it drop to her shoulders. It still retained the glossiness of the blowdry, more or less, and was still mostly ringlets. And getting the eyelash extensions had more than paid for itself; they made her blue eyes pop, even though her mother and her brother Alasdair both teased her about them. They were wrong – her mother was basically wrong about everything, so it was useful to listen to what she said, to give her a view from Opposite World – and she was right. She'd taken some tinted moisturiser out of her handbag – it would be very nice to have a drawer, frankly, but Connor gets a very haunted look if she mentions it, so she keeps all the essentials in travel size in her handbag so she can slip back to bed and pretend she wakes up gleaming.

Essie had admired the cornices as she put on a touch of under-eye concealer. This flat was so gorgeous. She is obsessed with property; her own flat is an overpriced shoe cupboard in an Instagram-gorgeous cottage in Stockbridge, the city's boho area, full of vintage shops and independent bakeries, where she tries not to get in the way of the owner, Persephone, who does quite a lot of performative yoga.

She can't envisage a place of her own. Everything in the city is crazy-making expensive, totally out of reach. Instead Essie often finds herself scrolling modern glass boxes with clean lines and no cupboards, with floating staircases and cathedral ceilings. Or she'll explore perfect little mews, cobbled and hidden behind the great terraces of Edinburgh, with planters outside and pastel doors. She looks at huge grand apartments with vast kitchens in dark blue; winding stone staircases; porticos in the sky; sunny balconies; private gardens which promise mysterious beauties and riches in the heart of the city. Despite the fact that her room at Persephone's has a tiny basement window that looks out over a pavement, she already has a view on whether a swimming pool in a home is too much trouble or not.

Of course house prices are astronomical, daydreams, but she so loves to have a sticky beak. Her mum has even said Carso prices were going up massively, and that's completely mad; who could possibly want to live all the way up there?

Early spring sun dappled the bathroom; they were higher than the trees in Moray Place park, the private gardens that only allowed entry to Feuars: local residents who held a treasured key. They had spent happy picnics there, long weekend lunchtimes with prosecco and expensive and delicious treats from Valvona & Crolla. She has liked Connor, his easy ways and his blond hair and rugby player's shoulders, ever since they'd met at some Young Financiers get-together at his office. And she fancied him rather a lot, she reminded herself, even before she'd seen his gorgeous apartment. Although he might have mentioned he lived in the New Town. Men who wanted to impress women normally did.

The first time they'd got together was one of the most romantic times in her life. On their third date, Connor had taken her back to his swanky West End offices, late at night.

'Come here,' he'd said. 'I want to show you something.'

And he had taken her to the back of the offices, behind the fancy flowers and polished dark wooden tables, to the old warren of servants' quarters, along the corridors and down a flight of ancient, forgotten worn stone steps.

'Look at this,' he'd whispered, and pulled open a back door she hadn't even known existed – and she'd gasped.

The door opened out of the back of the building, into the tiny cobbled mews behind. An old lantern glowed in the autumn dusk; there was not a soul in sight, nor a sound in the air, and the effect was akin to stepping out of the twenty-first century and into the seventeenth. He hadn't even known about her obsession with property; he'd got it right completely by accident.

'Isn't it amazing?' Connor had said as she nodded furiously. He'd opened another door just next to it – the original door had a code, but this was just an old wooden door you could walk past a thousand times and not notice it – and they'd found themselves, with the help of the torches on their phones, inside an old coaching loft.

Every other one of the buildings had, long ago, been converted into mews cottages and sold. This had to be the last one, so much money swilling about that it had never even been necessary; it had, in all likelihood, been completely forgotten about. There was a dusty earth floor, with, amazingly, an old carriage wheel, bolts and chains for the horses set in the walls and, up a very old rickety wooden flight of stairs, a hayloft.

'You are kidding me,' Essie had said, in shock.

'Roll in the hay?' Connor had said, his blue eyes sparkling, and she'd laughed, couldn't help it. For once, she'd found herself thinking less about potential and whether or not the property had good bones, and more about his big blue eyes, and obvious excitement. He had moved towards her and she'd pushed his blond hair off his face, and he'd kissed her strongly with his wide passionate mouth, and when they finally broke apart she had looked at him, flushed and full of lust, and said, 'Are you serious right now?' and he had hummed the tune of an old, old song, 'Little Red Corvette' at her, and his eyes had flicked upwards.

'How many women have you taken up to the hayloft?' she'd giggled.

'None!' he'd insisted. 'I'm just hoping the ladder holds!'

And he was so adorable that she'd decided that she would believe him. They had crept down later, covered in dust, giggling their heads off.

★

Connor works for a boutique firm for ultra-high-net-worth individuals, very closed and exclusive, which his friend Tris had set up. Her dad thinks it is a smart venture, and that matters a lot to Essie. Originally Essie had thought Connor's living and working with his old schoolfriend was very cute. That was before she'd spent much time with Tris. Connor is a sweetie-pie, everyone agrees. She likes his gentle manner, the way he puts up with teasing, his kindness. And what he stands for: money, security. After her dad left, her mum made such a hash of everything. Losing the family home; so many of their things had had to go. Essie wants something solid to come back to. Or she'll be like her mum: left with absolutely nothing.

Tris is another story. The fly in the ointment.

'Morning, Yoko,' he'd said this morning. It was meant to be an affectionate nickname but she hated it. He'd nodded over to the coffee machine at least.

'Would you like one?' she'd offered.

'Flat white,' he says, as if he's at Black Sheep. 'How's Sleeping Beauty?'

'Still sleeping.'

Tris had shaken his head. 'No stamina, that boy. I'm guessing you've seen the papers?' He'd smirked in a way she didn't like and turned his iPad towards her, and she had read the financial news headline, first in confusion, then in shock and disbelief.

And now, three hours later, here she is. Connor, she realises, hasn't contacted her. She can't call her dad as he's away with the new family. And soon her mother will hear the news and Essie realises she just doesn't know what to do.

4

'Okay, it's MOJO TIME,' says Lish, Janey's best friend at the hospital, shoving over the dating app. She has filled in most of it already. The problem is, Lish is a midwife, and a superb one, which means she has developed over the decades a certain way of telling you how to do stuff that you just obey without question. It's in the tone of voice. Mind you, as Essie is always telling her, and not as a compliment, she herself has been known to talk incredibly slowly and distinctly in order to make a point.

'I don't know how it happens,' says Janey, shaking her head and diverting her attention to the laptop and the app that is absolutely guaranteed to find her missing mojo, although she's not a hundred per cent sure she didn't pack it off to the charity shop when she moved. She got rid of a *lot* of stuff. 'But every time I have to write down my age, I think I'm thirty-five. I can't help it. Inside I am absolutely thirty-five.'

'You look thirty-five,' says Lish automatically.

'*You* look *twenty*-five,' says Janey quickly.

'You look like you're still at school,' says Lish. 'You could sneak in and re-sit your Highers.'

'Oh, lord, no thanks,' says Janey, who still occasionally has anxiety dreams about her exams, even though when she sat her school exams they all had perms.

14

'Well, anyway,' Lish continues kindly, 'stop worrying about it. Being in your fifties is cool now. Everyone is at it. J.Lo is at it. Look at Aniston. Bullock.'

'I don't want to look at them. They make me feel bad.'

'Gillian Anderson?'

'Oh, God, stop it. I'm just saying, it's fine; I feel fine about it. I just forget, that's all.'

'Uh-huh.'

'I just don't know why I feel exactly the same age I was twenty years ago. Do you think everybody does?'

'Of course,' Lish says, nodding wisely. Nodding wisely is also an exceptional midwife skill. 'Evolution doesn't need you to know how old you are. By the time you're thirty-five you've either reproduced the species or not. It has no more use for you. You can basically die now.'

Janey makes a long fuffing noise. 'Can I *identify* as young?'

Lish glances round the cafeteria. 'Come on. Before Milton gets here. You know he won't approve.'

Milton the porter tries his best not to look shocked about divorces and ribald talk; however, it is more or less unavoidable where they work, in a hospital full of women, dealing with very much the pointier end of the human experience, particularly the female experience, day in, day out.

Janey really does not want a single person more to know what she's doing, which is why they chose the special low-lit breastfeeding canteen corner the hospital built at great expense, whereupon everyone revolted about why they should have to cover up breastfeeding and started doing it in the middle of the foyer on purpose to set a good example, so hardly anyone ever goes there.

'Okay,' she says, pressing the button on her laptop. 'Let's have it.'

'MATCHES FOR YOU' flashes up on the screen.

'I think I'm going to be sick.'

'Come on,' says Lish, squishing her over. 'Maybe Pedro Pascal is passing through and has set his parameters to local.'

Janey nods. 'Probably.'

'Or for sure there'll be a stray billionaire who has left the shallow confines of the city in secret for some real people who love him just for him. Who wants to chop wood and stuff.'

'Of course most billionaires fancy women in their fifties,' says Janey. 'That's why you see them out with their middle-aged wives so much.'

Lish holds up her water bottle. 'To Pierce Brosnan,' she says, not for the first time, and Janey raises hers and clinks back.

'To Pierce. And Keanu.'

'Practically a trend,' says Lish.

Janey blinks at the screen. Then they both put their glasses on.

'Oh, God,' says Janey. 'Oh, lord.'

'Who?'

'That guy used to be Essie's modern studies teacher. Mr Harris. No way. Oh, my God. She hated him so much. She says he used to pick his nose at them while he was teaching.'

'It doesn't say that in his profile. It says he likes gardening.'

'NOSE-GARDENING!'

'You can't be too picky.'

'Tell *him* that.'

Lish smiles, but moves on.

'Is that Radge Jack?'

It is indeed the famously grumpy local groundsman. He is posing with a dog, which obviously someone has told him is the right thing to do for a dating profile, except that the way the photograph is angled, the dog is enormous and he looks absolutely tiny, as if he's going to ride the dog like a horse.

'I didn't know Jack was looking for a girlfriend,' says Janey. 'I thought he hated all humans. That's how he behaves, anyway. My God, these are slim pickings. Please. Please just show me somebody I don't know.'

'Everyone is famous in a small town,' says Lish. 'And Carso is such a very, very, very small town.'

★

Amsan and Milton spot them and appear with their trays. 'Why are you hiding over here?' says Amsan immediately, putting down her passive-aggressively large bowl of salad and oversized Stanley water bottle. 'Are you doing something weird like going on dating apps or something?'

'No,' says Janey hastily.

'Good,' says Amsan. 'Because my Yasmin put a profile up on one, against my advice, and she wrote as her last line in her description, "Also I have a tail."'

Janey is confused.

'She just wanted to see if men read to the end of the bios or just went by the photos.'

'And . . .?'

Lish blinks and says, 'Don't tell me. Not a single man asked her if she actually had a tail.'

'Not a single one,' says Amsan smugly, and cracks open her Tupperware as if this settles the matter.

'Oh, God,' says Janey. 'This just gets worse and worse.'

'You said—' begins Lish.

'I know what I said!' says Janey. 'That's before I got so old!'

'You said, in the depths of divorce misery, during which we were all extremely patient and sympathetic, you may recall . . .'

'I do,' says Janey. She does.

' . . . that once you were properly in your new house, we could do this . . . Has Essie seen the house, by the way?'

Janey shrugged. 'Oh, you know Essie. She'll probably send me something expensive and tasteful.'

Lish nods sympathetically as if she understands, but she doesn't really. Her kids still live in Carso; Willoughby is the pharmacist; Emma is expecting.

'She never tells me anything,' says Janey, trying to make a joke of it. 'She talks to Al more. I am glad she's happy. I am. Honestly. It's only my repulsive old neck that's giving me all the grief. And being fifty-five when every bit of me that isn't the mirror is absolutely convinced I'm thirty-five.'

'Write that you have a tail,' instructs Amsan. 'Yasmin got all the no-strings guys.'

Janey groans and lets her head slip to her desk. She gets salad cream in her hair and decides it counts as a conditioning mask.

5

It has been a long day, and Janey is happy to get home to the row of tiny stone cottages, which look as if they were built like an afterthought, a sentence petering out.

Once upon a time people came to Carso, which can be described as a town if you need to show a stranger you know how to order a complicated coffee, or a village, if you ever feel called upon to stress your *Outlander* credentials – to build holiday homes.

Big houses too. Carso sits on the very north edge of Britain, higher than the Highlands, where the swirling waters of the Atlantic and the North Sea meet, and do their best to whack the earth to bits.

The big sandstone houses there, all along the shoreline, were built by stout Victorians who were happy to breathe the clean air and never once anticipated that people would seek out sunshine to take a holiday – that people would even have holidays – or that women would, heaven help us, expose their bare limbs to get bronzed. On purpose! The very thought!

So: there are large, comfortable homes for trips that involved shooting and hunting and wearing rather a lot of heavy tweed, which were constructed with money from various nefarious places and means; and then, behind them, the old stone cottages that had been there to start with and were used for staff who did not live in, or people who did the everyday fishing and weaving, built with the crumbs that fell from the master's table. And although those Victorian homes still stand, proud against the storms, red sandstone blasted by salty air, their vast rooms and untuned pianos are hard to heat, the plumbing temperamental; they require maintenance and upkeep from a generation more interested in being somewhere warm, with cocktails.

But, oddly, the little cottages, the rough little homes, seem rather sweeter. If you don't look too closely and see the dilapidated paintwork. They are protected from the full force of the sea's rage by the large houses in front of them, sheltering them from the storms; they are on a quiet street because the road was paved so late – who, after all, wants to visit the cottages of the poor? – and nobody has ever bothered to lift the cobbles, which gives the street a pretty air, as does the old wrought-iron lamppost at the end that Janey adores even though it is rusting and faded, which is just as well, as it is where she has washed up, after a divorce that was not so much a bitter conflict as much as trench warfare that went on for so long that both sides eventually surrendered from sheer exhaustion.

The cottages aren't connected to the gas mains, and they added indoor plumbing extremely late; indeed, they all still have a shed outside that once held a dunny until the council, exasperated, came and took them away. It was pervasive for a long time, the idea that it was incredibly unhygienic to use the toilet indoors.

But the street itself . . . as you walk down it, the dusk settling in around you, pink cutting through the softest grey, a faint navy growing through the bottom of a clear sky, it feels as if you have strayed from the modern world altogether – something that already increases with every step you go above

Inverness. And there is nothing that underlines this feeling more than stumbling on this tiny little lane, untouched by time only by weather; unchanged by wars, by the break-up of the land, by the storms and warfare that swept over it. When you look at this street, Seagate, anyone could step out from one of the old weathered wooden doors: a Highlander off to fight the dreaded Campbells, a washerwoman, a young man off to war, a boy of twelve about to join the fishermen, or a young one off to join the great Victorian expeditions to search for the Northwest Passage; any one of them might seem equally likely, as if the tiny street were dropped out of time, completely oblivious to modern concerns, even as the grass grew between the cobbles, and most people clattered past to the main shore road and didn't even notice it.

And these days Janey tries to be proud of what she's managed to achieve here, from the ashes of the settlement. Hers is the only finished house next to the very run-down batch of four; it's the smallest, at the end, but the windowsills and door are in a pale, pretty, optimistic blue. You'd have to look very closely to notice that they are quite badly painted, possibly by a slightly annoyed midlife woman who has just gone through a divorce (window frames), and her slightly more practical son (doorframe), but they are painted nonetheless.

Alasdair, her son, is in fact standing there. This is unusual. She's used to seeing him on a Sunday for lunch, and occasionally a weekend night if he's hungry and his terrifying girlfriend Jacinta has served him up one single tiny bowl of salad, as per, but six p.m. on a Tuesday is a bit unusual.

'Have you seen this?' he starts, walking up to her. 'Also, answer your phone.'

'It's a soundproofed room,' frowns Janey. 'Shut up about the phone.'

She has actually had a good afternoon; she feels constantly sorry for her tinnitus patients, who come looking for a cure when she has little to offer them; but Big Mad Jim Eckles, father of Wee Jim Eckles, who is about six foot eight square in his stockinged feet and works the rigs, had turned up, smelling of engine oil and weed as per, but minus his usual glowering. 'Tell you what, doc,' he'd said (she isn't a doctor), 'those pointy needle things worked a charm.'

'You're kidding,' she says, genuinely delighted. Tinnitus is one of the few branches of medicine where they encourage any alternative remedy of any kind that might help people deaden the buzzing or whistling that lives in their ears, threatening to drive them mad.

'Sticking me full of pins aye right enough!' he chuckles. 'A few of my exes wouldnae mind.'

'Perhaps they could volunteer and take it in turns,' says Janey.

Big Jim frowned. 'Yeah, but they've got to be wee pins,' he says. 'Moira would come at me wi' a chisel. Again.'

And she had sent him off, happy he was finding a way of coping.

Now Al was brandishing his iPad at her, getting her to look at the *Financial Times* of all things.

STIRLING CAPITAL TO PULL OUT OF EDINBURGH BASE
Job Losses Expected

Janey frowns. 'Hang on, does this mean . . . I mean, is Essie going to lose her job?'

'Dunno,' says Al. 'She hasn't told me anything. But if there're going to be layoffs . . . '

Janey squints at the tiny text. Stupid thing. She puts her glasses on and tries it again.

'They're moving to *Berne*? Where even is that?'

'Switzerland.'

'She's moving to Switzerland?'

'I don't know; she hasn't called me. Has she called you?'

All of Janey's good feelings from the day slowly drain out of her. 'No,' she says, trying to keep any disappointment out of her voice, make it sound like a joke, which it doesn't. 'No, of course she hasn't.'

'She will,' says Al, stoutly.

He knows it was easier on him, a couple of years out of the house before the actual divorce. He lives in Caithness, in a scruffy little cottage. He has the family look, of dark curly hair and blue eyes, which along with his Highlands accent and Land Rover makes him absolute catnip to a certain type of generally blonde, sexy, very skinny posh English women. He can't resist them either. There's been an endless parade of Harriets and Juliets and Tamaras and Jacintas through the door of the cottage. When his mum and sister aren't there to take the piss, he's been known to wear his kilt to work, and not just for parties and weddings; it drives the girls wild. They generally retreat to somewhere with a Harvey Nicks eventually, and Janey has tried to befriend them, but normally without success. They are quite enamoured of a Highland lad with a rugged outdoor job and a twinkle in his eye, but they're notably less fussed about his mum, who has a comfortable bosom, a good recipe for chicken pie and an enviable number of points on her Boots Advantage card. They don't last for long, but they tend to buy Alasdair incredibly expensive gifts for Christmas. He has an unusually nice collection of watches for someone who works for the council.

Also, he has possibly a clearer-eyed view of Colin's behaviour than Essie, who idolised her dad. Colin's affair knocked the stuffing out of his mum, completely messed up her confidence, and it felt as though his dad then got annoyed with his mum for making him feel bad. They should have broken up years before. And he wishes Essie hadn't blamed Mum. She can be a right brat about it, even now.

'Let's call Essie,' he suggests.

They do.

She doesn't answer.

6

It is three weeks later, and Janey is telling herself yet again that she's not going to ask her daughter, as she drives home from work to the cottage. She has noticed that a For Sale sign has finally gone up on the crumbling cottages beside her. They're in a terrible state; it's partly how she was able to just about afford her tiny place next to them. But these were incredibly dilapidated, even if they looked pretty from a distance, or if you squinted. There was glass broken in the windows; cracks running down the outside of the ancient rendering. Old Mrs MacAleese, the last of the family to live in the cottages, hadn't had the wherewithal to look after them, and living so close to the sea is hard on buildings; hard on everything, the wind and the water and the salt.

But these days, it seems, housing is all anyone talks about. How much will they go for? Will a developer swoop in, splash some grey paint on them and turn them into short-term holiday rentals, which means instead of three families moving to the area to work and grow and have children and support the school, they will get rented a week at a time from May till September by people who drive up in their Land Rovers full of shopping from Waitrose and sit in the garden playing music, sloshing wine and loudly complaining about the midges and the lack of local amenities.

Janey will have to go online and see what they're on for. Which is a truly shameful habit that she would not confess to anyone she knows, even though she suspects everyone else does it too and in fact Googling how much other people's houses are worth might be the default for anyone with an address. She doesn't mention it just in case it's her being weird, like that time she said she could see what people saw in Jeremy Clarkson and nobody would speak to her for a week. That was when Lish started making the first noises about how she had to get back out there and brought up the whole dating app fiasco.

Janey gets into her wee car, tucking her dark hair behind her ears and trying to make a mental note to pick up some root dye plus something that will tame the frizz . . . Essie would know. Young people know everything about beauty products now, despite the fact that they don't actually need them. They know about phone filters too, something Janey wished she did. All Essie's selfies with her friends look like Bratz dolls, not something Janey had anticipated when she bought the pencil cases.

Still, she thinks. She has her car. It has taken her so long to pay off her debts after the divorce, plus Essie's university, that this is the newest car she has ever owned, or, well, leased at least, and she loves it dearly, even though it is the blandest, most common car on the road, just a wee Kia. But it is hers, and it isn't constantly terrorising her as to whether it is going to limp through its MOT, and it is, to her constant secret joy, bright red. Colin would have hated it. Every car he has ever had has been silver.

She pootles home from the T&C – their hospital serves a very large area and is called the Town and Country; affectionately known as the T&C, or the Tired and Cranky if you've been on a long Saturday night shift. She tries not to be smug that she specialises in audiology – she doesn't work on call, or Sundays, something all the others, particularly Lish in obstetrics, love to remind her of if she ever dares to complain about anything, as apparently she doesn't know she was born.

And it is true, she does love it: she mixes up in-hospital appointments with going out into the community, trying to help people do the best they can with what they have; and lots are grateful, and some not so much, but that's okay too. Some people get given a tough road. She feels she knows a bit about that.

But tonight, the drive, just as the sun is setting, with everything good ahead – long, light nights are coming; they are further north than Copenhagen and Moscow – and the colours of the hills on the single-track roads – there is an A-road, but it is dull and clogged with tourist campers – is beautiful and ever-changing. And if you get stuck behind a tractor, well, you get stuck behind a tractor, and can slow down and enjoy the hedgerows bursting into life, the early swallows swooping down on freshly planted fields looking for a feast, the copses of hardy trees starting to show their newest greens, or the bursts of pinkening sky throwing dramatic shadows through the immaculately planted geometric shapes of the fir trees.

And the earliest lambs are here! Which is troubling, really, as they are very early indeed. But even so: as harbingers of spring, these little creatures never fail to enchant. Today after rainfall there is a large muddy puddle at the bottom of McPherson's second field, and three brave ones are huddled, leaping over it, watched over by their attentive mamas standing back, looking exactly like women at a playground waiting for their children to give up on the slide before someone gets hurt.

She slows down – there isn't another car to be seen for miles; 'rush hour' is when a timber truck passes through – to watch for a little while. After some tentative baaing, the bravest takes a leap, and lands, with a comically surprised look on its face, right in the middle of the puddle, its immaculate white coat spattered with brown. *Your mum is going to be very cross with you*, she finds herself thinking, stupidly, before moving on again.

She wonders how Essie is. Al has ascertained that she's lost her job but maybe she's finding another one really fast? Or has lots of money saved? She was certainly making enough. Janey has asked her how she was getting on but has got the usual one-word answers. She can't imagine her parents ever did that with her, did they? They saw her all the time anyway. Her mum worried, of course; she never liked Colin. Did she listen? Did she stuff.

The stupid thing is, she remembers being Essie's age, not feeling terribly attractive, just a trainee nurse, not one of the fun party girls at all: mousy and awkward. She looks back at the photos now and she can see she was perfectly lovely: she had a nice slim figure – they wore proper dress uniforms in those days with the elastic belts, which were so flattering – and shiny hair and that fresh young skin. She was gorgeous! Why didn't she know it? She was always hiding what she thought were her big thighs. Honestly, she was insane. She should have worn nothing but slip dresses and heels and miniskirts and swimsuits the entire time. Not that that was incredibly conducive to living on the north coast of Scotland, it's true, but honestly, if she had that figure now she would run about half-naked the entire time and catch her death, who cares?

Of course she tried to tell Essie how gorgeous she was, all the time, but it never quite seemed to work. Essie complained she was trying to control how she dressed or something, and then she put herself into huge hoodies all the time that made her look as if she was incredibly sad about something.

Her Spotify shuffle in the car throws up an old Deacon Blue song Janey didn't like very much. It's the weirdest thing, she thought. The songs you absolutely love, well, you've played them half to death. You can't remember where you first heard them; you associate them with all the different times in your life because your desert island songs follow you wherever you go, from LPs to cassette tapes, to CDs to Napster – bloody hell, Napster, that makes her feel old – all the way to Spotify.

But the album tracks she didn't like, the singles she felt weren't worth her £1.25 at Woolworths – they're the ones that hurl her straight back into exactly where and who she was when she heard them; in this case, at the school dance, with big Alan, not to be confused with Wee Alan or the Allan with two 'l's. She smiles to hear it again, smelling Impulse Black in the air – they don't make it any more and Essie used to fall out with her if she bought anything that sprayed. But it took her back anyway. And reminded her just how very long ago it was. And how she hopes Essie is making a better fist of it than she did.

*

'Babe, you are going to be fine.'

It isn't Connor's fault, not really. Life has been mostly kind to him, and, as with many people who find life kind and are sunny in return, it works as a virtuous circle. He is finding Essie's worry concerning, but if everything went wrong for Connor he'd just move back to his parents' huge house in Perth, or they'd find him something, or someone from that posh school he went to would give him a job.

Essie on the other hand is looking, frantically; nobody is hiring, and Stirling Capital's move has had a huge effect on the market, as though the big ship has gone down and everyone is scrabbling for the same lifeboats. There are some entry-level accountancy jobs, nothing at all like the fun, fast-paced investment desk in the West End, with its free Nespresso dispenser and fresh orchids on the desk. These jobs are in great big industrial estate behemoths, way out beyond the reach of the tram, on the other side of the bypass, and mainly consist of adding up student loan payments.

Everyone, including Connor, assumes she has some savings from her well-paid job.

Everyone is wrong.

Essie can't believe it herself. Money had always been tight growing up; she had been so excited to find she actually had some. She had needed new clothes and of course there were the minibreaks with Connor, who assumed her family was well-off, more or less, because she had a nice accent; the nights out at trendy George Street nightspots, the Ubers . . .

And the rent on her beautiful, if tiny apartment, the little raised colony house down by the Water of Leith – where, if you ignore how tiny it is and just focus on the views, she can imagine herself living the dream.

Her mother had always been much more make-do-and-mend, and Essie has just been so keen not to have to do that any more that she hasn't put aside enough for a rainy day. She hasn't put aside a red cent.

Connor heads off to rugby training, kissing her on the head and giving her shoulder an 'it'll be alright' squeeze – which is, she has already ascertained, not at all the same thing as a 'move in with us for a bit' squeeze. They are only in their mid-twenties; it's a bit soon for all that. Plus it's Tris's flat and he has a strict bros code.

Essie opens her laptop, takes a deep breath, and once again starts searching for a cheaper place to live.

At first, she had thought it would be easy. She had started two weeks ago, and at first, as she pushed the button, loads of properties had popped up all over the map, right in town.

Then she looked closer. These were 'flats to rent', alright –
but they were only for a night. Or a week, at most. They were
all on Airbnb or other rental sites, all short-term, all completely
unsustainable. Some are as expensive as hotels.

That couldn't be right, she'd thought, looking closer. It
couldn't possibly be . . . there were flats she could see that she
had known were once rentals; had had friends staying in them,
long term. But now, they were all there for one-night visitors;
people coming into town for fun or a stag night or a brief trip,
who didn't mind paying a bit more.

Of course, she and Connor had . . . loads of times – gone
on minibreaks and stayed in other people's places, in Paris, or
Prague; they were often lovely and they'd congratulated themselves on getting to stay somewhere so cool when travelling,
cheaper than a hotel . . . but that had been then. She'd never
really thought what it meant back in the place she actually
wanted to live.

She had shut down that window; started again, looking for
long-term rentals.

There was almost nothing in the city. Nothing at all. It was
as if an entire sector had disappeared. Everything available was
miles away. And so incredibly expensive, so much so that she'd
realised she was practically getting a bargain in the lovely colo-
nies place in Stockbridge. All the flatshares she looked at – she
started off looking at studios, but ruled that out very quickly
– were hundreds and hundreds of pounds, and every time she
called one that had just come on, it was gone already. The couple she did manage to get to see were in scary old tumbledown
buildings, miles from anywhere, filthy dirty and with creepy
older men already ensconced there. And even then, they still
cost a fortune. And, whoops, they're gone.

Her college friends have scattered far and wide, many to much cheaper areas of the country where they have mortgages and, in some cases, babies on the way, and were mildly surprised to hear from her, which made Essie blush. Her new colleagues and work chums are acquaintances, either out of work themselves now or not in need of a flatmate. Plus, the whole thing is horrendously embarrassing.

Two weeks later, by the time she's been turned down by both a temp agency and an utterly nondescript apartment in Bruntsfield where she would have had to share a bathroom with three posh nineteen-year-old student girls who on the evidence of the bathroom floor left their hair extensions everywhere, she is deeply and seriously worried.

Essie sits in the lovely Stockbridge back bedroom, watching the evening light die over the water of Leith, which is thronged with couples walking, happy dogs, and small children on ethically produced wooden scooters.

She can't believe everything is crumbling so fast. She was meant to be going out to dinner with Connor, Tris and that lot tonight, but she already knew it would be a very expensive affair, and almost certainly end up with the rugby boys attempting to debag one another on the street or make themselves drink something that was already on fire, and it wasn't quite as much fun as it had seemed a while ago.

And her landlady, now she is at home all the time looking at job ads and heating up tinned soup, has started to make loud sighs and 'oh, you're here again' remarks whenever she is in the kitchen or the bathroom and reminding her that the rent is due and basically pass-agging the hell out of her.

The phone rings. It's her mother – of course it is. She looks at it for a while. Then she answers. What choice does she have?

7

'It's about hair-smoother,' says Janey quickly. 'I've got this weird frizz at the front that's appeared out of nowhere. It's sticking out like TV aerials. TV aerials are, uh . . . things we used to have on TVs.'

Sitting in her tiny, beautiful bedroom, with its tasteful old wardrobe and glorious view, as the evening sun hits the window frames, Essie can't believe the predicament she's in. Saying it is going to make it real. Her landlady had said, very casually that evening, that in fact she was going to start doing short-term lets for the room, so she'd need it back.

Essie had known it was coming. And she supposes she shouldn't blame the woman after all; she's just getting by, like everybody else. Which doesn't stop her hating her with the passion of a million fiery suns and wanting to spill red wine on her beautiful pale furniture, which wouldn't help matters as she desperately needs the deposit back. The agony of looking at horrible rooms on the same websites she used to idly browse for country homes is not helping either.

Essie takes a deep breath. She had known her mum was proud of her, going to university – first in the family, she'd told everyone – fleeing far away to the big city, away from that small life, and the awful atmosphere in the house, and her parents getting divorced the second – the *second* – she was out the door,

33

making it entirely clear that they had made their lives a living hell just because she was at home and wouldn't be doing it for one minute longer. Leaving her adrift in a distant city with nothing underfoot to moor her; just years of her parents wrangling about the house and money and every bloody thing while she and Al just had to get on with it. It had been hard to forgive. Essie isn't there yet. Janey knows it, and it cuts her to the bone, and Essie lets it. Dads . . . dads get away easier. And Colin is incredibly busy with his new family anyway.

'Ess?' says her mother's voice, in a way that always makes her feel reassured and slightly furious at the same time.

'Um . . . Mum, I was thinking . . .'

Essie finds herself, surprisingly quickly, on the brink of tears. She's worked so hard, come so far. Her mum is so proud of her. How will she square this with all her friends; with everyone in the village from the Scot Nor supermarket, all the way to the GP surgery and the hospital; all of them will know that her fancy daughter who went all the way to the big city was crawling back with her tail between her legs. The humiliation is going to be unbearable.

She takes a deep breath.

'Mum, I thought maybe I'd come home for a wee bit.'

★

Janey had stopped the car again to make the call. She knew theoretically she could just do it on the speaker, but she didn't like driving and talking at the same time. The light was deep pink on the long side of Ben Leven. She glanced back at the lambs, whose mothers obviously wanted them away, but who continued to frolic in the muddy water. She couldn't help smiling. She didn't say anything down the phone, though. Didn't want to jump in and get it wrong, as she always did.

But now she is trying to hide her delight as she parks outside her tiny house, the fading sun hitting the walls of the empty cottages on the corner.

She has got used to having the street to herself; it's going to be weird. Please, please, she thinks. Please let it be someone local. But it might be too late. It's too picturesque, has too much potential. They could whack it on the North 500 route, add camper van parking . . . oh, lord, please no. She likes tourists in the village, everyone does – you can't deny the joy of toddlers picking up their first crabs, their parents relishing the freshest fish suppers or listening to Struan McGhie's ceilidh band play in the pub, while lingering over a Badachro malt and staring at the bright, clear sky. It brings fun, and life, and colour. But she worries about a tipping point: the young ones vanishing off to the cities for opportunities, and nobody left to run the school or do the doctoring or clean the hotel rooms or work the farms. It's a good life at the end of the world, it truly is. But it can be a tough one too.

But it would be so nice to have Essie home.

'You're in a cheery mood,' comes a voice, and she starts and looks round. It's Johnson, the postman. He's married to Lish.

'What are you doing down here?' she says. 'I thought you were meant to be finished at lunchtime and playing snooker or whatever it is posties do.'

He chuckles good-naturedly. Johnson is a big ball of good nature.

'You need to sign for a parcel,' he says. 'I know when you finish.'

'Oh, Johnson!' she says. 'You can just leave it outside; nobody will nick it.'

'Can't take chances,' says Johnson, even though there is so little crime in the village that Pete, the policeman, spends most of his time giving parking tickets to tourists for reasons he has just made up. Everyone is very grateful he is not running for political office. 'Also . . . '

Johnson and Lish live out in the country, far away from the shops. She looks in his hands. Sure enough, there's clear evidence of a Fry's Chocolate Cream bar on there.

'Have you been to the Scot Nor?' she says.

'Don't tell Lish! She'll start going on about my cholesterol again. Do you want your parcel or not?'

Janey picks up the box and colours slightly.

'Don't tell me,' says Johnson. 'I am very good at this.' He concentrates. 'Some miracle skin cream you saw advertised on Facebook.'

'Lish told you.'

'She didn't,' says Johnson. 'All you ladies get it all the time.'

'Oh, really?' sighs Janey. 'Is it working, do you think?'

'I think,' says Johnson, 'you are all lovely and you shouldn't worry so much.'

'Well, Lish is a very lucky woman.'

'She is. Oh, also, look out for a big dog that's gone missing.'

'What kind of a dog?'

'How about, any big dog you see running free, you just call it in anyway?'

'Who needs Facebook when we've got you?' says Janey, smiling, as Johnson gets back on his electric bicycle and pedals off, grinning broadly, and she takes out the rusty old key to her very own house, and steps inside.

8

The little house is all hers now, and Lish and Johnson had been such a help to get her there.

'Don't be dumb,' Lish had said, that day back in the autumn, when they'd finally, finally taken possession of the new little house, and she'd had the chance to see how much stuff Janey reckoned she could move into the sixty square metres of the new place (including stairs).

The old lady she'd bought from had taken away her personal things but had, to their consternation, more or less left all the old trash, and Janey had been so terrified of losing the house, she hadn't dared make a fuss. The price of houses in their pic-turesque village had been shooting up over the years, faster than anyone local could possibly keep pace with.

Hence the gigantic mess.

The wallpaper was particularly dreadful. Amsan got her hands on a steamer, so they all took turns opening their pores as well. And gradually, bit by bit, filthy pail after filthy pail, the bones of the tiny place had begun to emerge. Her friends chipped in and they got Milton the porter, who kept boasting that he could do anything, to whitewash the front, and to be fair he did a good job, although they had to feed him so many steak bridies and so much Irn-Bru it might have been cheaper just to hire a professional. Which would also have saved the splashing of white paint on the grey head of the gull who had swooped down to see if there was any bridie left for stealing, although this had the useful knock-on effect of marking out the gull – who was the greediest in all of Carso, famous for swiping chips on the harbour's edge – so that people got used to seeing it and pointing it out and guarding their food, and eventually the greediest gull in Carso moved off to Thurso to nick chips in a place people didn't know him and they all lived happily ever after.

And Janey watched DIY YouTube videos late into the night and developed a raging crush on any gentle-voiced, comfortably shaped man who was happy to talk you through the ins and outs of plastering, and she in fact sometimes left plastering videos on autoplay just to have a nice man's voice around the place, a fact she would not have confessed under torture.

She plastered and painted the old walls in the colours of the shoreline: pebble grey, and clear low-tide blue and cold sand beige. But in the little sitting room she went for a dark, dark green and everyone tutted and said, well, but this is such a small dark room, don't you want it to be lighter? And she was happy for the kitchen at the back when it had all its old cereal boxes removed and the units stripped back (another lovely voice) to be painted a lovely sweet cornflower-blue, with jolly new yellow handles, and the windows were clean and suddenly letting in light over the dunes just beyond the end of the tiny garden, and just enough space to get in a little table and two chairs – one for me, one for a friend, Janey found herself thinking – and it caught the morning light in a way that lifted her heart every morning as she stumbled down to the coffee machine. That room was light. The sitting room wasn't; it was small, and the windows faced the other side of the street. From upstairs, in the tiny bedroom, you got the sunset, but down here there wasn't much of anything. So Janey decided to double down. She got curtains of thick velvet that kept out the draughts, and sweet-smelling logs for the grate, and she filled the alcoves with books they uncovered behind the piles of old chair legs and cat toys. The sofa she found on Freecycle was being moved out of a hotel that was doing itself up and seemed to Janey to be in fantastic condition, a deep mustardy velvet with tartan cushions, and she bought a thick rug that might have been wool if you didn't read the label. In short, she turned the room into a warm winter jewel box, because there was no point in trying to pretend she lived in a vast modernist Malibu beach house, but there was quite a lot of point in trying to be cosy the rest of the year round, and everyone nodded when they saw it and said, well, that definitely made sense.

Everything else, she was strict about. Dividing up the old house had been one of the hardest things she had ever had to do. The kids didn't care about their childhood paintings or school reports but she had sobbed over every last one of them. The Christmas decorations had nearly broken her. Finally her friends had taken pity and taken away all the old toys and clothes she was keeping for reasons she couldn't express and stuck them in their attics, because they were very good friends. Janey had managed to get the good old clothes to Barnardo's, the rest to the recycling. And then, on a sweet pink-skyed October evening, they had held a bonfire with the leaves and, with some ceremony and quite a lot of cider, placed her old wedding dress on it.

'I never liked it,' Janey had said, as they toasted it and it whooshed, horrifyingly quickly, into sparks in the air, moving as if there was someone still inside. It had given Janey a start, as if she was immolating that hopeful, anxious version of herself. Which, of course, she was. She wasn't quite sure what would emerge from the ashes.

'You looked lovely,' said Lish quickly.

'I thought I looked nice on the day,' said Janey. 'But it was the nineties, wasn't it? I had two big stripes in the front of my hair.'

'Everyone did!'

'And because it was strapless, all the wedding photos of us that are head and shoulders look like I'm completely naked.'

'There was quite a lot of . . . hoiking,' remembers Lish, who'd been chief bridesmaid and had had a sensational time. Janey had been young to get married and all their friends had dressed up as grown-ups who went to weddings – it wasn't until wedding four or thereabouts that it had stopped being a novelty and could become a bit of a drag – and everyone had got completely steaming but it had still been totally hilarious.

Looking at the dress go up in flames into the autumn sky, with everyone cheering and clinking glasses, Janey had tried to think back and remember the warning signs, the bad portents. But she couldn't. They had been young, and madly in love. Everyone was happy for them. They knew each other well; they came from similar backgrounds and families. Everything was set up for them to succeed. But they hadn't.

★

Janey had at first been terrified of living by herself; she had never done it.

But, to her amazement, she'd found that she loved it. Being able to buy food that wasn't immediately scoffed the second she walked out of the kitchen; having clean, dry towels to hand, and a phone charger that stayed where she left it. Oh, she missed the kids, of course; she still feels sad, some nights, coming home alone, lighting the lamps all by herself.

But when the lamps are lit, and the peat fire is burning merrily in the grate, everything is quiet and peaceful and she can kick back and chat to a friend and decompress her day, or have a couple of people over on the weekends to share a glass of wine. She has taken up knitting and has lively WhatsApp groups watching television shows together, and she cooks for herself or, sometimes, can't be arsed to cook at all and eats toast on the sofa. She takes long, foaming baths with novels, and avidly follows dog rescue social media.

Apart from Lish haranguing her to date again, for the first time in a very long time it feels as if she is sailing in peaceful waters. After the stormy seas of marital breakdown, children's adolescence, a ruinous divorce, Colin's new family . . . all of that.

Okay, she wishes with all her heart that her relationship with her beloved daughter could be better. And there is the menopause being an absolute arsehole at every conceivable moment, and her ever-wrinkling face, dried-out hair and broadening hips. But sometimes Janey feels this is a small price to pay for – at long last – a modicum of peace.

'Of course, come home, darling!' she had trilled to Essie on the phone that afternoon. 'Stay as long as you like!'

9

It's a chilly morning, as Essie grabs two huge suitcases. How and why did she accumulate so much stuff? Connor has agreed to store the rest of it, which would have been more impressive if he hadn't snuck the boxes into the cave under the dropped basement under cover of darkness and refused to mention it to Tris. But even so. He'd done it. And here he is.

'You'll be back,' he says, holding her close.

Waverley station is bustling as always, including the Flying Scotsman, the great burgundy steam train, which is leaving on one of its regular tours. A piper stands at the top of a tartan carpet that has been placed for the lucky travellers to walk up. Essie glances at them, feeling envious for once. That train would get her more than halfway home. There was a tiny plane that landed on the local airstrip, but with her bags it would be prohibitive, so the long train journey it was.

'I know,' she says. 'It'll be good to chill for a bit.'

'I'll keep my ears open,' he says. 'And I'll come up soon.'

She looks up into his frank, sweet face. 'Thanks,' she says. 'My mum likes you.'

'All mums like me,' he says, and she laughs, because it's true.

'Okay, back to my evil capitalist ways,' he says.

'Alright, off to chase the wild haggis running one-legged round the glens.'

'Don't forget to find a flannel-shirted woodcutter to teach you the true meaning of Christmas.'

She laughs, and kisses his adorable nose one last time, then hauls her bags on to the Inverness train to start the long journey to fifty-eight degrees north. It is a gloomy morning as the train pulls out of Edinburgh, the grey stone of the buildings and the rearing castle above her reflected in the monochromatic sky, so the world resembles a black and white photograph. But as they speed through the tram cuttings and past the Jenners furniture depository and hit the open country the grey starts to dissipate, and soon they are flashing past the lamb-dotted fields on the way to Dunkeld and Aberfeldy, the beautiful towns steeped in the Perthshire countryside, as pretty as a patchwork quilt, and on up as the looming slopes either side of the track grow steeper and the countryside rawer and more expansive, until there is nothing, it feels, but huge looming mountain ranges and dotted farmsteads and the train, piling onwards under a huge northern sky.

Essie meant to spend the journey hunting down job opportunities, and writing humiliatingly chirpy emails to friends in other firms who might hear of any openings, but it is dispiriting work, as every single kilometre sweeps her further and further away from the city she loves, from everything in the life she's worked so hard to build, and she can barely stop staring out of the window. She checks her messages and it's her mum asking her if she'd like square sausage casserole for her dinner, which had been her absolute favourite when she was about twelve, and Essie can't believe, genuinely can't believe for a second that she is going back. She could have gone and stayed with her dad . . .

She bites her lip awkwardly. She can't, not really. Lori, the blip who turned out not to be such a blip (she had overheard

Janey talking to Lish over a bottle of cheap wine one day), is nice enough, but it's a very surface kind of nice, lots of smiles showing her very small, neat teeth in a way that her dad thinks is charming – oh, Lori loves everyone, but Essie can see Lori's constant reckoning of exactly how much time and attention her dad is spending on her: a tally. Anything she and her dad might do just the pair of them – walking the dog, watching science fiction films – Lori now joins them, or insists Logan go too 'otherwise he fusses'. Fussing is the family word for Logan screaming and punching stuff for hours while everyone desperately tries to placate him.

Her half-brother Logan is cute and everything – he's a hearty six now, and she and Al had expected they would be very into having a new sibling – but Logan got everything designer and expensive and Lori clearly looked down her nose at anything they brought, and ever since he turned five he has been a football-kit-wearing thug in the making who was liable to go for your shins and doesn't seem to have grown out of his toddler tantrum stage quite yet. No, staying with her dad would not be a good solution, even if they did have a hot tub. Their new build looks fancy on the outside but on the inside has been badly finished and the walls are paper-thin. And she doesn't really want to sit in a hot tub with her dad anyway; it's hardly dignified behaviour. Especially since he complains a lot about his mortgage – hardly encouraging vis-à-vis Essie's own financial situation – and makes surreptitious efforts to find out how her mum is, and Essie certainly isn't going to be the go-between.

The train putters along through Aviemore, where all the hearty climbers and the very last of the optimistic spring skiers get out, leaving the carriage nearly empty. It is beautiful, but Essie can't help feeling sad. She changes at Inverness and goes to get a very large Starbucks, her last chance to have one for a while, she thinks, glumly contemplating an overlarge cinnamon bun she doesn't even really want.

The Inverness-to-Thurso stretch, while one of the most picturesque rides in the world, is also extremely long. The train takes four hours to travel eighty miles, so it is a little quicker than it used to be by horse, but not by that much. It is, technically, quicker to fly from Edinburgh to the island of Orkney then to catch the ferry back south to the mainland, but only if you don't have quite so much luggage.

Oddly, though, the fresh air blowing through the window vents, and the rattling of the old diesel carriages – there are only two – and the changing landscape as they skirt lochs, seaside and mountains, which she had thought would make her more anxious, actually has the opposite effect. As she passes through the familiar, lulling litany of stations – Dingwall, Invergordon, Tain, Lairg, Brora – and, after the many, many sleepless nights of worry and regret, Essie finds herself, quite to her surprise, falling asleep.

IO

Janey has finished slightly early today. Another client who was a hundred per cent sure their hearing aids weren't working, so they'd stopped wearing them. She wished there were a few more hearing aid role models. Gorgeous Rose from *Strictly Come Dancing* had helped a lot with Hearing Aid Barbie, but there were fewer for older people, who really needed them. In fact, a lot of her older clients said they didn't really mind a peaceful world, no youngsters playing their iPads too loud or people yelling into their phones. Janey has to find a polite way to tell them that wearing them will really help stave off dementia. There is, it turns out, no polite way to threaten people with losing their marbles.

'Hearing aids take time,' she repeats patiently, over and over. 'You have to let the brain adapt to where the sound is coming from. The brain is an amazing thing. It will adjust and learn to tune in to the hearing aid. But you have to wear it all the time to allow the brain to do that.'

To which the traditional response is, 'Och, no, I dinnae want to be wearing that about the place when it's just me and the coos/out for a nice night out' or, 'Ach, they're not comfortable/oh, I dinnae like the way they look/they make me feel like a right aul coot.'

And Janey has to smile politely and do her best to insist they continue, then, if they have brought a family member with them, try to signify desperately with her eyes how *incredibly important* it is that they enforce this. She always knows immediately from the way the client walks in at the next appointment whether this has been successful or not. Sometimes they bring the kit back, at least.

She is going to drive Lish home; her friend has been on an all-nighter with twins and doesn't feel safe to drive. Lish is also wearing a new bunnet, in pretty heather colours, as they stroll the long corridors together, nodding to staff they know, smiling sweetly at the latest intake of junior doctors getting lost. They'll figure it out.

'Carso babies?' says Janey, nodding her head towards the knitted bunnet. Lish yawns, nodding at the same time. Carso is mad for knitting. Extraordinarily for a town with one very small supermarket, the Scot Nor, it manages to support two yarn shops, in poisonous competition with one another, and if you're not in the right knitting circle it's on a par with being shut out of an American country club. Not a postbox is untopped. One of their knitters, Gertie from the airline, even had a scarf in *Vogue*. It's quite the thing.

'You wouldn't believe the delivery suite,' says Lish. 'It's basically insulated the entire room.'

'Oh, good,' says Janey, 'an even hotter hospital.' She says this with feeling. A lot of staff around her age have trouble with the tropical levels of warmth, and the failure of the new building windows to open.

'It's for the old folks and the bairns,' Lish parrots, as she has so many times before.

'I wish they'd knit me a handheld fan,' says Janey as they reach the huge revolving door, and she takes in great lungfuls of the cool March air, and it is absolutely delicious, which means Milton has been out doing his good work of kindly telling the smokers, who really absolutely cannot quit, even though they're in hospital, and even though you absolutely aren't meant to smoke anywhere on hospital grounds, about a secret spot around the side where the smoke won't annoy anyone, and you're near the furnaces so it's still warm.

'Oh, it's still light,' says Lish. 'Or is it light again? I can't tell.'

'Let's get you home.'

★

Sitting in the car, Lish is still sleepy but squints.

'Hang on, why are you leaving early?' she says, having finally realised what time it is.

'I'm picking Essie up from the train station.'

Lish blinks. 'Oh, yeah . . . You don't seem super-happy about it.'

'Of course I am,' says Janey, but her friend has known her a long time.

'Then why do you look like you've got spiders in your underpants?'

Janey sighs. Her eyes are on the road. It's funny how, often, it's easier to talk about these things when you're driving. Side by side instead of face to face.

'Well, you know Essie. She's never forgiven me for . . . well, Colin, or the divorce, or anything.'

'Yes, she's turned out gorgeous, with a nice boyfriend and an amazing job in the capital. How terrible a parent you must have been,' says Lish, because she is very much the best kind of friend. 'Anyway, that's why it's good you can spend time together as adults.'

'I know, but . . . it's taken me so long to get here, you know? With the house and everything. I just thought things might be stable for a little while. A bit of calm.'

Lish laughs. 'Oh, my God, you *jinx*! Midlife,' she announces, 'is just one continuous act of being kicked in the teeth.

I wouldn't be surprised if having actual spiders in your underpants was a real thing about menopause but nobody bothered
to tell us.'

'I just wanted a small period of peace and quiet. Before my
mum and dad start "having falls",' says Janey.

Lish smiles ruefully and pats her on the shoulder, offering
her lunchbox. 'Gingerbread?'

Janey smooths her clinical pinafore over her hips. 'AND I
CAN'T EVEN HAVE A PIECE OF SODDING FATTEN-
ING GINGERBREAD.'

'Would you like a knitted bunnet? I think there's some left
over.'

★

Despite how nervous she is, and although obviously Essie is
doing this reluctantly – her tone made it quite clear – in the
end, after she's dropped off a sleepy Lish into Johnson's waiting
arms, Janey cannot help getting a little excited. However big
and grown and, well, occasionally scornful she is – her baby
girl is coming home. Will be under her roof, with her expensive designer clothes and posh candles that cost a fortune and
knowing all about restaurants and, well, it is still going to be
good. Even though she hasn't got back to her about supper.
Maybe she'd like to go to the chippy; she has always liked that.
Even in the depths of her teenage miserableness, some hot fresh
fish with masses of vinegar and a big slug of Irn-Bru was usually pretty good medicine.

Essie's little train draws in, disgorging the last few remain-
ing passengers, stretching their legs after the long journey. The
wind is blowing down from the north – Arctic air, even in the
springtime, and the daffodils that are blooming in the city would
be nowhere to be seen up here just yet. Essie always complains
about the cold, but it is dry and fresh and the sky is a clear blue,

and the route home goes up and down over cliffs and past bays, each bluer than the last, and it is always lovely.

Essie is, to Janey's surprise, practically the last off. She's usually in such a rush. But she is yawning and stretching her arms, and hauling two vast suitcases of stuff that Janey cannot even imagine where they're going to store but she puts that thought to the back of her mind. They can stay in the car if they must.

She opens her arms wide and Essie, to her surprise, doesn't give her a pat or a kiss on the cheek. She gives her a great big hug back, even letting her head rest on her mother's shoulders as Janey pats her.

'There, there,' Janey finds herself saying, as if Essie is five and had skinned her knee.

Essie straightens up immediately.

'I'm fine,' she says, as if she's been caught out in something.

Together they haul the bags to the tiny Kia, which groans rather sadly under the strain, then beeps repeatedly because it thinks a person has climbed into the back seat, so Janey discards the car wardrobe idea and attempts to talk about anything other than the obvious: that Essie must have indeed lost her job and, from the looks of the suitcases, her flat as well.

Janey can't stop talking to her about dinner. She can hear herself doing it and wishes she could just shut up. But Essie looks sleepy and uncommunicative, so she finally lets the conversation peter out. As they drive, finally, into Carso, night falling, they pass the local pub, which has been repainted pale blue.

'That's weird,' says Essie.

'Oh, yes!' says Janey, seizing on safe ground. 'Shelby McFlynn took it over. Trying to make it some big Instagrammable thing.'

'Shelby McFlynn?' says Essie. It is ridiculous; she is a grown-up. Why does even just hearing the name make it all come flooding back? Shelby McFlynn, prettiest of all the girls in her year. Who had sneered when Essie had been caught crying in the toilets the day after a particularly bad fight at home. Who had pretended to make an apology when the teachers were called, and had pulled it off because she had blonde hair and big brown eyes and the teachers thought she could do no wrong. It makes her shudder even now.

She sticks out her lip.

'Is she really ugly now?' she asks, hopefully. 'Like, it all just went downhill and the suntans leathered up her skin and stuff. Or did she have some plastic surgery and it went terribly wrong?'

'Oh, no,' says Janey blithely. 'Oh, no, she's lovely-looking, is Shelby.'

'Mum!'

'What?' Janey is confused. 'I thought you two were friends.'

'She was a *total cow.*'

'Oh, no!'

'She was so obviously a total cow to me!'

Janey had always prided herself on being able to keep up with the serpentine twists of Essie's school friendship groups, but that had fallen away as Essie had got more monosyllabic.

'Okay,' she says, as they turn away from the harbour and go up the lane. 'I'll hate her now too.'

'Thank you,' says Essie.

'That's a shame, though,' says Janey, 'because they actually do a really nice set lunch. And they have a great knitting group. And it's kind of our Friday night—'

'MUU-UM!'

'No, you're right.'

'Can't you go to the Cedars?'

'It shut. Couldn't get staff.'

'Huh. What about the Red Lion?'

'Nope. No staff either. Couldn't get a chef to stay.'

'Why not?'

'Because most of the young people leave . . . and nobody else can find a place to live. Everyone's house is being turned into—'

'A holiday let,' said Ellie straight away. 'Edinburgh is exactly the same. It's just awful.'

'Yes,' said Janey. 'As soon as anything comes on the market it gets snatched up by some investor who doesn't even live here . . . and then it gets rented out for parties and hen nights and people being loud and annoying and who bring their own food and don't even shop here and then complain there's no restaurants even though they're staying in the house the chef used to rent.'

Their faces, for once, look very similar, even though Essie's long, ringlety hair is streaked expensively in gold and honey, and Janey's bust is low whereas Essie pays an expensive trainer to try to prevent this exact same thing from happening. Their jaws however are, right now, set exactly the same.

Janey shakes her head. 'It's not right.'

'It isn't.'

'You know when someone's looking to move in the village we have to do it all in secret?'

'What do you mean?'

'You have to tip people the wink. Otherwise if it goes on the open market it just gets snapped up by someone who doesn't give a toss and who we've never even met. And it's hard . . . it's hard for people to resist.'

'Why don't you do that with the cottage?' Essie can't help asking.

Janey knows she doesn't mean it in a callous way.

'Because I already got kicked out of one home,' she says, shortly, and Essie could have bitten her tongue.

'Anyway,' said Janey, parking right outside the cottage; in the city, Essie thinks, that would have been a miracle and they'd have had to have called the papers, 'where else would I go?' And she regards the little cobbled Seagate with pride. 'And why?'

★

The house is even smaller than Essie remembers. She had whizzed in and out last Christmas, barely stopping long enough to give her mum things she thought she should have, while mostly engrossed in her phone and refusing to eat anything so she could fit into a ballgown for the fancy New Year's Eve party Connor was taking her to at Gleneagles.

She can't help but notice, though, what her mum has done to it: the new flooring, wide oak-style beams on the little sitting room floor that Janey is incredibly proud of laying herself, and a floral rug in colours that match the walls.

'It's very dark in here,' she says, looking around. Janey looks stricken. 'But it's nice,' Essie adds quickly.

The two huge suitcases look bigger than the room and wider than the tiny creaking staircase. Janey not mentioning this makes everything even more awkward. She has made up Essie's bed, which is a lovely wrought-iron three-quarter frame that someone had been throwing out, and she'd managed to salvage it from a skip. She's made it up with fresh white linen and a soft pink blanket. There's a small white chest of drawers and, frankly, not much space for anything else. By the time they've put the two suitcases in, there's no room between the bed and the window. Janey's own bed is just on the other side of the wall, and the bathroom is across the landing. They'll be sharing it. They've never shared a bathroom before; the old house had two.

'I'll leave you to unpack,' says Janey.

'Where?' says Essie, despairingly.

'Do you want my room?' says Janey, anxiously.

'No, Mum, I'm not such a *horrible cow* that I want to put you out of your room,' snaps Essie.

She has been trying to hold off, promising herself she wouldn't break down, wouldn't cry and upset her mum, wouldn't admit to herself that she feels like a failure. But it has been a very long day. Her throat constricts; her eyes fill. She can't help it. She collapses on her bed and bursts into floods of tears.

'Baby girl!' exclaims Janey, taking her in her arms. Of course, this makes things worse. 'I thought it was just the job.'

This is the wrong thing to say.

'Well, even if it was,' howls Essie, 'my job meant a lot to me!'

'But I thought you were sick, or pregnant or . . . it's only a stupid job. You'll find another one in five seconds, you're so smart!'

'The company is moving to *Switzerland*! And they didn't want to take me,' says Essie.

'Good!' says Janey. 'You're far enough away as it is.'

This is met with more racking sobs. 'They didn't want me. And now I've lost the flat too.'

'Oh, darling. You loved that place,' says Janey.

'I did,' says Essie.

'You made it lovely. Was Persephone not more understanding?' asks Janey.

'No!' says Essie. 'She wasn't understanding at all! Which is odd, considering I was never there, did all my washing up, and never made a mess. It was a bit mean,' she adds.

'It was,' says Janey. 'I thought she was meant to be the glamorous laid-back hippy type.'

'Me too!' says Essie, suddenly sounding about fourteen years old. 'Apparently I was interrupting her yoga practice.'

'Well, you won't be interrupting *my* yoga practice,' says Janey. 'Because I think it's boring and keep forgetting to do it,' she adds.

'And you don't have any space to do it,' sniffles Essie, as Janey feels in her pocket for a tissue. Like all ENT specialists, she gets through an extraordinary amount.

'Well, exactly,' says Janey.

Essie tries to stop crying. 'It's very good for your mental health,' she says.

'So's a good cry,' says Janey, wiping her daughter's face. 'Come on, we're too late for me to cook. Chips it is.'

11

They both set out with such good intentions. They really do.

Janey wants to wrap her baby girl up in a blanket of love; protect her from the world until she's ready to take it on again. She buys her favourite foods ('full of additives' apparently), digs out their old favourite Meg Ryan films – problematic now – and is as soft and gentle as she can be.

But there is a fundamental misunderstanding between them: Gen X Janey has always worked in an environment where they are short-staffed and desperately in need of more people, terribly overstretched. She can't really envisage what it's like to not be able to get a job, not really. She doesn't understand why Essie can't just apply for a few things or do something else for a bit. She doesn't understand about internships and who you know, and Essie has given up trying to explain.

Essie is still begging Connor to help her, but his firm is very hush-hush high net worth and she just doesn't have the experience – or, she suspects Tris thinks, the background to work there. Also Essie is trying to keep from her mum how little money she has, which was to say, negative money: huge credit card debts. She is completely and utterly skint, despite having been making double her mum's salary plus bonus.

Janey tries not to ask why Essie appears to be so skint, in case it elicits a huff, which it will. She isn't sure what else to do, and feels as though she's panicking as Essie sinks from view into her phone and her laptop, an endless black hole that never ends, scrolling and typing; every time Janey asks if she wants to go out/take a walk/go for a drink she is greeted with 'I'm BUSY' and some noisy typing in a way that is impossible for her to refute. Meanwhile, all the towels have vanished. Also Essie has messaged her dad on the off-chance that he'd say, *Don't worry, darling, come over whenever you like, I've got a room for you and here's the deposit for a new flat in Edinburgh for you to get back on your feet.* But he hasn't. He's muttered about things being very busy and Lori's mum (who isn't much older than Colin) wanting to move in, and Logan going through 'a bit of a stage'. It's tough on Essie to not be able to think of her dad being the good guy all the time. The idea that her mum might have been right has exactly the opposite effect than it might have; it makes her even more trapped and resentful.

'I am doing my *best*,' Janey says at lunch, as everyone eyes her up expectantly for a mother–daughter update. She pokes depressingly at the salad bowl she has chosen. It's too cold outside for salad. Salad is for being drenched in lemon juice sitting outside under an umbrella somewhere. She hasn't been overseas since the pandemic; she doesn't know anyone living in a one-salary household who has. What she really wants is a pie.

Lish, who is having a pie, can think of nothing nicer than having her kids round all the time; they only live half a step away. Janey sometimes thinks if Lish could tuck her kids back inside her womb, she would be okay with that too. Milton's children are mostly in London, and one back in DCR doing wonderful work as a doctor, something which makes him incredibly proud. Few are the hospital doctors who don't stop, every so often, to pass on some new research or ask the quiet porter how his daughter is doing, and whether there is anything she needs. Much of the NHS is famously wasteful: at the T&C, every unused set of crutches, every nearly out-of-date packet of plaster makes its way to the porter's lodge, no questions asked.

Amsan understands: as well as the unlucky Yasmin, she has a son whose wife spends a lot of time with her family, who are rather wealthier and have a swimming pool, of all things, in Perthshire, which is ridiculous as basically the whole of Perthshire is more or less an ice rink and it's just showing off. But it's undoubtedly the case that when it comes to where the grandchildren want to spend their time, the swimming pool beats, unfortunately, any number of nice nature walks by the water in Carso. Amsan tries to keep her swimming-pool-based bitterness out of her voice, but it's hard.

'. . . but she just mopes about the place like she's fifteen again. And when she was fifteen at least I could give her some advice.'

'Essie listened to your advice at fifteen?' asks Amsan.

'No, of course not,' admits Janey. 'Obviously not. But theoretically I knew what the problem *might* be. Whereas I don't know how you get a job in super-weird clever-clogs finance in Edinburgh!'

She looks around the table but everyone shrugs.

'I don't know what anyone in an office does,' says Lish. 'I mean, hauling babies out of people – that makes sense as a job description, right? And pushing people about on trolleys?'

'Exactly. You can see an ambulance in Richard Scarry books,' says Janey. 'It's driven by a cat wearing Lederhosen.'

'Yeah. But being in offices looking at computers . . . I don't know what that is.'

Amsan holds up her hazelnut yoghurt. Someone had told Amsan once that hazelnut yoghurt would help you lose weight. Even though this can't possibly be true, and they work in a building full of scientists who could bear this out, she refuses to believe them. And she really loves hazelnut yoghurt; it's delicious. Which should have been an obvious clue in the first place, Janey likes to point out, but doesn't, after the whole 'Let's Have a WeightWatchers in the Hospital It'll Be Fun' débâcle of 2019.

'It's just . . . moving paper about?'

'I think so,' says Janey. 'Only the pieces of paper they move are somehow worth millions, and, if they don't move them right, the country can't afford hospitals.'

'They can't afford them now,' observes Lish, to a few hearty nods.

'Well, surely there are lots of paper-pushing jobs?' says Amsan. 'There seem to be a million people who do it here.'

'I know that,' says Janey. 'But somehow you get paid ten times more for looking at computer screens in Edinburgh.'

'Inside in the warm,' grumbles Milton, who has to circumnavigate the hospital buildings all day in all sorts of weather and does not always like it.

'We definitely got something wrong,' says Janey, smiling, but then she glances at her phone. She has an afternoon of community rounds, which means driving up into beautiful farmland to check up on how people are doing with their hearing, seeing so many whose quality of life it has massively improved or helped them work for longer, on a gorgeous chilly spring day, with the farms all grinding into life with the new buds on the trees and the daffs flourishing in every single part of sunshine they can find. She can see if old Fraser Ardmillan will be able to hear the tractor coming, and the birds singing in the trees, and which of his cows are lowing to him, and she can visit wee Abdul in Caithness, whose parents live in the loveliest house and always press on her food and treats to take away and she can't really say no, and he is so cute and has learned her name and is very proud of himself, in the way a four-year-old can be, at how brilliant he is at passing the audiology tests. She has absolutely learned to take along extra stickers for his twin sisters, who are six, and have truly earned them from long, long years of waiting on Abdul's appointments, his hospital stays; tolerating the fuss that was always made of their little brother while they just had to grow up and get on with things. Janey sees this a lot. She makes a special effort with the siblings. Then she has to pop into a GP clinic to schedule a late-night surgery of tests. It suits the poor overworked GPs, who work long days twice a week: it is knackering, but it's convenient for other people not having to take a full day off work, so she does it with a will.

No, she wouldn't swap it for moving paper about. Her poor girl.

★

Four long hours later, though, Janey's tolerance for her 'poor girl' is dropping significantly. She's exhausted from a hectic afternoon, despite Abdul's charms. She also had to manage an upset young man who constantly wears extremely loud head-phones, leading to hearing loss. He's very distressed about having to wear hearing aids before turning thirty, and Janey tries to balance being firm and being empathetic. However, he keeps making things worse by turning the volume up, which becomes more evident through the damage to his ear follicles. The young man ends up in tears, which is unusual in Janey's job, where she generally helps people feel better. Janey feels stressed and upset.

It's dark when she gets home, starving, hoping Essie has prepared dinner, considering they discussed having lamb chops, which are in the fridge.

When Janey enters the house, she's hit by the heat – it's on full blast. Janey usually keeps it low to save on heating bills, but now all the doors are wide open, and one window is slightly ajar. The kitchen is a mess, with teabags on the counter, and, in the sink, dirty plates piled up, a ketchup bottle lying on its side; laundry is dumped on the sideboard. The lamb chops are gone. Janey takes a deep breath, clenches then releases her fists, and wishes she hadn't been quite so dismissive of yoga.

*

Essie had a rough day too. She slept in, which is both good and bad, putting her out of sync with the rest of the world. Her phone showed no new messages, and it's as if she's vanished from Edinburgh. Her group WhatsApp chats continue without her, organising brunches and gallery events. Essie had typed *Just taking a little MH break, guys, back soon*, and left three groups, but now she regrets it, feeling isolated. It seems like the world is moving on without her.

Essie had scoured her mum's cupboards for food – nothing. There was no Uber Eats or Deliveroo either, and it was freezing. She managed to get the heating on and took a long bath to warm up. But then, back wrapped in her duvet, she checked Connor's Instagram. And there he was, at a party in a kilt, surrounded by others in kilts, trews or black tie, along with girls in ballgowns. He'd told her he was going, but she'd been too busy complaining. It should have been her at the event, but she'd forgotten about it. They would've had a fun weekend together.

Then she spiralled down a rabbit hole of what happened if you weren't in a committed relationship by the time you were thirty and what to do when the head-hunter hasn't called you and looking for big bank jobs that didn't require German – there weren't any, although there were plenty of pension administrator jobs – and tortured herself reading articles about how impossible it was to get on the housing ladder and how it wasn't going to get any better, ever, because the boomers would die and hand their city houses to their kids, who could then get all the good jobs, and otherwise all jobs were open to every human being in the entire universe, and AI would filter your CV before anyone even bothered reading it.

She didn't even get dressed, just mooned around, eating everything she could find, throwing her phone down in disgust, then picking it up again. She was absolutely in the depths of misery, barely noticed the day slipping away. She had a Zoom call with her recruiter at three p.m. and did her best to at least dress her top half.

'So. A lot of the jobs we're looking at,' said the recruiter, 'they need an MBA?'

'Seriously?' said Essie, who had spent a lot of time at Sinclair feeding figures into algorithms and looking for differences in results. It didn't feel quite like MBA behaviour. 'I'm not sure I can get one of those in time.'

'Then the normal procedure is four or five interviews and a presentation.'

'Four or five interviews in Edinburgh?'

Essie had got her last job by doing work experience, turning up hours early, staying hours late, and being so cheeky to Hari that he had taken her on as an assistant. Once again it really stung that he wasn't taking her to Berne. And she couldn't afford to intern again. Last time she'd only managed by working two jobs through the summer and being a student guidance counsellor so she could live cheaply in halls. This seems . . . impossible.

So she is not in the best of moods when she hears Janey come in and slam the door behind her. Oh, God. She isn't in the mood to face her mum right now, she really isn't. Things are already bad enough. She feels terrible.

'Essie?'

Her mum's voice sounds pissed off. Oh, for God's sake. She's in a rotten situation, she's been home for five minutes; can she not have someone else be annoyed with her too?

'Essie!'

'Yeah?' Her voice is full of truculence.

'Could you come down a sec?'

Huffily, Essie gets up and brushes down the crumbs from her pyjamas. Okay, it was a bit mad that she hasn't got dressed all day but . . . come on, she's clearly depressed. She needs a duvet day, not a row. And she doesn't want to tell her mum, and she doesn't want to ask, but she hasn't heard from her dad at all, apart from a *You'll be fine!* message, which was frankly the reverse of encouraging.

'Hi,' Essie says in a gloomy Ross-from-*Friends* voice, descending the stairs.

Janey can't help her face getting pained when she sees her gorgeous, messy daughter. 'Oh, sweetie,' she says.

'What?' says Essie, irritably.

'Nothing,' says Janey quickly. 'It's . . . how was your day?'

'It was awful,' says Essie, sullenly.

'I know,' says Janey. Then, 'Err . . . can I ask you not to mess with the heating too much?'

'But it's a stupid complicated mechanism.'

'I know,' says Janey. 'I'll put instructions on it.'

'Also, I'm in the house all day. I can't freeze to death.'

'I know,' says Janey again. 'But you can burn the peat to keep warm, it's much cheaper.'

'But it's hard to light . . . '

Janey struggles to hold on to her patience. 'Come on, sweetie,' she says. 'You had to open a *window*.'

'Fine,' says Essie, rolling her eyes and closing the window.

'So, dinner . . . ' Janey says. It's seven-thirty in the evening.

'Oh, yeah, can we order in?' says Essie.

'Where from?' said Janey, incredulously.

'Isn't there a Domino's? I thought surely you'd have one by now.'

'Well, no, there isn't,' says Janey. 'And if there were, I probably wouldn't want to eat pizza on a Tuesday.'

'Fine,' says Essie. 'It's my fault. Sorry if my life is in ruins and that interferes with your precious eating schedule.'

'Essie,' says Janey. 'That's not what I meant.'

'I know I should have moved in and just started behaving like your servant. I know I'm not welcome here,' she says.

'Of course you are!' says Janey. 'Of course you are! Now you're just being dramatic.'

'But a very dramatic thing has happened!'

Janey can't help her lips twitching. 'Yes . . . to my lamb chops.'

'Oh, for God's sake,' says Essie. Then, grudgingly, 'I'm sorry I ate your lamb chops.'

'That's okay,' says Janey. 'I shall call it fasting.'

Essie sniffs. 'I ate them quite a while ago,' she says. 'You don't keep any food in this house.'

'I don't,' agrees Janey. 'If I have it, I eat it, so I find it's best not to have it. Why didn't you just go to the Scot Nor?' This is the local supermarket, which does a fine line in Empire biscuits and extremely localised crisp flavours.

'I didn't want to get dressed.'

'Frankly these days I think they're not that fussed,' says Janey. 'People started wearing their pyjamas to the Scot Nor during the pandemic and it kind of caught on.'

'Classy,' says Essie.

Essie doesn't say the real reason: everyone in this town knows her, or at least knows Janey, who is popular, and they'd all want to know what was up. But Janey realises.

'What do you say,' she says finally, 'to baklava for supper?'

And she digs out the baklava Abdul's grateful parents had pressed into her hands as she'd left, and boils the kettle, and puts Kirsty and Phil on the television, and they pretend everything is fine, though the ways in which they both feel they are failing are like pins in the sofa.

12

It is a sweet-scented, settled evening in Carso, after a winter full of towering storms, great sweeping gusts of snow and rain pounding them relentlessly from the west, gathering fury over the Atlantic. There is a bleak excitement to it, Janey always feels: to watch the waves leap up, higher than the walls of the esplanade; to see the ocean boil in fury – it's fun if you're properly dressed, and on your way home to your nice wee cosy house from which you can already see the woodsmoke coming; then it's nice to marvel at the extraordinary power of the sea, as the windmills out in the water whizz endlessly, harnessing power under noisy skies. It's exciting, when it has a nice hot cup of tea and a biscuit at the end of it. Not so much when you have to go and fish in it for thirty-six hours, as Janey's father had done, once upon a time.

But tonight it feels as if the winter gods have blown themselves out, at least for now: the evening is soft and gentle, with just a breath of chill beneath it; there is a sense on the air that summer will come, a promise often made in Scotland, in its ravishing springtime, even if this is not always fulfilled in its rainy July (as many a bride, telling everyone it really didn't matter, it was the people who were there that counted, could attest).

Janey has made a decision. She can't keep on like this with Essie; they will end up rerunning her teenage years, and surely neither of them wants to do that. Even though they are theo-retically both adults, she knows it doesn't feel like that to Essie, holed up in her room with Pot Noodles and wearing her dress-ing gown all day.

And it is the night of the Carso quiz. They have ditched the unreliable needle gauges after a fight nearly broke out, and the rounds about identifying aeroplanes and airports by their codes after Morag MacIntyre and her grandfather Ranald, who run the tiny planes that hop around the local islands, gleefully cleaned up every single time. It is a very popular village event, but not without its controversies.

Suggesting Essie just come along to the quiz worked precisely not at all, so Janey is going to have to bring in the big guns: Essie's beloved brother Alasdair, who takes life lightly, who is always fun and popular, and who is just, in general, easier; abso-lutely not, as Essie screeched at her mother many times during her adolescence, her mother's favourite, but he is certainly easy to get along with. It is almost impossible to say no to him.

And so it proves. When Janey gets home from work that Thursday, she hears something she hasn't heard in a while: Essie is laughing.

'Come on, sis,' Al is saying, both of them hanging out in the tiny kitchen in an easy way that makes Janey's heart soar. 'Come on. It will be the formidable triumph that starts us on the road back from *Pyjama Land*.'

'Maybe I like Pyjama Land,' Essie is grumbling, clutching her cup of tea.

'No, you don't,' says Al. 'You think you look like a cute Amer-ican college student in a television show. But you look like a depressed person who's nearly in their late twenties.'

If it were Janey saying that, she'd have had her head bitten off, Janey thinks, as she sticks her bag down in the kitchen.

'That's what I'm *going for*!'

'Hey, you guys!' says Janey. She always thinks, with secret pride, that the fact that her children get on means she couldn't ... it couldn't have been all bad. Of course they'd had to rely on each other maybe more during the divorce . . . no, she wasn't going to think like that. They had a lovely relationship. Maybe, just once, she could stop exhausting herself with everything she'd done wrong and enjoy one of the few things that had gone well.

Al turns to her with a grin. 'Hello, Janey.'

'Just call me Mum, thanks. Mummy is also acceptable.'

When they'd been younger they had thought calling her by her Christian name was utterly hilarious, and Al has never quite shaken the habit, even though he's here in his work clothes, look-ing like a proper grown-up. He works for the council, managing the deer populations, which is a euphemism, he has to point out quite often, for killing all the deer before they strip every last leaf in every last forest and decide to move on to eating babies.

'Is Zara not coming?' she asks pleasantly. She tries to keep a handle on Al's posh girlfriends, and knows Jacinta has passed by the wayside, but they come and go so regularly. Sometimes she worries about Al messing about too much with his busy 'hot kilted woodman' internet nonsense (thank God Lish had set the parameters firmly out of his age range); sometimes she thought it was amusing, and sometimes she thought it was his own way of dealing with the divorce, which, while worrying, wasn't quite as bad as Essie's territorial warfare.

'She's in Klosters,' he says, then adding, 'That's in Switzerland?' for Essie's benefit.

'*Too soon*,' says Essie, frowning.

'Well, you can't come to quiz like that,' Al says decisively to Essie, simultaneously kissing his mother on the top of her head.

'Good,' says Essie. 'Because I'm not actually coming at all?'

'Yes, you are,' says Al. 'We need you on young person stuff. Everyone else going is a gazillion years old.'

'Oi!' says Janey. Then she wrinkles her nose. 'I just feel like a gazillion years old. That's not the same thing at all.'

'Well, if it helps, you don't look more than a billion, billion and two, tops.'

Essie sighs.

'There'll be wine,' says Al.

'There'll be the kind of wine pubs stock up here,' says Essie.

'You are such a *snob* now. Oh, my God, I knew it!'

'That's not fair,' says Essie. 'It's not being a snob if the wine literally says, "Product of Several Countries" on the label. And "Do Not Feed to Livestock".'

'Yeah, it is,' says Al.

'And it's not being a snob if it's got the sugar concentration of tablet.'

'The sugar concentration of tablet is perfect; what's your problem? Come on. Go and get dressed. Have a shower first. I'll buy you a gin and tonic if you're going to flap about the wine. Gins and tonics, plural.'

Essie frowns. Janey realises she is holding her breath, so much does she want her daughter to take even a baby step towards getting out of her slump.

'But Shelby McFlynn.'

'I'll handle Shelby McFlynn,' says Al, who had always done well with the girls, and even more so these days now he has a trim beard and a job that requires a suit and tie and, for the more deer-killy days, a Barbour jacket and a Land Rover.

'You couldn't get Shelby!' says Essie. 'No way, man!'

'I could get Shelby!' says Al, horrified.

'Prettiest girl in the school? No chance.'

'Ah, that was school. And all those football club losers she was into then are now still losers. Whereas I . . . '

' . . . shoot Bambi with a gun.'

'Provide an important environmental service. While still in full possession of my hair.'

He shows her a picture of Zara.

'Bloody hell,' says Essie.

'Yeah,' says Al complacently.

'Well, my boyfriend is lovely-looking.'

'Does he know you're wearing monster slippers right now?'

Essie has forgotten she is wearing her old monster slippers. She and her mother remain in a war of attrition over the thermostat.

'Some men like feet,' she says, frowning.

'Yes, *feet*, not *claws*.'

Essie frowns to think what, exactly, Connor would think of the way she looked right now, her skin breaking out, wearing grungy old jimjams. She sighs. Janey looks the other way in case they catch eyes.

'Come on, sis,' says Al, his voice warm, as if he's trying to coax a scared foal. 'Come on. Get dressed. We're going out.'

Essie makes the face again.

'What is the big deal with Shelby, anyway?' asks Al.

Janey immediately pretends desperately hard not to be listening and goes into the next room. Fortunately, as the house is the size of a well-appointed rabbit hutch, she can hear perfectly well.

'Ugh,' says Essie. 'She was . . . when the divorce was happening, and my mates were being nice and the teachers were doing their best, she would walk in and go, "Oh, boohooing again? Poor little Essie," and all her horrible mates would laugh. All the time. Wherever I went. "Oh, everyone, be sympathetic to poor top-of-the-class Essie." I was absolutely *terrified* of her. Every day.'

Janey's heart drops. Essie had spent those years yelling, sulking and slamming doors. She had tried so many times to get her to open up – always, obviously, wrongly. She should have got Al to do it.

'She was probably just jealous,' says Al.

'Of my misery. Yeah, whatever,' says Essie. 'Anyway, even if she was, loads of people are jealous. I don't go up to Taylor Swift and say, "Oh, boohoo, you only got to date Harry Styles for five minutes," do I?'

'I bet you would.'

'I would not,' says Essie serenely. 'Taylor and I would make friends straight off.'

13

'So, all it took,' says Janey quietly to her friends, as they all give her meaningful looks at seeing Essie up and about, 'was for me to keep completely silent and hide in the next room.'

They are in the End of the World bar – the name of the place makes both Essie and Al roll their eyes, which annoys Janey, because at least someone is making an effort. It's hard up here. Shelby had the little low white house painted up nice and fresh, and the doors and windowpanes are pale blue; it looks lovely, even though it faces the sea so will need to be painted every five minutes to have a hope of staying that way.

'Look, sis,' Al is teasing, pointing at a chalked-up menu. 'They have avocados! You're alright! You haven't been kidnapped!'

Essie gives him a look. Considering how dire she's been feeling, having a shower and getting dressed, even if it's only in jeans and a top, has made her feel a little better, as has putting make-up on, as has the prospect of the local gin and tonic Al is currently buying her. She looks around, feeling edgy as she waits to see Scary Shelby McFlynn. When she appears, behind the bar, Essie feels a sudden chill.

Shelby does look well, as her mum said. She's bigger than she was at school, but she's bosomy and shapely, so it rather suits her, particularly working behind a bar. Her brown eyes have been further enhanced by huge false eyelashes that curl up, and she has a deep tan, which isn't really the first thing that springs to mind when you think of the winter just past in Carso.

Essie blinks and tries to slow her racing heart. She hasn't thought about what she might say – well, that's nonsense: she has thought about it loads, mostly along the lines of effing off out then effing back in again so she can eff off once more, and ideally it would have taken place while she, Essie, was swanning down George Street in a ballgown and lots of handsome friends on their way somewhere exotic (she's not quite sure where), while a now acne-ridden and miserable Shelby has come up to see *Menopause the Musical* at the Playhouse and can only stare after her wistfully.

And yet, here they are. Back in Carso. And Shelby is looking straight at Essie with a look on her face that is almost defiant; as if she is daring Essie to say something, to bring it up. She recognises her, alright; she's practically reading her mind.

Essie realises she can't do it. She isn't going to speak to her school bully. She can't. Instead, she turns around and folds her arms and looks defiantly around the room, at the groups of gossiping knitters and cheery quiz teams, and makes her face into something not exactly like a sneer, more a kind of pitying glance.

Al comes up, wondering why she hasn't ordered.

'Hiya, Shelby,' he says, and Shelby turns to face him with a huge, sticky lip-glossed grin. Her teeth are very white and even, again slightly belying Hector, Carso's only dentist, a well-meaning man but not exactly *au fait* with dental fashions.

'Hiya!' she trills, as if lit up. Essie smiles gratefully at Al, while looking over at the tiny wooden table with her mum's friends from the hospital. Their team is called the Ancillary Justices. Nobody understands this except for one intense young man called Owen, with long, greasy black hair, who sometimes manages to look skinny but have a potbelly at the same time. She keeps an eye on Al.

'Can I get a bottle of white and two G&Ts? How's Dwight?' says Al.

Shelby and Dwight's parents were big fans of line dancing, hugely popular in Scotland. Essie remembers them at the village ceilidhs, persuading the band to play 'Achy Breaky Heart' and then all doing their special walking-about dance while the old folk found it adorable. Some years they got a few people to do it with them. Essie remembers being very small and feeling jealous of Shelby in a white lace shirt, pink cowboy boots and lip gloss. And Dwight, all freckles and cowboy hat.

'He's alright, yeah. He's coming in.'

'What's he up to these days? Roping cattle?'

'Ha bloody ha, Alasdair Munroe. He's just come in off the rigs, if you must know. Made a fortune.'

This was said loudly enough for Essie to hear, and was almost certainly deliberate, thinks Essie gloomily.

'Good for him,' says Al, meaning it. It wasn't an easy life, on the rigs.

'Not sitting in a nice warm office like you.'

'I resent that remark,' says Al. 'Sometimes I have to go out with a crossbow.' He nods at Essie. 'You remember my sister.'

Shelby turns towards her as if she's just noticed her for the first time. 'Gracing us with your presence from the big city,' she says, not pleasantly, but with a big grin to cover that up.

'Something like that,' says Essie, trying not to sound over-eager, or over-anything, in fact.

'You went to the university, aye?'

'Yeah,' says Essie, unwilling to elaborate, so the conversation dams up like water slowing to a trickle.

'Well, alright for some,' says Shelby, serving up the G&Ts.

'Wow,' says Al, as they head back to the table. 'Okay. You were right and I was wrong. She really does hate you.'

'I never *did* anything,' says Essie.

'You went off far away to university and shook everyone off your shoes like they were cat poo!' says Al, grinning.

'Yes, because of horrible people like her!'

'Uh-huh.'

Al sets the wine down and Janey smiles at Essie. 'See, I told you you'd be fine in here.'

'I am not fine in here!' says Essie immediately. 'She looks like she wants to bar me! God, this town.'

Janey can't believe it's quite as bad as all that and looks around the room expectantly. She knows nearly everyone in here. That's one thing. People were so sympathetic after the divorce, and it really helped. Milton is sitting on her left, frowning. He gets nervous on quiz nights and says it reminds him too much of the citizenship test, but he comes anyway to keep them company. Lish is texting her Emma, who wants to know what she thinks of her new curtains. Amsan is drinking coke and telling her about how worried she is that her son is getting into crypto, which is Amsan's way of also telling her that her son has enough money to be getting into crypto.

Suddenly she sees an oddly familiar face appear at the door. He's tall and thick-set and burly and looks like he doesn't quite know what he's doing there.

Al sees him too. 'Oh, God,' he says, frowning.

'What? Who's that?' says Janey. It's tugging at the back of her mind but she can't quite place him.

Meanwhile, Essie finds herself seated next to Owen, the only man her age. She's feeling a bit guilty about slagging off the town to her mum, but really.

'Hi,' he says in a doleful voice.

'Hi,' says Essie. 'Are you here for the quiz?'

Owen snorts. 'Well, *obviously*,' he says, which is quite rude if you think about it.

'Uh, good,' says Essie. Owen sniffs again, loudly.

'The problem here,' he says, glancing round at the warm room full of happy people greeting each other, who all look pleased to be out on a lovely spring evening, and are passing trays of bottles and glasses along the throng, and ordering chips from a very young waitress, and wandering among tables to chat to their neighbours and discuss the upturned tractor on the B47, 'is that these people don't look like they're going to be taking this seriously *at all.*'

His droopy face droops even further, and he folds his arms. He is wearing a short-sleeved shirt that has sharply ironed creases in it. Essie wants to ask him if his mum had done them but didn't think it would be quite polite.

'Isn't that okay?' says Essie. 'Isn't it supposed to be fun?'

Owen snorts again. The way he clearly thinks he is too good for all this is, paradoxically, making Essie want to defend it.

'If your idea of fun is . . . *losing a quiz*,' he says, glancing at his watch. 'Look at that. We should have started five minutes ago.' He looks at her. 'Have you even got a pencil?' His tone is accusatory.

'No,' admitted Essie. 'I need a pencil?'

'No, not if you always write the correct answer down *first time*,' he says with something that might be laughter.

Meanwhile, Janey is still looking at the man who has just walked in the door and is now standing at the bar.

'I'm sure I know him,' she says.

'No, you don't,' says Al. 'I've worked on his land. He's an absolute grouch. Does nothing but complain about us.'

'No, I definitely know him,' says Janey, frowning. Stupid menopause brain. She can never remember anyone. 'He's got a weird name.' Then she snaps her fingers. 'Oh! He had a kid.'

'Well, he definitely lives alone,' sniffs Al. 'I know because I have to go to his big stupid house and explain to him that he's got to stop feeding the deer. And I know he has a weird name. It's Lowell.'

'He feeds deer?' says Janey. 'What a monster.'

It is all coming back to her. A little girl, congenitally deaf. Gosh, that was a long time ago. He had been . . . he hadn't had as much grey hair then, and his wife had been much younger . . . Something had happened – she racks her brains. Oh, yes! They had been lined up for a cochlear implant; the child was just lovely, and then . . . nothing. They'd moved away or the files had been transferred or something. How strange. He was English, she remembered that, and his wife was . . . Albanian? She can't quite recall.

The man stands at the bar looking awkward, then relieved when Shelby bustles over to serve him. He orders a half-pint, then looks around, a little nervous, at the noisy room, full of people who knew each other.

'Look busy,' says Al, just as the man's gaze sweeps over him.

'When are we starting, please?' comes Owen's voice, loudly.

'Why?' says Lish. 'Where are you headed after this, String-fellow's?'

'You're right,' says Owen. 'Silly me. Just because they advertised a quiz at seven-thirty and chalked-up "QUIZ SEVEN-THIRTY", imagine me thinking there's going to be a quiz. What a moron I am.'

Essie and Janey exchange glances, and almost smile at one another. It's a feeling Essie hasn't had in quite a while, and Janey ducks her head, so it doesn't turn into a thing.

The quizmaster, Hector the dentist, is standing up and attempting to get people's attention – he has Owen's, raptly – and clearing his throat and tapping the mic. Even though he always does the quiz, he always also manages to behave as if he's never handled a microphone, a crowd, or written English before.

'Good evening, ladies and gentlemen, and, um, everyone else . . . '

Hector does his best to be up-to-date but doesn't always manage it.

'So, um, hi,' the strange man Janey recognises is saying to Al, who is grimacing and trying to be polite back. Everyone else is shushing each other and taking their seats.

'SIT DOWN,' booms Owen, suddenly, looking up under his beetle brows at the strange man.

'Um . . . ?' says Lowell, looking confused.

'So if you'd all like to sit down, it's straight into Round One,' continues Hector.

'I didn't really come for a qui—'

'Question one. Which English monarch was believed to have ordered the deaths of the princes in the tower?'

'Richard III,' says Owen promptly, snatching the answer sheet from the middle of the table, and wielding his pencil, one of four lining his top pocket.

'Actually,' says the strange man mildly. 'I think historians now believe it was Henry VII . . . '

Owen turned round his face scornfully.

'*Do they*?' he says. 'Are you even in this team?'

Milton glances over. 'I think it is Henry VII also,' he says, politely, then stretched his hand out to shake the man's. 'Milton,' he says.

'Lowell,' says the man, and before he knows it, he's sitting down.

The round finishes and they swap papers with the table behind them and, sure enough, the answer is Henry VII.

Owen goes pink.

'Well, this is nonsense,' he says. 'It's in a *Shakespeare play*. I challenge this answer!'

'Evening, Owen,' says Hector, with a certain world-weariness.

'Might I buy a round of drinks?' says Lowell, standing up. He glances at Janey and suddenly his face looks puzzled. 'Sorry . . . have we met?'

The entire table looks at them expectantly.

'I'll come and help you with drinks,' says Janey, unwilling to share a patient's medical history with half the town. The local knitting circle are at the next table. They are all terrible at the quiz – they keep knitting when they're meant to be filling in the form – but they love a night out and they all have ears like bats.

'Janey Munroe,' she introduces herself once they're at the bar. 'I was . . . ' She can't remember the child's name. 'I was briefly your daughter's audiologist.'

He inhales deeply. 'Of course! That's it. Sorry. Sorry, I didn't realise . . . out of context, you know. And I'm getting old.' He shakes his head.

'That's okay, but . . . why are you at our quiz night?'

'I'm really not,' he says. 'I'm so sorry. Would you like me to leave? I was just passing and . . . a quiz night kind of happened to me.'

Owen and Hector were by now having quite a noisy dispute about Catherine Parr.

'No, not at all . . . how's your daughter?'

He wrinkled his nose. 'Uh,' he says. 'It's complicated.'

And Janey feels immediately that she's crossed a boundary. 'I'm sorry,' she says quickly. 'None of my business, of course.'

'No, no, not at all.' He has that slightly clipped way of speaking, as much English as Scottish, with an accent you don't hear much on television these days. It sounds as if it is from a slightly different age. 'Verity is wonderful. She's great. Thriving.' He bites his lip. 'Her mother isn't crazy about me, that's all.'

Shelby comes to serve them.

'Is that . . . is that the only white wine you have?' he asks, with a slightly pained expression, and Janey wants to smile; maybe Essie has a point.

Shelby folds her arms and looks at him as if he'd just asked if she was serving squirrel juice. 'Yeah.'

'Okay . . . a couple of bottles of that, then.'

'That's very generous,' says Janey, surprised, but Hector is already starting a new round, the first question of which appears to involve listing rugby teams, and Milton is gesturing for Lowell to come over quite urgently. Owen is sullenly taking dictation with his special quiz pencil.

'How many Doctor Whos . . . ' begins Hector, and Owen's eyes slowly begin to close. This is turning into the worst quiz night of all time.

'Are you okay?' asks Essie, slightly worried about him.

'This is . . . an impossible-to-answer question,' says Owen. 'I feel I should start the steward's enquiry now to save time.'

'Why?' says Essie. 'Count up the number of actors.'

'Audio, film or television?' says Owen immediately. 'And what about Doctor Moon?'

Essie does not have a clue what he's talking about, only that he looks as if he might get some spittle on her. She remembers, very briefly, going to the launch of a new perfume on the fourth floor of Harvey Nichols on St Andrew's Square. There were amazing-looking people there, and lots of Scottish celebrities. It had been extremely exciting and there had been a specially

created cocktail just for the occasion. Alright, so a haggis mar-
tini probably wasn't going to catch on everywhere, but, even so,
it had been so very jolly that evening, looking down from the
glamorous balcony on to the wet punters on the square below.

Just as she is thinking perhaps she should just sneak out on
her own, as Owen has now counted up to two dozen Doctor
Whos, Al leaps to his feet.

'Yo!'

14

The new arrival is not particularly tall, walks with a swagger as though he owns the place, and looks slightly annoyed, as if he hadn't expected so many people to be in his living room. Essie looks up at him. There is something familiar about him, but then she always sees something familiar in this town: faces repeating, generation after generation. He is the most ridiculously dressed person she's ever seen, and she wants to laugh. Simon Cowell-style cowboy boots under incredibly tight Levis, and, of all things, a cowboy hat. At first she thinks he's a stripper sent as a joke; but Al is already moving forward.

'Dwight, man, how's it going?'

The man nods. 'Al. Alright, aye. Shelby, can I get a beer?'

'No!' says Shelby. 'This isn't your bar. You can wait in a queue like everybody else.'

Dwight frowns crossly, and Essie realises who he is: Shelby's brother. Of course. Both their names are completely mad. But he can't . . . he can't *still* be dressing like this. Oh, my God. It's the most embarrassing thing she's ever seen. He's not big, but he's wiry, and his clothes absolutely cling to him. She looks away, only to be confronted with Owen scratching a pimple that's peeping out through his moustache. Oh, lord.

'How you doing?' says Al to Dwight.

'Well, beerless, mostly,' says Dwight, still frowning. His eyes rest momentarily on Essie and he nods quickly, and she nods back just as quickly. Then he actually tips his hat to her. She stifles a giggle, which her mum notices, crossly.

Janey comes over to the boys. She's always had a soft spot for wee Dwight, with his silly name and cowboy boots and enforced line-dancing. He'd always taken it all in reasonably good part, and even when he was small he used to tip his cowboy hat at ladies he passed, which made her laugh. He doesn't have freckles any more, but you can still see the cheeky little boy within the man. And now she is far too old to have useful opinions about it, she thinks he fills his jeans out rather nicely, if anyone would ever think to ask her, which they wouldn't, in her sensible hospital lanyard.

'Hello, Dwight,' she says warmly.

'Howdy, ma'am,' he says, because he knows she likes it, even though it makes her feel about a hundred also.

'You off the rigs, I hear?'

'Oh, yeah,' he says, brightening.

'Excuse me?' says Owen, bright pink and shouting over from the table. 'But we have three minutes to work out which of these names are Grand National winners and which are Crufts winners.'

'Yeah, I'd had enough,' says Dwight, ignoring Owen completely. 'And I've got a plan.'

'He thinks he's going to be Billy Big Bollocks of Carso,' remarks Shelby loudly.

'Shut it, you,' says Dwight crossly.

'Mr Property Developer,' says Shelby, rolling her eyes.

'Ooh,' says Janey, impressed. And, it's property. Always interesting. 'Whereabouts?'

Dwight shrugged. 'I've bought Seagate. Going to do it up for holiday cottages.'

Janey blinks. 'You've bought the houses next door to me?'

'Is that where you are, aye?'

'Yes! I thought they'd just gone up – the For Sale sign arrived yesterday!'

'Aye,' smiles Dwight. 'But there's a . . . ' He obviously can't remember the word. 'There's a condition on them – they can only get sold locally. So I just swooped in and . . . swoosh!'

Janey raises her eyebrows, which is a bit harder to do since she'd gone to Caithness for Botox. Hector the dentist does it in town, but the idea of entrusting her face to Hector, and going in and out of his office in front of everyone, is a bit much for Janey. It isn't that she lies to her mates about it specifically. Every-one politely doesn't ask the questions, that's all. Well, she'd once tried to bring it up with Lish, but predictably Lish has never had anything done and has completely wrinkle-free skin and couldn't understand what Janey was on about or why she should mess with her perfectly serviceable face, so Janey had retreated timidly. It's a nice thing, Janey sometimes thinks, to have a friend who is so confident and secure in everything. But it is also, quite often, incredibly annoying. Janey tries to watch what she eats, so she can still get into her jeans. Lish thinks this is ridiculous behaviour, eats cake whenever she feels like it, and just wears a larger size.

'Hang on,' Janey says, frowning, which she can still do. 'Does this mean I'm going to be living next to a building site for the next year?'

'We will be quiet as mice, ma'am,' says Dwight, cocking his ridiculous cowboy hat at her again. 'And by the time we're done, your road will be the smartest in Carso.'

'Hmm.' Mind you, she can't help thinking, it will be nice to have the street tidied up, and everything fresh and nice.

'Well, well done,' she says finally in genuine admiration. 'There must have been loads of vultures circling.'

'Aye,' says Dwight. 'There was a bunch of consortiums wanting them. *Codicil.* That's what it's called. Something written in the will.' He smiles, looking cocky. 'I did pretty well on the rigs.'

'You must have done,' says Janey admiringly. Essie looks up. She couldn't help hearing her mother's admiring tone, something she hasn't heard applied to herself for quite a while. So Shelby is running the bar and Dwight is clearly doing well. Essie remembers, with some bitterness, being smug about the fact that she'd got her qualifications and was moving away, and these guys were stuck here. It doesn't seem quite like that now. Her student loan is still enormous. Whereas these guys won't have any.

'Grand National,' she says automatically to Owen, who is pushing a piece of paper in her face.

'Lord Floss-Floss of Cardingdale?' he says. 'I shouldn't have thought so. What do you think to Prince Nero Verashan dell'Antico?'

'Foreign is horses, local is dogs,' says Lowell unexpectedly. He has proven to be a quiet yet valuable member of the quiz team, killed it on architectural terms, and is the only person Owen can currently look at with respect, even though they are all getting thrashed by a team of out-of-town ringers, all men, who are sitting in the corner not talking to anyone and pretending to be local even though they clearly aren't. Hector had taken many complaints about ringers in the quiz night (admittedly many of them from Owen) and had attempted to establish a ten-mile village perimeter from where people were allowed to enter, but it didn't work well for visiting relatives and friends and people having to dig out utility bills, and frankly absolutely nobody could get on board with it, so the £50 fish shop voucher was still at risk from the shark ringers. The only good thing anyone could see was that all four were drinking, which meant they'd be catching the bus back to wherever they'd plotted the evil scheme from, and that bus was always late, incredibly draughty and meandered round the houses for hours, and that was without factoring in the upturned tractor on the B47, so they had to hope it was worth it for their stupid fish voucher.

'Huh,' says Owen, as Hector reads out the answers and Lowell is proved to be right. Janey, meanwhile, on a few glasses of the white Lowell had bought, is doing that thing where you try not to be an idiot in front of your children, but somehow you just can't help yourself. She can hear her own voice in her head, sounding ridiculous.

'Dwight, you remember my daughter, Essie, don't you?'

Essie is shooting her a look she knows only too well, and doesn't even stand up as Dwight ambles over, sticking out his hand.

'I sure do – hi there. Aren't you in the big city now?' he says, still with that politeness Janey remembers from his days of talent shows and town fêtes. He never got tall, she notices; he's wiry, not big like Shelby. He's a little taller than Essie, but then his boots probably have heels.

'I'm back. For a bit,' says Essie, giving an 'and now we're done' thin-lipped smile in a way that makes Janey want to shake her. Shelby is watching all of this, her face like fizz.

'Oh, good,' says Dwight, amiably enough, then, to Al, 'Let's catch up, eh?' just as Hector says, 'And now, the round is Eighties song lyrics' and the entire table of quizzers says 'Ooooh!' and (finally, thinks Owen, darkly) starts paying attention.

*

Owen sits with his arms folded as the final tally comes in. Everyone else was more or less completely uninterested, and a couple of people who'd hit the wine quite hard had appeared to have forgotten they were in any kind of a quiz altogether. The Ancillary Justices have come in third, to Janey's evident surprise; they never normally win anything. There is even a prize, a bottle of prosecco, which Shelby hands over rather reluctantly, but they open it right away in delight.

'You got all the questions!' Janey says, grinning at Lowell, who had obviously made the difference.

'That's not true,' says Lowell, cheerfully allowing her to slosh the cheap fizz into his empty glass and smiling despite himself. 'You were very, very good on Eighties song lyrics.'

'I was rather,' agreed Janey, a little carried away. 'I used to memorise them all from *Smash Hits*.'

Lowell grins again. 'I couldn't even read that text these days,' he says. 'Didn't they used to print in white on top of photographs?'

'I didn't have you down as a *Smash Hits* fan,' Janey says, looking at his slightly shabby waxed jacket.

'I wasn't,' says Lowell. 'I was definitely an *NME* kid. Although I had never heard of any of the bands.'

'I was scared of the *NME*,' Janey finds herself confessing. 'They were so mean to everyone. And the bands were all called things like "Scraping Babies Out of the Abyss".'

'I think I saw Scraping Babies Out of the Abyss at Caithness Pleasure Gardens,' he says. 'They weren't as good as Super Big Nuclear War or the I Hate Thatchers.'

She laughs immediately.

'I did love music then, though.' Lowell is warming to his subject. 'God. Once I went to Glasgow and I bought an album from Fopp and I kept that plastic bag – I took it everywhere with me, until it was falling apart. So people would think that I was in Fopp every weekend when I lived in Thurso.'

Janey shakes her head. 'Don't start me!' she says. 'I am *furious* about the vinyl revival. You know Fopp is back?'

'Is it?' says Lowell. 'I think I still have the bag.'

'I genuinely can't believe I got rid of all my vinyl. I can't believe it. My daughter wanted a *record player* last Christmas. There's even an HMV in Edinburgh.'

Lowell shakes his head. 'Wow. I am behind the times. Or so far ahead of them I have no idea what's going on.'

'And,' says Janey, 'having basically given away all my albums to a jumble sale, I thought, oh maybe I'll just buy *Hounds of Love* again.'

He smiles. 'All the girls I used to fancy at school had that album.'

'That is not true, because all of us girls who had that album never got asked out one single time. The boys were busy asking out the girls who had Def Leppard albums.'

'I'm not saying I had the courage to ask any of them out.'

She grins. 'Anyway, I took it up to the cash desk . . . you won't believe this.'

'Go on,' says Lowell, squeezing his eyes shut. 'Everything is *so expensive.*'

'It cost thirty pounds.'

'No way!'

'I thought six pounds was expensive the first time.'

'It was.'

'Not for that album,' says Janey fiercely. 'But paying it again really hurt.'

'But worth it, though?'

'No!' says Janey. 'Because I put it on Essie's record player and guess what? They've remastered them and cleaned them all up. So you don't get the breaths and the crackles and little noises. It didn't sound the same at all! It sounded exactly like Spotify!'

'Almost as if,' says Lowell, 'getting older is an endless series of disappointments.' He looks at her suddenly, then drains his drink. 'It's been really nice to meet you.'

'Janey,' she supplies.

'No, I knew that,' he says. 'I remember you. You were . . . very kind to us.'

'I'm sorry I couldn't help . . . '

Again he looks awkward and she doesn't want to intrude, and anyway Owen is getting up and putting on his anorak that he zips right up to his neck, still complaining about Hector's mispronunciation of Eastern European capitals, and Essie is looking at her mother in an accusatory way that Janey is sure has something to do with her re-introducing her to Dwight, and she really ought to call it a night.

'How are you getting home?' she finds herself saying, again feeling stupid. She is sure she used to be charming. When did she forget how; when did it all become so difficult?

'Oh, I have my bicycle,' he said.

'I didn't have you down for a MAMIL,' she says. He looks confused, and then she doesn't want to say 'Middle-Aged Man in Lycra' because it will sound so weird. 'I meant, what kind of bike do you have?' she gabbles.

'I don't know,' he says. 'I think it belongs to the gardener. I just borrowed it.'

'That's my favourite type of bike,' she gushes, going red – is it very hot in this bar? – and Lowell looks confused.

'Okay, Janey,' says Al, coming up behind her. 'You're all flushed. Better get you home!'

15

Janey has the next day off and hooray, she thinks, pulling back her curtains: it is a pretty one. She cranes round to see the dilapidated windows of the other houses in the close. Goodness, Dwight will have his work cut out. She immediately jumps on a property website to see what they are asking for them, but they haven't appeared.

Al had gone to Aberdeen first shout to discuss a new tannery. Sometimes Janey does not like to think too deeply about what her eldest actually does in his highly successful job; the day she'd asked to pop in to see him at work and he'd been getting everyone in the office to test out new electric fences sprang to mind.

It is a lovely spring morning, just coming into bluebell season, when the astonishing heavy scent of the flowers coats the woods, so lovely it is almost impossible to believe they are real. Certainly it doesn't matter how up-to-date your camera is; you won't manage to catch their loveliness or the way they appear to hover just above their green stems, like a carpet. You can put lots of filters on it before you post it on Instagram, but you know it's not the same, not really, as drifting in that soft blue cloud, feeling privileged to be inside it, scowling if you see anyone dare to pick one, even though you know they only want the same thing as you do: to hold on to that sweet scent a little longer, bring it with them wherever they go, as a talisman. Janey has bought every type of bluebell scent ever since, from very expensive candles to basic room plug-ins, but none of them, none of them even gets close. At best it's a harsh reminder, outside of that precious three weeks when they bloom so briefly.

As she gets older Janey feels these things are more important, more special for being transient. If the bluebell cloud settled over the world permanently, it would lose all of its magic. Likewise Christmas, even though that seems to come round every fifteen seconds these days. Whereas, the young, of course, have so many years ahead to appreciate it . . .

But she isn't old, she reminds herself. She is middle-aged. She has absolutely yonkingtons.

'Hey,' she says up the stairs at nine-thirty, as she feels the day slipping away from her; her precious day off and she really doesn't want to spend it scrolling or catching up on housework or trying to work out which of the nine thousand new shows to watch on television and ending up with *Sex and the City* again, astounded anew at Carrie constantly lighting up cigarettes indoors and nobody even mentioning it.

There's no reply. She had felt the quiz night had marked something of a thawing in general relations with her most beloved, gorgeous, wonderful, utterly infuriating daughter, but it was possible Alasdair was being a buffer, and so it proves.

'*What*?' comes a voice, finally, and it sounds so like Essie at fifteen on a school morning that Janey has to check herself.

'Well,' she says, clearing her throat and telling herself it is ridiculous to be slightly scared of your own daughter, 'it's a glorious day and I was going to go and walk through the bluebell wood and thought you might like to come.'

'Neh, I'm working on my CV,' comes the default response, as it always does these days.

'You aren't,' says Janey, feeling slightly shaky. But this can't go on. 'You're lying in bed staring at your phone.'

She goes up the stairs, knocks on the door and goes in.

'Mu-um!'

The bedroom is in a right state. Clothes are strewn everywhere, along with dirty coffee cups. The suitcase is a floordrobe.

To her credit Essie does look shamefaced at the state of it; she knows Janey has worked very hard to get the cottage into shape. The dusky pink walls might not be to everyone's taste, but Janey thinks they are soft and lovely and suit the evening light, and she chose the colour with care and painted the room herself. And now it's just a scrap heap.

'I've got stuff to do,' says Essie, angry and defensive. 'You don't even care.'

'Of course I do,' says Janey.

'But you don't understand what it's like out there. You think it's me not doing it properly, not doing the "get a job, get a place" thing. But everything's changed! It's not like that now! You don't just walk down the road and get a job! You're up against everyone in the world! And everyone else can do internships . . . '

Essie's voice trails off. She knows this is unfair. Her family have never had the money for her to undertake unpaid internships in big banks, but that's not her mum's fault.

'You don't just get a job, then get a house. Everything . . . everything is different.'

'You're right,' says Janey. 'I don't understand. The whole world seems mad to me.'

Essie harrumphs.

'So maybe . . . a wee walk to clear your head and get your focus on? You're meant to get out in nature every day, aren't you? We could call it a forest bath?'

She attempts a conciliatory smile. She doesn't think Essie is depressed, clinically depressed; she has worked with particularly elderly people who lose their hearing and withdraw from the world, and Essie is not in that place. But she recognises her beloved daughter is very, very sad, and incredibly upset about this halt in her hitherto glittering career. Janey understands completely, and wishes Essie could talk to her about it. But obviously she's too proud and can't, or won't. And Janey feels so bad that things have got to this state. But you can respect that people are sad and feel sorry for them, while also finding them quite annoying, that's for sure.

'Anyway, you need to strip your sheets, it's a perfect drying day.'

This is true: it is breezy and bright, and also, giving Essie an ultimatum might help. Janey glances down at Essie's laptop. It is open on the same property website Janey was looking at.

'Were you snooping at the houses for sale next door?' she asks immediately.

'No!' Essie scoops up the laptop. 'Maybe.'

'They're not on there,' says Janey.

'I know. Why not?'

'Well, I happen to know the answer to that,' says Janey. 'I'll tell you if you come for a walk. Fancy buying one?'

'Of course not!' chokes Essie, horrified.

'I was only joking,' says Janey. 'Come on. A wander through the woods and I'll buy you a hot chocolate at the shore. With marshmallows. You love them.'

'Mum!' says Essie. 'I'm not nine!'

'Marshmallows are not ageist,' says Janey, conscious that for once she appears to be winning a battle. 'They are the only thing in the world that isn't. I'll see you downstairs in half an hour.'

★

Of course it's nearly an hour, and the glorious morning is nearly gone and the afternoon, as is so often the case, looks as if it might not be nearly so nice. But even so. It is a victory of sorts, compounded when Essie rather clumpily brings down her coffee cups and stuffs her sheets in the laundry basket, which is not the washing machine, but close enough for government work.

They agree to go together into the cobbled streets of the town, heading down naturally, as your feet take you, towards the harbour. They'll skirt it, then turn south into the woods, following people walking their dogs – it's a happy life in Carso for dogs, although depending on your standards of dog cleanliness it can be tricky for their owners, as dogs like nothing better than a good splash about in the waves in the morning followed by running into the forest for a quick roll in the mud, plus some fox poo if that's available, which it always is. There are plenty of West Highland terriers, and terriers in general, with short wiry coats, who don't mind the cold but dislike swimming, which is useful. The people with long-haired wave-loving spaniels learn very quickly to give up on any ultra-high standards of non-muddiness for their cars, hair, houses, clothes, etc.

The children had been desperate for a dog when they were little, but Colin had not had time for it, didn't want the fuss. In fact, Janey reminds herself, that big dog that Johnson was talking about is still missing. An Irish wolfhound, it turned out; it was sitting, looking gormless, on the local Facebook page while people offered up various hopes and prayers but, tragically, no sightings. It isn't a dog she recognises, but it appears to be the size of a small horse, which leaves an obvious question as to how it could be missing, unless someone had accidentally jumped on it for the Grand National.

They walk in what Janey would call a companionable silence. She wants to say something normal, like did Essie have fun at the quiz, but doesn't want Essie to snort and say *of course not* like she did when she'd made a mild remark about buying the house next door. Also, Janey herself is still feeling slightly too touchy about making a slight idiot of herself in front of that man to really think about it.

'Sorry you got Owen yesterday,' she offers.

Essie blinks. She doesn't want to admit it but going out last night – even with Shelby there, grumpily eyeing her up from the corner – and being out in the fresh sea air this morning – she has had a shower and is wearing jeans and a jumper and is not, amazingly, freezing to death, even though the jumper was incredibly expensive and therefore has holes and fraying bits all over it, thus making it not very good at actual jumpering – is doing her a little bit of good. Obviously last night was terrible: but it had stopped her missing Connor and her lost life for five seconds, particularly as they had to put all their phones into a basket as apparently there had been some fairly rampant Google cheating from ringers in the past, and Hector was having a crackdown.

And today there is a clear blue in the air, and the wind has dropped. The wind doesn't ever really drop in Edinburgh; the whole place is effectively a wind tunnel, designed that way to keep the English out, someone once said, in which case it has been quite spectacularly unsuccessful.

'I thought you were setting me up,' she says, but not in an angry tone.

'I know I'm a terrible mother,' says Janey, 'but even I would not inflict Owen on you. I'm just surprised he works in a hospital rather than running the prison service.'

'What does he do in the hospital?'

'Why, you interested?'

'From a psychological standpoint, sure.'

Janey laughs. 'Guess.'

'IT? Or would that be too obvious?'

'It would,' says Janey. 'Owen looks after the fax machines.'

'The *fax* machines!'

'The NHS is the largest user of fax machines in the world. Our IT systems don't talk to each other and faxes are relatively secure.'

'He's the world's last fax repairman! That's actually quite romantic when you think about it.'

As they turn back along the harbour, Essie looks back up to Seagate, their tiny street full of cottages. The trio for sale really do look like they're falling down.

'I can't believe Dwight's bought these,' Janey muses.

'Dwight?' says Essie, who hadn't thought much of him the night before apart from cringing at his stupid hat.

'Yeah, he's bought them.'

'What do you mean, bought "them"?' She stares at the For Sale sign at the end of the row.

'He's bought all three of them, to do them up. Some kind of local arrangement.'

'Why did they put the For Sale sign up, then?'

'I'm not sure,' says Janey. 'Maybe it's like banns?'

Essie shakes her head and moves closer. 'Unbelievable,' she says.

'What?' says Janey.

'He's bought . . . *three* houses!'

'Well, three wrecks,' says Janey. 'I mean, seriously, look at them.'

But Essie seems wretched suddenly, and Janey is genuinely worried by the look in her eyes.

'What's up?'

'I . . . ' Essie shakes her head. 'I don't . . . ' She suddenly can't go on. She finds herself almost in tears. 'I'm never going to be able to buy a house. Never! And he's bought three! And he doesn't even . . . he doesn't have student loans, he's got no brains in his head except . . . *line dancing*! I can't believe I'm never going to live anywhere except stupid shared rentals while that lughead—'

'What?' comes a voice suddenly.

Essie whirls round in despair. 'What?' she says, panicking, her heart dropping through the floor like a plummeting lift.

'What will that lughead do?' comes the voice.

Dwight is standing there, thumbs entwined in his jean belt loops, which must be a childhood boot-scooting habit, and looks completely mad. Although at least he is *sans* hat today. His hair is scruffy.

'Hey, Dwight,' says Janey. 'Sorry. Essie was just venting.'

'I was,' says Essie. 'Sorry. I just . . . I can't afford . . . '

'You're in Edinburgh, right? No wonder. Crazy prices there. Nuts.' He shakes his head. 'But then again, what would I know? I've got no brains in my head.'

'I'm sorry,' says Essie again. 'I'm really sorry.'

'It's okay,' shrugs Dwight. 'I heard from my sister that things had gone totally to shit for you.'

Essie shrivels inside. What has Shelby said? She doesn't have to wait long to find out.

'She says you've had some kind of breakdown. Had to come home with your tail between your legs.'

'Shelby seems to know a lot about me,' says Essie, trying to reclaim some dignity.

Dwight shrugs. 'Well, you're here, ain't you?'

'Did you just say, "ain't"?' says Essie, her voice icy.

'There's a lot of work to do on the houses,' says Janey quickly, figuring that the fastest way out of this conversation is changing the subject.

'There is,' says Dwight. 'I'm not afraid of hard work.' He jangles a set of keys in his hand. 'Want a peek?'

'No,' says Essie sulkily, at the exact same moment as Janey, genetically incapable of not having a look around someone else's house, says, 'Yes, please!'

Essie nudges her hard.

'What? Come on. I visited Mrs MacAleese there, you know. I want to see what you're going to do. And how much it's going to disrupt me, in particular.'

'Sure,' says Dwight equably.

'Am I right in thinking,' says Janey, catching him up, as Essie dawdles behind, furious with everything, 'that Mrs MacAleese didn't have indoor plumbing? That's how it seemed back when I was here, but surely they sorted it out?'

'They never did,' says Dwight. 'She didn't like the thought of it, said it was unhygienic to go to the bathroom in the same place as you ate your meals.'

'Ha,' says Janey. 'My grandad thought that. But won't you need, like, en-suite bathrooms to every single room including the other bathrooms? If you're going to let it out.'

'They're going to be holiday lets?' says Essie icily.

'Haven't decided,' says Dwight, unlocking the first door.

Janey pokes her head inside. The house smells very unpleasant – cold and unoccupied, with the suspicion of rats – and, as the door creaks open, a bird rises up to the rafters and disappears.

'Well, it's getting out somewhere,' says Dwight, following her gaze upwards.

The floor is littered with old magazines and pieces of stained carpet, and there is a boarded-up fireplace. Wallpaper has been pulled off the wall, and the spray-painted signs on the far wall indicate that this place has seen some use, presumably by local teens.

'Goodness,' says Janey. 'You've got your work cut out. This is worse than the state mine was in, and mine was bad.'

Dwight scratches his head. 'I know,' he says. 'But there's a load of lads doing two on, one off, yeah?' He is talking about the men who go on the rigs; tough, hard grafters, the lot of them. They work two months on for every month they have back at home, with their families, or, sometimes, in the pub. 'They can do with a project, aye?'

'I know,' says Janey. And she does; she sees them all the time. The constant roar of the drill is hard on the men's ears. They're issued with protectors but they won't wear the damn things; they're young, they think they're untouchable. She sees them at fifty, when they can't hear the TV, when the world feels like it is becoming unreachable. She tries, always, not to make a big deal out of how preventable it could have been. The money on the rigs is good, but she never wanted Alasdair to go.

'Make them wear their ear protectors, okay?'

Dwight looks at her. 'Yes, ma'am.'

Janey glances around. The house is laid out like hers, only the other way around.

'Think how many generations lived here,' she says. 'It's two hundred years easy, just like mine.'

'Two hundred and thirty,' says Dwight, not without pride. 'Every stone put in by hand.'

Janey peered into the ancient fireplace, charred black. 'I think she still cooked in a pot.'

Dwight smiled. 'Aye, you're probably right about that. Probably why she lived until she was ninety.'

'Probably is.'

Essie is looking around, taking in the beautiful old walls, the rickety floor. Nothing has been changed or replaced here over the years. She shivers, thinking of the blur of humans who have been born, grown old and died here. She glances out of the filthy back window of the very basic kitchen. You can see the sunlight glinting off the waves, right from here, through a crack in the big houses on the front, which you can't from her mum's.

'How are you doing the decor?' she says.

Dwight shrugs. 'Dunno,' he says. 'Just going to clean it up a bit, figure it out. Probably nip down to B&Q Inverness.'

Janey and Essie turn to look at him and at this moment they look extremely alike, both horrified.

'What?' he says. 'What's wrong with it?'

'But the bones of this place . . . ' starts Essie. 'What you could do with the northern light . . . you could make it so beautiful and maybe Scandinavian.'

'Or give it a nice beachy vibe,' says Janey. 'Everyone likes that.'

'No, Mum,' says Essie. 'Oh, my God, you'll be putting up a *Live Laugh Love* sign next.'

'I quite like those signs that say *To the Beach*,' says Janey mildly, because it's perfectly okay to like what she likes. 'And pale blue. And slatted wood. And ticking.'

'Happy 2011, Karen,' says Essie.

'Ach, well,' says Dwight, turning away. 'I wouldn't know, I don't have a brain in my head.'

Essie thinks about how in the city you hardly ever run into anyone you know, and how much she prefers that way of doing things, and turns to head back when suddenly she hears a noise from upstairs.

It's an odd noise, not a cat, but not unlike a mew or a howl. They all freeze. Essie feels the hairs on her neck stand up.

'Did you hear that?' says Janey, and Essie wants to roll her eyes because her mother always has to be the queen of whether or not people can hear things.

'Ssh,' she says, and then the odd, unearthly sound comes again.

'Sounds like Mrs MacAleese doesn't want you to take over her cottage,' says Janey, and Dwight starts for a moment.

'What?' he says.

Janey grins. 'I'm kidding.'

'Well, don't kid,' he says crossly. 'You see some strange things on the rigs, I'll tell you that.'

'I'm heading out,' says Essie.

'You can't,' says Janey. 'What if it's an animal in distress? Come on.'

Essie frowns. 'It'll be a stupid seagull shouting at another seagull. You know what they're like: total thugs.'

Seagulls *are* thugs; this is indisputable.

'Yes, but if it's stuck?' says Janey.

'One less seagull in the world, oh, no,' says Essie, but she knows when she's beaten. 'Are the stairs safe?'

Dwight shrugs. 'They carried Mrs MacAleese, and she was the size of a Highland coo.'

'Dwight!'

'What? I'm estimating. It can't have been far off. Took me long enough to clear the Tunnocks teacake wrappers out.'

'Actually they're surprisingly low-calorie,' says Janey.

Essie looks at her, having delivered many lectures about diet culture over the years.

'Stop with the accusing glances,' says Janey. 'You'll have a fifty-year-old metabolism yourself one day. You'll need to know these things.'

The noise comes again and Janey heads towards the stairwell. 'Please not bats, please not bats,' she says. Essie quickly ties her hair up in a bun. Dwight turns the torch on on his phone. All of them nervous, they advance slowly up the stairs, quietly.

When Essie gets to the top and peers in – there is light streaming in from missing slates on the roof; it is genuinely incredible Mrs MacAleese lived here for so long – she isn't sure at first what she's looking at. Her brain, ludicrously, thinks it is a dragon curled up in a corner, with wings sticking out of it. This makes no sense at all.

'Oh, my goodness, poor lamb,' says Janey suddenly, and Essie thinks, *that isn't a lamb!* just as her mother bolts forward, across the rickety floors and under the sloping roof.

As her eyes adjust, she realises what it is: a huge dog.

The dog is trembling and groaning, and as they get closer they understand why. Stuck coming out of the dog's rear end – what Essie had originally thought was a separate appendage – are the closed eyes of a tiny creature.

'She's whelping!' says Janey. 'Oh, you poor dear. This must be the missing Irish wolfhound! It was on Facebook.'

Dwight pulls out his phone and looks it up.

'Her name's . . . Felicity.' He frowns. 'That's a weird name for a dog.'

'Alright, *Dwight*,' says Essie.

The dog is in distress and wants to twist away but Janey speaks low, comforting words and her tail thumps, just once, on the floor.

'Mum, you're an *audiologist*; you can't birth a baby.'

'Managed two of my own,' says Janey, still in a sweet, calming singsong voice, moving closer still. 'Dwight, could you run and see if the vet is about? Essie, feel like giving me a hand?'

'*No.*'

'Well, is the water still on?'

Dwight nods.

'Run me some hot.'

'There's no hot.'

There is, thankfully, a scrap of pink soap from downstairs, and Janey soaks her hands in the cold water and lathers up as well as she can, before gently getting hold of the tiny creature stuck in the birth canal.

'Come on, baby,' she whispers gently, getting as much soap into the canal as possible. She's spent enough time with Lish for some of it to rub off, and Al's birth had been an at-home-at-incredible-speed affair – he'd come careering out like a runaway train and has barely stopped since – so she knows the basics.

Essie can't help being a bit impressed by her mother's calmness, as she gently twists the tiny form the right way up and pulls, ever so gently, until with a slither the tiny creature, covered in streaks of blood and goo, finally drops on to the ground. Essie wouldn't go near a dog's vagina in a million years.

Janey is reasonably sure, given she doesn't know how long it was stuck for, that the puppy will be dead, but Felicity noses round and starts licking the tiny bundle with a sandpapery tongue, great long licks, and to Janey's surprise and delight, and Essie's astonishment, the tiny mouth falls open, a little pink tongue appears, and with the tiniest of snorting noises the creature takes its very first breath.

'No way!' says Essie, grinning and dashing over. 'Mum, look!'

And Janey glances at her girl, her darling daughter, delighted and engaged.

'Watch this,' she says, moving the bundle down to Felicity's tummy as, sure enough, the brand-new thing snuffles, eyes tight shuts, its nose in the air, nestling and pushing until it finds and latches on to one of Felicity's nipples and, after a few moments of snuffling misconnections, finally settles down and starts pulling contentedly, as Felicity continues to lick and lick.

Essie finds she has tears in her eyes.

'I can't believe something so disgusting can be so beautiful,' she says.

Janey smiles. 'I think you've just described womanhood,' she says, and puts her arm around Essie, squeezing tightly. 'Now,' she says to Felicity, who looks tired and unhappy but appears to be heaving again, moving to try to expel something. 'Dogs don't have babies in ones, do they?'

By the time Dwight thunders up the stairs with Ahmed the vet, who has been tending to an illegal albino crocodile in Wick and wasn't best pleased about it, Janey has helped with pup number two, and it looks as if number three is well on its way.

Ahmed smiles.

'Good midwifery,' he says, washing his hands. 'That was a breech. It's strange such a big dog should have such trouble giving birth. She looks old for a litter.'

He pats her gently, as the last three pups arrive without incident and Felicity keeps up her constant licking routine, despite looking as exhausted as a dog can look, and flopping back on what Janey has finally realised is a mattress. A mattress that is now good for nothing but being set on fire, but it makes sense that Felicity found her way here.

'I know this dog,' says the vet. 'Mr Meakin looks after her for the big house. He hasn't been to see me for ante-natal though.'

'Maybe he didn't know,' says Janey. She knows Jack Meakin, a tough, solitary outdoors type. She tries not to think about his dating profile.

'How could he not know?' says Essie, who is already, unavoidably, down among the puppies. Ahmed had warned her to be careful, that mum might be defensive, but in fact Felicity's tail is beating lazily; she seems very happy to be showing off her new babies. Ahmed handles them quite casually, stuffing them on to Felicity's nipples; they form a double decker layer of pups, half grey, half white, all falling all over each other, each one blind to anything but the need to suck.

'Two boys, four girls,' says Ahmed. Then he looks at Janey again. 'You know, if you hadn't been here and the first had got stuck for much longer, all of these dogs might have died. Felicity included.'

Janey beams with pride. 'Well,' she says. 'And look at them!'

Dwight has found a number for someone to go and knock up Jack Meakin, who, when he arrives, lets out a mighty sigh, after complaining vigorously about how dusty the stairwell is all the way up. Janey thinks he will be thrilled they've found his dog, plus VAT. She is completely incorrect about this.

'Felicity!' he hollers, even as the dog wags even more to see him. 'Oh, my God, you absolute *slut!*'

'All those years of dog church, completely wasted,' Janey whispers to Essie, who giggles.

'You terrible girl,' Mr Meakin is saying now, shaking his head at the dog, who is desperately excited to see him, but unable to get up, held down by six very busy puppies. 'I can't believe you let those dogs do things to you. I guess we'll never know who the father is.'

Dwight grins. 'By the colouring, I'd say you want to have a word with some of the Westies.'

As they are just north of the West Highlands, the little West Highland terriers are extremely common around town, mostly called Jock, with the occasional Hamish thrown in for good measure.

'How?' says Essie. 'How does a West Highland terrier have sex with that . . . pit pony . . . ?'

'Excuse me?' says Mr Meakin, whirling round.

The room goes quiet and undoubtedly, everyone is currently completely unable to prevent themselves from picturing it. Essie suddenly thinks she might have hysterics.

'Aye, there's a chest of drawers left over there,' points out Dwight, and at that point it's too much. All three of them explode laughing.

'I'm so glad you find it funny,' says Mr Meakin fiercely. 'Now I've got these puppies to deal with and she's not even my bloody dog.' He turns to Ahmed. 'I mean, what's the usual procedure.'

Ahmed looks at him with thinly disguised disapproval. 'The usual procedure,' he says carefully, 'is that if you don't want your bitch to have puppies, you have her safely neutered.'

'It's not my dog,' Jack Meakin says instantly. 'I'm just minding it.'

'Well, then, I believe we should probably inform whoever's dog it is.'

'Isn't there a way we could just make this . . . go away?' he says.

'No way,' says Dwight. He had left the room, but reappears, with the bowl filled up with fresh clean water. Felicity laps at it gratefully and Janey feels bad for not remembering how incredibly thirsty breastfeeding makes you.

'Well, she can't come home with me, not like this,' says Mr Meakin.

'Did you not even notice she was pregnant?' asks Ahmed, genuinely astonished.

'She's a very hairy dog,' says Mr Meakin ferociously.

There's a silence, apart from the tiny pants and squeaks of the brand-new babies, and nobody feels like laughing any more.

'There's a pound,' says Ahmed, reluctantly. 'But they only hold on to them for . . . '

Janey can't bear to think of it. 'Whose dog is this?' she says.

'The Thomases',' says Mr Meakin. 'I'm his gardener. I took their dog in when she left.'

'Well, I think this makes it his problem,' she says mildly, keen to stop Jack Meakin picking up tiny puppies and drowning them, or whatever it is he has in mind. 'Can you call them?'

Jack tries, on his aged phone – which, oh, Christ, has Tinder on it, Janey notices in horror. He hadn't put 'possible puppy-drowner' on his profile, that was for sure. But there's nobody picking up.

'We'll go to the house,' offers Essie, out of the blue. Janey looks at her, and is surprised to see how affected her daughter is. She looks genuinely frantic, terrified that something bad is going to happen to the puppies, and suddenly very young.

Meanwhile Dwight has usefully dug up some old blankets from a back room somewhere, and is tucking Felicity in. She looks up at him gratefully, tail still thumping. The puppies have stopped mewling and are either still sucking, blissed out, or fast asleep, making a pile. Nobody needs to say what's on everyone's mind.

'We'll go and find the owner,' says Janey. 'I'm sure they can sort this out.'

Nobody mentions what happens if they don't want to sort it out.

16

The house address is on the edge of town, and turns out to be the large, crumbling Victorian schoolhouse Janey herself attended for a couple of years until they built a brand-new pebbledashed flat-roofed one, which itself has now been pulled down. It is looking very worn – weeds growing out of the path – but is still standing. The old playground is now a garden – a beautiful one, she sees, looking closer, with new bougainvillea popping out of the corners like fireworks.

'Mum!' says Essie. 'Mum! He was going to kill those puppies!'

'People do,' says Janey, sadly. 'Sometimes.'

'Evil people.' She looks at her mother. 'You have to take one.'

'I'm in no position to have a dog,' snorts Janey. 'I work twenty miles away!'

'Dogs love going in cars.'

'In a hospital!'

'Dogs are therapeutic in hospitals, everyone knows that. Anyway, you don't work in a hospital, you work in a shipping container in the corner of the car park.'

'It's a prefab, thanks,' says Janey, although for once Essie is right. 'Anyway, I think I have enough on my plate for now, don't you?'

Essie frowns. 'What, you mean with me?'

'No, of course not. Look,' she says, changing the subject quickly. 'This is my old school. I knew they'd made it into a house but I didn't know people lived here now.'

'Who?' says Essie.

'I don't know.'

'You! Not knowing someone in Carso?'

'It's a town!'

'It's a . . . hamlet.'

'It has a Scot Nor,' says Janey. 'I don't want to have this conversation again.'

'It doesn't have a railway station.'

'It has an airport!'

They step into the garden. The wind has died down. It is overgrown, but filled with spring flowers, randomly scattered: tulips everywhere in different colours, and some early-budding roses. Janey bends in to have a closer look and can hear the buzzing of industrious bees going about their business among the thick grass; under the clear sun it looks an enchanting world to be in. In the shadier parts under the trees, wild white mushrooms are growing, in fairy rings, and, here and there, small patches of bluebells.

'What a pretty garden,' she says.

'It's a mess,' points out Essie.

'Yes, but it's a pretty mess.'

'Like me,' says Essie, to make her mum smile, which it does.

'You're not a mess!' says Janey. 'The world is a mess, and you got stuck in it.'

'Nobody else is,' says Essie, quietly.

'Everyone else is!' says Janey. 'Some people are just better at hiding it than others.'

'Like Shelby McFlynn.'

'Shelby McFlynn doesn't have a passport,' says Janey. 'Everyone's scared of something. Everyone's got a mess.'

Then she grins.

'Although not quite as much as whoever lives here and is about to find out they now own seven dogs.'

★

They go round to the back door, being friendly locals, Janey explains, and not religious salespeople.

'I can't believe you've never been here,' says Essie.

'I haven't! It was empty for a while I think, once it stopped being a school, then rented. Honestly, my life has a bit more going on than Carso gossip.'

Essie gives her a look.

'Okay, it also has hospital gossip.'

The back door is pale green, peeling, with four glass panes through which nothing can be seen. Outside sits an ancient bootscraper and next to it a very large pair of wellingtons, next to a small pair of wellingtons, pink with purple flowers.

'They won't be in,' says Essie. 'It's the middle of the day.'

Janey shrugs. 'As someone who works in the community, I can tell you that you'd be amazed by just how many people are home in the daytime these days.'

She knocks loudly.

'HELLO!' she hollers, being used to turning up to people's houses and to those people not being able to hear particularly well.

Essie winces. '*Mum!*'

★

However, to Essie's surprise, it does the trick, and soon they hear a thudding noise in the hallway and a large figure opens the door, an enquiring look on his face.

Janey is completely taken aback. It's Lowell, the man from the pub quiz.

★

'Oh!' she finds herself saying. The man himself looks slightly uncomfortable and Janey finds herself gripped by the horrible thought that he thinks she has tracked him down to his house and is one of those creepy middle-aged stalkers who falls in love with vicars and whatnot and he'll have to get a restraining order.

'Ah,' says Lowell in return, then glances down at himself, as if he's checking he remembered to put his trousers on that day. He did, but his large jumper has toast crumbs on it, and he brushes them off hastily.

'Yes, sorry . . . Jane, is it?'

'Um, Janey,' she manages to stutter out. 'And this is . . .'

But Essie has disappeared in pure embarrassment and is back in the garden staring at her phone, her ears pink.

'From the quiz,' says the man carefully, as if there's a possibility that she's come to take him hostage, and he's trying not to upset her by using a soothing tone of voice.

'Yes,' says Janey, regaining her composure and feeling quite irritated. She's a middle-aged woman, not an unexploded bomb. Although some days the difference isn't that big. 'But this isn't about that.'

'Good,' says Lowell. 'I'm not sure I can handle any more questions about Spitfires.'

'Do you have a dog?' asks Janey, feeling this is a bad angle to come in on but not quite sure where else to start.

He looks confused. 'Well, kind of, but Jack Meakin looks after it for me, has done since . . . '

His gaze unavoidably strays to the small pink wellingtons parked by the front steps and Janey tries not to notice.

'Why?' He looks concerned, and Janey realises he thinks she's about to tell him she's run over it.

'Good news!' she says, quickly.

'What?'

'You're . . . a dog grandfather!'

'I'm a—?'

'Your dog's had puppies!' She smiles, hopefully. 'It's amazing!'

17

L owell heads back into the house and grabs a waxed jacket to follow them down into town. Janey is glad about this. Okay, he's a bit of a weirdo who treats her like a crazed stalker, but at least he didn't say, *oh, who cares*, or, *let Jack Meakin handle it* (she doesn't want to have to explain exactly how Jack Meakin would handle it) or, *I'm busy right now*. He just grabs his coat.

'How did you . . . ?'

'We were having a look at the Seagate cottages. She was in there.'

He shakes his head. 'Must have gone looking for a quiet spot. Oh, poor Felicity. I should never have let her go to Jack's.'

'Why did you?' asks Janey, curious.

He glances at her quickly. 'It was a bad . . . ' He checks himself, as if he doesn't want to talk in euphemisms any more. 'My marriage broke up, if you must know,' he says, quite shortly. It sounds to Janey like the kind of thing a therapist would have told him to be more upfront about.

'I'm sorry,' she says.

'And I had to work, and it didn't seem fair on Felicity. She couldn't go with . . . well, anyway. So Jack offered to take her for a bit, he's always had a bit of a soft spot for her . . . well, I thought he had.'

He sighs.

'The divorce, obviously,' he says, carrying on, 'had a terrible effect on Felicity as well as everyone else in this family. Do you think she was acting out?'

Janey frowns. 'I think she was doing what dogs do,' she says. 'And I think you were very irresponsible not getting her fixed if you didn't want this to happen.'

He sighs a little. 'I always . . . I always thought we might have a litter from her. She's such a beautiful dog, and wolf-hound pups are worth their weight in gold.'

Janey smiles tightly. 'Not necessarily these pups, I don't think,' she says. 'Didn't you see she was missing, on the local Facebook group?'

He looks at her with a hunted expression. 'You're on the local Facebook group?' he says with some fear in his voice. To be fair, the local Facebook group has a lot to say on . . . well, pretty much everything.

'My mum did the birth,' says Essie unexpectedly, coming up from the garden, and Lowell looks up.

'You did?'

Janey shrugs.

'I thought you were an ear specialist.'

'Turns out when you're used to sticking your hands in awk-ward parts of anatomy, it starts to feel quite normal,' says Janey, and instantly wishes she hadn't when she sees his face. She realises that one of the freedoms of getting older – being able to say whatever you like – isn't always ideal. Just because you can, it doesn't always mean you should.

'Well, thank you,' he says. 'I think.'

★

They reach the Seagate cottages. By now word has got around, and there is a small clutch of children on their way home from

school, hanging about on the off-chance that they might get to
see some puppies. Jack Meakin is standing outside with a face
like fizz, as if he's somehow been denied the opportunity of
having some fun drowning wee dogs.

'Yon vet's upstairs,' he says. 'Will cost you a pretty penny,
aye.'

'I thought Janey here did all the work,' says Lowell.

'She did!' says Dwight, bounding down to the doorway.

'Excuse me,' says Ahmed as they enter, drying his hands on
a towel. 'Someone made sure the afterbirth was safe and all the
puppies were healthy. You're welcome.' He sees the faces of half
the town, every single one of whom will need a vet at some point
for something or other, and decides discretion is the better part
of valour. 'Actually, delighted to be of service, don't worry about
it,' he mutters. 'Now I have to get back, I have a musk rat surgery.
Your pups are all fit and well, Lowell.'

'So what do I do with them now?' says Lowell, looking
astounded.

Ahmed shrugs. 'Some puppies make a lot of money on the
open market . . . some crossbreeds are very valuable,' he says.
Then he frowns. 'I'm not sure about wolfhounds and Westies,
though. That's more of an—'

'Offence against God,' chips in Jack Meakin.

Lowell blinks as if he's having a very surprising afternoon,
as indeed he is, and the entire party proceeds upstairs with the
exception of Jack, who is looking, not angry, just disappointed,
and rubbing his weather-cracked nose dolefully.

Dwight has clearly been unable to help himself, and is sitting
down, stroking Felicity and being a lot less bullish than he normally is. Essie glances at him.

'Must make a change from rounding up all those cattle,'
she says.

'Aye, yeah, good one, aye,' he says lazily, not looking at her, then turns back to Janey. 'Can Felicity have some food?' he says. 'I reckon she's absolutely hanging for a scran.'

Nobody wants to leave the puppies, but Janey finds a cereal bar in her handbag – she always has snacks in her handbag, never quite lost the habit from when the children were small. She checks it for raisins then hands it over. It vanishes into Felicity's big hairy maw in two seconds flat.

'I'll get some more,' says Janey, but Felicity has now obviously smelled Lowell approaching, very gingerly, and her tail starts thumping again. Dwight gets up as Lowell moves forward.

'Hello, my sweet girl,' he says, stretching out his hand. 'What have we got here, then?'

Felicity bends her large grey head and forces Lowell to start scratching her ears.

'Oh, my girl,' he says quietly, and Janey can hear a slight crack in his voice. 'Oh, my darling girl. I am so sorry. So sorry.'

But Felicity doesn't look sad at all. She is butting his hand, then licking the squirming pups then butting his hand again. It is clear as day that she's saying, *Look! Look what I have! Look!*

Lowell picks up one of the tiniest white pups and it squeaks, its tiny paws flailing. Felicity watches him, but he doesn't take it far.

'It's beautiful,' he says, stroking the velvety head with his finger. 'It's absolutely beautiful.'

'I can't believe this town is going to be terrorised by giant Westies,' says Essie. 'Or tiny Irish wolfhounds. Hard to say.'

'All the nippiness and feistiness of a Westie, but in the body of a vast Irish wolfhound,' says Dwight. 'Nothing can possibly go wrong.'

'It's like the plot for a horror film,' says Essie. 'Maybe a kind of Jason Statham-y one.'

'Oi!' says Dwight at once. 'Don't diss on the Statham, what's wrong with you?'

'Be quiet, the pair of you, and make yourselves useful and get some dog food,' says Janey. She nearly gives them a pound coin each but restrains herself just in time; they're grown-ups. And she watches them go down the stairs and thinks, this is the most animated she's seen Essie since she got here.

'Well,' she says, as she and Lowell are left alone with the dogs in the room.

'Well,' he says, shaking his head. 'God. I don't . . . I don't know what I'm going to do.'

'I wonder . . . ' says Janey, not wanting to pry but even so. 'Do you think your daughter would be excited to see them?'

He blinks. 'Oh, God, yes. But I go there, normally.'

'Where's "there"?'

'Galloway.'

Janey winces. Galloway is just about as far from Carso as you could possibly get. A solid eight-hour drive on very narrow roads, or about eighteen hours by public transport. She might as well be living in Canada.

'Well, surely she'll want to come up and . . . '

He shrugs and Janey feels the issue is immediately closed, like a door being slammed shut. 'Well,' she says. 'First things first. Where is she going to stay?'

Lowell looks concerned. 'Will she need looking after all day?'

'I don't think so,' says Janey. 'I think dogs have been having puppies for a really long time without going into hospital or anything.'

'Yeah, she looks absolutely fine,' says Lowell wonderingly.

'I know,' says Janey. 'After Essie I lost three pints of blood and couldn't walk for three days.'

117

'Christ,' he says, and Janey regrets mentioning it. He is a complete stranger who probably doesn't need the image of her gushing blood from her vagina in his head. 'No wonder you knew what to do.'

'Yeah, dogs definitely have it easier,' says Janey. 'Hey, maybe she could stay here.'

She is Googling frantically on her phone. All new dog-mums need is somewhere reasonably cosy – the house isn't heated, but it is sheltered, and the weather is warming up outside. With plenty of blankets they should all be okay.

'Do you think that cowboy lad would mind?'

'Mind?' says Janey. 'I think he's already choosing a pup.'

'But what about . . . won't they poo and stuff?'

'Well, I regret to inform you . . . ' says Janey, and hands him the phone. He holds out while he fishes around for his glasses, and uncovers a horn-rimmed pair in his black pocket. They suit him.

'Let's have a look . . . oh. Yuk.'

'I know,' says Janey. 'Barely worth the glasses.'

The web page informs them that the puppies will pee and poo, and the mother will eat it, to cover up their tracks from predators.

'I wish I didn't know that,' says Lowell, rubbing his rumpled face. 'Today is proving something of a steep learning curve.'

'Well, if we all popped in, I'm sure we could manage it.'

Lowell looked at her. 'Seriously?'

'Yeah – my Essie is just hanging around at the moment and we're only next door. Dwight will be here. If you pass him some cash, I'm sure he wouldn't mind.'

'And then what will I do with the dogs?'

'I think,' predicted Janey wisely, indicating the children still hanging around outside, 'that problem might solve itself.'

★

'This is getting ridiculous,' says Essie. 'And very expensive.'

'Naw!' says Dwight. His enthusiasm is genuinely quite appealing, Essie thinks. Today his jeans are stonewashed. Where do you even *find* those, never mind get them on? 'It's alright, I've got money.'

'I thought you were being a big housing investment guru?'

He shrugs, as if slightly self-conscious that he's been showing off. 'Aye, whatever.'

'Well, then, you should be watching costs like a hawk.'

He looks down at his basket, which contains some pouches of the most expensive dog food the Scot Nor had to offer, plus a blanket and a pillow from the expensive gift shop at the top of the town which has had an extremely slow start to the year and whose owner had been completely delighted by the arrival of Dwight and his jeans, which, Essie thinks, clearly show he will waste money on any old crap. Most adorably of all, Dwight has a set of six tiny Velcro collars in different colours, so they can identify the pups. Even Essie melts at these.

'So you're the banker, are you?' says Dwight, pinging his card without even looking at the total, which makes Essie frown even more.

'Yes,' she says. She may be bad with her own finances, but she's watched a lot of good businesses go bad over the years. 'Tell me you watch your building costs better than you watch your completely-strange-dog-that-is-nothing-to-do-with-you costs.'

He gives her a sidelong glance. 'Huh,' he says.

'What?' says Essie.

'Nothing. This is my first project.'

'Well, watch your costs!' says Essie, slightly panicked for him.

'Neh, it's alright. I've got money, plus money from the bank.'

'Yes, but people go through it like you can't believe . . . '

She doesn't realise quite why she's so concerned – who cares? But even so, she saw him helping Felicity and is less inclined to think he's awful now. And it would be even worse for the village if the Seagate failed and got left to rot; her mum would basically be living next door to a slum.

'Well, you don't need to listen to me,' she says.

'Free advice from a banker? I think I will, actually,' says Dwight.

'Okay. Well. Watch your costs. Sit down with your accountant.'

'Oh, yeah,' he says, making a shrug.

'You have got an accountant?' says Essie, suddenly worried.

'Neh,' he says. 'It's just doing up some wee houses, yeah? I'm going to get some mates round, we'll be done in a couple of months.'

'Haven't you ever watched *Grand Designs*?'

'Has it got Jason Statham in it?'

'No!'

'Well. No, then. Sounds boring.'

They leave the shop and are soon back outside the Seagate cottages. Essie looks upwards. The houses are adorable, but they are crooked and leaning up against each other. The coving is coming away, likewise the guttering.

'And you want to let these?'

'Yeah,' says Dwight. 'Or flip them for absolutely loads. Down to B&Q, quick bish bash bosh and I'll be rolling in it.'

Essie frowns, torn. She has spent long enough in her last job looking for weaknesses in companies to exploit, in fact exactly like this kind of thing, to know a recipe for disaster when she sees it.

On the other hand, in this current climate, he's probably right. If he throws a coat of Turnkey Blue over every surface he can find, he probably can flip them for a fortune.

120

But to whom? To nobody round here. These are poor cottages, built for people with next to no money at all, living a subsistence life from the vegetable patch, working their lives in all weathers. They weren't meant to be a rich person's plaything, popping in twice a year, complaining that the Scot Nor doesn't stock saffron, or, worse, driving up with a huge pile of groceries they've already bought in their car so they don't have to spend any money in the town at all; complaining they can't find a cleaner, because cleaners have nowhere to live.

Essie realises she is sounding exactly like her mother. She's only been back a couple of weeks and she's been infected already. Why shouldn't Dwight, who left school at sixteen and has done nothing but graft ever since, in some of the most difficult conditions known to man, make a killing? There are very few ways left for guys like Dwight to do well in life; most of the routes have been closed off, as she knows only too well, scrabbling in the sea of publicly educated kids in Edinburgh whose parents had got them sinecures and internships at the banks they and their lawyer friends all worked at; who had secured the tutoring necessary to get their dumbo children into the right universities, then given them a place to live in the city while they got a foothold. The system is totally rigged against the Essies and Dwights of this world, as she can see only too clearly, stuck back here by one turn of misfortune, while the Connors and Trisses of this world sail on regardless, happy that their rent is covered by Mummy and Daddy while they 'make their own way'.

So yeah, screw them, and screw anyone who dares to tell Dwight what he can and can't do with the meagre opportunities he has. The system is rigged, so he might as well get on board with it, and if some of those posh wankers from the city end up with a boiler someone's mate stuck in on a free weekend from bevvying off the rigs, well, they've got it coming.

On the other hand . . .

'Are you thinking about the puppies?' says Dwight, as they push open the garden gate.

Essie doesn't want to admit that, no, she's been thinking about him, and his business. But she can't help herself.

'If you like,' she says shyly, 'I could help. I'm on . . . gardening leave.'

She's never quite understood what gardening leave is but has figured out that nor does anybody else, and it's a good cover-all word to use whenever anyone asks what she's up to.

'I could . . . have a look at your accounts if you like. Just. Maybe. Help you out with your budget and stuff.'

He looked at her, shouldering the door. 'Aye, Shelby says you were a right swot,' he says, considering it.

Essie feels her fingers tightening into her palm.

He holds the door open for her behind him as they head back upstairs to where the puppies are. 'Mind you, she also says you're a stuck-up cow, and she was right about that.'

And he grins and lets Essie's furious face follow him up the stairs.

'That's a yes, by the way,' he yells back down.

'You . . . you can STUFF IT!' shouts Essie, loudly, as Janey and Lowell cover the puppies' ears.

★

'Hey, sweetie . . . '

'And there were pups! Born right away! Just there! Did you not look at my Insta?'

Connor laughs down the phone at Essie's enthusiasm.

'Sorry, I called to speak to Essie? Down-in-the-dumps, depressed-at-living-in-a-hole-in-the-sticks Essie?'

Essie glances out of the side window, to the end of the road, where in the distance she can just see the sun starting to set over the fields, the wind blowing through the long grass, the lambs hippety-hopping up and down. On the street, closer by, she sees Struan McGhie, the local music teacher, pass with his girlfriend Gertie, who's a famous knitter. He is wearing a knitted bobble hat, a knitted scarf and a knitted waistcoat and is carrying a knitted music bag, all in lovely, matching but different spring tones of blue and yellow. She smiles to herself. They seem pretty happy. Johnson the postie whizzes by. He has been given a new electric bike to help with the hills and is a frankly terrifying sight on it.

'It was cool!' she says, and tells him all about it.

'Three houses, wow,' says Connor. As for all Gen Zs, even comfortable ones like Connor, home-ownership is still pretty amazing: on a par with 'and then a unicorn appeared, tapdancing on the Northern Lights'.

'I know,' says Essie. 'There was a codicil in the will stipulating they could only be sold locally.'

There's a slight silence on the other end.

'Interesting,' says Connor. 'So, he's not a professional developer or anything?'

'No,' says Essie. 'He's made money on the rigs and he's putting it into this.'

'Very interesting.'

'How is that interesting to you? They're basically falling-down sheds in the middle of Carso. The nearest cappuccino is miles away. It's not three Georgian townhouses.'

'I know, I know, I'm just interested in property.'

'You and everyone else. Well, come up and have a look,' says Essie, teasingly. 'I really want to see you.'

'I want to see you too,' says Connor. 'I'll make a plan.'

And Essie feels better all over again, and applies for four more jobs, trying not to even mind that none of them will get back to her. Her mother doesn't even realise employers don't have to get back to you these days; that everyone ghosts every-one all the time.

To put her in an even better mood, as she is about to close her laptop an email pings – a new vacancy has been posted! With a capital management group! In town!! She is so happy she even goes downstairs and doesn't look at Janey's pasta, with the ear-liest green beans from the garden, which Janey is so very proud of, and fresh herbs from the window ledge, and forgets to even mention that she thinks she is probably gluten-intolerant. She doesn't think she is gluten-intolerant; she is just annoyed that her mother doesn't believe in it, so is striking a blow for truly gluten-intolerant people everywhere. Fighting the good fight.

*

Janey discusses it with everyone at work. There are vague plans to start a rota to make sure Felicity is alright – Lish's kids are keen – but in fact it doesn't prove remotely necessary: local Facebook page readers start popping in at all hours, lots of them to make their opinions known but also, it being Carso, lots to help too. Of course Fred Wilson from the butcher's gets his usual snit on and starts wanging on and on about health and safety and rabies, which quickly degenerates into a shouting fight about dog vaccinations and foreign wars, but everyone is used to that and just ignores it. Morag the pilot comes down and tries to persuade Gregor, her other half, to get one. They puppy-sit for over an hour while Gregor patiently explains to her in English and in Gaelic that dogs and ornithologists are a terrible mix unless you get the breed exactly right, and what-ever these deadly hellspawn are, they are not the correct breed.

Dwight has to be careful to lock the doors every day so the pups can't roam, as they start to get more mobile – and so that Felicity can't get out again, observes Jack Meakin gravely, seeing as that dog is basically a whore, and he is told to hold his wheesht by the ladies from the knitting circle and he says he can only say things as he sees them so they can blooming well hold theirs and Jean nearly punches him in the face, which would have proved his point so everyone is glad she didn't.

But the person who is over every day is Essie. Making sure the children don't get too handsy; that Felicity is fed and comfortable and, unavoidably, to hear Dwight stamping about, touching things. Essie cannot help but wonder if he has the faintest idea what he's doing.

18

'Oh, lord.' The man makes a groaning noise of pure delight. 'Stop that, please,' says Janey.

'Honestly. I think . . . I think this is the best thing that's happened to me in ages . . . '

It is a running joke with her friends that, apart from the real sickos, audiology is the only department where people have a really great time. People really love getting their ear wax removed, it turns out. Something to do with the hot water, Lish avers. It reminds them of being washed as babies by their mothers. Plus, of course, the miraculous and instantaneous improvement. The heart surgeons and neurologists at the hospital get all the glory, they always reckon, but what gives patients the largest measure of happiness is undoubtedly a toss-up between getting their ears cleaned out and getting their toenails sorted when they can't reach them.

'Well, I'd rather they didn't do the moaning and groaning,' says Janey. 'Especially the men. In fact I'd rather they just cleaned their ears properly so my waiting list could go down.'

'You love it,' teased Lish.

'I do not,' says Janey. 'Also, it reminds me it's as close to action as I've had in a while.'

Amsan pouts. 'What about that puppy guy? He's alright. Bit big.'

'Ooh, I like a big man,' says Lish. 'Something to cling on to.'

'I agree,' says Janey. 'I do too. It's reassuring. I don't think I would like someone like Timothée Chalamet. I'd be scared I'd break him.'

'Yes,' says Amsan. 'That is for sure the only thing stopping you and Timothée Chalamet being together.'

'Well,' says Janey. 'I don't know. Puppy guy . . . he's nice. But I think he's a bit sad.'

Milton looks at her. 'Divorced?'

'I think so. Or separated, anyway. His wife and daughter don't live with him.'

Milton frowns. 'Is he a bad man?'

'You're asking me if they're under the patio?'

'You are kidding,' says Amsan. 'You live in that tiny village and nobody knows the gossip?'

'It's a town, not a village,' says Janey quickly.

'Come on, *someone* must know.'

'Also best you find out now rather than later. About the patio,' adds Milton.

Janey finds she is perking up, just at the way people are talking about it. Like, why shouldn't she date him or want to; why wouldn't she? It's a perfectly normal thing that might happen.

Then she remembers her imminent birthday, and it brings her back down to earth.

'Oh, don't be daft,' she sighs. 'I'm an old lady to him.'

'Isn't he about your age?'

'Yes, that's exactly what I mean,' says Janey. 'His ex-wife – I remember her. Really pretty, and young. He's tall and he's got his own teeth and hair and a house – oh, my God, he's like an endangered species. Of course he's going to want some lovely juicy thirty-something; he's a human being.'

Milton frowns. 'This seems strange.'

'Milton,' says Janey, 'you have to realise how bad it is out there. He literally *could* have buried his wife and daughter under the patio and women would still be like, *well, yeah, but he's so cute though.*'

'There's nothing wrong with you,' says Lish. 'You look lovely.'

'I look okay *for my age*,' says Janey, spooning her fat-free yoghurt disconsolately – they'd all started it. 'That's not actually the same as being a comfortably-off fifty-something guy with hair. If he started dating a super-hot thirty-five-year-old everyone would be like, *oh, obviously.* Whereas if I did . . . '

'Timothée is twenty-nine,' says Amsan.

'Could you shut up about Timothée?' says Janey.

'Don't talk about him like that, please,' say Amsan.

'Okay. Well. Anyway. You get my point. I'm just the middle-aged woman walking past. I'm completely invisible to him.'

'Maybe he just has to get to know you,' says Lish.

'And please,' says Milton. 'Find someone who can tell you about whether he has killed his family. If that makes a difference.'

★

As it happens, Janey has to get her hair cut anyway. Well, she doesn't *really*, she does her roots herself – who has three hours to sit down in the middle of the day? But maybe she will just go. Self-care. To her surprise, Essie has been out that day and the house is basically the way she left it. Well, thinks Janey, a bit of puppy-cuddling won't exactly go amiss.

Jean, hairdresser, knitter supreme and local gold standard busybody, beams as she enters the salon, her thickly lashed Liza Minnelli eyes a look she decided to like in 1973 and has seen no need to update since.

'I never see you!' she says.

'I know,' says Janey. 'I never seem to have the time. Plus I hate sitting looking at myself in the mirror for an hour.'

'Don't be daft,' says Jean.

Janey picks up a magazine. 'And I hate the magazines. "How to Make Your Menopause the Best Time Ever"!'

Jean laughs darkly. 'Ooh, they lie, they lie. But they lie to young women worse. At least we know the truth.'

'Indeed we do,' says Janey, putting on the unflattering hair-dressing shirt, the wrong way round as always. Ugh, her neck looks awful. She doesn't know why; it's not as though she's creased it up by nodding *yes yes yes* to all the amazing things life has offered her. 'It doesn't stop us dreaming, though.'

They both look at a picture of Jennifer Lopez looking incredible on a yacht.

'She's probably miserable, right?' says Jean.

'Probably,' says Janey, sighing.

'Want a Jammy Dodger with your cappuccino?'

'*Yes*,' says Janey resoundingly. 'Then I would like you to make me look like Jennifer Lopez. Or if that is no use I will settle for Jennifer Aniston.'

'How about you look like a lovely version of yourself?'

'What, you're going to make me twenty-two?'

'Did you think you were lovely at twenty-two?'

'No,' says Janey reflectively. 'I thought my thighs were too big for me to ever be loved. That is the one thing young people have right now: liking big thighs.'

'Yes, and all they had to lose was the housing ladder, job security and cheap nursery places,' says Jean, expertly pulling over the dye. 'I'm going to mix you up something honey-like in strands and cut shorter for body.'

'Okay,' says Janey. 'Jennifer Aniston, right? Nothing that screams "Minor Stand-in Royal".'

'Wouldn't dream of it,' says Jean, whose own hair is a jet black not found in nature and backcombed towards the sky. She also knits all her own clothes, favouring a batwing design last seen in about 1986, so, you know, you really have to make triple sure she understands.

'So,' says Janey, as *faux*-casual as she can make it. 'I was just wondering . . . you know the guy who was at the quiz . . . '

'You were hanging out with Lowell Thomas at the quiz!' says Jean. 'We all noticed. Good for you! He never goes out, I don't think I've seen him for a long time.'

'Why?' says Janey. 'Did he bury his wife under the patio? Has he been seen buying a lot of spades and stuff?'

'No, but she definitely left him, though,' says Jean. 'Took the lass as well.'

'Why?'

Jean shrugged. 'Dunno; they didn't live here very long. Bought the old schoolhouse as a fixer-upper, I think – not sure what they did with it. I'm surprised he's even still here; I haven't seen him in so long.' She frowned. 'I wonder who's cutting his hair?'

'Nobody, by the looks of him,' says Janey, remembering the thick mass of it.

'Why? You like him?'

'I don't like anyone,' says Janey. 'I think I've frozen up from the waist down. Apart from having to pee in the middle of the night.'

'Don't be daft,' says Jean, who is dating the retired head of the tiny airline, so is feeling very proud of herself. 'There's years in you yet!'

'Um, thanks?' says Janey.

'And it's never too late.' Jean smiles to herself, and Janey feels both a little jealous and a tiny bit hopeful.

Jean starts tearing up the foils.

'Think Jennifer Aniston,' orders Janey.

'Yeah, she's single too,' says Jean.

19

Essie brings over the kitchen scales to weigh the pups. It's incredible, the rate they grow; she can't get over it. Janey won't get over losing the kitchen scales either; she'll keep missing them and forgetting to buy new ones.

The pups are squirming and wriggling, and one of them, the largest, white and grey, with the tiniest, most beauteous, gorgeous pointed ears starting to show, is moving around on its tiny paws, clumsily bumping into things. Essie has bought some puppy milk and has put out a bowl shaped like a doughnut that the baby is trying to get to, to lap at. She cannot resist picking him up, one hand under his warm little belly. He eeps and Felicity looks up, but she is only mildly concerned, because it's Essie, and soon the baby has its snout burrowed in the milk trough, absolutely delighted.

'That will take the pressure off you, eh, old girl,' says Essie to Felicity, whose nipples look swollen and sore. Felicity does her huge tail-thump, and gracefully accepts a snack from Essie, who is revelling in being able to give a dog as many snacks as she wants. A sunbeam comes through the window and illuminates them all, warm and soft, and Essie feels something bubbling, and it might be . . . well . . . happiness, of a sort. She must prepare that job application, though.

Alasdair turns up, and is full of animal know-how in a frankly rather annoying way. He and Dwight exchange nods.

★

'We're naming them,' says Essie, holding up the bag of differently coloured soft Velcro collars they got at the pet shop.

Al frowns. 'You shouldn't get too attached.'

'No, that's the Velcro,' says Essie. 'We just need to tell them apart. And stop thinking you're the animal expert.'

'That's right – how could having a degree in animal husbandry make me any kind of expert?'

'Shut it.'

'Well, maybe give them fairly basic names to start with,' says Al.

'We could name them alphabetically,' says Essie, picking up the two smallest bitches.

'How about Argyll?' says Dwight.

'Not bad,' says Al, as Essie snaps a pink collar on Argyll and a yellow one on . . . Bute, she decides.

'Good choice for this one; she has a massive butt.'

It is true: Bute is all Westie at the back and scrawny wolf-hound at the front. She looks like two different dogs who've been caught up in an evil experiment.

Al holds up the next two, a bitch and a dog. 'Caithness and Dingwall!'

'Dingwall?'' Essie pats the tiny creature. 'That's not a very pretty name.'

'Dingwall is lovely!'

Caithness gets orange, Dingwall gets purple.

'Eriskay . . . ' Al picks up another dog.

'I think Eriskay is more of a girl's name,' says Essie.

'I thought you were a bit more up-to-date than that,' says Al. 'Are you assigning gender to that pup?' He gives a grin of satisfaction as Essie is forced to agree. 'And Freuchie,' he says, pointing to the last one.

'Where's Freuchie? I haven't ever heard of that made-up place.'

'It's where the Scottish Deer Centre is!'

'Wait a minute,' says Essie, her face confused. 'They have a place you can go and see *more deer*? Are we trying to get rid of the things or are we trying to encourage them? Make your mind up.'

Eriskay gets the blue, even though it is incredibly gender-essentialist, points out Essie, and Freuchie gets the green, and Al and Dwight head out for lunch without Essie, who has job application prep and is going to stay behind and do it, and not play with the dogs. Freuchie is the only one who looks remotely normal, like a lovely white cuddly Westie, just on a vast scale. All the others, Al has pointed out cruelly, look as if they've broken out of the Island of Dr Moreau.

Essie looks up Mergers and Acquisitions specialist, and tries to think like a Mergers and Acquisitions specialist. She isn't sure how much time passes, but it's hard to concentrate, as the puppies scramble around and Felicity stretches out in a sunbeam.

'Teeny weeny dogs,' she suddenly finds herself singing. 'In a loft somewhere . . . teeny weeny dogs . . . who will grow a lot of hair . . . teeny weeny dogs . . . like to sleep all day . . . teeny weeny dogs . . . who were born in the hay.' Technically they were born on a mattress, but it doesn't really matter. 'Teeny weeny dogs . . . will grow big or small . . . teeny weeny dogs . . . we don't know because your mum is big but your dad we don't know at all . . . teeny weeny dogs . . . you are squeaky and wee . . . teeny weeny dogs . . . I can't believe that your mum . . . licks your pee . . . '

She starts as she hears a sudden noise behind her. She glances around, and it's Dwight. She doesn't know how long he's been standing there and is mortified that he's been listening to her ridiculous singing.

'Oh, uh, hi,' she says, carefully putting Bute down and scrambling to her feet. She's wearing her oldest jeans, for dog-cuddling purposes, and brushes them down hastily.

Dwight, it has to be said, had rather enjoyed the girl, the sunlight in her hair, her voice sweeter than she knew, crooning a little song to the dogs. It looked oddly timeless, in the old cottage there. He was not a particularly sentimental man, except when listening to Wichita Lineman and thinking about his dad after a few Jack Daniels, but. Well.

'No, go on,' he says quickly. 'I liked the verse about the dog licking the pee.'

He comes over, carefully lets Felicity sniff his hand.

'Aye, they're something, eh. Did they get bigger again?'

'Dingwall's on the move.'

'I can't believe you gave them all names. Which one is on the move?'

Essie indicates Dingwall, who is still snuffling around the milk bowl, not quite managing to figure out how to get his head over the top of it, but very excited to find a drip.

'Alrighty, then,' says Dwight, picking him up. 'You are obviously the strongest and the smartest. You are going to be mine.'

'What do you mean?'

'What do you mean, what do I mean? I'm taking this hound.' The pup was one closed pair of eyes and a vast black button nose in a scraggy ruff of black, white and grey. 'I'll call him Smokey.'

'Well, one, he's called Dingwall, and two, you can't just *take* a dog. They're not objects.'

'I'm afraid he was born on my property so I think that makes him mine. And someone's gotta take them.'

'It's "got to",' says Essie. 'You're not American.'

'Git down then, my boy Smokey.' Dwight is ignoring her and playing with the dog, getting him to bite on his finger.

'Well, that's not good for him,' grumbles Essie. 'I think you'll have to ask that schoolhouse guy anyway. They're technically his dogs.'

Without stopping playing with his finger around the puppy, who is squeaking with happiness, Dwight fumbles out his phone and calls Lowell, who actually picks up. Boomer, thinks Essie instinctively.

'Hey, man, it's Dwight,' says Dwight on speaker.

'Hi, there,' says Lowell, sounding harassed.

'Hey, I'm going to take one of your pups, okay?'

'Oh, my God, that's wonderful, that's brilliant news. Thanks so much, Dwight. You won't regret it.'

He is still being grateful as Dwight hangs up – smugly, thinks Essie. 'Yeah, I think he's okay with it,' drawls Dwight, looking annoying.

'Well, you can't take him from his mother for another four weeks,' says Essie.

'Oh, he'll be ready before then, won't you?'

He leans down until the tiny creature is nose to nose with him. The pup sticks out its tongue experimentally and gets Dwight on the nose.

'Then you and me are going to go get ourselves into some trouble,' says Dwight, hypnotised by the tiny creature.

'If you're so great with dogs, why haven't you got one already?' says Essie.

'Weirdly, dogs and North Sea oil platforms aren't a very common mix,' says Dwight, without looking up. Then his phone rings and he sighs. 'Right, I gotta get down the builder's yard. Do *not* let anyone else have this dog, you understand? This is *my dog* and his name is Smokey.' He taps the purple Velcro collar the pup is wearing. 'I mean it: don't swap him out; he's the best dog. Don't you go taking him.'

'I shan't take your stupid "best dog",' says Essie, rolling her eyes.

Dwight takes a bunch of photos from different angles, clearly just in case. 'Right,' he says. Then he frowns. 'What colour house paint should I get?'

Essie looks at him. 'You haven't thought of this?'

He shrugs. 'Neh.'

'Do you even have an account?'

'What do you mean?'

'Do you have a business account with the builder's merchant?'

Dwight shrugged. 'I'm sure it will be fine.'

'It will not be fine!' Essie looks around at the wind blowing through the cracks in the warped window frames, the missing tiles on the roof. 'And paint is the last thing you should be thinking of! Where's the builder's yard?' she says.

'Caithness.'

She frowns and looks at her watch, which is stupid, because she has absolutely nothing planned for the rest of the day that won't be trying to spot Connor in the background of other people's house parties from the weekend, when she's sat in the house all day listening to her mother complain about her neck as if, oh, my God, that shit even mattered or would ever happen to her.

'I'll come with you. You can show me your budget. I can't bear watching you bugger this up. It's not fair on Smokey.'

Dwight nods as if he can see the sense in this. 'Okay,' he says. 'I mean, I haven't got a budget, so . . . '

'Have you seriously never ever watched a single property show?'

Dwight shrugs. 'Nope,' he says. 'On the rigs we watch . . . ' He looks faintly embarrassed. 'Other things. Shark films and that.'

'You watch shark films out at sea?'

He shrugs. 'Don't you watch, like, bank heist films?'

'Sometimes,' says Essie. 'That's not the kind of bank I work in, though. Hang on, let me get my laptop from next door.'

'Can I bring Smokey?'

'*No!*'

★

When his car pulls up in front of the house, Essie is pondering whether to change. After all, it's not a date; she is perfectly happily coupled up. It's just her first chance to escape the village in weeks, but on the other hand she is in her scruffiest clothes. She knows for sure he's the kind of person who will notice if she changes, and will probably make a remark about it. But she is so desperate to get out, to do something that isn't just obsessing over her life and watching, terrified, as rents increase week on week.

Janey is back, admiring her new hair in the mirror, which Essie doesn't notice and charges past. Janey tries to keep her face completely straight, as if the idea of Essie going out in the afternoon with Boot-Scooting Dwight McFlynn is a perfectly normal situation she had always expected her beloved daughter to be part of.

'Stop that!' she hollers from the doorstep, as Dwight honks the horn. Everyone is used to Dwight's ridiculously shiny black Dodge Viper car that is his absolute pride and joy, bought as a shell and meticulously fixed up week by week.

Janey comes out and Dwight steps out of the car. He's wearing black cowboy boots and supertight black jeans, ostensibly to go with the car.

'How's the roadster?' she asks, smiling. 'Still getting three miles to the gallon?'

Dwight smiles in his good-natured way. 'Why yes, ma'am, yes I am.' He looks at the little doll's house, with its pretty pale green front door and Crittall windows. 'I like your house,' he declares, as if surprised.

'Glad to hear it,' says Janey.

'She says I have to think about things like windows and that.'

'Who's she, the cat's mother?'

'Essie. She knows her sh . . . her stuff.'

'Does she?' says Janey, genuinely pleased. 'Oh good!'

Essie clatters down the narrow stairs, looking pretty and apprehensive, particularly, it seems, about what her mum might have been saying while she was getting changed. Then she sees the car.

'Oh, my God,' she says. 'What the hell is that?'

'It's the "That Don't Impress Me Much" car!' says Janey, but neither of them is old enough to really remember Shania Twain, so it goes right over their heads and she finds herself muttering, 'Okay, so you got a car' to herself.

'Does the horn play La Cucaracha?'

'That's a great idea,' says Dwight. 'I'll get right on that.'

'No!' says Essie. She gets in. It's incredibly low-slung and she has to basically dip and shimmy to manage it, even as Dwight holds the door open for her. The car is a left-hand drive.

'You could have pointed that out before I crawled in,' says Essie.

Dwight gives a slow look at Janey. 'I figured you wanted to drive.'

Janey smiles at the pair of them. 'Have fun,' she says. 'I'll check on Felicity.'

Well, well, well, she thinks, heading back in as her phone starts to ring, feeling genuinely optimistic.

20

A ringing phone, Janey is to think later, used to be such a wonderful thing. So full of excitement and possibility. A boy, some gossip, just a friend for a chat.

Now it is almost certainly someone attempting to scam you out of your life savings, and nobody younger than her ever picked up the phone for anything. This definitely is not an improvement. Also, you'd think it would make public transport more pleasant, but it turns out the last guys on earth who still think having a mobile phone is magical and impressive are businessmen who like to bark things about paradigms into their phones in the middle of train carriages. On speaker.

But now, the phone is ringing and it's Lish and she picks it up without thinking too much about it, even though Lish and she usually WhatsApp each other 'worst patient of the week' awards, while feverishly hoping the hospital will never have a reason to subpoena their WhatsApp messages and promising faithfully to one another that if this happens they will both throw their phones into the sea.

She is listening to the ridiculous roar of Dwight's car tearing off down the sea road – and feeling slightly envious of her daughter, which isn't a good look but even so, it isn't every day a cowboy comes to whisk you out on a sunny afternoon, even if

it is to the Caithness Builder's Merchants – and idly considering another cup of tea when she presses hello.

'Hey, you!'

At first Lish isn't saying very much. But gradually, her choked
voice starts.

'Janey? It's Lish.'

Janey knows immediately. 'What is it? What is it? Not the
girls?'

'No, no . . . it's Johnson.'

Lish's sweet, rotund, gentle husband, their postie. Everyone
knows Johnson; he is beloved in the town. It's rare the week he
doesn't come home with a dozen fresh eggs, or the joys of some
overflowing plum trees, or, on one memorable occasion, a brace
of skinned rabbits hanging in the larder that made Lish scream
her head off.

'What? What?' The worst things ran through Janey's head: his
red van, upside down in a ditch. A stray shotgun across a field.

'He's had a stroke.'

'Oh, my *God*! Are you at the T&C?'

'Uh-huh.'

'On my way.'

★

Janey gets there in super-quick time and pulls her hospital pass
to charge past the reception desk in the stroke unit, who know
her, thankfully – she was often there, assessing hearing damage in stroke patients. She glares at her phone en route. This is
midlife, in a nutshell. The phone ringing only means something
awful has happened. To children, to elderly parents, to dear
friends. Ask not for whom the default ring tone tolls.

Johnson thankfully isn't on life support but a drip, staring
ahead, vacant, but conscious, Janey is pleased to see. Lish has
him by the wrist, as if she is feeling for a pulse and has simply

140

forgotten to stop. Their assorted grandchildren are causing mild chaos under the beds, but the staff are turning a blind eye. Everyone knows Lish, has been the recipient of a cake or a kind word, even on the craziest shifts, her way with the NRNs directly responsible for the hospital's having a far better retention rate than most others.

After the first long, tear-mingled hug, and a quick squeeze from Milton, who is there, and a tender stroke of Johnson's unreacting cheek, Janey assesses the situation. Lish is staring straight ahead, nodding her head, clearly in shock.

'We got him here,' she says, her voice quiet. 'We got him here in time for the drugs.'

'Thank God,' says Janey, wholeheartedly.

'But if he hadn't been at home . . . if he'd been at the other side of Luff Fen . . . '

'I know.'

'Or up in Larbh.' She names the next island up on the archipelago. He would have needed to be Medi-vacced out.

'You can't think like that,' says Janey, looking around. 'Emma, could you get your mum some tea, my love?'

'Actually,' says Lish, looking up, 'sorry, my darling girls – can I have five minutes just to chat medic stuff with Janey and Milton?'

Amsan charges through the curtains. 'I'm on my tea break. They're going to have to wait for their poo samples.'

'Did you wash your hands?' says Janey.

'This is *not* the time for jokes,' says Amsan.

'It is very much the time for clean hands,' says Janey, but Amsan still isn't smiling.

The rest of the family departs, leaving Lish with her friends, and Johnson's hand in hers.

★

'They got to him in time,' says Janey, in her most reassuring tone of voice. 'It'll be rehab, physio . . . we'll know a lot more in a couple of days, right? But it's still great news that he's here and in time. Yeah?'

'It really is,' says Amsan. She squeezes Johnson's free hand, and gets a reassuring tiny pressure back.

'Oh, you sweetie,' she says. 'You are going to be just fine. Don't let Sandro be assigned as his physio. He's a dickhead.'

'How does that affect whether he's a good physio or not?'

'Evil comes down through his fingers.'

'That sounds like quite a good superpower.'

Janey is frantically trying to joke because she remembers how it saved her. When Colin had gone, for good: the fights, the mediation, the money, Essie blaming her for driving her beloved daddy away – all of it. The only thing that saved her was her mates, with their stupid jokes and prosecco nights and attempts to distract her, so she wouldn't have to think about it every single second of her life.

'BUT,' says Lish suddenly, and they are all so surprised to hear her raise her voice; she never does. Janey stops babbling immediately and there is silence in the little space made by the drawn curtains around the bed. 'I know he's going to . . . I know they're going to do stuff . . . '

They all murmur in agreement.

'And you're right about Sandro, he's a nob.'

'He *is*!'

'But . . . I thought . . . I thought . . . ' Her voice is cracking. 'I just thought at this age . . . God. I thought we'd have it worked out. That we'd have our careers, and know what we're doing and have learned a bit about the world and raised our children, God save them, and they'd all be launched . . . '

Janey makes a sceptical face but the rest of them nod.

' . . . and then there'd be some *space*, do you know what I mean? Some time. To look around on your life, in the middle of it, and think, well, phew. Here we are. This is cool. This is great. Okay, the menopause is a pain in the fricking arse, but otherwise these should be calm waters now. We've done the career, the finding the guy, the babies, the teens . . . now it's time for us.'

She tears up again.

'But it never is. It never is. There's always, *always* something. Now it's my Johnson. But then next it's going to be my mum, I know it, she's already forgetting things and she's four thousand kilometres away and I don't know what the hell I'm going to do about that, because for damn sure my brothers are utterly fricking useless. And one of Emma's . . . '

She tails off, obviously not quite ready to share whatever that was. Janey looks at her, surprised. And slightly worried. Lish is the friend who always has everything figured out, who knows who she is, who lives so comfortably, cutting through the world like a steady ship. It worries her suddenly. If even Lish feels this way, what hope is there for any of them?

Lish's voice is tailing off. 'I just wanted . . . I just wanted five minutes of fucking peace and quiet,' she says, in a voice so quiet it is almost a whisper. 'I take on all the obligations of love – I do. I always have.'

'But . . . ' Janey is more flabbergasted by this than by the terrible thing that has befallen Johnson. 'But you're always so calm.'

Lish rolls her eyes. 'Of course I am! I have to be! I've seen anxious mothers in childbirth and I've seen calm ones, and you know who makes it through the best? I watch terrified mothers, older mothers, IVF mothers leave hospital, fretting over their babies, and guess what – the babies fret right back. Those babies are going to be screaming every night – for years. You work hard and project calm out into the world and that's the only way you're going to get through.'

Janey nods. It isn't advice she's always been able to take, that's absolutely for sure. But she recognises the truth in it.

'I thought we'd have longer.'

Lish squeezes Johnson's wrist again, and his fingers flutter.

'He is going to recover,' says Janey.

'He is,' says Lish. 'Very slowly. And then it will be something else. And then something else. And then we'll be old.'

Janey gives her a hug. 'You know that chart that always shows women's happiness peaking and going upwards after sixty?' she says. 'We need to cling to that.'

'Don't be daft,' says Lish. 'That's because their husbands die. And I really like mine!' And she bursts into wails again.

21

By the time they've made it out of the shop Essie has signed them up for a builder's account, for which Dwight gets ten per cent off immediately, and he has therefore immediately decided she is some kind of financial wizard.

'I have seen multi-million-dollar companies go down,' she says, conscious she is showing off a bit. 'And tiny ones. Because they couldn't control their costs. It doesn't matter how big or small you are.'

'You sound like Alan Sugar.'

'So you do watch some TV.'

He shrugs, starts to speed up as they pass the schoolhouse at the edge of town.

'What about manpower costs?' she says

'Well, Wee Jim Eckles will do it for a hundred quid.'

'Do what?' says Essie.

'Whatever needs doing,' Dwight says, looking over at her spreadsheet.

'Keep your eyes on the road!'

They are zooming along at nearly seventy miles an hour on the curving country lane. Dwight handles the ridiculous car with an insouciance born of one who started driving old bangers in the fields at age thirteen. Essie would have been embarrassed to admit she rather likes it. Connor would bark at every pedestrian cyclist and other motorist and tram and complain, entirely without irony, that Edinburgh was becoming impossible to drive in, which Essie could only agree with, as they were doing it on purpose. Cars were nothing but a hindrance in the middle of the city.

Out here, though, the sky is huge, a bright clear blue with wispy white clouds, and they are cresting the moor road; they can see for miles in every direction. The huge gullies and cliffs of the very last of the Highlands; kestrels circling in the drafts; newly planted fields full of yellow rape, long lines waiting to be sown with summer crops; and everywhere, sparks of green in more shades than you could imagine; everywhere new life: baby ducks in duck ponds; lambs waking up, hopping joyously on the sides of the mountains, cast into shadow or sun as they flit past. The air smells heavy with a combination of gorse and thick petrol fumes from the car which normally Essie would disapprove of but the feeling of extraordinary speed, the wind whooshing through the open windows . . . There is of course no air-conditioning, no GPS. It doesn't feel quite as dumb a car as she'd thought it might. Obviously, she disapproves of great big gas guzzlers on principle. It's a disgrace.

On the other hand . . . it's fun.

There is a tape player in the car, of all things, and Dwight is playing something that sounds like fifty-five banjos having a fight, and someone hollering 'yee haw' over the top of it. Essie lets her gaze drift from her laptop for a moment, out of the window into the empty spring air. Suddenly she feels like shouting; feels, bizarrely, free. With nobody else around, nobody asking how she is, or, just as bad, ignoring her; nobody to talk to about the pathetic hurts and disappointments in herself that her mother doesn't understand; that as a white, educated girl from a good home, more or less, in a nice part of the world, with a nice boyfriend, she has absolutely nothing, at the end of the day, to complain about. Not really. Not at all.

'Aaaah,' she tries nonetheless, experimentally, out of the window into the vast landscape all around them, making them tiny, the sea a turquoise stripe on their left between the clifftops.

Dwight glances at her. 'What are you doing?'

'Singing along to your music.'

'Okay,' he says, cheered. 'Go ahead.'

'Can I just have a holler?' she asks.

He grins. 'Be my guest,' he says, and guns the car even harder as she leans out of the open window and screams into the wind. A field of auburn Highland coos, their beautiful russet locks blowing in the breeze, glance up at her as she passes, idly wondering, Essie thinks, what this huge black howling raven is . . . and then they are gone, over the crest of the next hill, doing an incredibly dangerous blind takeover of a wide farm truck carrying silage as Essie closes her eyes and yelps in quite real terror, seeing as Dwight is on the wrong side of the road to see properly around the bend.

'Playing the odds,' says Dwight, his cowboy voice back, and Essie rolls her eyes and laughs in nervous horror as they hit the straight again, the car bouncing over the middle line, but she feels alive.

She hasn't worked much more on the spreadsheet yet, but she had come back to it. From the price he'd paid and the money he'd made . . . well, he would do well on the cottages, it's a sure thing. And, she tells herself, they were lying empty before. They haven't been looked after for a long time. So maybe a young family is going to come and use one of them for their holidays and make happy memories . . . once or twice a year. Maybe Christmas and Hogmanay too. That would be alright, wouldn't it? Maybe they'd spend money . . . when they came. The pandemic had stopped so many people travelling, of course; that had been tough. When all the holiday homes had sat empty year on year and people had got out of the habit, and they'd started to deteriorate and there wasn't anyone around left to fix them up . . .

Anyway. There is definitely a way to do well on this project, and to make it look lovely. Dwight just needs to be careful.

But she doesn't think he is a very careful person.

She is dreaming of reclaimed fireplaces, and how well the flooring might scrub up (once you'd got the puppies off it) when they pull into the car park. As she gets out, the phone rings. It's Connor. She feels oddly guilty, for no reason, as if she's been doing something other than just having a ride in a car.

'Hey, you,' she says.

'Thought we might come up for the weekend soon?'

'We?'

'Yeah, you know, me and the lads? Bit of a stalk.'

'A what?'

'A deer stalk! Tris got it all sorted out. And I get to see you!'

'Um, great,' she says. 'Want to stay? The house is . . . it's quite small.'

'No, Tris has booked us somewhere posh.'

I bet he has, thinks Essie. 'Can I come?'

'Stalking?'

'No! I want to hang out in the nice hotel and have a big deep bath. My mum's house is stifling me.'

'Well, I would like it if you did that,' he says, and they both smile down the phone.

*

'I just wish it wasn't deer-killing,' says Essie to Al on the phone later, taking a walk so her mum doesn't overhear every word then give her that pained expression and head-tilt when asking for further details of her bolloxed life. Temporarily bolloxed life, she tries to tell herself.

'Painlessly destroying an old or malformed animal that needs to be culled,' says Alasdair. 'Essie, I've explained this a million times. They will eat every leaf in the forest. They will eat every crop in every field. They will eat every sapling – that's a baby tree, Ess. They'll eat every baby tree. Do you know what happens next? They starve to death. Want to watch Bambi starve to death, Essie? Because it takes a long time, so you can go and watch it crying.'

'No!' says Essie, crossly.

'Well, then,' says Al. 'Stop being a bloody hypocrite. Deer have no natural predators.'

'Except us.'

'That's right, except us. To make the ecosystem workable.'

'Deer are like us,' says Essie. 'Just growing and overrunning and ruining everything. But occasionally cute.'

'That's exactly right,' says Al.

'We have no natural predators either.'

'Yes, that's why we've invented AI. Can I get off the phone now?'

'Can I ask you something?'

'What?' he says.

'Will you go stalking with Connor?'

There's a groaning noise.

'What? Don't you like him?'

'I don't know him. I just . . . gangs of posh young guys are, it will amaze you to hear, not my favourite clients.'

'He's very sweet.'

'What's he doing with you, then?'

'Ha ha ha.'

'How's Mum?'

'Blah blah blah laundry blah blah blah money doesn't grow on trees blah blah blah I'm a million years old it's terrible.'

'Essie! That's cruel. Go and stay with Dad if it's that bad.'

'Oh, God, Lori is always on a diet and Logan's a thug and Dad works all the time and looks haunted and sad every time she gives him more kale salad. At least at Mum's I know how to use the coffee machine.'

'Lucky old Mum.'

'It's alright for you! She thinks the sun shines out of your behind!'

'It does,' says Al seriously.

'Whereas I'm just . . . a problem.'

'I was going to say pain in the arse.'

'*Al!*'

'Come on, sis. It's temporary. Soon you'll be able to piss off back to Harvey Nicks or whatever it is . . . '

'I'm not like that.'

'Okay,' says Al. 'But you hate it here.'

'I did,' says Essie, looking back at the cottages, and down to the harbour. In the pinkening sky the tiny propellor plane that serves the archipelago circles down, almost fluttering down to a halt on the little airstrip, right on time as ever. Morag must be back from her rounds. Essie wonders if she's managed to talk Gregor into getting a pup yet. 'But it was such a bad time. I had to get away.'

Al's voice turns serious. 'I know. I was there too, remember.'

There's a silence as she looks out to sea, both remembering the horrible nights of hearing her mum cry.

'I just wish . . . '

'It wasn't Mum's fault.'

'I know, I know,' says Essie, and she kind of does on one level. But on another, she still feels: how did she let it happen? Why wasn't she nicer to Dad? More fun? Why did he have to look elsewhere? She had always been so frustrated, niggly with him. Just as she was with Essie now. She sticks out her bottom lip.

'Okay,' says Al finally. 'I'll only take him to where the really mean right-wing deer are.'

22

It is, inevitably, Smokey who is first to wriggle himself under the makeshift barrier at the top of the stairs, trying to find his mum when Essie has taken Felicity out for a slow wander and a bit of me time – something Felicity seems to revel in. Although she fulfils the internet definition of being a good mother, in that she hasn't tried to eat any of the pups, she is clearly over the whole situation, and sometimes swipes the pups away from her with a gentle paw. They are getting huge and feisty, apart from Argyll, who is clearly the runt, and getting good at finding their way to the milk bowl. Essie is completely entranced, particularly with Bute, who can only walk with a Marilyn Monroe bustle. Freuchie remains the snow-white beauty, and almost certainly the only one they could easily sell.

Essie cannot bear to think about selling the pups.

'Hello, baby girl,' she whispers to Bute, stroking the hound's pointy ears even though wolfhounds were meant to have floppy ears. Freuchie aside, these dogs are not going to be bonnie by any standards. But Essie is madly in love with them all regardless. 'Hello, my sweetest girl,' she whispers.

Bute snuffles and eeps, tiny tongue creeping in and out.

'How odd: I'm the first thing you've ever seen,' says Essie, amazed, as Bute snuffles into her for a warm cuddle; the sky is clear but the day is cold. Essie sits with her for a while, feeling calm, as she hears Dwight arrive downstairs with Wee Jim, who is six foot eight and as wide as a barn. 'Christ,' Essie had whispered to Dwight the first time she'd seen him. 'How many raw chickens do you think we'll have to feed him? This will really eat into our budget.'

Most of his available energy goes on walking and standing up without the blood rushing to his head, as far as Essie can tell, because he speaks as little as possible at all times, mostly by grunting. He also has the best-looking girlfriend Essie has ever seen. She hadn't even realised women like this existed in Carso; she makes Shelby look plain.

'Hi, guys,' she says. 'Hey, look, Bute's eyes are open.'

Dwight sniffs. 'Smokey's have been open for days. Got to start training you up as a fighter, Smokey,' he says, cuffing the wee dog playfully as it stumbles towards him.

'Don't you dare!' says Essie.

'As a guard dog!' says Dwight. 'In case someone tries to attack us.'

'Who's going to attack Wee Jim?' asks Essie in consternation.

'Ugh,' agrees Jim.

'Aye, well,' says Dwight, his hand instinctively caressing the tiny creature. 'We need a proper guard dog. Like Felicity.'

'Yes, but he might end up looking like his dad,' points out Essie. 'Those Jocks couldn't hurt a fly.'

'No chance. Right, what are we doing?'

'You're seeing what's under the old wallpaper. Stripping it.'

'Who put you in charge?'

'What were you going to do?'

'Slap some paint on.'

'There's six layers of wallpaper on there! And you have to plaster. Oh, and I have boiler news.'

'What boiler news?'

'There isn't one. Did you check *anything* about these properties before you took them on?'

'There's no boiler?'

'Nope. An immersion heater, and a kettle.'

Dwight sucks his teeth in. 'This sounds expensive.'

'Yes, not costing things is very expensive.'

'I think we'll start with wallpaper.'

'Urgks,' says Wee Jim.

'We've just been to the bakers, Jim,' says Dwight, looking
weary.

'URGKS!'

'Be right back,' says Dwight, looking rather haunted.

Essie hears a noise at the bottom of the stairs and realises that
Janey is coming up. 'Hey?' she says, scrambling to her feet. She
is still holding Bute.

'Don't you get too attached to . . . ah,' says Janey. 'Am I thinking it's too late?'

'How's Johnson?' says Essie.

'Ach, it's a long road,' says Janey. 'But thanks for asking. And
we have all had to promise to give up salt in everything, and it's
making me cranky.' She looks down. 'Goodness, the pups have
their eyes open!'

Indeed, her arrival has stirred them up and they have
hopped out of their cardboard box and are pootling around
her as close as they could get. Smokey even nips the toe of
her sandal.

'Ow! Oh, lord.'

'What?'

'Well, look at them. We can't keep them in a cardboard box
any more.'

Essie shrugs. 'No. And the boys will need to get in here to
work anyway. The dogs can't be here while they're sanding.'

'Are you working here too?' says Janey with a grin, but Essie immediately takes it as a slight that she isn't working at all.

'No,' she says fiercely.

'Okay, just wondered. Goodness,' she says, as one of the pups does a massive pee on the floor.

'Oh, yeah,' says Essie, 'and the guys will have to strip that floor.' She pats Bute. 'It might be time to get Daddy involved.'

'Custody disputes,' says Janey. 'Great. Love 'em.'

'He's got a big garden,' says Essie.

Wee Jim comes up the stairs with a full bag of sausage rolls, whereupon the tiny dogs start yipping. He gives some to Smokey and the rest of them go bananas.

'You wean them on Weetabix, not pasties,' says Janey.

'We have to move them,' says Essie.

'Has he even been in to see them?'

'I don't think so.'

'A dog-hater.'

'A dog-hater with a big garden,' says Essie.

'Yeah, maybe he doesn't want dogs digging anything up,' says Janey, and Essie makes a confused face. 'I'll go and see him.'

'Did you not swap numbers? Are you, like, one hundred?'

'We just forgot,' says Janey, refusing to mention that actually Lowell had offered to give her his number and she hadn't had her glasses on and had been too vain to pull them out as her nice ones were in her handbag and all that was in her other bag were the 1970s serial killer ones she'd bought in an emergency one day at a petrol station, and she really didn't want him to see her in those, so she'd faked taking down his telephone number, assuming she'd get hold of it later, then completely forgetting to do that. 'You're right, he's got plenty of space in his garden. I'll talk to him. You coming?'

Dwight has taken his shirt off to shovel crap out of the kitchen into the big black bin outside. Goodness, thinks Janey. Wee Dwight. It feels rather indecent to be looking at someone she knew as a boy, but this doesn't seem to have stopped Essie. He isn't large, but he is wiry, and his muscles are firm and incredibly well defined. He's brown from being outdoors; a thin trickle of sweat is running down his hairless chest.

'I'll just go myself,' says Janey, but Essie hasn't heard a word she just said.

★

In fact Janey finds Lowell outside too, in the beautiful scruffy wildflower garden. His early azaleas are out and they are big and red and glorious. He isn't topless, though. Janey finds herself wondering idly what that would be like. The opposite of Dwight, probably. But broad; she likes that in a man. Colin's shoulders had sloped. She'd kidded herself he had other qualities. She wonders if Lowell is hairy, considering how much hair he has on his head. She likes a hairy chest, even though Essie thinks they are an offence against all that is holy, like all of her generation. Hmm. She tries to find something neutral to say that won't betray what's on her mind.

'Nice azaleas,' says Janey, just as he stands up, wearing a rather tattered old straw hat and says, 'What?' and she wishes she hadn't.

'Oh, hello,' he says, blinking slightly and rubbing his hands on a very old holey gardening jumper. Possible ex-rugby player, although his eyes both point in the same direction, so possibly not.

He mistakes Janey's distracted imaginings for disapproval. 'Sorry,' he says. 'I'm wearing gardening clothes.'

'You should see what some people turn up to my surgery in,' says Janey, truthfully. 'So. We have to talk about . . . '

'Oh, my God, the dogs. Of course. Sorry. I meant to get down and check on them and then . . . work . . . and . . . '

He doesn't sound terribly convincing and they both know it.

'Well,' he says, looking around his lovely wild garden. It isn't, Janey is realising, the mess she'd thought when she first approached it. In fact it has been allowed to grow in its own distinct order: flowers, rows of vegetables, with ratcheted green leaves; some strawberry plants under nets. The field beyond the grey stone rear of the house has been left to run as a wild meadow, and Janey can see deer cropping away at the end of it.

'Wow,' she says.

'I know, aren't they beautiful?' says Lowell, following her gaze towards the deer. 'They'll come and eat fruit out of your hand.'

'Ah,' she says. 'You do know I'm Alasdair Munroe's mother?'

His eyebrows rise. 'I was not aware of that, no. The deer-killer.'

'Culler,' says Janey. 'There's a difference.'

A young stag bucks around the green grass, revelling, Janey thinks, in simply being alive on such a beautiful day; in being able to tear around so fast and jump so high. It feels like nothing but joy.

'Well, anyway,' says Janey, 'we have different animal problems to talk about. I need to move the pups over here.'

Lowell stretches out his back, then nods.

'Okay,' he says. 'This is all my fault.' He looks around his garden. 'Well, I should probably say goodbye to all this. They'll ruin it, won't they?'

'No!' says Janey. 'The deer would; they'd eat everything. Dogs don't like fruit. You can make a run on the lawn for the pups.'

'Won't they dig a lot of holes?'

'They're babies. They'll just roll about,' Janey says, hoping this is true. 'But they can't stay in the cottages any more.

They're about to start eating real food, which means they're about to start to poo.'

'How many of them are there again?'

'Six puppies plus Felicity.'

'Pooing in my garden?'

'Um, yes,' says Janey. 'That's why you should probably have a run.'

He straightens up, unhappily.

'Is this what you do for a job?' says Janey.

'Oh! No, I'm an architect. Semi-retired now; they call me in when—'

'Their domes fall off?'

'Ha. Not exactly.'

'Do you do the twiddly bits?'

'I don't really like twiddly bits,' he says, looking serious.

'No, that's the problem: you all just like big, horrible blocks, don't you?' says Janey.

Lowell takes on the slightly fixed expression of a man who has spent a lot of time listening to people's ill-informed views on modern architecture, and Janey spots it and shuts up. His own house, the old schoolhouse, she can't help noticing, is Arts and Crafts. It's completely covered in twiddly bits.

'Well?' she says. 'Can you pick them up?'

'Put seven dogs in my car?' he says frowning. 'I'm not sure. Not by myself.'

There's a brief pause. Then he says, quite casually, 'Can you help?'

Janey nods, suddenly feeling nervous. 'I get back from work around six tomorrow?'

'Perfect,' he says immediately. 'I'll see you then.' And he smiles, and looks slightly embarrassed in a way, she thinks, that you wouldn't be, surely, if you were only discussing a car. Or would you?

23

'It is absolutely and definitely not a date,' says Janey, peeling a tangerine at lunchtime, rather than opening a Tunnocks teacake, which is their habit on a Thursday. They come in boxes of six, but that works out well, as Milton and Lish like the crunchy bottom biscuit and Janey and Lish like the marshmallow top bit, so they get a whole one each, then a half.

All three of her friends look pointedly at her tangerine.

'That doesn't matter,' says Lish eventually. 'Have sex with him.'

'Without even dinner?'

'You used to have sex with Colin after you'd made *him* dinner. And washed his grundies.'

'Oh, yeah,' says Janey. 'But if it helps, I don't think either of us enjoyed it very much.'

'I hope you have a nice date,' says Milton, trying to change the subject.

'Stop it!' says Janey. 'I am moving seven dogs in an estate car.'

'That wouldn't even be the worst date,' says Amsan.

The others turn to look at her. 'Surely not.'

'Surely yes. Someone matched with Yasmin on a dating site and says they had a tip slot booked and would she come with them and by the way did she have a car.'

'Ooooh!'

'That is bad,' says Milton, shaking his head sadly at the state of the world.

'I can never do them,' says Janey. 'I just can't.'

'You can't because you're too busy having sex with a very hairy man who only owns one pair of trousers,' says Lish. 'You have to do it for me. Johnson is on a ban for six weeks.'

'So he should be!' says Janey in horror. 'Seriously, you want to do it with him when he's ill?'

'I do,' says Lish, stoutly. 'He's lying *right there.*'

The others regard her with a certain amount of respect, which she ignores. 'What are you wearing? Don't say black.'

Janey is in her smart black trouser suit, which is kind of just about smart, but also, trousers. 'Just this?'

'Well, that's stupid.'

'Why?'

'Seven dogs – you'll be covered in hair. You'll look like a burst cushion!'

'Oh my God,' says Janey. 'Stop it.'

'We'll stop it,' says Lish, 'when you agree to go home and change. We know you have time.'

Janey smiles apologetically. She must offer Lish some more time sitting with Johnson. He's a mean Scrabble player.

'Just do your last appointment by phone and say you're checking to see if they can hear down the phone,' offers Amsan. 'Nobody will notice.'

'You're all terrible,' says Janey, used to being ribbed about her supposedly easy job. 'Anyway, look at all the gifts you get, Lish.'

It was true. Lish gets showered in thank-you presents and chocolates by grateful mothers, even if she sometimes darkly observes that they are really grateful to whoever it was had just got them their epidural but they couldn't remember her name.

'I've got to stop that,' says Lish. 'Johnson is too heavy. That's what got us here.'

'That's just Johnson shape,' says Janey. 'Doesn't he walk it all off anyway?'

'No,' says Lish. 'It's bad. Since they replaced his bike with an electric one, for all the hills.'

'No,' says Amsan, pretending to beat her head on the desk. 'What were they thinking?'

Milton just shakes his head slowly. As a porter, he covers about fifteen thousand steps a day, pushing a heavy trolley.

'They were thinking, let's make all our posties get sick,' says Lish, shaking her head. 'He's going to need new shorts when he goes back to work.'

Nobody asks if this is an 'if'.

'Well, he can practise round your house,' says Janey carefully.

'Not really,' says Lish. They live out in the sticks, a beautiful house in the middle of nowhere, but it's right on the road with no pavement; you have to drive to get anywhere. 'He's missing the fruitcake the most.'

'One whole fruitcake?' says Amsan.

'Some people like fruitcake.'

'Don't ask whether she still puts a pound in it.'

'You . . . bake him a fruitcake and put a pound in it?' says Amsan.

'No,' says Lish. 'I bake everyone a fruitcake. Then it's just a race against time.'

Everyone digests this around the table.

'It didn't matter when he was cycling twenty miles a day.'

'Well, anyway, got to go,' says Janey, and Milton's bleep goes off.

'Call it a date!' says Lish, desperately, as she goes. 'Shower! Lipstick! Hair! Breath spray!'

'*Breath* spray?'

'Preventative, you idiot.'

'Yasmin met someone for a date off of the internet whose tooth was brown and he asked her to pull it out for him as he couldn't get an NHS dentist and was too scared to do it himself,' starts Amsan, as Janey heads off, groaning.

★

She changes into her nice jeans with the turn-ups and a red stripy top with a boat neck. Then she looks at her neck more closely and puts on a white shirt and a tank top Essie bought her for Christmas instead. It is from Brora, an incredibly posh Edinburgh brand, that Janey would never consider, and also she has never worn a tank top in her life and doesn't get the point of them. It is navy with a thin burgundy trim and actually as Janey slips it on over the shirt she slightly sees the point of it. It is neat and slick and keeps her shirt tucked in, and the colour brings out her eyes. Huh. She had been so willing to write it off as Essie buying her stupid and impractical things just to show off how much money she has, and making some point to her mother that she never goes anywhere remotely fancy enough that she could justify spending this much money on a jumper that doesn't even have any sleeves. But in fact it is flattering and pretty and she feels nice wearing it.

She adds some lipstick in a colour that matches the trim, pulls on a nice pair of trainers, and figures that, okay, she's a little dressed up, but she's not wearing a ballgown. It occurs to her that the nicest and most expensive item of clothing she owns is now almost certain to get peed on by six puppies and she should probably keep it for best. Then she reminds herself that keeping things for best is a total waste of life and energy, and heads downstairs.

Essie frowns. She was having a slight reverie about Dwight's bum in his tight jeans, which is crazy because she thinks tight jeans are ridiculous. Connor dresses as though he's in a Hugh Grant romantic comedy, which she absolutely thinks is the correct way for men to dress, not like Woody from *Toy Story*. But they cupped him so very well and . . .

She tells herself this is just because she hasn't seen Connor for so long. And their hayloft days were behind them quite quickly. It was very sexy and romantic at the time, but she was finding hay in very odd places for quite a long time after that, and bed is more comfortable after all. It's become . . . very sweet, and quite conventional. Which is absolutely fine of course, she's not complaining . . . she just can't believe how very fixated she got on that drop of sweat rolling off Dwight's tight chest.

Which is why she has now found herself sitting here ordering grouting for him, and checking everything off on the spreadsheets. Which she said she would never do; she never meant to get so involved. But there's so much to do. She has to give Wee Jim a timeline, otherwise he's going to keep sanding the same bit of banister for eternity. The beautiful finished homes she loves to look at never mention all this stuff. They're all terribly vague about moving out to other places, or employing project managers . . .

She looks up. Oh, God. Is that what she is?

Her mum comes down the stairs, smelling perfumey.

'Where are you going?'

'I'm going to move the puppies – fancy it?'

'No, I'm going to call Connor,' Essie says, loudly, as if Connor can hear her and she is just proving she isn't thinking about anyone else. Which she isn't, as, one, that would be stupid, and two, she has heard Wee Jim discussing Dwight's success with women when they didn't realise she was upstairs, and Dwight had said, *I do explain to these little ladies that I just can't be tied down*, and Essie had snorted so loudly he'd heard her and said, *What was that for?* and she'd said, *Oh nothing, little laddie*, and he hadn't liked that at all.

She shakes her head and turns to look at her mother. 'Is that the tank top I got you? It's from . . . '

'I know. I love it.'

'You're wearing it to *move puppies*?'

'I thought it would be nice . . . '

'Yeah, whatever.'

Janey bites her lip. 'And I thought it might be nice to . . . spend an evening with a guy . . . '

Essie's face is the worst; she looks . . . not disgusted, or interested. She looks completely and utterly bamboozled, as if her mum could not *possibly* have an opinion on the opposite sex in any way at all.

'Thanks for the vote of confidence,' says Janey, upset and flustered, and heads out the back door.

'I thought I was meant to be the moody one,' Essie says to the empty kitchen as she goes.

24

Lowell is waiting outside by his big old estate car. The boot has almost nothing in it at all.

Janey's boot contains her unused yoga mat, her unused gym kit, her unused swimming costume – basically anything she might need if she felt a fit of emergency exercise come on, which it hasn't yet – a torch, a first-aid kit despite the fact that the car spends nine hours a day parked outside a hospital, some cereal she keeps forgetting to take out, four pens, three charging cables, two of which aren't working but she can never figure out which ones, and a bulk-buy of loo roll that she keeps there because there genuinely isn't enough room to store it in the tiny house, particularly as Essie has filled the bathroom full of her incredibly expensive La Roche-Posay products. Inside the car are either a hundred and seventy-five pairs of cheap sunglasses, or zero pairs. There is no in-between.

'You ready?' says Lowell. He is, she notices suddenly, wearing his gardening trousers.

'Are those your only trousers?' she asks, before cursing the fact that a side-effect of the menopause appears to be blurting out the first thing in her head. She can't avoid the fact, though, that's she a bit disappointed. She's gone to an awful lot of effort.

Sure enough, he looks completely nonplussed.

'No,' he says mildly. 'But I thought to pick up puppies, perhaps I wouldn't wear my best trousers.'

'It's just, those are the only trousers I've ever seen you wear,' says Janey, trying to make things better but not necessarily succeeding.

'Well, yes. One night I was cycling, one day I was gardening, and now I'm picking up . . . '

He looks down. The old cords were once bottle-green but are now wearing through with softness and age.

'You're right,' he says, sounding surprised. 'I live in a muddy country. I probably need more than one pair of working trousers.'

Janey smiles. 'Is everything else in your house, like, morning suits and stuff? Fancy architect clothes? Strangely shaped metal glasses?'

He smiles. 'No, I don't really like having too much stuff.'

'Except in your garden.'

'Oh, gardens are different,' he says, warmth in his voice.

'Is this why you don't own your own bicycle?'

' . . . or a second pair of trousers. Yes, I think we can agree I've taken it too far.'

Janey wonders what is in his house.

'Well,' she says, 'you're about to very much maximalise on dogs.'

He nods. 'I am. Shall we?'

'We should probably take something to cart the dogs in – have you got a bucket?'

'A dog bucket?? Is that a thing?'

'I think any kind of bucket will do.'

★

The cottages are deserted – Essie and Dwight are choosing bathroom fixtures. Janey briefly wonders if there is anything going on – they seem to be spending a lot of time together – but dismisses it immediately. Connor has such lovely manners and is just so perfect for Essie; they make a lovely couple. Unsophisticated roughneck Dwight is not her type at all.

Wee Jim is outside, and grunts at them and continues what he is doing, which appears to be something with a hammer and a sink. Janey cannot imagine the circumstances under which it makes sense to take a hammer to a sink, but doesn't mention it. Once they open the door, however, it's a different matter. Instantly there is a paddle of excited paws rampaging on the floor above them, and an excited woof from Felicity. By the time they climb up the stairs, having found a bucket in an unplumbed bathroom downstairs, one of the pups has already managed to squirm its way around the barrier and is tentatively making its way down.

'Oh, no, you don't,' says Janey, at once. 'Into the bucket with you.'

She can't believe how much they've all grown. Every day they seem to leap ahead. No wonder Felicity looks utterly exhausted. Their hair is getting long and straggly already. About half have Felicity's pointed floppy wolfhound ears, flat against their tiny heads, and about half have proper Jock Westie ears, perfect triangles popping out of their skulls. They're all a combination of grey and white but already it is becoming obvious that they are going to be the most curious mixture of shape and sizes: there are sturdy bodies with long giraffe legs, and Bute has a long furry torso with tiny legs and a big arse which makes her look like a hairy sausage dog. Freuchie is pretty, a perfect white Westie that has been blown up like an air bed, but Argyll also has an underbite, as her huge wolfhound snoot doesn't quite match her small Westie skull.

Janey loves them all.

'You are the most gorgeous things I have ever seen.'

Felicity has bounded over towards Lowell, who is cuddling her and, Janey notices curiously, turning his head away.

'I'm sorry, old girl,' she hears him murmur. 'I'm so sorry. I thought it was for the best.'

'Did you not want to give her away?'

'I didn't,' he says shortly.

But Felicity is a forgiving sort of animal – in fact, she's a very easygoing girl all round, as a few people have observed before – and is burrowing into his armpit and making tiny pleased noises and rubbing her huge muzzle against his face in the manner of someone very in love with him. Much to Janey's surprise, eventually Lowell gives in and, despite being a large man, simply lies down and stretches on the dirty floor, whereupon Felicity leaps in delight – this is obviously an old game – and jumps up and down across him, sticking her nose into his neck and tickling him, while he giggles uncontrollably. Janey can't stop smiling; it's very unexpected. She feels a jolt immediately, seeing him lie down like that, free, relaxed. She is almost tempted to lie down next to him, but doesn't, of course. She wonders what he would do if she did. His great head is laughing, and naturally the puppies note that something is going on and join in, a great many-pawed mass of hair and noses, hopping all over him, sniffing, and occasionally giving him daring little nips. Janey watches him, feeling . . . she can't help it: in that moment, on that dusty floor, she finds him incredibly attractive. She can't stop staring. She wants to, absolutely wants to clamber on him like one of the pups.

'Okay, okay, enough of that!' he shouts eventually, and she blushes, feeling as if he's talking to her. Still laughing, he is sitting up and carefully brushing the pups off. 'Felicity, I beg your forgiveness and mercy, will that do?'

'I think you're forgiven,' smiles Janey. She can't help herself: it's the first time she's seen him smile, properly. 'Okay, now we've got everyone wildly overexcited, shall we try and get them to sit nice and calmly in a bucket in a car?'

'Felicity's good in the car,' avers Lowell.

Janey looks at him. 'Why didn't you come before? She's so obviously your dog.'

His face falls. 'Well, I've been away. And she wasn't . . . isn't my dog. Not really. She's my daughter's. I just felt . . . '

He breaks off. This is clearly a very difficult subject.

'Have you even told her there are puppies here? I couldn't have kept Essie from it for love nor money.'

'Yes, she's . . . hopefully she's coming up for Easter.'

He doesn't seem to want to elaborate, so Janey doesn't say anything more and they busy themselves. She pops the small shaggy bundle – Smokey, as it happens – into the bucket, which, naturally, he immediately tips over. They are so much bigger than she was anticipating. They find another bucket among the building materials and stick half in each, which works a little better. There is some growling from Smokey's bucket, and Janey predicts, correctly, that he is causing trouble, but they somehow manage to get them downstairs.

It has been a brisk, clear type of a day, and all over Carso sheets are out on lines flapping in the breeze, tumble-drying being so expensive and frankly entirely unnecessary when you live on the north coast of Scotland where the two tides meet. And with evening they are beginning to shake off the deep black troughs of long winter nights, when the light starts to trickle away as early as two-thirty in the afternoon, and you often take much pleasure in hunkering down in the cold, the dark, fires lit, heavy curtains pulled, with a book and a cheese scone and a cup of tea big enough to swim in.

Now, spring is appearing – very, very tentatively, it must be said, shy and demure, a nervous maiden, as she often is in this part of the world, easily cowed and sent scurrying home by an Easter blizzard, May sleet sometimes indistinguishable from petals.

Janey sits in the back as Lowell drives as carefully as if they have real babies back there. Felicity rides shotgun, occasionally raising her great wolf head to check what's going on over in the back seat beyond the netting. Janey cradles each bucket and finds she is speaking in a soft crooning voice to the pups, telling them it'll be okay, very much in the same way she talks to infants in her clinic when they are dealing with the unexpected sensations of waking up to a frightening, unfamiliar hearing world for the first time.

'Are you alright back there?' says Lowell, who cannot deny rather enjoying listening to her gentle voice. He doesn't hear a lot of gentle voices.

'It's nice,' she says experimentally. 'To try new things.'

They both feel the cold breeze when they get back to the old schoolhouse. Lowell looks at her, faintly alarmed. They look at the chicken wire run he has built. It's not unimpressive. He has filled the kennel with blankets.

'After all,' offers Janey, 'puppies have been growing up in the wild for thousands of years.'

'Yeah,' says Lowell.

'Like when they try and sell you tooth chews for your dog and stuff. Dogs have been kind of alright without toothbrushes for a zillion years, like, literally up until the invention of marketing departments?'

But she has no conviction in her voice; she doesn't believe it and neither, she can tell, does he.

'You must have a laundry in there,' she says. She's a little nosy to see inside the house – she has already checked, and if it was ever on the house-moving apps it isn't any more, which makes her crazy. She considers it very rude not to list your house and let other people have a peek at it.

She thinks it will almost certainly look like a bachelor pad, and not a cool one either: socks on drying racks; miserable ready meals in the fridge; a well-worn armchair in front of the fire that has a bum shape impressed into it, and a mark where the sweaty back of his head goes; remote control in easy reach. She's seen a few, from being asked out – rarely, but from time to time. And going because that's what you're meant to do, isn't it? Then listening at some length to a man insist that he is absolutely over his ex, that cow, for two hours, not have people demur when you offer to split the bill and then . . . well. The divorced man's flat. It's generally a terrible disappointment. Would make up for the fact that she rather likes the way he drives; not fast, not aggressively, but with a certain control. Men would be amazed, thinks Janey, if they knew how much being a good driver is the most incredible turn-on for women.

'Well, yes,' Lowell says, as they stare into the squirming, fuzzy, adorable bundles in the buckets. 'It's where I make stuff clean?'

'Have you got a boot room?'

'I don't, but I can't imagine shutting puppies in with shoes is best practice anyway.' He sighs. 'This is my fault. I let Felicity out of my sight, and some wee Westie Jock parachuted down on to her.'

'I assumed he got lowered on, like Tom Cruise in *Mission: Impossible*.'

Lowell grins. 'I wonder if that's how Tom Cruise does it in real life.'

They both laugh.

'Okay, fine. I submit. My life, which was already pretty grim, is now going to be made rather more . . . '

Janey picks up one of the wee girl dogs. Lowell stops in his tracks as the tiny thing, grey and white, long eyelashes, tentatively wags her tiny nub of a tail and experimentally puts out her tongue to lick her hand.

'Oh, lord,' he says, his voice changing completely, and for the first time, it seems to Janey, he sees the dogs as dogs, rather than a problem for him to solve. 'Hello,' he says. 'Which one is this one?'

'Argyll,' says Janey, examining her. 'She's going to be huge. Wolfhound body, and shrunken Westie head, like a cut and shunt.'

Lowell frowns. 'I think she's perfect.'

He holds the little pup gently in the palm of his large hand, while she carries on licking and making pleased noises.

'Alright,' he says, picking up another bucket with the other hand. Felicity bounds around his legs, wagging wholeheartedly, sniffing around the garden, relieving herself joyfully on a plant-pot and generally looking absolutely delighted after her many adventures in the big city.

Janey picks up her bucket full of dogs and follows him in, as if it's the most natural thing in the world.

25

At first Janey reacts as though she's just walked into the TARDIS. That, more or less, is what seems to have happened.

'Hang on,' she says, and walks back out and in again.

Nothing has changed outside. The blinds are still drawn. The brickwork is still chipped and the pointing needs done, and the window frames are peeling.

Lowell smiles rather awkwardly. 'Ah, yeah,' he says.

Janey puts the bucket of puppies down, to some disgruntlement.

'Oh, my God.' She shakes her head. 'Nobody in town knows about this.'

'I . . . I quite like it like that,' says Lowell, looking at her.

'But . . . how?'

The space inside has been hollowed out. Where once there were, as Janey well remembers, two classrooms, three sets of toilets – boys, girls, teachers – a staff room, a cloakroom and a gym/canteen/makeshift theatre – all of that is gone.

Instead, there is one, vast space, made almost entirely of wood – there are wooden ridges along the back wall – with the side completely made of glass. There is very little furniture: a large wooden dining table; a large fireplace glassed in; but then a full set of steps running into the eaves of the building, from which is suspended a beautiful wire and wood mezzanine, lined with bookshelves, with a vast double bed. In the far corner on the right is an office space with a tilted desk and a large wooden storage unit for rolled-up plans. On the other side, by the glass, is an immaculate small kitchen with a wooden bar for sitting at and looking out on to the beautiful wild garden in the fading light. It is warm; the entire space is warm, no mean feat in a space this size in Scotland, particularly in a Victorian building that can't be properly insulated. As she looks closer she sees that the windows have an inner pane that double- or triple-seals them; that there are few doors, but the ones there are are heavy and sealed.

'I couldn't imagine this was here,' says Janey.

He smiles politely.

'But why do you leave the outside such a mess?'

'I don't think it is a mess,' he says. 'I think it's normal wear and tear; it's exactly how the house should look. I'm happy to respect the exterior and all the lives its been through. I think it's beautiful like that. Then . . . the interior is mine.'

Janey takes off her shoes without even thinking about it, apart from a brief check in case she's got a hole in her sock. The floor is blissfully warm under her feet after the windy chill outside. Felicity has made her way over to the front of the fire and, with a happy, exhausted sigh, has collapsed in front of it. Janey feels rather like doing exactly the same thing. The puppies are meeping.

'Well,' says Janey. She was so proud of her own little place, she thinks now, just because she chose nice colours. She would like to pretend not to be so impressed, and that she walks into amazing, design magazine-type homes all the time, but it's too late – she already did a mega-TARDIS reaction, so she's lost the cool points. It strikes her, quite forcefully, that a man with a house this nice and all his own hair will probably be quite well-off for female company, but she squeezes the thought down. It's pointless. He has a house this beautiful but still, whenever he sees her, deliberately puts on the same pair of trousers. Maybe it's intentional, to stop her falling for him; he's just being polite about it. That's a very depressing thought.

'Where were you thinking, for the wee guys?' she says, regarding her bucket rather dolefully.

'I *was* thinking outside, with the chicken wire,' he says. 'However . . . '

He nods, and heads to the right-hand wall. Fitted flush into the wall are practically hidden doors: one to a laundry, one to a small bathroom, then one small larder.

'Oh, this is why you leave all your shoes in the porch,' she says. 'So you don't have to bother with stuff.'

'I don't like stuff,' he says. 'I know, it's a cliché.'

Janey doesn't like thinking back to how hard it was to throw out all the stuff. All the endless bloody stuff, fighting, dividing, dwindling piles, impossible choices. Christmas decorations, school reports; holiday albums that now seemed to be laughing at them and the mythic happy family they represented. All of it, just . . . stuff.

She turns to him, frowning. 'But architects . . . why do you live in this beautiful house but build horrible miserable blocks for people?' she says, in a more accusatory tone than she'd intended.

'I don't, not really,' he says. 'But I think there's a lot to be said for high-density. We just really must get it right, which we don't always do, but when we do . . . people like it a lot.'

'And making everything so plain and dull?' says Janey. 'Like the new wing at the hospital.' The turrets and big clock of the old-fashioned hospital are now hidden behind a big, ugly, antiseptic block of metal and glass.

'Well, all the fiddly things you may like – stairs, and fancy doors and handles and whatnot . . . they're just not very helpful if you're old, or in a wheelchair, or can't climb stairs or are visually impaired. It really helps for access to make things as clear as possible. Think about the iPad . . . most people think that is beautiful, and it's as empty and clean as possible.'

Janey folds her arms as she would really have preferred it if he didn't have a point.

'You didn't do the new hospital wing, though?'

'No, I didn't,' he says. 'I've seen it. I know what you mean. Unfortunately beautiful buildings cost money, and it's their responsibility to spend as little of our money as possible.'

'Stop making good points,' says Janey.

He leads her over to the drawing board and shows her what he's working on. There are two large screens, one enormous, that show the project in three dimensions. A pair of round horn-rimmed glasses sit neatly at the top of the drawing board.

The screen shows a long line of tall, narrow houses with pointed grey roofs, which looked like Dutch houses lining a canal; they nestle near each other and have cubes of grey and white colour cut out of them in different places to individuate the houses, which have large glass windows that take up most of their first floor. The effect is soothing but surprising too, the rows of houses looking pretty in the same line, but also as if each is individual just to you. Janey can't help but look longingly at the well-insulated glass, the heat pumps lined up, the solar panels on the roof. She bets those houses are always cosy and toasty.

As if reading her mind, he says, 'A-rating.'

'That's not possible,' she says. 'I thought that was a myth.'

'What are you?'

'D,' she says. 'And that's if I fill in all the cracks with freezer bags.'

He grins. 'Well, then.'

The pups are getting restless and Smokey is making a clear bid for freedom.

'Alright,' he says, and opens one of the almost invisible doors on the side wall. Beyond is a laundry with a butler sink and the original flagstone paving.

'Oh!' says Janey, in recognition. 'That was the . . . '

She is about to say cloakroom, but as she does so she realises that in fact along the far wall are a line of old-fashioned hooks, on a long stout wooden rail, just as she remembers it, now hold-ing tea towels. He has kept them.

'Oh, my,' she says. 'This is really . . . this is where I used to hang my blazer.'

He smiles.

'I had a sticker, though. You got a sticker in case you couldn't read your own name.' She pauses for a moment. 'I don't think Jamesie Carnyne ever did learn to read his own name.'

'Wonder what happened to him?'

'He's on his dad's farm, of course. Well, his farm now. Good man, Jamesie. Not much for the reading, but he's a good man with the coos. One year the dairy truck couldn't get through the snow, and his dad sent him down with fresh milk for all us weans.'

'That sounds lovely.'

'It was terrible! All warm, with, like, bits floating in it. It gave us all the boke and we pretended we were going to be sick . . . then I think Carmel Wilson really was sick. Oh, yeah, and Mrs Hegary gave us all a row and that was it, we were in big trou-ble.' She laughs, remembering. 'Jamesie was *fuming*. His dad had gone to all that trouble, given away a bit of his day's takings too, and we just took the piss.'

He smiles to see her laughing.

'Oh, goodness, we called him Bokie Jamesie for ages. Oh, God.' She puts her hand to her mouth. 'We were terrible.'

He crouches, letting the puppies squirm over his hands, dropping them when they started to nip.

'I can't imagine you as a naughty schoolgirl,' he says, and Janey is suddenly conscious that the laundry room is not huge, and is very warm, with heated dryer rails – oh, the luxury – and she suddenly finds she has gone pink and begs herself not to have a hot flush, not now, of all times, please.

'I wasn't!' she protests. 'I was very well behaved!'

'Were you a big swot?'

'Well, I wasn't a big enough swot to go to *architect school*, no,' she says. 'Where did you grow up anyway?'

'St Andrews,' he says.

'Oh, my God, that's swot capital of the world!'

'Well, quite.'

'Why aren't you wearing a diamond-pattern jumper, in fact?'

He smiles. 'Yeah, yeah.'

'And your trousers should be red—'

'Please, please can we not start on my trousers again?'

He looks around then opens a unit in the sideboard, inside of which are piled lots of towels, all a soft grey.

'That is the most anal thing I have ever seen,' says Janey, then regrets even referring to the 'a' word.

'What, owning towels?'

'Owning them all the same colour.'

'Why would you own different-coloured towels? How does that make you . . . whatever.'

He obviously doesn't want to say that word either.

'Well, you have some daft beach towels . . . and some from an old place that are so worn through they're super-soft and comfortable and dry really well and . . . I don't think I've ever thrown a towel away.'

'Fascinating,' he says, pulling two from the bottom of the pile.

'No!' says Janey. 'They're going to get ruined! The pups will mess them all up.'

'They're *towels*.'

Janey would offer to go home and get some of her old ones – she has some right shockers, it is true, even though she did her best at the clearout. She couldn't get rid of the dinosaur towel Al wore all summer for a year when he was four, in lieu of actual clothes, his scaly tail swinging behind him wherever he went. Plus it was useful for wrapping your hair in, as long as nobody was there to see, obviously, which generally nobody was apart from Essie, and she wouldn't notice her mother if she walked down the stairs wearing a Joan Collins turban festooned with diamonds and grew an extra foot.

'We need newspapers too,' says Janey. 'Cor, I haven't bought a paper for ages.'

'Not even the Sundays? I love the Sundays.'

Janey realises she used to love the Sunday papers too. Then, recently, they started to get her down: so full of films she will never watch, music she will never hear, recipes she will never try . . . With a start she sees it for what it truly was: a slump, a real slump, when everything seemed so gloomy, when she lost so much fun, so much joy in the normal things of everyday life. Everything must have faded to grey.

'Oh, yeah,' she says, quietly. 'I kind of assumed people just buy them for puppy-training these days; that's what's keeping the industry going.'

'I used to have a paper round,' says Lowell.

'On the gardener's bike?'

'Good point,' says Lowell. 'I seem to have gone downhill in the area of owning my own bike.'

He lets the puppies out, and they immediately start to squirm and sniff their way around. One bumps into the bottom of the washing machine and cries, and Felicity comes in from the fire and graciously bends her neck down from a great height like a giraffe on the veldt, to sniff and make sure everything is okay. Janey pulls out their doughnut feeding bowl and Lowell fills it with milk; they are all able to lap it now, pretty much.

'This is great,' says Lowell. 'Look at them! Look at their wee noses!'

All the tiny tails stand rigidly up as they concentrate on lapping busily.

Janey reads off the printout Essie has made for her.

'Next you have to start putting baby cereal in their bowls.' She glances up over her glasses. 'Uh-oh.'

'What?'

'That's when they start to poo properly.'

'I see,' says Lowell, taking it manfully. 'Better get those newspapers.'

Janey gives all the wee dogs, now completely milk-drunk and staggering around, a small kiss on their tiny noses. Felicity is very keen to go out of the laundry and leave them behind, so Lowell lets her. He frowns and vanishes outside for a second.

'Jack brought back her bed,' he says, pulling out a rather chic large grey suede dog bed and settling it down by the fire. 'He says he wants nothing more to do with her.'

Janey laughs, as Felicity bounds towards the bed with glee. 'Do you think his pastor has told him to cast her out of the community?'

'I think,' says Lowell, 'we are meant to throw stones at her whenever we see her. Glass of wine?'

He says it so casually. He can't have realised, Janey knows, what a seismic effect it would have. Why wouldn't they have a glass of wine? Perfectly normal thing to do. Nothing to read into it. But she is having some kind of internal panic attack, and immediately escapes to the bathroom.

The bathroom is as bare as everywhere else. She inspects her face. Oh, lord. This used to be . . . oh, goodness. She looks bright red. The lighting is gentle in the main room, but she fumbles in her bag for make-up. Mascara always helps. And a bit of blotted lipstick. Not so much as to make it obvious or go into the irritating little puckered lines around her mouth . . . and does she smell of dog? But if she adds perfume she will be that overbearing too-perfumed middle-aged lady of the kind who likes to asphyxiate small nephews and the like. Christ. Plus it might mingle with the smell of dog and seem as if she liked putting dog-scented perfume on.

She realises her hands are shaking and tells herself to calm down. This is ridiculous. It's just a drink, for God's sake.

With this very attractive man. Alone in his house. His very attractive house.

She looks down at herself and sighs. So why the hell would he be interested in her? Stop thinking like that, she tells herself. And get out of the damn bathroom before he assumes the absolute worst.

Back in the big room, Lowell has poured two very large glasses of red wine, and Janey takes one gratefully, even though she knows it will make her look redder than ever. She sits down on the surprisingly comfortable corduroy sofa, and worries immediately about spills.

'I'm amazed you allow red wine in here,' she says, and he looks confused again. 'You know, in case someone spills it?'

'Are you likely to spill it?' he says. 'I can get you a towel as well.'

'Well, normally I don't,' she says. 'But now you've mentioned it, I'm worrying about it.'

'You brought it up!'

Janey takes a large slug to bring the level down in the glass, then sets it carefully on a coaster on a side table.

Lowell blinked. 'I don't have people round very often,' he confesses.

'I've never seen you around the town,' says Janey. 'You're not in choir or anything.'

He laughs. 'You've obviously never heard me sing.'

'Honestly, being able to sing is very low down the priorities for being in the choir. I'm not a hundred per cent sure you need a pulse.'

His eyes stray to the mantelpiece, and Janey notices for the first time that there is a picture on it.

'Oh, there's Verity!' she says, jumping up and going over to examine the picture.

Verity is a very serious-looking child. She has her father's dark eyes, but otherwise there isn't a huge resemblance; she has a pointed chin whereas her father's is round; russet hair and a petite build where her father is dark and sturdy.

'She's beautiful,' says Janey.

'She looks a lot like her mother,' says Lowell, and his face is pained.

'How is . . . '

'Oh, well,' says Lowell, and takes another long swig of his wine.

It feels rather as if the evening is slightly hanging on a knife edge. It strikes Janey that a different, less bruised person than her might say, *Oh, we're not going to talk about our families tonight. We're not going to talk about our pasts, or any of that,* and stride across the lovely room and put his glass of wine aside (carefully), pull off his glasses and simply sit on his large, comfortable-looking lap. There is, in fact, quite a lot of Janey who would have liked to do that. To do exactly that, right now. So much. But she has never been confident in that way, not even when she was younger. What if she terrifies him? What if he goes, *Christ, what the fuck?* What if? What if?

So instead she gives him a warm, encouraging, pretty much professional smile, and doesn't say anything, which is the way she encourages people to open up to her in clinic about their hearing loss; the way she's been good at her job for years and years and . . . well. Lots of years. Being a good audiologist means being good at listening, in more ways than one.

She sits back down, still wearing the smile, and picks up her wine, physically holding it, as if it is a barrier to her marching across the room . . . his look of shock and horror as she disports herself like a hussy . . . no, she can't bear to think of it. But she wants him so badly, it frightens her.

'Oh, you don't want to hear this,' he says, interrupting her train of thought.

'Of course I do,' she says, looking around again to hide her pink face. Felicity is snoozing gently in her lovely bed; the puppies have settled, it appears. The fire is flickering, the room is warm, the wine is delicious, the lighting very flattering. It would have been such a nice evening for a seduction, truly. Is it too late?

'Well, if you're sure. I was married, working in Aberdeen . . . '

She wistfully lets it go. And listens, which she has always been so good at.

They had been in Aberdeen, but his wife had had an affair with a colleague, so they had moved to the country to have a second chance, which was when they'd enrolled in Janey's clinic. But Thalia had been increasingly unhappy – she was young, Lowell says. He'd married a lovely young woman but she'd had to leave all her friends behind, and – he winces – her social life. She was miserable. Started picking fights with him about everything.

'It wasn't your fault,' says Janey gently.

'It *was*,' he says forcefully. 'It was entirely my fault. I married her, knowing there was an age gap, pretending it didn't matter. I figured it would be fine, she wanted children, and we'd settle down together – but it was like, after Verity arrived, she immediately became terrified. About what she'd missed out on, what was going on without her. I had made her old before her time. She said that.'

'She wasn't a teenager, though,' says Janey, frowning.

'Oh, no, she was thirty-two when we met,' says Lowell. 'Christ, no. I was an idiot, but not a pervert. I hope.'

'And you were . . .?'

'Forty-four. It didn't . . . I didn't think that much of it. I mean, it was a bit of a gap, but I wasn't old enough to be her dad or anything.'

Janey nods. 'I get it.'

She does. If he were to date a forty-four-year-old woman now, nobody would bat an eyelid. It was unlikely anyone would even notice. Hell, he could date a thirty-two-year-old now and it would be completely fine. She, on the other hand, would be in the *Daily Mail*, next to the lady prison guards who kept copping off with armed robbers.

'But no: I was the boring old fart tying her down, burying her . . . ' He gestures around. 'I know you think I'm some kind of crazy minimalist, but I'm not that weird, honestly. I just thought she'd fill it with paintings and pictures and cushions and . . . stuff. But she never did. She never brought a thing in. She hated it so much. She was just online all the time . . . '

'Did Verity like it?'

'She did,' he says. 'She loved getting a dog – they'd go for miles in the forest and Felicity was so gentle, but protective too. You have no idea: having a differently abled child, you worry about them so much – what if someone takes advantage, what if they don't notice something or become aware of something . . . but here, she could roam for miles and we didn't have to fret about her. And the school was great, and she made a friend, and we really were considering the surgery.'

'I seem to remember her lip-reading being very good.'

He smiles in pride. 'It is,' he says. Then his face clouds again and he refills their glasses.

'So what happened?' asks Janey. 'Did she move back?'

'Well, first . . . ' says Lowell. 'And God knows I'm not blameless. I travel a lot with my work, you know. We build things all over. There's a lot of meetings in London and Amsterdam and stuff.'

'And you live in the middle of nowhere.'

'Well, there are big chunks when I'm at home all the time, but she wasn't crazy about those bits either.'

Janey nods.

'But she wasn't working . . . we'd agreed that was okay, that someone could look after Verity. But she wasn't; she was online all day. And I mean all day.'

He swallows, and suddenly Janey knows what's coming. She's seen it before. Many times. He looks at her, and sees her tiny nod, and the relief in his eyes as he realises she already knows what he is going to say is absolutely immense, as if he's been carrying it for a very long time; as if he can't believe he is about to be able to put it down.

'The activism . . . ' he says.

She nods again. 'I know.'

He bows his head.

'There is nothing . . . nothing wrong with being deaf,' he says. 'I believe that. I truly do. I truly think Verity is perfect. I wouldn't change the tiniest bit of her.'

'I completely agree with you,' says Janey.

'But I also don't think she's deaf because she got her vaccinations, or I got mine or Thalia got hers, or because they're deliberately putting stuff in drinking water, or it's because they chlorinate, or because the one world government is in the pay of pharmaceutical companies . . . She went so fast from completely reasonable questioning, to absolute . . . she believed *everything*. She thought having a cochlear implant was Bill Gates putting a control chip in your brain. She absolutely believed that. Believes that. Fervently.'

'Internet poisoning,' says Janey. 'I've seen it again and again and again. People come armed with their YouTube videos.'

'Some of it *is* completely reasonable,' says Lowell again, desperately trying to defend his wife. 'But a lot of it is just absolute . . . *pish*.'

'You don't need to tell me,' says Janey quickly.

He's running his hands through his hair, very agitated. 'And she believes all of it! She thinks she can cure deafness with diet!'

'You can,' says Janey. 'If you've got carrots stuck in your ears.'

He stares at her for a moment and then, finally, laughs and breaks the tension.

'Ha,' he says. 'You're funny.' He rubs his head again. 'Thanks,' he says. 'I'm so sorry. For going on and on about it. You're such a good listener.'

Good listener and *funny*, thinks Janey to herself. Two of the least sexy female things in the history of the universe. Never mind. Never mind.

'That's okay,' she says.

'I've stopped now,' he says. 'I'm really sorry. I don't talk about it much. It's no excuse. Can we change the subject? What do you like?'

I like you, thinks Janey, suddenly terribly sad. At everything and everyone that has passed her by. But you are a million miles away, thinking about your ex-wife and worrying about your daughter, and you are not remotely, not even nearly, anywhere near that space, even if you saw me as something other than a frumpy clinician-stroke-dog-pee-specialist.

'Actually,' says Janey gently, 'it's getting late.'

'Oh, God, I'm so sorry. "Man Yammers On" shocker.'

'It's not that,' says Janey. 'It isn't, not at all. But I have work tomorrow. And you're about to be very busy.'

'Of course,' he said, sitting back, more businesslike. 'So, how long are these puppies going to stay? What do I have to do?'

'Another three weeks?' says Janey. 'That's assuming you find homes for them all. I think Dwight wants one.'

'Okay, wow,' says Lowell. 'But I have to work. And I'll need to go and visit Verity.'

'Didn't you say she was coming here for Easter?'

'Well, I hope so, but Thalia isn't keen . . . says this place has bad . . . there's a 5G mast somewhere around here.'

'There is,' says Janey. 'I strongly recommend not looking up what the local Facebook group had to say about it. But surely once Verity hears about the pups . . . Anyway, you know, I'm sure Essie would pop in and help. For cash, probably. Just to make sure they're all okay, feed them, take them out in the run . . . '

Janey has absolutely no idea how her daughter will respond to the suggestion, but she'll figure that out as they go. She likes the pups anyway; they make her happier than she has been in a long time.

'Yeah, okay,' says Lowell. He looks at the bottle, which is empty.

'Phew,' he says, and they stand up.

Janey rises with the strong sense of stepping away – from one way of being a woman into another: of being a woman, alone with a man, and a bottle of wine, and the old possibilities and dreams and titillations and chances. But tonight she didn't get to feel like that. Tonight she was a sympathetic ear, nothing more, and it troubles her more than she would have ever thought or could have admitted; as if she is shedding the skin of her fundamental adult self, even when inside she feels exactly the same as she ever did. And always will. For years and years and years stretching ahead. Even as she stands to meet him, his bulk looming above her, she feels it: a quick spurt of attraction, an almost overwhelming desire to touch his jumper, to see him smile that gentle rumpled smile at her; his comfortable size, his slightly distracted air, as if he's building houses in his head all the time; the hair that he runs his hands through, a gesture which immediately makes him look younger in a way she can't quite put her finger on.

For a second, as they are facing each other, she catches something, or thinks she does: something in his eye. As if, for the first time, he sees her. Woman her. The person she thought she was. She can see it. It's like a tiny hole in the universe, a pause that stretches longer than it should do. He's confused; blinks, looks nervous. Then he returns to himself, and she thinks he is thinking how horrified she would be, a comfortable middle-aged lady, after all, in sensible trainers, with a Boots Advantage card.

Oh, and he had a twelve-years-younger wife, of course.

'Thank you, sorry,' he says, both things at once.

'What for?' she says, meaning both.

'For . . . for monopolising your time. But for letting me . . . I don't talk about it to many people,' he says, rumpling his face.

'You haven't thought about a real therapist?' Janey asks delicately.

'I don't . . . I mean, honestly, I don't think I'm that interesting. And I think . . . I think I'm not feeling bad for any mysterious reason, you know what I mean? My wife left me because I'm a boring old fart – what is there to say about that? People wanging on about themselves for hours on end doesn't make them any less boring either, in my experience. So, again, my apologies.'

'None needed,' she says, smiling at him.

★

The puppies are scrabbling in the laundry and they go to check on them. They are playing a game which appears to involve tearing their tiny claws up and down on the expensive towels, pulling loops out of them. Little puddles of pee are starting to form. Felicity is showing absolutely no interest in coming over to see how they're doing, even though they are absolutely desperate to bolt over to her. But they are tumbling around happily enough; it's a warm, cosy spot for them.

'Do you think puppies have existential problems?' Lowell says.

Janey bends down and picks up Bute, the little girl with the big bum, whose hairy tail stub wags furiously when she recognises a familiar scent.

'I think,' says Janey, 'that puppies might be the *answer* to existential problems.'

And she goes out into the chilly evening, walks – despite his gallant offer to accompany her – by herself back across town. The last thing she needs is to be spotted by people who know her, given that that is practically everyone, or for people to start to gossip. Particularly, these days, when there is absolutely nothing to gossip about; nothing at all.

26

'Burnt Otter.'

'That's not what it says, stop being ridiculous,' says Essie, grabbing the paint chart off the table in front of Dwight. 'Oh. It is. They should add a health and safety line that says "no otters were burnt in the making of this paint".'

Dwight throws his hands up. 'This is all nuts. I don't want Rabbit's Arse colour.'

'Well, maybe you do.'

They are technically having a planning meeting in the End of the World bar when it is shut, on a Friday morning, and Shelby is – Essie has checked carefully – off in Inverness doing some shopping and getting her roots done, as Jean in the village is not up to snuff, apparently. Jean has a lot to say about this, little of which is repeatable, and, unusually for Carso, nobody has repeated it, because everyone is completely terrified Shelby will get the huff and leave the village and close the bar and then they'll be stuffed because absolutely nobody is moving to open any hospitality venues – there's no staff; all the seasonal young Europeans have disappeared.

They also technically asked Wee Jim to the meeting but he was not being much use, just sitting there looking so much like he didn't understand why nobody wanted him to hit anything with a hammer that Dwight ended up sending him round the back of the Seagate cottages, where they're putting the stuff they've pulled out that Essie has decided they can't sell on, which is almost everything: cheap little falling-apart MDF cabinets and the type of old, heavy furniture riddled with woodworm that weighs an absolute ton and nobody wants in their house any more, even if houses need sideboards for wedding crockery. Essie saves all the old wood for the wood-burner, and Dwight is astonished that they don't have central heating and that anyone could conceivably prefer a stove with real wood they have to light and use kindling for rather than something you can just turn on with the touch of a button, much in the same way as he was astounded that Essie thinks wooden floors will be more popular than patterned carpet.

'I'm just telling you what people like,' Essie is saying.

'Yeah, by people you mean *snots*,' he says. 'Christ, I can't tell you the difference it would make if there was carpet in the rig.'

'Is it cold?'

He shook his head. 'Outside is fucking nightmarish, but inside is just about alright. Twenty-five degrees.'

'They heat it to twenty-five? Aren't you all stifling?'

'No, that's a normal level of warm.'

'Bloody hell,' says Essie, who has adopted the Edinburgh practice of pretending that cold houses are much classier, actually.

'I really don't care,' he says, finally, gesturing at the paint charts. 'Also I'm colourblind.'

'Dwight!' says Essie. '*What*? We have sat here this entire morning looking at paint colours and . . . they all look the same to you?'

He is clearly quite embarrassed about it. Being colourblind possibly doesn't go with his cowboy image, although it would explain all the black clothing. Today he is wearing a two-tone shirt, with a cow's head bootlace tie. Normally Essie would be in hysterics. Now she feels like pulling the tie gradually towards her, grabbing his hat and sticking it on her own head. Which would be an absurd thing to do.

'Not *exactly* the same!' he says. 'Just . . . '

Essie picks up an odd aubergine colour he'd put aside as a definite maybe. 'What colour is this?'

'Titmouse,' he says immediately.

'No, I mean, what normal . . . Titmouse, really?' She reads the writing on the card. 'Huh. Anyway. What actual colour is it really?'

'Brown,' he says. 'I thought that would be fine given the door-frame is – you know. Wood colour.'

'It's not brown!' says Essie. 'Oh, my God. It's purple.' She bursts out laughing.

'Don't laugh at me!'

'Why didn't you say?'

He shrugs. 'You wanted me to choose one.'

She looks at him then. He is normally so confident and bull-ish about everything; it's unusual to see him cowed in any way.

'Yes, but not if you can't . . . '

'I can.'

'This is a horrible colour.'

'Is it?' He shrugs. 'Purple's not a colour I can see.'

She moves closer. His eyes are a distinct green, just like Shelby's. But Essie isn't thinking about Shelby right at that moment. She's not, if she is being one hundred per cent honest with herself, really thinking about Connor either.

'What can you see? Is the world black and white?'

He shakes his head. 'Naw! I can see fine.'

'It's just . . . '

'You call it purple, I call it brown, that's all.'

'Well, I suppose you do,' she says. 'Is it brown you'd like?'

'You choose,' he says, finally. And holds her gaze.

'I like green,' Essie finds herself saying.

'I'm not too good on that either,' he says. 'Red and green are a bit . . .'

'You can't tell the difference between red and green? Is this why you never pay any attention to traffic lights?'

'Traffic lights are for pussies,' he says.

'*Traffic lights are for pussies* is exactly what I'm going to have put on your tombstone. When I have to order it, next week.'

'Would you be sad?' he asks, looking at her with a challenging glance.

She returns it. 'I would wear mourning colours,' she says. 'Purple and brown, together.'

He hitches an eyebrow at her and Essie suddenly realises she is twirling a ringlet on her finger in front of him, which is not like her, not at all.

Suddenly there's a commotion at the door.

'Coo-ee! Dwight, love, can you grab my bags . . .'

A bustling, highly scented Shelby, hair coloured a bright, gleaming blonde, piled high on her head, comes in through the pub's side door. She stops short on seeing Essie there, and Essie is conscious how close she and Dwight are sitting, and moves away, which, she realises belatedly, looks even more suspicious.

'Hi,' Shelby says in a pointed tone that is very much the opposite of friendly. Essie finds herself simultaneously a bit freaked out but also annoyed. Shelby used to bully her, for goodness' sake. It should be Essie who gets to be snotty now.

'Just leaving,' she says quickly. 'Dwight, I'm going to order some samples, have a look.'

'You choose, eh?' he says. 'I don't really care about all this stuff.'

Then why have we just wasted a morning? thinks Essie, then it comes to her that she might already know.

★

To her surprise, Shelby walks her out.

'You're hanging out a lot with my brother,' she observes, icily.

'I'm helping him on a work project,' says Essie, cursing her need to try to connect rather than keeping an icy-pure Zendaya silence that would be much cooler.

Shelby snorts. 'Yeah, whatever,' she says. 'You're just playing about up here, laughing at the country bumpkins?'

'I am *not*,' says Essie, exasperated. 'I'm from here, I was born and raised here and I have every bit as much of a right to be here as you do!'

'Except the second you can leave you'll piss off back to *Edinburgh*.'

She says Edinburgh the way one might say 'Sodom'. Essie doesn't have anything to say to that.

'I'm not remotely interested in your brother. I've got a boyfriend.'

'Really? You certainly seem interested in gaining access to his bank account.'

Essie rolls her eyes. 'To *help him*, for God's sake. He doesn't have a clue what he's doing.'

'No, how could he, coming from Carso? How could he, having saved up enough to buy three properties before his thirtieth birthday, which I'm sure you're also doing. How could we, when I run this place single-handedly. How could we possibly know what the hell we're doing? Thank *God* Miss Essie Big Boots is here from the big city to show us all up for the idiots we are.'

'You're *impossible*,' says Essie, too upset and angry to speak. She wants – oh, how she wants – to think of something quick and witty to say off the top of her head, in the spur of the moment, but goodness, she just can't. She marches down the street instead, her whole body shaking, terrified and filled with adrenaline. 'AND YOUR HAIR LOOKS STUPID,' she shouts back behind her.

'No, it doesn't,' says Shelby. 'It looks brilliant. You're wrong, as usual. Just as you are about everything.'

And she slams the door.

27

'Hmm,' says Amsan at lunch. 'Did you ever treat a Verity Thomas?'

Janey starts. Lowell has been in her thoughts. She is thinking of his handsome shaggy head, his worried smile; the pleasing heft of him. It is a good distraction from looking at the packet of Caramel Wafer bars someone left in Amsan's staff room, which she has stolen to pass on to her daughter as Yasmin just had a date with a man who had seemed perfect until he told her he liked to spend most weekends dressed up as a unicorn and did she have a problem with that, and needed cheering up. Janey has spent the morning with another family who want their deaf child to sign and have turned down the operation, where she had to do the tricky balancing act of supporting their decision without having a point of view about it. By definition she is there to help people hear, but she understands the agony completely. And she agrees. There is nothing wrong with their beautiful, perfect baby. And life has a way of being very tricky.

She glances at Amsan, and, slightly, the Caramel Wafers.

'Yes, ages ago, why?'

'She has a check-up coming.'

'I thought she'd been discharged from the service. She doesn't even live here.'

'Yeah, it's a request referral,' Amsan shrugs, glancing at her iPad. 'Dated two years ago.'

Janey goes a little pink. 'Um, I know her dad. I'll tell him.'
Something strikes her.

'She's not moving here?'

'No, no, her address is miles away . . . ' Amsan squints at the iPad. 'Oh, lord, I think this should have been sent over.'

Suddenly there is a squeaking noise. Owen has materialised and is squeaking over to their table on his wheely chair. He obviously thinks it looks cool, but overshoots and heads straight back.

'Hi, Owen,' says Janey.

'What's this about a patient mix-up?'

'It's nothing, just someone who should have been transferred to another region . . . '

'Uh-huh,' says Owen, stroking what is beginning to look like a deliberate beard, which is useful, but appears definitely oily. 'And how was this done?'

Amsan hides her iPad. 'You can't see that, Owen.'

'I can, actually,' says Owen. 'My clearance is, like, ultra-everything?'

'But this isn't your patient.'

'It isn't anyone's patient if they shouldn't be here.'

There's not a lot of arguing with that.

'TC-MED,' says Amsan, referring to the regional IT service.

'Uh-huh,' says Owen. 'And there's a paper trail?'

Amsan stabs, uselessly, at the iPad, which has frozen up again.

'Because you see,' goes on Owen, relentlessly, 'if this had been properly backed up *on fax* it would be in the file.'

He strokes his beard in a satisfied way, and kicks his chair back to his own table, where he is playing Dungeons and Dragons with the phlebotomists.

Amsan and Janey look at each other.

'Don't say it,' says Janey.

'He's ri—

'DON'T SAY IT. What are you doing this weekend?'

'Oh, Yasmin has a date with a Sorku guy so I'm taking her to learn how to ride. I think Sorku guys might be the way forward, yeah? No new technology, old traditional ways? You should try them.'

Sorku was the benign local cult that lived in a settlement at the foot of Ben Alton, politely fending off the hordes of keen young people who arrived every year wanting to make podcasts about them.

'Well, one,' says Janey, 'I think they see women over forty as witches. Even more than normal men do, I mean. And two, they have more than one wife.'

'That could be seen as efficient.'

'I don't not appreciate their lustrous beards, wood-chopping bodies and carriage-driving skills,' muses Janey. 'But I think the vow of enforced female silence and the menstrual hut might prove a bit of a test. Oh, God. Actually, the menstrual hut probably won't be necessary.' She sighs. 'Hang on, why are they even on dating sites?'

'What are you up to?' says Amsan.

'Essie's boyfriend is coming up.'

Amsan frowns. 'Well, you don't need to show off.'

'I apologise,' says Janey, immediately. It's really not worth getting on Amsan's bad side.

'Your house is very small . . . '

'Oh, he's not staying with us,' says Janey, half embarrassed, half relieved. '*Far* too common. He's very posh. They're staying at Harcourt House.' This is the smart estate country house hotel up the road.

'My Yasmin met a posh guy on a dating app,' says Amsan. 'He wanted her to wear a tail and prance around like a pony.'

'Okay, out,' says Janey. 'I mean it. I have to get very busy with dying alone.'

28

Essie has worked so hard to stop seeing Dwight so much. It's Saturday morning and Connor is coming. Her lovely, gorgeous boyfriend will be here in just a few hours. She doesn't need some hard-bodied, rough-handed scruffbag with the neatest, tightest—

No. She needs to concentrate on the next stage of the refit. The problem is, they need more manpower, they need people, and the people they have, like Wee Jim and his mate, aren't specialists. The electrics are going to be next, now that everything is more or less cleared out, and she doesn't really know anyone she trusts not to blow them sky-high. She needs a specialist.

Janey is very anxious even making the offer, but she has to. Essie is back to being at home all the time, which isn't doing anyone any good, not least her electricity bill.

'I told Lowell you might puppy-sit,' she says. 'He'll pay. It's only pin money but . . . '

Essie looks up, and Janey steels herself for a sarcastic refusal.

'What does Lowell do for a living?' she says. 'Isn't it something buildery?'

'Well, he's an architect.' Janey frowns. 'Is this for next door? Because, you know, I did this place mostly by myself.'

'Who did you get to do the electrics?'

'No one; the electrics were okay.'

'What about the plastering?'

'Johnson did a lot of it.' Janey frowns again. 'Oh, lord, I shouldn't have had him lifting his arms above his head.'

'How is he?'

'They're putting a care package together,' says Janey. 'It's slow-going. He wants to be completely back to normal straight away and that's exactly the kind of thing that makes people fall over. But he's going to be fine.'

She doesn't mention Lish, who she found yesterday crying in the linen closet. Lish finding things too much was incredibly unsettling. She takes everything in her stride. If *Lish* is under too much pressure . . . She decides not to talk about her abortive night with Lowell right now.

Essie leaps up. 'Yes!' she says. She has a lot to ask this guy. Her dad has not been remotely helpful, although he did ask if she would come over and babysit Logan while he took Lori away to New York for the weekend.

'Okay,' says Janey, surprised. 'Well, let me know how you get on.'

'Give me his number.'

'Ah,' says Janey, 'I still don't have it.'

'Oh for heaven's sake!'

'Just walk over there.'

'No way!' says Essie. 'What, just turn up out of the blue? God, Mum, you are so Gen X.'

Which feels not remotely fair, as Essie had adored every *Friends* rerun when she was a tween, and had always said she was envious of the way people just turned up at each other's houses without a hundred and seventy-five WhatsApp messages needing to be sent first.

'It'll be fine.'

'A strange girl turning up on his doorstep. No way. Come with me?'

Janey was going to tell her not to be daft, she's a grown-up, but oh, how often does Essie want to do things with her? Plus, it might be ridiculous but . . . she wants to see Lowell. She isn't young; she's certainly far too old to have a crush. She thought she'd grow out of it. She thought, when she was younger, that surely only the young felt terrible yearning. Grown-ups couldn't possibly feel it. And she doesn't, for the most part. She can appreciate a nice-looking young man, but this is different somehow. It's the smell of him, the gentle timbre of his voice; the way he thinks deeply before he speaks; his beautiful house, and the clear reflection of his character drawn upon it; his deep love for his daughter. She has it bad. Not that he would be looking at her. But she has it far too bad not to traipse past his house, like a teenage girl going out of her way to get on at a different bus stop.

'Sure,' she finds herself saying. 'Plus I want to see Bute.' She quickly amends this to, 'All of the puppies.'

'Has her arse gone back into proportion with the rest of her body yet?'

'She's the Kim Kardashian of dogs,' says Janey. 'Only a bit hairier.'

★

Outside in Carso it is a day to make you sing. The birds are everywhere, chattering with excitement, and everything is yellow and bright; the grass, after the long winter rains, as green as a jewel, and, if you look closely, buzzing and humming full of life. Clematis bursts like slow-motion fireworks from hedgerows, and the streets are full of Saturday people; early tourists, excited to have beaten doom-laden weather reports: locals just going for a stroll, feeling the luxury of being able to discard their big winter puffas; considering leaving the house without one of Gertie's knitted berets on. Unfurling their instinctive hunches against the north wind; embracing its sweeter, sunnier cousin.

'See,' says Janey, following Essie and shading her eyes. 'If it was like this every day you'd get bored. You'd get fed up of all the lovely weather and you'd hate the sunshine. Whereas when it happens like this, it has a rarity factor that brings you far more joy . . .'

'Hmm,' says Essie. 'Rather than horrible then amazing, can it not just be "not bad", and average everything out?'

'No,' says Janey. 'I love the horrible too. That's what the peat stove is for, and the big curtains, and a good book and the telly.'

Essie looks at her, uncharacteristically open. 'You really love it here, don't you?'

Janey nods at old Mrs Patterson on the high street, hoping she's solved her feedback issues. 'Of course I do . . . oh. Yikes.'

Lowell is in front of them. Janey immediately flushes hot, completely flustered. She hasn't even had a chance to put some mascara on.

She is so attuned, she had already recognised him, all the way down at the harbour's edge; the bulky shape of him, getting out of an electric Volvo. An electric Volvo was exactly, she thought, what a stupid architect would drive.

She thinks back to the night before. When nothing happened. When they shared a bottle of wine on a weekday night, and the thought that they were a man and a woman in the same room did not even cross his mind. She feels her body slump. Even more than it slumps normally.

'Oh, is that him?' says Essie, craning her eyes and starting forward.

Lowell has gone to the back door of the car and is opening it, and a slight, short figure with long, dark hair is getting out. Janey feels her heart-rate speed up.

'Ooh,' says Essie. 'He's got a girlfriend.'

Janey feels faintly hurt – not that he has a girlfriend, because she already knows that the figure is not at all his girlfriend; but that Essie might not consider it of the slightest concern to her whether he does or not.

'Don't be daft,' she says, as they squint in the sun. 'That's his daughter.'

'Okay. Well, good.'

'She's deaf,' says Janey.

'Oh, right. Has she got an implant?'

'She doesn't.'

'Oh, no.' Essie stares at her hands. Janey had made both her children take basic courses in BSL when they were small, but they hadn't practised it or kept it up.

'You'll be fine.'

'Don't make me,' says Essie, and she makes the one sign she does remember at her mother. It is not polite.

The girl is sallow, and as soon as she gets out of the car stands as far away from Lowell as she possibly can, facing away from him. As they get closer it's clear that she is about nine or ten; when Janey last saw her she was five.

She glances at Essie.

'Are you going to say hello?' Essie says. 'Can I go and get buns?'

Janey smiles, remembering how hard Essie had always found it when she was small, running the gauntlet of how many people her mother had to stop and chat to on a completely average walk through the town. Janey ran the hearing tests at school, so every kid knew her and would often shout out a cheerful 'beep' as she passed; or people would stop to let them know how their grandparents were getting on. Essie would writhe with boredom, swearing over and over to herself that she was going to get out of this town the second she was able.

Now, however, Essie spots Gertie, the knitting genius who'd been in her class, and Struan, the cool musician of the school. She wouldn't have put those two together in a million years, but Struan is a teacher now and they look incredibly happy together. They wave cheerfully and Essie looks suspiciously happy about it. 'I'll be back in a minute!' she calls as she darts off.

Janey carries on by herself down to the seafront. The harbour is busy: a van sells fresh lobster rolls and chips on a Saturday, as fresh as could be pulled from the water, and you had to be quick or they sold out; on lovely sunny days like today, there is even more of a crush. He's been lucky to find a parking space so close to the water; people are coming in from miles around for a stroll and a snack on such a gorgeous day. There is clean salt in the air, and the pleasing aroma of coffee, ice cream, chips.

'Hey,' Janey says, approaching with a smile.

Lowell turns round. Instead of a smile, he looks awkward. The child doesn't turn around at all and is standing at right angles to her father; she can't hear her, of course. Facing away from her father is a very clear display that she currently has no interest in communicating with him.

Janey manoeuvres herself around to the girl's left side and signs, 'Hello.'

The girl stares at her blankly and doesn't respond. She is very thin for her age, Janey can't help but notice.

She smiles cheerily and signs, 'Are you Verity? I saw you in my clinic once when you were very small.'

'Verity has had quite a long drive,' says Lowell, coming round. He speaks and signs at the same time. 'Haven't you, sweetie?'

Verity stomps away from them, off further up the harbour wall, towards the lobster shack, scowling. Janey and Lowell share a glance.

'Hey,' says Janey, and Lowell only winces. She is suddenly glad he told her the situation last night. 'Is this her first time up here with you?'

'I just . . . with the dogs and everything . . . I thought it would be a good idea. It has been made very clear to me that it isn't, and that there are quite a lot of things she'd rather be doing today, none of which involve me.'

'Tough day?' she says, lowering her voice.

Lowell looks around, makes sure there's nobody about. 'Tough everything,' he says, and for a moment, as he watches his beloved daughter storm off with all her ten-year-old might, his voice catches, just a little, and Janey's heart goes out to him.

'You wouldn't believe how vile Essie was as a teen,' she says, consolingly. 'She was pure vileness. All the time. Like, she would not stop until I was completely crushed to the floor. I'm sure there's some evolutionary reason for it that temporarily escapes me . . . '

She's aware she's babbling, but fortunately Lowell smiles. 'Oh, lord. She's not even a teen yet. How much worse is it going to get?'

Janey opens her mouth to mention the piercing wars, then wisely decides against it.

'How's your ex?'

'Bonkers as conkers,' says Lowell without elaborating. 'How's yours?' he adds, politely, and Janey can tell he is trying to make up for the one-sidedness of the night before. She finds this quite touching.

'Someone else's problem,' says Janey. 'Have you thought about buying Verity some chips?'

'She's vegan now.'

Janey frowns. 'I hope she's getting everything she needs. I'm not a nutritionist but she seems awfully . . . '

'She's fading away,' says Lowell. 'She gets a lot of messages from her mother about food. Mostly, avoid it at all costs, I think.'

Janey winces.

'Oh, sorry. I am trying, Janey,' he says. 'I know I sound bitter and awful and mean, but I am trying so hard, and God, I don't know what to do.' He looks at her. There are heavy bags under his eyes. 'Do you think . . . would you mind . . . ? I'm sorry, I'm leaning on your good will . . . '

He is. Janey wished she minded more. 'What is it you want?'

'Well, you speak her language, and she won't talk to me . . . I know this is a terrible imposition, but do you think you could hang out with us for a little? You must be sick of the sight of me, I realise.'

'Actually,' says Janey, 'I was just bringing Essie over to check on the dogs.'

Her phone pings. It's Essie, telling her she's going to lunch with Gertie and Struan, is that okay? Lowell clearly doesn't need her this weekend. Of course it is okay. Essie doing something that isn't lying indoors staring at her phone is always okay.

Janey makes up her mind. 'Sure,' she says. And he smiles at her so gratefully and, well, gratitude isn't as nice as fascination, she supposes, but it might have to do for now.

★

Janey and Lowell move rapidly to where Verity is standing, staring out to sea.

'I'm a friend of your dad's,' signs Janey. 'And we were going to get some chips.'

'Are you his girlfriend?' signs back Verity, and both Janey and Lowell frantically shake no. Didn't need to be quite *that* fricking frantic, thinks Janey, but keeps it to herself.

'No, I used to be your audiologist.'

Her face crinkles a little in faint recognition.

'You were very tiny. And the cutest thing I ever saw.'

There is a tiny twitch in her mouth. 'Was I?'

'Adorable,' says Janey. 'I'd have taken you home.'

Verity smiles, then her thin face stiffens. 'You wanted to cut my brain open and put a computer thing in it.'

Janey blinks. 'We wanted to help you the best way we could,' she says. 'Your parents always did. Everyone wanted the best for you.'

'Well, nobody cut my brain open.'

'And that's fine,' signs Janey. 'Chips?'

'I'm vegan.'

'So are chips! I thought that was the first thing everyone learned when they went vegan!'

Lowell waves from in front of the food truck. Janey signs to him rather than speaking aloud. 'Three bags please. And some Irn-Bru.'

'What's that?' signs Verity.

Janey considers how best to translate the bright rust-coloured national soft drink of Scotland, rumoured to be made from iron girders, and simply cannot manage it.

'It's a drink,' she signs. 'I hope you'll like it.'

Verity looks extremely uncertain. 'My mum doesn't like me eating processed foods,' she signs.

'Well, this is a drink,' signs Janey, and Verity seems not unhappy with that.

Lowell comes back with the delicious chips – Janey would have dearly loved a lobster roll too but doesn't want to upset the vegan – and they sit in a line on the harbour wall, Verity kicking her feet against the stones, like any other kid in the world. They watch the passage of a great container ship, and Janey, as is her habit, looks it up on her phone. 'Off to Singapore,' she signs.

'How do you know?' signs Verity, who seems alright talking to her, but is still studiously ignoring Lowell.

Janey shows her the app, and they spend a happy twenty minutes tracing the boats that come past, covering Janey's old Samsung with greasy fingers, taking bad smudgy photos of the boats, their vastness dwarfed by the sea and the great horizon.

Verity regards the Irn-Bru dubiously.

'I cannot believe you have a Scottish child who has never tasted Irn-Bru,' signs Janey. 'What is wrong with you?'

'Thalia was never keen,' says Lowell out loud.

Verity reads his lips, and clamps her mouth shout. 'Mummy won't like it,' she signs, her hands nervous.

'That's okay,' says Janey, glancing at Lowell.

'Of course that's fine,' he signs. And goes off and gets some bottled water.

'Are you looking forward to seeing the puppies?' signs Janey after he's gone.

She nods. Then leans towards Janey, looking over her shoulder to make sure Lowell is queuing at the van a good distance away.

'Daddy is not allowed to open my brain.'

Fortunately Janey has long experience of children, and often children who are confused or distressed by the process of living in a noisy world with limited or zero access to what all the noise is about. Calmness is a skill she managed to conquer, she often thought glumly, in every part of her universe except for when dealing with her own beloved daughter. Other people's children, of course, were always easier.

'Of course he isn't,' she signs back. 'He's not allowed to if you don't want him to.'

'I don't.'

'I get that completely.'

Verity kicks her heels loudly against the harbour wall as if venting frustration.

'It's okay if you can't hear,' she signs. 'You'll get no arguments from me.'

'Medical companies are just trying to make money.'

'Then I would like a nicer car,' signs Janey, and the girl looks at her, not cross, just curious. 'Sorry, bad joke.' Then she points at Lowell. 'He just wants to see you.'

'He's old. He's not like other daddies.'

'That's not his fault.'

'Mummy says he had bad ideas about things.'

'I think,' signs Janey carefully, 'both your mummy and your daddy tried their best. I don't know your mummy but I know your daddy loves you very much. Sometimes people have different ideas about what the best thing is.'

'I miss Mummy,' says Verity, and she looks younger than ten suddenly.

Janey nods. 'I bet.'

'Daddy doesn't want me here.'

'He does. He really does.'

Lowell comes back over, the worried expression still on his face. 'Hey, sweetie,' he signs, handing over the water.

'I don't want single-use plastic,' Verity spells out, quite laboriously. Lowell squints to follow it.

'Ah,' he says out loud. Then, 'Well.'

Janey decisively crumples up her empty chip wrapper and pops everyone's in the bin.

'I think,' she signs, 'it is PUPPY TIME.'

The sign for puppy is literally a dog but small, and she deliberately over-pantomimes the smallness of it, hunching her shoulders over and even sticking out her tongue, until Lowell laughs, and even Verity smiles reluctantly, and they get up and head for the car.

'Thank you,' mutters Lowell as they get in. 'Thank you. She's still not talking to me . . . but she is talking.'

'Nnnnnnn,' says Verity from her seat in the back, a sound which Janey recognises immediately as almost any deaf child telling people to face them while they talk, but which seems to startle Lowell. He absolutely has not spent enough time with this child, she thinks, and feels sad. She nudges him and he looks at Verity in the car mirror.

'I'm sorry, darling,' he signs, turning round awkwardly from the driver's seat and freeing up his hands.

'WHAT ARE YOU SAYING?' she signs furiously.

'Nothing! Just seeing if J-a-n-e-y wants to come to see the dogs with us.'

'That's all?'

'Of course.'

'You're not going to do treatment?'

Lowell's face sags again. 'Of course not. Of course not. I never would. Your mum wouldn't let me take you if I was going to do something bad would she?'

'She's gone away without me,' signs Verity. Janey is impressed by her fluency in signing – she is beautiful to watch, her hands flying through intricate patterns as if conducting a tiny orchestra – but she would normally be a little concerned about how little effort Verity makes to speak along with it.

Then she reminds herself that she is not responsible for this child, and it is absolutely up to Verity how she lives her life. Or Verity's mother, she also thinks, but tries to quell the thought. One thing about getting older, she has found, is that you may not share people's points of view, but you can learn to understand. There's always a reason for it. People aren't as black and white as the movies would like you to think. Which is a shame.

'She'll be back very soon,' signs Lowell, and the devastation that his only child believes that to spend time with him is the same as being abandoned is writ large across his heavy features.

★

Once they reach the house, Verity leaps out without waiting for a signal.

'You should put the child locks on,' Janey murmurs to Lowell, who nods.

Verity is obviously not scared of much. She looks up at her old home without interest. It is weird, Janey thinks, just how incredibly aggressive an act turning your back can be. Lowell is rubbing the back of his head. Then he goes and fetches her bag.

'I can head—' says Janey.

'Please don't,' he says, with feeling. Janey finds herself stiffening a little. She's a health professional, but she's not here in a professional capacity. She's not staff.

He realises immediately. 'Sorry,' he says. 'Sorry. I didn't mean it like that.'

'You are going to have to get on with her at some point,' says Janey, as kindly as she can, without trying to sound like their bloody social worker.

'I know, I *know*.'

'I think I know a few creatures who are ready to help.'

It's a nice enough day that the puppies are in the out-side run but of course Verity hasn't heard them scrabble and yelp, tearing about. Felicity has stayed inside. But Lowell has already opened the door, and the large shaggy beast tears into the sunshine, a ball of huge hairy energy, flopping ears and tongue.

'Of course!' says Janey, amazed at herself for not realising. 'Verity and Felicity. Of course. Truth and Happiness.'

She turns to Lowell to tease him for calling his dog and child matching Latin-based names, but he is not listening: in the dead centre of the lawn, buried in one another, heartbeat to heartbeat, are one little girl, and her enormous dog.

Janey sees that his eyes are full of tears. Oh, no, she thinks. She can talk herself out of anything, tell herself she is too old and too daft for everything. But it is very hard to watch this huge man cry and not want to go to him with every fibre in her being.

She remembers, briefly, that some men cannot bear to show weakness, or to get caught in the act of it, and that these men, if seen undone, can be dangerous. But she does not think Lowell is this type of man. She moves towards him, stands side by side, lets her hand graze his. Sure enough, almost as if he doesn't know he's doing it, he grabs hold of it, squeezes it, surprisingly hard, and a tear runs down his large cheek.

'It's okay,' she says, soothingly. 'It's okay.'

'I miss her so much,' he says.

Verity and Felicity have recovered now, and are now examining each other, inch by inch, Felicity sniffing everywhere. She starts licking Verity's ear.

'Look,' says Janey. 'She's saying, you won't *believe* what happened to me. I was just hanging out with this wee guy, right. He was short, but . . . you know, good with the banter.'

Almost despite himself, Lowell smiles.

'Next thing I know . . . six of the buggers, driving me crazy, playing me up half the night . . . '

He looks at her. 'You're funny,' he says. They're still holding hands, they both realise at the same instant, and Janey is so enjoying – cannot help it – the heel of his large rough hand in hers. Rough from gardening, she supposes. It is a reassuring hand: huge, not sweaty. The top has black hair on it, but not too much, and she finds herself wondering about his chest again. She lets his hand drop.

Dog and girl start to walk around the garden, Verity's fingers knotted in Felicity's white-grey fur.

'She used to do that when she could barely walk,' says Lowell, unable to tear his eyes away.

'Did you never let her ride her?'

'Don't,' says Lowell. 'For years you couldn't turn your back without her trying to climb on. Felicity never minded. I think she would have carried her if she could.'

He steps forward and opens the chicken wire gate where the pups are in the run. There is an instant commotion: Felicity looks round, then Verity follows her lead. The puppies have found them, tumbling, bouncing in the green spring grass. Verity lets out a squeal, then, oddly, does exactly what her father did: she lies down flat, spreadeagled on the grass; happily relinquishing and giving herself up to being pawed over, sniffed. Smokey nips at her buttons, and Argyll and Bute start a tug of war over her shoelaces. It is clear from Felicity's wagging tail and Verity's heaving ribs that she is laughing.

Lowell stands still.

'Go,' says Janey, softly. 'Go and talk to her. I think you'll be fine now.'

He starts.

'Of course,' he says. Then he turns, looking her up and down. 'You're a remarkable woman, Janey Munroe.'

'Yeah, yeah, whatevs,' she says, brushing it off like a joke. Inside, it pings, lights her up like a fairground bulb. 'I'll send Essie over next week,' she promises, and then she watches: the tall burly man, the thin pale girl, who has jumped up as soon as he got there, brushing the little yipping dogs off her. He starts talking. Janey can see every word they say. She turns away. This is private; she turns and leaves.

She doesn't see his eyes following her as she goes.

29

'Now,' Al is saying. 'On to gralloching. Gralloching is the hygienic removal of the internal organs of the animal . . . '

It is a chilly early Sunday morning but the mist is rising, which is unfortunate as it means conditions will be clear enough to carry on with the shooting, Essie thinks to herself. Everyone else is in ridiculous Barbours and wellies. She's in a black puffa she last wore in secondary school, with what her mother calls her 'torn' face to match it. She doesn't have to go on the deer stalk, she knows. But if she doesn't, she won't see Connor at all, and that is driving her crazy.

*

When she'd met Connor at the tiny airstrip yesterday afternoon, she'd been so excited: he was as handsome as ever. If his stupid friends hadn't been there, Essie would have run towards him. Instead she'd just grinned.

'It's me!' he'd announced after he'd kissed her. 'Your money-obsessed Big City Boyfriend. Have you discarded me for a sensitive woodsman who's taught you the true meaning of Christmas yet?'

'It's April,' Essie had pointed out, rather guiltily quashing any thoughts of Dwight. Because nothing had happened at all, she reminded herself. Absolutely nothing. She had spent the evening trying to explain fire regulations to him, that was all.

'Oh, yeah,' said Connor.

'But apart from that, you are more or less exactly right.'

Tris and Trumpet came up, hefting their identical bags, guffawing. They looked like overgrown kids on a school trip. Connor immediately stood back with them. He was, Essie thought, still bound to his school gang. *Bros before Hos* was the most ridiculous thing in the whole of the world.

Anyway. He was there and that was what mattered. And oh, my goodness, they had the hotel to look forward to. They were staying at Harcourt House, a local hotel so posh that Essie had never met any of the guests, who came in and out without seeming to leave a trace in the village. It had once been a family home – the daughter, Serena, was about her age, Essie knew, and she'd had a huge eighteenth birthday party there, with fireworks, long parades of cars queuing up through the driveway, the house dramatically lit, and not a single Carso child invited. The entire year group, including Shelby, Essie remembers, had gone down to the sea wall – it had been midsummer so not even dark until well after eleven – and eaten fish and chips and passed round vodka-Bru. Even among natural enemies there was solidarity in the face of an implacable enemy, i.e. a fabulous party stuffed full of handsome posh boys, to which not only were they not invited, but nobody had ever considered inviting them for a millisecond.

'Well, we know Felix and Serena,' said Tris when Essie commented. 'From school, you know.'

'I did not know. Did you go to Serena's eighteenth?'

'I assumed you'd know them,' he said. 'This is basically a village.'

'It's a town!' said Essie, then realised she sounded exactly like her mum. But then of course that family had moved away a long time ago; Felix had gone into rehab, she'd heard.

Now it is a smart hotel where you pretend you're going to spend a weekend at a friend's country home.

Now she thought about it, it really was a bit naff. Triss was wearing plus fours, for God's sake. Everyone's wellingtons were bright polished green. She was wearing her mum's, which have flowers on them. Triss had already noted them and scoffed.

They're larping, she thought. Live-action role-playing as posh, rich people from a world that no longer exists. Larping a world like *Bridgerton* or *Downton Abbey*, faking their way all the way to the top. Pretending Britain, the world, doesn't look the way it really is.

'So, you shoot?' Tris had asked, exactly as a character would in a film. She'd looked at him and realised that in her back yard – on her territory, not his – she didn't care quite so much what she said to him.

'Of course not,' she'd retorted. 'Where would I learn to shoot?'

'You're from the Highlands!'

'I'm not – you're far higher than the Highlands up here,' she'd said. And Tris had turned and walked off.

★

'You look good,' says Connor now as they follow Al in the car to the place where they're all starting out. 'Country life agrees with you.'

Essie realises she hasn't put smoother on her hair – she ran out and can't afford to buy more, even if you could buy it in the Carso semi-chem, which you can't – and she hasn't used her straighteners in yonks. There's absolutely no point, when the wind will blow your hair every which way two seconds after you step out the door, plus you need to wear a bunnet every day because, well, you just do, it's generally freezing at some point very late into the spring. There is a girl in town who makes beautiful cashmere ones – Janey managed to snaffle one from her hairdresser and now Essie wears it every day without really noticing. Connor notices, though; there is colour in her cheeks, and freckles from the early spring sunshine, and her face isn't looking quite so pinched. She's put on weight – he decides not to mention it, but it suits her, takes away that hungry look. She looks softer.

'It's good to see you.'

'How's work?'

'Hectic,' he says. 'Nuts.'

'Well, that's good,' she says. 'At least you won't get outsourced to Switzerland.'

'Put the willies up everyone, that did, your lot closing,' he says. 'I think that's why we're working harder, just to stand still.'

She'd crammed them into her mum's car, reluctantly lent. They had made some reasonably predictable jokes about Noddy and Essie found herself uncharacteristically annoyed on her mum's behalf. She was allowed to slag off her mum's beloved car, but nobody else was. Also they didn't – apart from Connor – know how hard her mother had saved to buy it, and how intensely proud of it she was.

To her surprise, when she parks up beside Al's battered old Land Rover on Lochouire Fell – obviously this is a much more acceptable vehicle – there's someone else in the car with him, who soon reveals himself to be Dwight.

The lads get out of the car and stare at him, in his black hat and boots. He's notably shorter than all of them. Dwight is completely oblivious and hails her.

'Oi! Essie! I got those wallpaper samples, hon!'

At this the boys start to giggle.

'The only gay cowboy in the village,' says Trumpet quietly. Essie wishes, for possibly the only time in her life, that Shelby had been here, to hear him say that.

'Shut up,' she says, meaning it to sound jokey, but it doesn't, it sounds as if she means it, because she does.

Dwight hasn't noticed a thing and strides over. 'Hey, darlin',' he says, and Essie can feel Connor stiffen.

'This is Dwight,' she says. 'He's developing a row of cottages.'

'And Essie is helping me,' says Dwight, cheerfully. He passes over the wallpaper samples. 'But I leave the girls' stuff to her.'

'Oi,' says Essie. 'Honestly, Dwight.'

She looks through them anyway before throwing them in the car. Tris narrows his eyes. 'You're doing a housing development?'

Dwight shrugs.

'I mean, with the new planning laws . . . how did you get round it?'

'Well, it's local,' he says. 'Local houses. I'm local.'

'You're the codicil guy,' says Connor suddenly.

'Interesting,' says Tris. 'How many houses?'

'Three . . . but they were sold as one lot. Paid the down-payment in cash.' Dwight can't help puffing up his chest and Essie really wishes he wouldn't.

'Did you, now?' says Tris. He sticks his bottom lip out. 'Clever old you.'

Dwight beams at this approval from the Big Lads up from the city.

'So what are you going to do, flip them?' says Trumpet. 'This place is cute, man. Golf, lots to shoot, plenty of fish. Plenty of out-of-towners are always looking for second homes.'

Dwight looks at Essie, puzzled.

She shrugs back. 'The thing is,' she says, 'your accounts are a mess. You know that's true.'

He nods.

'I just don't want you to lose it all. I've seen it happen.'

'You need to talk to me,' says Tris.

Essie looks up, surprised. She just wanted him to get some advice, and for everyone to tell him to stop spending his budget without a spreadsheet, but Tris seems serious, even as Dwight shows him photos on his phone.

'You could get round that codicil, form a shell, flip those places for a fortune,' says Tris. 'We could totally help with that.'

Essie is amazed. The super-secret fund that she never gets to work for or have a say in . . . they're going to let Dwight walk right in! It's a boys' club.

Dwight looks completely bamboozled as Tris pulls him aside.

'What's going on?' Essie asks Connor.

'What do you mean?'

'Well, I thought your fund was high net worth only. Dwight hasn't got a pot to piss in, just three falling-down buildings.'

Connor glances up. 'I think Tris wants to get into more property; he was talking about expanding.'

'Oh, no way,' says Essie. 'We don't want him living up here.'

'What do you care?' says Connor. 'You're coming back, aren't you?'

Essie shrugs. 'It's just – it's not fair,' she says. 'I can't even get a job, and he gets taken seriously immediately.'

'Ach, it's just money,' Connor says simply.

'I know,' says Essie. 'I'm just saying. Did you even mention me possibly getting a job with you?'

Connor looks at the floor.

'No,' says Essie. 'I thought not.'

'It's not personal!'

Al is clearing his throat in front of them. They are all lined up on the side of the fells. The mist has risen, dissipating into little puddles of smoke at the bottom of the valleys. The browns and greens of the hillsides are glowing; there are shades of purple on the higher slopes. Essie finds she is looking around with some pride, and takes a deep breath of the fresh air.

The ghillie is giving them lots of safety instructions, mostly about making sure there is something behind the deer – a hard stop – and to go for the chest, not the tiny head, and never to shoot in motion. Everyone has a licence, including Dwight, who probably has holsters at home, Essie thinks drily. She's not shooting, of course.

'Reds, fallows and sikas,' the ghillie was saying. 'Nothing moving, and make sure you look at me for the go.'

The proud wolfhound by his side, sniffing, reminds Essie of the pups, and she finds herself being for once resentful for being away from the puppies. Normally she loved hanging out with Connor and feeling one of the gang, doing posh grown-up things. But she isn't sure if she wants to do this, even though Al is obviously pleased she's there.

She looks out over the early morning fields which run to the cliffs overlooking the very top of the country, and out to the islands beyond. White birds are shearing up and down the edge, eyeing up the fish and the fields, happy in the bounty. The faint burr of a tractor sounds, but in the great expanse of land it could be coming from almost anywhere. The air is cold, but still, for once; the land is in a dip from the cliff edge and they are sheltered. It is a cold day, but beautiful beyond imagining; so clear, she can see the little puddle-hopping aeroplane her friend Morag runs, taking off again from their tiny runway, en route to delivering post and vegetables and happy tourists and reunited family, and the occasional transiting farm animal. White vapour trails across the light sky and Essie feels a lightness in her, looking down into the little town, where, back in Seagate, Wee Jim is stripping window frames with a blowtorch, a tool that makes him possibly too cheerful, if no more talkative. It is, undeniably, a lovely morning, and despite Connor still being avoidant on the job front, she is feeling more optimistic than she has done in quite a while.

'Do you know where the nearest Starbucks is?' Tristan says loudly. '*Oslo!*' Then he laughs heartily at his own joke.

The ghillie watches them patiently. He's seen it all before. Al doesn't mind so much; Zara makes quite a lot of the same jokes, all the time. Nonetheless, he looks up and casually says, 'You know deer have excellent hearing, yeah?'

'What, and they'll think I'm disrespecting the neighbourhood?' says Tris, but he settles down as the men start to space themselves out as they've been told.

Essie watches them, lets them go ahead. She finds herself thinking of Felicity as she looks at the ghillie's dog, Bran. They've been warned not to touch him; he's a working dog. Essie finds herself thinking that Felicity should have coupled up with him, they're much more suited, which is a ridiculous thing to think about dogs, but then she looks at Connor, tall, pink-cheeked, handsome. Obviously she and he belong together. Whereas Dwight, tanned and wee and crazily dressed – it was ridiculous.

'Are you coming?' asks Connor quietly, turning his head.

'Only to watch,' she says. 'I leave the whole deer-killing business up to Al.'

'Hypocrite,' says Al, smiling. 'You'll like the venison stew.'

'I will,' she says. 'Get over yourself. I'm not denying being a hypocrite. I'm admitting to being a total wuss.'

★

The forest is a light covering of spring green, humming and bouncing with new life; tiny streams tumble; new leaves unfurl on every branch. There are nests visible high in the trees; a woodpecker can be heard, far off. Old trees fall apart beneath their feet, rotten to the core from their wet winter as nature discards and builds again. The sun dapples through the trunks.

Essie follows the paths, here and there, careful not to make a sound; it feels like a game, a magical exploration. She remembers her parents trying to drag her here for walks when she was young, on Sundays, and her vociferous complaints. But the silence of people tiptoeing and the gentle pad, pad, pad of the dog's feet against the rippling, crackling life of the wood feel almost holy on this sunny morning; the forest is enchanted; the circles of toadstools absolutely ready for a fairy with a fishing rod. She feels as likely to see a human-faced faun as a deer.

Then, suddenly, the ghillie holds up his hand, and everyone freezes.

Nobody breathes. Nobody moves. There, over by the tiny burn, the beautiful stag's great head lifts as it sniffs the wind. And the world stands still.

Essie has been completely in her own world, utterly enchanted by the deep Scotland she has found herself in, and her eyes grow wide as she remembers what they're here to do.

She glances at Al, who is entirely concentrating on the animal and slowly raising his gun. Tris and Trumpet have their guns pointing now, each with one eye closed, trained on the great beast. Connor is starting to raise his, but reluctantly.

Essie can't believe it.

They all glance at the ghillie, who drops his arm . . .

'NO!'

Essie surprises herself by the sound of her voice; by the shout she had had absolutely no intention of making. The guns go off, above the treeline, skewed by her noise; the stag bounds, faster than seems possible without being able to fly, over fences and tree trunks. There is a flash of red in the trees and the stag is gone, nothing but an incredibly fast bob of white as his tail vanishes.

Everyone stands for a moment, frozen in disbelief. The guns come down. Essie has that sinking feeling you get when you realise you have made a terrible, unwarranted error you really didn't mean to make.

'Oh for fuck's sake,' says Tris, in a terrible temper.

Essie doesn't care. She whirls round. 'Don't kill that beautiful creature!'

'We've been through this, sis!' says Al finally in anguish. 'Don't come if you can't handle it!'

The ghillie is sucking his teeth, clearly profoundly unimpressed. Tris is tutting audibly. Connor is bright pink. Dwight is messing with his toothpick again, seemingly unconcerned. At the noise, there is a great flutter of wings overhead, as birds take off into the early summer sunshine.

Essie is tearful and furious at the same time. She wants to stamp her foot on the moss underfoot. Everyone is staring at her.

'Seriously,' says Al. Tris is sneering.

Essie is burning bright red now, full of embarrassment.

'What if we'd swerved our shots and injured him? What then? And he'd taken off with his leg hanging off?' Al is genuinely upset, very unusually for him. Essie sees, suddenly, that he means it when he says he cares about these animals, even if it looks perverse from the outside.

'I know,' says Essie, staring at the ground.

'You never thought about that!'

'No,' she mutters.

'You never think about anything or anyone, do you? Spent enough time making Mum's life a misery.'

'Oi,' says Dwight, wandering over with his cowboy stroll, gun casually tucked across his shoulders in a way the ghillie had already expressly forbidden at the safety briefing. 'Leave off her, alright?'

'I'm talking to my sister.'

Dwight takes his stupid toothpick out of his mouth. 'Not like that, you ain't,' he says.

Essie looks up, astounded. Tris bursts out laughing in a highly stylised sarcastic fashion. Connor blinks. It would never, Essie thinks, occur to him in a million years to stand up for her like that.

Al takes a deep breath and simmers down. It's not like him to fly off the handle; he just spends so long defending his job.

'Okay. You're right. Sorry, sis. I mean, you're still a moron.'

Dwight nods as if he's the sheriff keeping the peace.

'S'okay,' mutters Essie. 'Don't tell Mum.'

'I won't.'

'You will.'

'I will.'

They are all standing around the forest glade.

'Do you know what: I think I'll just head down,' says Essie.

The ghillie ignores her, indicating another group of deer cropping young tree shoots by the side of a clearing. The boys stealthily move off.

Essie retraces her steps, down across the lichen-covered logs, the uprooted trees, the tangles of daisies and budding nettles, as furious as she has ever been. Doesn't fit in in the city, doesn't fit in here. She is angry about everything. She comes face to face with a fawn at the bottom of the tree line, who stares her in the eyes, then immediately bucks off at an incredible rate. 'You're welcome!' she shouts after it.

Halfway down the green hill, heading back to the car – Al can drop off his new best friends, she is thinking crossly – she hears footsteps and turns round, half-expecting another bollocking from Al. To her genuine surprise, it's Connor. He smiles awkwardly.

'Hey,' he says.

'Yes?' she says.

He looks at her. 'I'm using you as my excuse,' he says, reaching out and taking her hand. His gun is gone, she notices; he must have handed it back to the ghillie. 'I don't have the stomach for it either. They're so beautiful.'

'So you had to say you were going to look after your girlfriend?'

'Is that okay?'

She beams. 'It is. Did they not rag you something awful?'

'They can do it later.'

And she joins her hand to hers, even as they hear gunshots. Connor winces.

'I am a terrible coward,' he says.

'Good,' she says.

30

They creep in later, after a perfectly pleasant, if rather vanilla, afternoon in the lovely country house with its freestanding bath in the black and white tiled bathroom, warming up after the chill of the forest. Essie had nearly fallen asleep, before being reminded that the lads would be back by now and they should all head out to meet them in town for a meal. She does, though, go through every nook and cranny of the nice hotel, looking for ideas: striped wallpaper she likes, but isn't sure whether it will make the tiny cottages even smaller; the automatic bathroom light in the en-suite she wants right away; and she wonders if she could get tiny coil versions made of the pretty chandeliers. It is amazing how much time she spends thinking about the project. She wants to text Dwight with the photos but contents herself with taking pictures, as she doesn't want it to get weird. They can discuss it when she's back tomorrow.

Essie truly does not want to go and meet the boys for supper after her little display that afternoon, but it is either that or not see Connor again till goodness knows when, so she drives them both to the End of the World quietly, wearing a plain black dress. It would probably be good if Shelby sees her with Connor any-way, so she snuggles under his arm. The look on Shelby's face makes it perfectly obvious that Shelby thinks she is instead an industrial-strength slutbag, but there is not much that can be done about that.

She is determined to be on her best behaviour. She has been distracted, that's all. By stupid cowboys and the joys of working on the new build. But she knows what she really wants. She wants to get back to Edinburgh. With her sweet boyfriend and a real career, not dabbling about with grouting. Although she did have fun when Wee Jim let her use the power hose. But no. She needs to get back . . .

She hoists up her bra as a distraction and lets her hair hang loose around her shoulders the way Connor likes it, even though it is eminently impractical on a windy evening and it is, frankly, always a windy evening on the winding sea lane to Shelby's bar.

The boys are in the corner, already well into the rough red wine, telling Connor wild stories about shots fired and derring-do and the size of the stag that got away as he nods appreciatively. She appears to have been forgiven for her inter-vention, and it turns out Dwight was a crack shot – well, he would be; she assumes his parents taught him to shoot on the back of a horse – and everyone's freezer will be stocked through the summer. Dwight is still wearing his cowboy hat, but nobody seems to be taking the piss out of him any more; in fact Tris is asking him again about the cottages in all seriousness. It doesn't make any sense; Tris always makes a point of only going after big money.

'So who are you going to sell them on to when you're done?' he's asking.

Dwight shrugs. 'Whoever wants one.'

Tris shakes his head. 'No. That's not what you want. You need to slap some nice grey paint everywhere, get some pic-tures done, make sure it hits the smart Edinburgh estate agents. Or even London, place as pretty as this.'

'He's not allowed,' says Essie, firmly, interjecting. 'They must go to a local family. That's the whole point of the codicil.'

Tris sniffs. 'Oh, come on, think big. Yokels,' he says. 'That's easily sorted. You just form a shell company, make sure it has a local address so you adhere enough to the codicil they won't check. Then you borrow money off the shell company, you own the company, then the company can rent it to whoever it likes. Bob's your uncle. You make a fortune.' He looks around the bar. 'Completely under-utilised, the Highlands of Scotland. People up here don't even realise what they have.'

Essie wonders if he knows something. Maybe there's going to be some huge redevelopment and he wants to get in on the ground. Maybe there's been a new oil field discovered, just over their heads.

Dwight looks completely bamboozled. 'Wouldn't that be illegal?' he says, looking at Essie.

'No,' says Essie. 'Not technically. But it's . . . not very ethical.'

'As opposed to all the other ethical ways of making money there are,' says Tris, rolling his eyes. 'You know, Essie can't shoot a deer but she can certainly get round the tax regulations, can't you, love? Her job is basically persuading people to do stuff like this. Or should I say, her ex-job.'

'Yeah, enough, Tris,' says Essie. She is already letting him wind her up, exactly what she told herself not to let happen. 'Is something happening around here?'

Tris shrugs smugly. 'Wouldn't mention it in here if I did,' he says, and Essie realises that the knitting circle are in the corner of the pub, faces keen to know more. 'But there may well be a fortune in it.'

Dwight rubs the back of his neck, already brown this early in the year.

'How much . . . how much is a fortune, though?' says Dwight. Essie finds she is incredibly annoyed for the second time today about something she has, truly, no reason to be annoyed about.

Connor sees her face. 'What's up with you?' he teases. 'You look really bothered.'

'I am bothered,' she says. 'It's not right, if he's up here planning things without local people being informed.'

'So you're "local people"?' teases Connor.

'Yes. No,' says Essie, taking a slurp of her wine crossly. 'But I'm from here.'

'It's money,' Connor says simply, as he had earlier. 'Money just does what it does.'

'Well, maybe sometimes it shouldn't.'

'I know, I know: we should all still be ploughing our own gardens and bartering spades.'

'I don't mean that,' says Essie.

'I know, but you know how these things work.'

'How things work in Edinburgh.'

'Ha, you *are* sounding local.'

Essie just gives him a look, and he laughs, trying to mollify her. 'Essie, you realise . . . the money people like us make . . . you realise it funds the whole of Scotland? Every hospital? Every pensioner? Every school place?'

She does, of course, know this. 'Yes, but we're meant to be ethical!'

'Being ethical means not laundering money, it doesn't mean "don't restore a holiday cottage".'

'But people around here need homes.'

'We're not in the business of building homes. That's the council's business. They won't do it.' He shrugged. 'Your cowboy friend worked damned hard for that money.'

'He did.'

'So, what, he should just hand the houses over to people who can't be bothered working at all?'

'You're such a Tory.'

'I'm not!' says Connor, looking uncharacteristically worked up. 'I'm literally standing here defending increased public housing provision and opportunities for the working classes!'

'Ooh, trouble in paradise,' says Tris, glancing up. 'What are you two bickering about?'

'Nothing,' says Essie sullenly, just as Connor says,

'The global economic system.'

Tris raises his eyebrows. 'How very undergraduate of you,' he says.

'Oh, shut up, Tris,' says Essie crossly, without even thinking about it.

Tris gives her a look. 'Time of the month?' he says pleasantly.

It's the kind of banter he resorts to often – out of working hours, obviously; he doesn't want to lose his job. It's silly, naughty, over-the-line, knowingly ironic stuff.

And today, Essie is done with it.

'Seriously, just shut the fuck up,' she said.

'Are you okay?' Connor says quietly. 'You've been on edge—'

'*No!*' says Essie. 'Your patronising mate is being . . .'

'Being what?'

'Nothing.'

'No, really, we'd all like to know,' says Tris. 'After your little display earlier today.'

Essie is flaming red suddenly and doesn't know how she got here. She stands up.

'I'm going home,' she says quietly and urgently to Connor, who is looking just as pink as she is and equally irritated and has already had to follow her out of one stramash today.

'Um,' he says, 'aren't we going for dinner?'

'I'm not hungry.'

'You'll let the boy have his dinner, though,' says Tris.

There's a long silence.

'Can I . . . can I catch up with you after dinner?' says Connor, finally.

Essie glances at Tris. He is enjoying all of this.

'Sure,' says Essie eventually. 'Not a problem.'

She swings her expensive handbag over her hips, turns around, does not say goodbye.

★

Shelby is outside the pub, having a cigarette. They give a small nod to each other. Essie is so sure Connor will be outside in a moment that she doesn't want to head off quite yet. Then, as the minutes pass, and Shelby takes a drag and stares flatly at her phone, and the large moon gleams down on the black maw of the harbour, Essie realises something terrible, but something she has always known; Connor is choosing his mates over her. It was one thing when she was being funny about the deer. But when it comes to money . . .

She pulls her coat around herself against the cold northern wind and slowly makes her way up the high street, back towards the tiny bedroom, not even hers, in her mother's house. What more can she even lose?

Shelby, she can feel, watches her all the way.

31

'Um, Essie?'

Janey is running late and has a packed day, as well as a kitchen that is covered in late-night toast crumbs. Janey just shouts up the stairs. If the girl is going to behave like a grumpy teenager, she's just going to have to treat her like one. 'Essie, where's the car?'

Essie has tossed and turned all night. Every time she nearly dropped off, she remembered all over again. Were they broken up? Was this a fight they could fix? Why had she ever come back here?

'What?' she growls.

'My car. You know. That you borrowed yesterday for all your smart friends and promised to bring back home clean and full of fuel?'

Essie sits up.

'Oh, crap,' she says. It is, of course, still sitting outside the End of the World. She'd meant to wake early and go and get it . . . she'd thought she'd be waking up with Connor, in his beautiful room with the rolltop bath . . . oh, crap.

She checks her phone and sees lots of missed messages. He wants to talk, thinks he should come back and see her by himself another weekend. She's still utterly livid. With Connor, with herself, with Tris, with Dwight and his stupid greedy look; the entire bloody situation. She needs quiet to think. She's trying to work out what had happened last night. All the boys, talking about money, talking to *Dwight* about money, while she was sitting right there. Oh, God. And she had stropped out, and what had that gained? Precious little, except the question in her mind: however sweet Connor was, did he really see her as something serious? It didn't feel like it. She finds herself wondering, too, was she trying to prove something to herself? To see how much she could make him care? Make him stay? Because there was a man in her life before who, the second she moved away, vanished immediately. Ugh.

'ESSIE!'

'For God's sake, Mum, it's at Shelby's bar, stop freaking out.'

★

Janey walks up the stairs, trembling with rage. She doesn't know where this rage comes from suddenly, this towering fury. It's like a volcano going off inside her, hot and bitter to her very core. She never thought of herself as an angry person – sad, of course, when her marriage broke down. But jaunty, on the whole; cheery. This rage monster is absolutely blinding her.

'Essie!'

'Whaaat?' Essie says through the closed door, sounding like Kevin the Teenager.

'It's my morning to go and see Johnson! To bring him his breakfast so he doesn't start eating stuff he shouldn't be eating, because Lish is working all night at the hospital. Then I've got a full clinic! Essie, how could you?'

Janey has had such a disappointing few days. Getting to know Lowell, getting to know his family, even, feels like being shown a gift that is never ever going to be yours. *Here's what you could have won. If you were younger and sexier. Thanks for the sympathy though!* She is feeling profoundly down and disappointed, and the last thing she needs is this – a fully grown adult in her house behaving as though *she's* the unreasonable one because she needs her car. She erupts like a volcano.

'You're not even LISTENING to me,' says Janey, almost in a shriek. 'I run EVERYTHING for you, I run myself RAGGED shopping and washing and doing everything round here for you, and you treat me like absolute scum. I spend my whole life bending over backwards for you and terrified of upsetting you and I've just trained you to be completely selfish!'

She regrets the words the second they're out of her mouth. There is an ominous silence. Then the door opening. Essie looks absolutely numb.

'I know.' She nods. 'I know how you feel about me.' She is deathly white.

'Don't start with that CRAP,' shouts Janey. 'Haven't you had enough self-pity yet? How long are you going to keep blaming me – not Colin, of course, not your dad, just me – for every stupid bloody thing that happens for the rest of your life? Well, have fun, because I am OUT.'

Janey is so blinded by tears she is not even sure she can drive by the time she stumbles to Shelby's bar. But she manages to go to see Johnson, who is insistent he can do everything himself – is better, even as he growls at her for not bringing him contraband cake. She goes round the kitchen putting things he likes out of reach; he is still not steady enough on his feet to climb a chair to get at the chocolate biscuits. She takes him out for a wobbly turn around the garden, and then hands over gratefully to Emma, who gives Janey a big hug that makes her feel worse instead of better. Other people's daughters seem to have no trouble hugging her. Then off to her clinic.

★

'There is literally nothing wrong with you, and this is an NHS appointment. Other people need them!'

She is trying, but it is very difficult to be cross with Mr Zandisky for very long.

'There's nothing wrong with your ears,' she says, examining them at some length. Although his large old nose has white hairs bristling out of it, there aren't any in his ears. He has obviously had them groomed specifically for this visit.

'I can't hear so well,' says Mr Zandisky.

'You're eighty-six,' she says, not without sympathy. 'This is just what's going to happen.'

'I think I have some wax.'

She looks again, and sees a little stick of something white. Frowning, she fishes it out with her blue clinical gloves and rolls it between her fingers.

'Ah, yes, you see,' says Mr Zandisky.

'It's wax.'

'Yes, is wax.'

'Mr Zandisky . . . is this *candle wax*?'

He looks at her with a wide-eyed expression of innocence. 'I do not think this can be.'

'Have you been putting candles in your ears?'

There had been a fashion some time before for 'ear candling', a total load of hooey that involved people sticking candles in their ears to supposedly bring out wax and impurities from the brain, a physical impossibility, or so Janey most fervently hopes. This resulted in a rash of burnt ears, stuck candles and even, in Aberdeen Royal Infirmary, someone who'd managed to puncture their own eardrum.

'Well?"

'I just think it is nice,' he says defiantly. 'To have very clean lovely ears. I am sure you agree with me.'

'I do,' says Janey. 'But not to the extent of you cluttering up my surgery.'

Mr Zandisky looks sad and Janey immediately feels bad. This trip to the hospital has probably been the highlight of his week. He lives alone, all his friends back in Poland long dead, his children hugely successful and living in Paris, London, Sydney. He worked incredibly hard all his life to raise a family and is now on his own, his smart suit and tie indicating a man who very much still has his pride. It makes Janey's heart slightly ache to see him, when there are so many who expect everything to be given to them. Mr Zandisky expects so little.

'Let me just double-check,' she says, and takes a surgical wipe and wipes it around his ear, removes the ear candle detritus, and puts in a little ointment, for absolutely no reason.

'You have,' she says, 'the best ears for a man your age that I've ever seen.'

Mr Zandisky beams.

'But no more sticking candles in them. It's dangerous and ridiculous.'

He nods seriously.

'Well done.'

'I make other appointment?'

'In two years,' says Janey. 'You'll get a free hearing test.'

'That is long time,' he says.

'Because you're doing so well,' she says, smiling encouragingly and standing up. She has a long list to get through. 'You should be very proud.'

He nods, then brings out – oh, no, she thinks. Please no. But yes. A Tupperware of Polish sugar cookies he has baked for her.

'You don't need to do this,' she protests.

'But I wish to,' he says gravely.

She knows he does, but now she will have to decant the cookies, he'll want the Tupperware back, and then show them to everyone and she shouldn't be eating sugar cookies anyway, she just can't get away from it, miserable as this may seem, and he's so kind . . . maybe I should just date him, she thinks. Make my life a lot simpler. But instead she takes the better lesson. Don't lose contact with people that you love. Don't ever lose contact with the people that you love.

So she smiles as she ushers him out; races through the rest of her appointments. And finally, just as she's going to call her daughter, the phone rings. She grabs it in relief. But it's not Essie. It's him.

★

It takes a long time for Essie to leave the house. She reads the messages. Connor is going home early, is the gist. He doesn't say come. He just says he's had enough and he's going home. She feels so trembly and upset inside and doesn't know what to do. She should call Al, but he's still furious about yesterday.

Everyone has gone.

The early sea mist is rising. The haar muffles the sound of the town, the tolling of the harbour bell, the chugging of the fishing boats, the shouts of the men, their boots stomping on the cobbles, as they head off to the tiny airport to take Gavin's helicopter out to the rigs – Brent Spar, North Cormorant, Ninian Central – for eight weeks of solid toil in punishing conditions before they get back to dry land, swaying slightly to steady themselves.

She doesn't even know where she's going. Where is there to go? Nobody wants her.

The very first ray of watery sun comes out just as she leaves the house, looks at the row of Seagate cottages. They look a mess, but they aren't: they're her mess. Done to her spreadsheet, to her timetable, they had stopped Wee Jim banging stuff with a hammer and got him and his mate, the diver, to work on the pipes, installed long ago and never used. It's kind of amazing: outside are three toilets, ready to be connected, under swaths of plastic. There'll be a boiler too, shiny and new. Everything going in in order, just how it should be, beautiful inexpensive pieces of kit, chosen by her, with Dwight's input. The houses are going to be lovely. One day. Assuming they don't get immediately sold off by some dodgy scheme of Tris's. Or even, she concedes reluctantly, if they do.

Dwight is leaning over the garden gate, with his stupid hat on, not waving, or talking. No toothpick. No Wee Jim. Just Dwight, standing in the frame, watching her pass by.

'Morning, ma'am,' he says, and picks the hat up again.

'Dwight,' she says, still embarrassed about the day before.

'Well, thanks for introducing me to those city folks,' he says, surprisingly. 'Tris is going to look after all of this for me. The money, the deeds, everything.'

Her heart sinks. She's so conflicted. Is it a good thing? She thinks of herself, unable to find anywhere to rent; Johnson and Lish's daughter, about to have a baby and living in a converted shed in the grounds of their own house. The closed-down restaurants in this town. The way life is getting harder. Everything she's noticed since she got back. But then again, look at Dwight getting his chance. There's only so long he can live on the rigs; a drilling hole costs the bodies of its men, everyone knows that.

'I'm not sure . . . I mean, you don't have to do this.'

'But I'll have enough to buy a new car,' says Dwight. 'And more houses, then I can do it again, and grow it all. And look how good we are. As a team. We can do it together. With the money from Tris . . . we could go and get more, it'll be great.'

'But . . . what if it goes out of the village and nobody has a place to live?'

Dwight raises up his hands.

'I have had nothing,' he says. 'Oh, yeah, it was okay for you, going off to the big city. You forgot about those of us who were left behind. Come back sniffing like there's cow pats every-where, making judgements about the rest of us.'

'I do not do that!'

He looks at her with an 'oh, come on!' face, and she feels more furious than ever.

'Anyway we're not talking about me!'

'Yes, we are! You and those guys and everyone like you who think it's fine to come when it suits you! Who never thinks that the rest of us are here, trying to get by, leading decent lives but feeling like we have to feed off crumbs from the big table.' He breaks off and turns round. 'And you'll be off again soon enough out of this dive, and forget you had a sudden crisis of conscience when you're back with all your posh friends at New Town dinner tables and you remember it's the government that didn't build enough hooses, not me.'

They are both breathing heavily and Essie can feel her cheeks go very pink.

'You don't know how I think,' she says.

Suddenly he is standing in front of her. She has not realised, until now, that although he is not tall, they are exactly the same height, and face to face she is level with every inch of him; his body is as tight and strong as she had always thought, now pun-ishingly close.

'What do you think?' he says, gruffly, and she realises that, for the first time in so, so long, she isn't thinking of anything at all; her entire mind has gone blank, and she is confused and excited and overwhelmed, and before she knows anything at all he is kissing her, hard and fiercely, completely out of the blue, in broad daylight.

★

After a moment she breaks away and steps back. It has been a very surprising morning.

'I'm sorry,' says Dwight, not sounding remotely sorry at all. 'I apologise. I should have asked.'

Essie just stares at him, furious at her betraying, racing heart.

Then she moves closer to him, and she does not just let him; she welcomes him, pushes herself against him, and what she had dreamed of, if she had let herself realise it, or given in to it, she finally has: his tight chest, his narrowed, bright blue eyes, the long hair. The toothpick is gone. It's just him. He smells of fresh sweat and leather, and suddenly, like a roaring train, Essie forgets everything: the problems, her life, her boyfriend; everything is completely gone. There is nothing in her at all except an intense animal yearning, a strength of extraordinary desire she has never felt before, that feels both overwhelming and completely inevitable.

They have staggered inside: a ray of sun hits them through the empty window frame that faces out towards the sea. His tanned skin looks beautiful and Essie finds she is desperately pressing herself up against him, ferocious as he kisses her, hard.

He is tugging up her T-shirt now, pressed against the wall, and before she knows it he has his hand under her arse and is grinding her hard against the stiff fly of his jeans, and oh, my God, it has never occurred to Essie before that to be exactly the same height as someone has extraordinary benefits, even as she finds herself desperately rubbing against him.

'You wanna?' he snarls into her ear like an animal, and she nods, furiously, absolutely: yes. 'It's not too dirty?'

'It's not dirty enough,' she says, looking straight at him, not giving herself time to think, and in an instant, with some expertise, he has pulled down her skirt and has taken a large, calloused hand and slipped it inside her knickers. She nearly shrieks. Suddenly it feels as if the wall cannot hold her up. He increases the pressure a little, watching her face intently to see how she responds and what she likes. She likes it all.

'Oh, God,' she says, leaning over, as if she's going to fall. He holds her up and she is absolutely streaming and cannot wait even a second longer.

'Put it . . . '

'What?'

'Put it . . . I want it . . . '

She can barely articulate it.

'Yeah?'

'Please . . . please . . . '

'Well, I hate to see a lady beg,' says Dwight lazily, as if he's not fussed one way or another. Unbuttoning his jeans, though, which have been uncomfortably containing his massive bulge, tells another story completely.

Without thinking, Essie drops to her knees, taking him, and herself, by surprise at her desperation to stuff him in between her lips. She looks up at him, opening her mouth wide, and it is all he can do not to grab the back of her head and ram himself straight in, but he doesn't, even if she looks as if she might welcome it. Instead he pumps several times, but holds himself back, and gradually moves an aching, desperate Essie back up again until she's braced against the wall. The lack of a height difference between them means she is at exactly at the right level as slowly, carefully, he takes his large cock, rubbing it

241

up and down slowly across her sodden opening, and she finds she is making the most ridiculous noises, pushing herself forward, desperate for him to take her. They are both panting as he waits several terribly, agonisingly long moments, and then, with a grunting noise, finally pushes right up, deep inside her, endlessly and relentlessly, pushing her and pummelling her, hard and ferocious. Essie is loving it, vociferously so; she puts her hands on his buttocks and drives him hard into her, screaming for it harder, and for more of it, which he willingly gives, until she finds herself collapsing forward on to him like a rag doll, as he pins her to the wall and keeps on driving into her without mercy.

Afterwards, they sink to the floor. Essie raw, horrified and delighted all at once.

Dwight is clearly falling asleep. Essie glances at him. Ridiculously, even though she is exhausted, she can't help herself: she genuinely wants him again. Right away. This time, on all fours. While she gets filthy.

After sex with Connor she usually felt a slightly odd sense of relief. This isn't the same thing at all. This is not even in the same ballpark.

Oh, my God. She had thought things were complicated before. She leaps up. Dwight stirs. She wants to grab his bicep and Christ, those hands of his, and God . . .

'I have to go,' she says.

'Why?'

'I . . . I promised I'd speak to Lowell about looking after the puppies,' she stammers.

'They'll be alright,' he says. Then, more seriously, 'Come back here, you.'

'Wee Jim will be back.'

Dwight looks at her, his sleepy eyes half shut, in a way she finds very difficult to resist.

'If only you lived nearby.' He grins.

'In my *mum's house*.'

'Nothing wrong with living at your maw's,' says Dwight, and Essie wants to hit the side of her head. Oh, lord. He lives with his mum. So does she. And she has a boyfriend. And she and Dwight are meant to be working together. Oh, God. This is just awful.

She pulls her T-shirt back on, in a frenzy now to leave before she has to think too much about what she's just done. And how much she wants to do it again.

'So, your friends . . . ' he says. He seems infuriatingly uncon-cerned about Connor. Which reminds her that of course, in the scheme of things, it's not actually Dwight's problem. He pulls himself up to sit against the wall and suddenly she wants to sit on him. She quashes the thought.

'Yeah,' she says, shamefully remembering her outburst. So much of it, truly, comes from jealousy. That he was chosen and she wasn't.

'I mean, it's going to be alright, aye?'

She shrugs. 'It's your money.'

'But if I give him the money and the deeds . . . He makes money for folk?'

'He does,' says Essie. Everyone, it seems, except for her.

Dwight looks at her squarely. 'Wanna do that again?'

She does. More than anything. Anything in the world.

Her life is an unbelievable mess, and this is only going to make it worse.

Her life is an unbelievable mess, but for a very, very short time just past, it felt as if it made sense.

Wee Jim and the plumber can be heard approaching the door and having a loud argument about doughnuts. The spell breaks; Dwight leaps up and pulls back on his jeans at lightning speed – practically professional, thinks Essie briefly – and she turns.

'Just dropping the latest project deadlines,' she says loudly as the men come in. 'Oh, no, I forgot them . . . '

They grunt at her. 'Jam or fudge?'

Dwight looks her straight in the eye.

'Honey,' he says.

She finds herself looking straight back at him.

'Cream,' she says. Then leaves before she can make things even worse.

32

Janey curses her teen excitement that her crush is phoning her.

On the other hand, after the awful morning she's had, it's nice to have something nice. Clinic hadn't been much better; one of her lovely clients, Bettina Murray, had been brought in by her distraught daughter. She kept pulling out her hearing aid, claiming it was aliens controlling her. Hearing aids were brilliant for slowing the path of dementia. But she could tell from the slumped shoulders of Bettina's middle-aged daughter that they had got there too late.

'I'm so sorry,' she had said.

'We'll manage, won't we, Mum?' the woman had said.

'I need to get to work,' the old woman had muttered. 'I'm late, I think. I don't want to be late. Do I work here? Where are the children? I should be at work.'

'She was a teacher,' says her daughter. 'A great one.'

'Conscientious,' says Janey, and they share a look. 'I'm so sorry.'

'Do you want them back?' says the woman.

'Keep trying,' says Janey. 'I promise, it can really help.'

'I'm LATE FOR WORK,' shouts Bettina, terrifyingly loud suddenly. She stamps a tiny foot, smart in court shoes.

'It's okay, Mum,' says the woman, at full volume, gradually standing up and tenderly putting Bettina's coat on her. 'It's an inset day. Come on, I'm going to take you to the Costa and get you a wee cup of tea.'

'AND A WEE BISCUIT.'

'Always a wee biscuit,' says the woman, leading her out, and Janey doesn't want to ask herself if Essie would, could, ever be like that for her.

★

'I'm so sorry,' Lowell apologises immediately. Even just hearing his deep burring tones, the soft East Coast tinge, somehow makes her feel better. 'I know you're working.'

'It's okay, it's my lunch break,' Janey says. She almost says, *you are the only good thing that has happened to me today.* But she doesn't need to add hysterical to the adjectives she gloomily imagines already accompany his opinion of her – comfortable, dependable, all the sexy ones.

She notices she hasn't had a message from Essie. She is, she realises, still too upset to call her daughter. Because part of her is still angry, and she knows that's dangerous. She needs to wait for the flame to burn out, in case it flares up again. Her daughter is so hard on her.

'Oh, then—'

'No, it's okay. I'm running early; I have time. Is it the pups?'

'It's Verity.'

★

She meets them by the war memorial park. Felicity flops out of the back of the car, obviously happy to have a break from the pups. She's not quite back to normal; her nipples are hanging down very far, and her belly is covered in loose, floppy skin. It's the first time Janey has smiled all day. 'Welcome to your new body, sweets,' she whispers to the hound as she comes up to lick her.

Lowell is signing for Verity to get out of the car, but nobody is emerging.

'What's up?' murmurs Janey.

'Her mum wants to take another week on her yoga retreat and for Verity to stay here, through the whole Easter holiday,' says Lowell. 'Verity is taking it very personally.'

'So this wasn't organised or . . . '

'I don't mind,' says Lowell immediately.

'I know you don't,' says Janey. 'I wasn't implying . . . '

She steps towards the car. 'Hi,' she signs to Verity, who has glanced up from her iPad, and scowls. Then she drops her head into the iPad. She can't hear if she isn't looking at you.

'You're going to have to wrest that thing off her for starters, I think,' says Janey.

Lowell looks as if she'd just suggested he wrestle a bear for a jam sandwich. He screws up his face. 'Do you think?'

'You're her dad! How's it been? I thought it was going better.'

'So did I,' says Lowell. 'Then I tried to get her to eat supper and she found some bacon in the fridge and it kind of unravelled from there. Then she wouldn't go to bed and sat up till four, so she's probably not at her best. Neither am I.'

Verity gives them both a side-eye so intense coming out of her little pale face that Janey is quite discomfited. This child is so unhappy.

'She hates me,' says Lowell in despair.

'She doesn't hate you,' says Janey patiently. 'She's upset with other things in her life and you're the safest person to take it out on . . . oh.'

'What?' says Lowell.

'Nothing. God. I am the worst person to give parent–daughter advice at the moment.'

'What do you mean?'

'Essie and I had a big fight. She did one small, totally under-standable thing and I blew my stack.'

'You?'

Janey is slightly comforted by the surprise in his voice. 'Oh, yeah, she's just . . . it's been a tough . . . I thought I'd be so happy when she moved back in. I thought we'd have such a lovely time.'

She realises she is snivelling a little, even as Lowell is nodding his head in agreement.

'Sorry,' she says. 'You don't need this.'

'So you're telling me it might never get any better?' says Lowell. 'Jings. This is why people drink at lunchtime.'

'No. No,' says Janey, rubbing her eyes. 'We're not bad people. Are we?'

Lowell shrugs. 'I'm a privileged white man, Janey. I'm liter-ally the worst person in the world.'

And Janey chokes out a giggle and wipes the mascara from under her eyes.

'Maybe you should do Verity,' she says, 'and I should do Essie. Like a reverse *Strangers on a Train*.'

She gets in next to the girl on the back seat of the car and watches the game she's playing, jewels tumbling in a line. It's beautiful and hypnotic.

'You like the iPad?' she signs, after a while.

Verity nods and signs that it's her dad's. 'I want to keep it,' she adds, obviously in case Janey has any pull in that department.

'I imagine there's a way,' signs Janey, figuring that given how beautiful Lowell's house is, he can afford it, 'but it would involve stuff like having to put time limits on it and stuff.'

Verity is far too smart a kid not to realise she's been played, but also, she accepts Janey as a competitor, and lays the iPad down beside her. Janey pretends not to notice or care. God, kids were so much easier at this age. She has no idea why she thought it was difficult at the time.

'C'mon,' she signs. 'Let's walk.'

They climb out and Lowell locks the iPad in the car, looking at Janey as though she's a fearsome magician. She'll explain later. At this point she's more interested in what's eating Verity.

'What's up?' she signs, keeping her hands as relaxed as possible, as if she absolutely couldn't care less if Verity was currently being gnawed by a wolf.

And Verity tells her.

★

After she's finished explaining, the child seems different, as if a weight has been lifted off her. Janey, for her part, is amazed and delighted, and deeply nostalgic for the days when her own daughter's problems were so easily solvable. Would give anything for it. Still no messages.

They've entered the fullness of the wood now, a giant clearing filling up with a purple blue sea. Verity has stopped, her eyes and nose full of the colours, the heavy scent of it all, completely enthralled, and dashed off ahead with Felicity, to bound among the blue.

'Well?' says Lowell, catching up with her.

'I'm sure she meant well,' says Janey diplomatically. 'But your wife was worried that Verity would start her periods while she's here.'

'But she's not even eleven!'

Janey shrugs. 'Perfectly possible, I'm afraid.'

'Oh, lord,' says Lowell, shaking his head. 'I never thought of that.'

'Unfortunately, Verity's got hold of the wrong end of the stick. Thinks that means it's definitely going to happen and she's not very well prepared.'

'What did Thalia give her?'

Janey screws up her face. 'It's not . . . I mean, it's not a bad idea. It's called a moon cup. But it's definitely for what I'd call . . . advanced menstruators?'

Lowell's face makes Janey want to laugh. If she could get any less sexy than the dog pee bit, or the counselling bit, perhaps it's now.

'Lowell, your face!'

'Sorry,' he says, lumbering onwards. 'You're right, of course. I'm the wrong generation for all that.'

'You are not!' says Janey. 'You're my age. Which means you just weren't listening.'

'I've got two brothers,' says Lowell. 'It never really came up.'

'Where are you in that line-up, out of interest?'

'Where do you think?'

'I don't know . . . if I had to guess, I'd say . . . sandwiched in the middle, trying to get on with everyone at once?'

He smiles. 'Exactly right! That's how I feel.'

'Me too,' says Janey. 'Squished.'

She has been focusing on him, and keeping an eye on Verity and Felicity, who have raced ahead, and realises suddenly that she's trampled on a load of bluebells.

'Oh, no,' she says, looking down in dismay. The bluebells have so brief a span; to make it even shorter through carelessness feels terrible.

'There's plenty more,' says Lowell, looking ahead. He turns around the wood, a woodpecker in the distance; early swallows overhead. They both look around for a while. 'I was trying to think if there was anything I could possibly say; anything about these bluebells that a million people haven't said before, a load of poets and clever people and all that.'

'I know,' says Janey. 'But it doesn't seem to capture it, does it?'

'When I was wee,' says Lowell, 'I didn't notice them at all. I mean I'm sure my dad pointed them out but . . . ' He waves his hands around. 'It was boring, *go out and play* stuff, you know.'

'I do,' says Janey. 'You wanted a BMX.'

'I had a BMX,' says Lowell.

'You posho.'

He grins. 'I'm not even going to mention the ponies.' ·

'Good,' says Janey. 'Wait – ponies, *plural*?'

'If you're after me for my money,' says Lowell, 'I can assure you, it's all long gone. Tax and care homes. My mum's body held out a lot longer than her mind.'

He winces; he's tried to make light of it, but he hasn't quite judged it right. Janey likes this in him, his obvious discomfort in getting it wrong.

'What was she like?'

'For the last ten years, absolutely fucking furious,' says Lowell. 'But before that . . . she was nice. Fun. I was just the one in the middle; they didn't have to worry about me so much. Not like only having one.'

'Or two,' says Janey, but she's smiling.

The sun strikes through the trees on to a wide tree stump and she sits down on it, checking for bugs first. It's an old coat; it'll survive. Verity and Felicity have found a fairy circle and have sat down on the ground, child and dog intent on something crawling along a branch.

Lowell is standing, enjoying the sun on the back of his neck.

'As I got older, and when Verity was little, we thought – I thought – this was just the most magical place in the world. I told her that fairies came here to show you bells if you couldn't hear them and she believed me completely.'

Janey sees his hands unconsciously sign the words for fairy and bells; he doesn't even know he's doing it.

251

'That's beautiful,' she says.

He looks at her. 'I don't think she cares now.'

'I don't know,' says Janey. 'She's interested in something.'

'Getting an iPad,' says Lowell.

'Essie wouldn't be interested either. She might take a picture of it for her Instagram.'

Her shoulders slump.

'Tell me more about Essie,' says Lowell.

'She just . . . she's out of work and has no direction, and she just . . . she treats me like garbage and I don't know what to do. I know she's hurting, but I can't get through to her and I don't know what I did wrong . . . well, we got divorced. But I didn't . . . '

She swallows hard and says the next thing very quietly.

'My ex had an affair. I tried to save it, but I couldn't. Essie despised me for it, for not being able to hang on to her beloved dad.'

'You were brave to leave,' says Lowell gently.

'I didn't,' says Janey, frankly. 'He wasn't a bad guy. He didn't hit me or anything. He just . . . ' She doesn't know why it's coming out now. Choking out of her. 'He just didn't want me enough.'

There was a long silence, broken only by talkative birds.

'What happened to us?' says Lowell finally, in his soft growly voice. 'What happened to the young people we were, so full of it?'

'What?'

'Joy. Hope. Springtime.'

Verity and Felicity are now jumping around at the other end of the glade, Verity holding up a stick Felicity can reach easily. The dog's great silver tail swishes through the greenery.

'I don't know,' says Janey.

Lowell is still staring at the flowers. 'They bloom so beauti-fully, and for such a short time.'

'Well, I know that feeling,' says Janey, and for a moment he looks at her, and she feels herself being looked at, and tries to hold it, to not bustle or turn away, or panic, like when she acci-dentally has her phone camera facing forward. He can't possibly be thinking what she is thinking. He is perfectly well-preserved – well, perhaps rather stout, but nonetheless he is tall, has a house and has all his own hair, which means he is worth everything on the market, could get any woman he likes, could even have more babies with a hot, yoga-loving thirty-year-old. Whereas she, at the same age, feels like a joke. A stupid, middle-aged, foolish joke, most likely to be found at home sending money to strangers on Facebook who pretend they're doctors in the American army.

She smiles at him. He isn't moving.

'Well,' she says finally, trying to sound insouciant, running her fingers through the flowers, 'I know there's no point in picking them. I know they only last a day, and actually it feels cruel to pick something so lovely and so fragile, and I know in fact that, if I do, the fairies and the hares will come and curse me . . . '

He smiles. 'Uh-huh?'

'But I'm going to pick some.'

She gets up, cursing her own yearning; finds a hidden patch behind a rotting tree that nobody would ever call a beauty spot.

'And I'll take them from here so it doesn't spoil anything.'

He nods. 'Although won't you only be upsetting the really malevolent fairies?'

'Malevolent is an excellent word. You don't hear it much these days.'

'Because nobody under forty can spell it.'

They both laugh, and she wanders over and bends down.

253

'I'm sorry,' she says. 'You are very beautiful wild, and it's self-ish to want to carry your scent with me, but that's how humans and flowers co-exist. And I'm going to pick you and you'll die but you were going to . . . '

She stands up.

'I can't.'

Both Verity and Lowell look at her.

'You can't pick the bluebells?'

She shakes her head. 'We don't know, do we? What if they scream when we pick them?'

'You eat lamb!'

'I know,' she says. 'I have no moral consistency anywhere. I'm worse than Essie, and sometimes she pretends she's a vegan.'

'Do you kill spiders?'

'No! Oh, my God, only monsters would do that.'

'And you won't even pick a bluebell.'

There is a long silence, and now there are only the birds chirping, noisily, in the woods far above their heads, the rustling of leaves with gentle breezes making their own sweet way, and just for a second, for the tiniest of seconds, Janey isn't thinking anything at all. Isn't making a list in her head of what she needs to be doing that day, what needs to be done, laundry and shopping and dinner and her children and work and the car and that wobbly banister that keeps catching everyone out and the state of her neck and the nice coat she has been meaning to take to the dry-cleaners for eight months . . . all of it evaporates, on a cloud of pale purply blue.

And she feels it once again, like a surge of sap that comes when she's with Lowell: that tearing excitement – how can she have forgotten it after all this time, forgotten what she had spent so many of her teenage years dreaming of, fantasising about; so much of her twenties searching for and fumbling about with; what she had found, or thought she had, once or twice, then lost it, or been disillusioned, sometimes quickly, and finally very, very slowly, a deflating balloon of years and years and years until she had felt completely shrivelled.

The back of her neck prickles. Lowell looks at her for a long, steady second and this time she holds it, bathes in it, moves closer towards him.

'*Ah!*'

Verity appears, Felicity bounding beside her, great armfuls of bluebells in each hand. She ceremoniously presents them each with a huge bunch.

'Thank you,' signs Janey, rather clumsily. The spell is broken. 'And I'll bring you the things we talked about and show you how to use them. But honestly, I think you'll be fine.'

Verity nods.

'Oh, yeah,' says Lowell. 'Um, and is your girl going to help me with the pups?'

'I think so,' says Janey. 'If she ever speaks to me again.'

33

The house is tidy – that's something. Janey walks in quietly, once she gets home from work, incredibly anxious, which is a ridiculous way to feel about walking into your own home. Although, after years of walking on eggshells with Colin, not a new experience.

Essie is in the kitchen. The kitchen is clean. Essie has been scrubbing, something she thinks is not without irony. She is trying to distract herself. She can't make nice chat with Connor and she can't listen to the hammering and whistling going on next door, so the vacuum cleaner seemed the best thing to drown everything out, including the commotion in her own head. Today was startling, astonishing in so many ways. She cannot repeat it.

'Hey,' says Janey.

'Hey,' says Essie, staring at the floor.

'I'm . . . I'm sorry we shouted,' says Janey. 'I'm sorry *I* shouted. I don't want us to shout.'

'I'll . . . '

Essie had called Connor, terrified of herself, absolutely terrified he'd be able to tell she'd cheated just from her voice. He had asked what had brought it on and she had just said it was her time of the month. He went to an all-boys' school; he's scared of periods. 'Yeah, that's just what Tris thought,' he'd said. Then a pause.

'I'm sorry,' Essie had said again, heartfelt and guilty.

'That's alright, babes. Tris is really happy he's taking over this deal from Dwight.'

'I think Dwight is too.'

'I think there'll be some consulting work in it for you,' says Connor. 'If you like.'

And, all at once, her heart had leapt. And it had leapt even more when she'd checked her email, which she'd almost given up on, to find out she had an interview in the city for the Mergers and Acquisitions job. She had put her noble thoughts about serving Carso to the back of her mind immediately. She could make it okay. She could find her way back. Back to the city. Back to her life. And her very suitable boyfriend, who did not live with his (delightful) parents; who was sweet, and thoughtful, and appropriate. And okay, could not . . . could not . . . she flushed even to think of it. Could not make her feel what Dwight had made her feel. But that – that wasn't everything. And if she is working on the project still, doing some consulting, well, she can oversee it, can't she? Make sure it goes somewhere good . . .

'I'll be gone soon,' she says now.

Janey's heart is breaking. Her darling girl. And this gulf she cannot cross.

'I don't want you to go.'

'Doesn't feel like that,' says Essie, shortly, her mind still beavering away. She has so much going on now. Her mum is still bleating about the car and this morning's argument, not even noticing the seismic changes in Essie's life.

Janey rubs her eyes. 'I . . . '

'I'm going to Edinburgh next week,' blurts out Essie. 'I've got an interview and I'm going to stay at Connor's.'

'Okay, good, that's great . . . ,' says Janey, genuinely surprised.

'I can't believe you're surprised,' says Essie.

'I'm not . . . honestly, I'm not. I think it's wonderful.'

'You weren't expecting it.'

'I can't win,' says Janey.

'I didn't realise it was about winning,' says Essie.

★

They put on a property show and eat in silence, not even passing the usual remarks about how attempting to put in a circular all-glass extension is a disaster and a divorce waiting to happen.

Janey breaks first.

'So Al tells me Dwight's going into business with your city friends?'

'Oh, my God, this town,' says Essie.

'I'm surprised . . . I thought he'd be small fry to them.'

'It's property, isn't it?' say Essie, not betraying that she'd thought the same thing. 'Get in, leverage, take over the world.'

'Hmm,' says Janey. 'I'm not sure Dwight is really the taking-over-the-world type.'

'Dwight can do anything,' says Essie without thinking, and Janey looks at her curiously. 'He's lucky to be in Tris's fund,' she adds, quickly. 'It returns twelve per cent. Nothing does that.'

'But doesn't that mean Tris will own those houses, really?'

Essie scowls. 'It'll be fine.'

'I don't trust anything that I don't quite understand,' says Janey.

'I can tell,' says Essie, looking round the tiny room.

'So you're not going to go to Lowell's, then?'

Essie frowns. Among everything else happening, she'd pretty much forgotten all about it. But she really, really needs some pin money though, for going back to the city.

'What does he need me to do?'

'Just help with the dogs, of course.'

'Last employment: puppy-wrangler,' says Essie.

'Are you saying that in a happy way or a sarcastic way? I can't tell with young people. And anyway, he might also need some babysitting.'

'Better and better.' But Essie's face is losing its hostility as something occurs to her. 'Are you going to keep a pup?'

'Hahaha,' says Janey. 'Under absolutely no circumstances.'

'If you had to choose, which one would you go for?' says Essie, thoughtfully. It is a truce of some kind.

'Bute,' says Janey instantly. 'I like a bit of booty on a girl.'

'Don't say "booty",' says Essie, habitually, and there is, finally, a semblance of normality in the room, and still so much unsaid.

34

Essie pulls on a pair of jeans, a T-shirt and a jumper and barely stops to put on make-up when she leaves the house first thing the next morning. Did it really used to take her nearly an hour to get ready? It must have been the most ridiculous faff. She doesn't miss the eyelashes that much, that's true.

She didn't think she'd sleep for thinking about Dwight, but she did; she slept well. She supposes she knows the reason. And she wants to get out from under him – literally – to remember where she is. Things are heading along the right track. She has a job interview right after Easter with a nice, respectable firm in the West End. Connor is happy. He'll be so pleased to see her. Once she's got the job, she can start looking for a flat, or maybe they can look together – it will all be fine. Yes. She can put the whole of Carso behind her. Maybe she can gift those knitting needles Gertie made her buy.

She wanders up along the hedgerow; she hasn't seen a car for a while, just old Wull on his tractor, who had slowed down even further just to wave to her and wish her a fine morning, which it is.

She has startled a fawn in a field, and it darts off, white tail the only thing that can be seen by the naked eye. 'I'm on your side!' she says, remembering Al is yet another person she has yet to talk to. She wonders if he's still cross with her. She'll take him out for a nice lunch in Edinburgh, when she's back there.

She is eyed up by some fairly belligerent geese as she walks over the small wooden bridge by the burn, which keeps getting washed away in heavy storms and rebuilt by locals, as it had taken the council about nineteen years to do an assessment on what it might be replaced by and whether or not it would displace any precious animal life, at a cost which would have already replaced the bridge about seven times.

In Edinburgh, she muses, she could walk down George Street and dematerialise, and her mum would just think she was hard to get on the phone, and Connor would assume she was at a party and her friends would assume she was just too busy, and Al would just never even think to ring her even though he is mostly happy to see her when she does turn up. In Edinburgh she could vanish and it would be days. In Carso, people are probably discussing where she is headed right now. In fact, she'd waved to her mum's hairdresser going past, which means that every single person who goes in and out of Jean's salon today will have a full appraisal. She used to mind a lot. She doesn't so much now, on this pretty day.

Thank goodness nobody will have thought anything of her coming out of Dwight's houses yesterday. Even though it is beyond their imaginings. She shivers. No. Focus on Edinburgh. The life she truly wants. And the first step is finishing this project, so everyone can see how efficient she is and wants to work with her and her mum won't think she's a failure and her dad will pay her more attention and . . . well, everything will be better. She walks towards the old schoolhouse with renewed purpose.

★

Janey hasn't told her what to expect in Lowell's house, hoping her daughter will enjoy the lovely surprise of it as much as she had. In fact, she is rather unflatteringly astonished.

'Bloody hell, you don't normally see anything as nice as this round here,' Essie had rather spluttered. 'This could be . . . '

'Somewhere else?' Lowell enquires drily.

He is not having a good morning. He was trying to get on with work. Thalia is . . . well, she very much wants to stay longer on her very expensive yoga retreat in Bali, seeing as Verity seems to be enjoying herself so much, so there's that. He's not sure what has precipitated the change of heart. For years she has been tricky with visitation rights, one of the reasons, he thinks, that Verity is so suspicious of him; for years, he has believed that if there were a hell, it would be him spending long nights without sleep in the Travelodge round the corner from his ex-wife's new home, as she insists that the vibrations aren't right for his visit that day after all, that it would be disruptive and he'd better not try. He would move to Galloway but there is no work for him down there, which would mean a lot less money for the guru retreats. So he is rather stuck.

He has refused to get drawn into a narrative that Thalia is the baddie and he is the goodie. He knows he tried to impose on her the life he had wanted; assumed she would be happy to follow his lead. He had loved that quirky, uncompromising side of her when they'd got together, had thoroughly enjoyed the free-spiritedness, the creative side of her nature, and he feels guilty that motherhood and marriage had squashed her; that he had squashed her, and the internet had fed on her disgruntlement, as it does, and converted it to poison.

He thinks about Janey, desperately trying not to upset her daughter. They are two sides of the same coin.

But this is new. He has done what he had sworn he wouldn't do. Gone and looked at Thalia's Instagram. And sure enough, there was a man, a bendy, muscular-looking man with long hair in a bun, just out of focus in the distance of the shot. Could be anyone.

Of course he had known she wouldn't be single forever; she is young, and gorgeous. He doesn't love her any more. It's completely to be expected.

He feels as if he's been punched in the stomach.

And now there is someone on his doorstep being rude about his house.

'I didn't mean it like that,' Essie says, in a tone of voice with enough penitence in it to make him realise he's been sharp.

'Sorry,' he says. 'I'm a bit distracted.'

He pays more attention. It's funny: Essie looks like Janey, he realises suddenly, but as if she isn't finished yet. It's odd; there's definitely a resemblance. Essie is pretty, certainly, but fuzzy round the edges, undefined, whereas you can see everything about Janey the second you look into her open face. Funny, that. Mind you, everyone under about forty looks fuzzy to him these days, he finds more and more, and every female younger than that makes him think rather uncomfortably about his daughter. Essie looks like a copy, Janey the original.

'I'm not surprised,' says Essie, who can hear, in the hushed cathedral space of the beautiful house, the excited yips of puppies who can sense someone has just walked through the door and like the scent of who they think it is.

Lowell indicates where they obviously are, and she goes in, instantly bursting out laughing, crouching on to the floor and being entirely engulfed by a clutch of small, frantically wagging lunatics who recognise her smell as the first secure thing they learned about on this earth, and are patently delighted to be reunited with something they recognise in this whole wide, confusing universe. The tiny breaths pant and there is some yipping from Argyll, who as the runt of the litter as usual finds it a problem to get to the front.

'Come here, baby girl,' says Lowell over the top of her head, scooping up the tiny scruffy pup, who licks his face off.

'You seem to have taken to her,' says Essie.

'Absolutely not,' says Lowell, absentmindedly tickling Argyll's tummy. 'I really don't have time for a dog. That's why you're here.'

Essie smiles knowingly.

★

Essie does a remarkably efficient job of replacing the newspaper, only briefly stopping to read the headline, which was, predictably, about the housing crisis and how young families were having to move into the caravan park on the next bay along, while homes that might once have belonged to them were sold at eye-watering prices to be used for holiday lets, or as second homes for people who lived down south to visit for a couple of weeks a year. She makes herself not look at it. A local person is going to be helped.

Then she takes the dogs out into the garden. The speedwell is coming up through the grass; it needs mowing. She wouldn't blame Lowell for giving up while it has a clutch of noisy puppies charging through it at all hours of the day. She gives the chicken wire a thorough check all round the edges. Nothing seems too gnawed so far, but she wouldn't put it past Smokey to be able to jump over it quite soon.

As she's straightening up, she senses a presence behind her, and whips around. Outlined against the old Victorian schoolhouse, at first she thinks she's seeing a ghost: a school-age girl with long, dark hair, standing with her hand buried in the neck fur of a huge dog.

Of course, the dog is Felicity, which means the child must be Lowell's daughter, Verity. She hadn't come out before and Lowell hadn't thought to introduce them.

'Hello,' she says, then remembers Verity doesn't speak, and waves to her. Her mum tried to teach her a little sign language when she was younger but she had loudly protested that it was boring and pointless because she wasn't going to do the same job as her mother. She winces, now, remembering that. She didn't want to be cruel to her mother; sometimes she was just upset about other things and it just came out.

Anyway, her mum had been right: it would have been useful. She waves again, limply.

Verity stares straight at her with huge dark eyes, very like her father's, but she doesn't say anything. He's an old dad, Essie thinks. He's older than her stupid dad. Mind you, her stupid dad has a six-year-old. They're all at it, dirty old men.

'I'm here for . . . the puppies?'

Brilliant financial fixer by day, she thinks, puppy poop-scooper in the mornings. Modern all-round woman.

She expects Verity to come and play with the pups – they couldn't be any more adorable right now, eyes open, tugging and playing with a selection of toys, rolling around the grass, eating some of it in chunky little Bute's case, then realising that it was not meant to be eaten and coughing it back up again melodramatically – but she hangs back, standing with Felicity, who is avoiding her pups in case they try – as they always do – to fix their painful teeth on to her still-drooping teats in the hopes of a feed, even though those days are gone and the dogs are now on cereal, a development that is to prove not much fun for Essie in the mornings and cause a sharp spike in bleach sales at the Scot Nor.

Essie beckons her over to at least give Bute a cuddle, but Verity quite slowly and deliberately turns away with Felicity and walks her to the other side of the garden, the part that the pups can't get to. This isn't, Essie reckons, about being deaf. She is in a definite mood. Essie can empathise, being in a fairly massive mood herself, and wishes she could figure out a way to bridge the gap.

Presently Lowell emerges with a coffee for her.

'Thanks,' he says, passing it over and taking a sip of his own. 'It's . . . a bit much in the mornings. No? Too hot for you.'

'Wait a minute,' says Essie, as a small, shiny black nose emerges from his cardigan pocket. 'How come you've still got Argyll?' She looks at the other pups. 'God, I counted wrong. Shit, I could have lost one.'

'Well,' he says, 'she's so wee. It's not really fair to let her compete with the other pups; she doesn't get enough food.'

She appears to be licking butter from his fingers.

'Uh-huh,' says Essie.

'How's your mum?' he asks.

Essie sighs and he looks surprised.

'Really?' he says. 'She's . . . she's dead nice, your mum.'

'Oh, yes, everyone just loves her,' says Essie, not without bitterness. She's still feeling stung and almost misses the implication of Lowell asking about her. No, she thinks, that's just ridiculous. Not her dumpy mum. She discounts it immediately.

'I'm sorry,' says Lowell, glancing at Verity, who, as soon as she notices, turns away quite dramatically. 'I know a bit about what it's like to be a disappointment to your offspring.'

★

Essie looks over too and smiles, but Verity scowls back. Essie glances up at the sky. It is black and threatening. It's going to rain today, no doubt about it. Not a lot of fun when you're cross with a parent.

'Is she missing her mum?'

'I think so. It isn't going to help, me having to work today.'

'I have a plan,' says Essie, because, suddenly, she does.

The rain comes on and they stick the pups back in the laundry, then Essie feels around her bag. She has let her personal grooming drop quite considerably since she's been back, but it doesn't mean she's forgotten. She heads into the main room.

Verity doesn't hear her come in until Essie approaches carefully, waving. She doesn't smile.

'I brought you something,' says Essie as clearly as she can.

Verity doesn't pause the TV. Lowell looks up, but doesn't interfere, in case, no doubt, he makes things worse, which is entirely possible. He is wearing a towel on his trousers, which means, Essie knows for a fact, that he still has a dog secreted about his person. Well, if he gets Argyll, she thinks, she's going to find Bute. Although Bute's arse is already too big to fit in any of her pockets.

She holds up the box and peels back the corner. The colours of the polish and the UV dryer sparkle in the light. Verity blinks a few times.

Essie shows Verity her nails, then says clearly, 'I'm going to do mine. Would you like me to do yours?'

Verity darts a glance at her dad, who nods. She signs very quickly.

'Mum says it's toxins,' Lowell interprets.

'Well,' says Essie, 'we shan't eat it.'

She pulls out another towel ('I see now,' says Lowell, incomprehensibly, 'what your mother meant about all the towels') and spreads it on the low wooden coffee table.

Verity willingly puts her thin little hand out and Essie starts with her; they choose a light pearly pink. Essie explains carefully what she's doing at each stage, and although Verity nods solemnly, she finds it very difficult to stop her fingers from moving instinctively every time she wants to say something.

Lowell stops working and comes over.

'You don't really need me,' he signs, and says to Verity at the same time. 'You can speak.'

Verity gives him a look and signs something even Essie can understand.

'It's not stupid,' he says. 'It allows you to talk while you're getting your nails done.'

Verity stares at the floor where she can't see him. Lowell puts his hand on her shoulder and she flinches; he heads back to his desk, looking defeated.

Essie finishes the job in silence, apart from gently telling her what she's doing. When it's finally finished, Verity stares at her beautiful new nails in rapture, holding them up to the light and turning her fingers round and round.

'They look lovely,' says Essie, grinning. The child has beautiful hands: long fingers, smooth muscles made longer by constant motion. 'You have lovely hands,' she says, simply.

Verity stops looking at them for a second and turns to Essie, and she smiles, puts a flat hand to her chin, and pulls it away. And Essie smiles and does the same thing in return.

★

Essie goes in every day that week with a will – it feels good just to get out of the house, and Lowell has pressed notes in her hand that will at least feed her when she gets to Edinburgh, and Verity is taking her job of teaching Essie sign language very seriously, and the pair of them roam the woods, and Bute does not exactly fit in Essie's pocket but she is the pup Essie pulls close in the evening. The best thing is, it keeps her away from Dwight and out of trouble. Every day she asks Lowell more questions about project management and he has been explaining to her, more and more, the importance of using local staff who understand the buildings and even the way the land lies, and local materials that suit the territory and the climate, even if, he says wryly, no local people will ever live there, which makes her frown and change the subject. She is going to finish this project brilliantly and on time, prove to Connor and his bunch of lads that she isn't some hysterical moron, take a brilliant job back in the city and get everything back to normal.

So she sends emails, and books flooring, and sends samples to Dwight, all of which he okays. It's even better than that: Verity helps her pick out tiles and, as it turns out, has an extremely good eye for colour and pattern. Essie wonders if it comes from her world being so very visual; she's intensely in tune with which colours go together, so much so that they sit down with a colour wheel and work out everything from curtains to doorknobs. Meanwhile, Lowell kindly offers to cast an eye over her building and completion estimates and announces himself surprisingly impressed by how well she's done – she's thorough and realistic and has a talent for project management. They could probably do with someone like her at the practice, he says; they have the same retention issues as everyone else in the Highlands. Nowhere for young people to live.

And Janey – she is incredibly relieved. They haven't made up, not exactly. But at least Essie is busy, and distracted. One night she even brings Bute home, which Janey completely realises is cold-hearted bribery, when the dog hasn't even had its vaccinations yet, but she is such a – well, it would be nice to say such a beautiful puppy and also something along the lines that all puppies, just like all babies, are beautiful, but the fact is that Bute, with her narrow deerhound face and very long schnozz plonked on top of her round, supersized Westie chonk, looks like nothing more than A.L.F. the friendly alien in dog form.

On the other hand, she is unusually sweet-natured (unlike Smokey, who appears to be all unreconstructed terrier feistiness in the body of a horse, much to Dwight's delight), and Al comes over too, and they all eat fish and chips and let Bute have a chip, which bodes very badly for how spoiled the dog is going to be if Janey is ever going to keep a dog which of course she one hundred per cent is not, and the evenings are lengthening out, spilling over the sides of nine p.m.; the world is a dazzling array of shades of green. Johnson is limping up and down the high street when they bring him in, unable to go more than two steps before being greeted by someone he knows. Amsan's daughter Yasmin has met someone through an app. They illegally breed alligators in their spare time, Amsan has mentioned, almost casually, but apart from that they're very nice, and Janey has put her foot down and insisted Yasmin at least meets Owen; he would always keep her in fax machines, and he's punctual and knows a lot about the Second World War.

Essie concentrates hard on trying to keep everything steady. On Good Friday she has to go by the cottages and check they have the fire safety regulations in, and measure up for curtains. Dwight is standing there, leaning cockily against the newly installed sliding windows at the back, looking smug.

'Hey,' he says. Essie flushes immediately and he smiles, as if this is a totally expected thing to happen. He follows her over to the back wall and puts his arm up so they're face to face. She feels herself go weak at the knees.

'Missed you round here,' he says.

Essie feels her breathing quicken. But she's off to Edinburgh. *Focus, focus, focus*, she tries to tell herself. *Focus*.

'You have to stick to the plan,' she says. 'I'm seeing Tris and everyone next week; they'll want to know it's all going ahead.'

'With you I can get it sorted, yeah?' says Dwight, moving in closer. 'We're a good team.'

She shoots out from under him. 'I don't think . . . I think this should be professional. I don't think we should mix business with pleasure.'

'Well.' Dwight thinks about this for a moment. Eventually he says, 'I'm very glad there was pleasure.'

'Okay, well, bye,' says Essie, cursing her betraying blush.

'No, hang on,' he says. 'I'm coming with you. I need to see Lowell.'

And he walks her to Lowell's. They don't speak much. Essie keeps shooting glances at him, wishing it weren't so vivid in her memory: the feel of him, bucking against her. Dwight for his own part seems completely happy to be walking down the beautiful lane, the hedgerows growing higher every day, wild meadowsweet everywhere, tumbling over, an orgy of green and fresh planting, shining in the leftover diamonds of the morning dew. He doesn't check his phone very often, Essie notices, or feel the need to fill empty spaces with conversation. He seems perfectly happy in his own skin, walking his own road with his wide cowboy swagger. It's unnerving, but undeniably attractive.

Lowell frowns at the sight of him.

'Hi?' he says, then glances at Verity, who is signing at him. It is undeniably funny and very obvious that she is asking who the cowboy is – the sign for cowboy is someone taking pistols out of the back pocket of their jeans and shooting with them. She scowls immediately in case they are laughing at her and Essie straightens her face.

Dwight kneels down to her level and speaks directly into her face.

'I'm Dwight,' he says.

She points at his hat.

'You want my hat?'

She nods. He puts it on her head.

'You can't give her your hat,' says Lowell stiffly. 'She doesn't need special attention. There's nothing wrong with her.'

Dwight straightens up, winking at Verity.

'I'm not giving her my hat,' he says. 'I'm swapping it.'

Lowell looks confused.

'I want Smokey. Ahmed says he's big enough for his jabs.'

Lowell looks for a moment as if he's going to disagree, then he remembers suddenly what a bully Smokey is.

'Um,' he says, 'okay.'

'Let me do it,' says Essie quickly, as he heads to the laundry. There is a lot of anticipatory barking. When the door finally opens, the puppies charge like maniacs. They are now huge, and seem to move like a cresting wave of hair. The noise is tremendous. Verity is smiling.

Dwight reaches into his jacket pocket and pulls out a black leather collar with studs on it, and a black lead, also with studs.

'Oh, my God,' says Essie, 'That is *so* . . . '

'Like a bit of black leather, do you?' says Dwight to her, quietly, where Verity can't see. Lowell is bending down and cuddling Argyll and apologising to the runtiest dog (even though she is still pretty big, and almost pure white) for making her sleep in with the rough boys.

The effect on Essie is instant and devastating. Essie wants to ignore Dwight or tell him he's utterly ridiculous. Instead, she feels a bolt of pure lust shoot through her. She wants him to take the leather and tie her up and . . .

She quickly turns away.

'Okay, I'll take Bute home tonight,' she had said. 'Cheer up my mum. God knows *I* can't.'

Lowell looks up.

'Say . . . say hi from me,' he says.

35

The hospital had attempted parking charges, and quickly changed its mind when confronted with the evidence that adding parking wardens to areas with limited public transport and ill and stressed-out people was having profound negative effects on the overall health profile of its base, so had reversed its policy lickety-spit. The new car park, however, was about a kilometre from the actual hospital building, and everyone who worked on site covered their ten thousand steps in corridors alone, so it was still doing them some good.

Unusually, Lish, Janey and Amsan meet up at the same time, closely followed by Owen.

'Unbelievable,' he is muttering in the way people do when they pretend they are talking to themselves but they really want you to ask what's wrong.

'What's wrong, Owen?' says Lish, who is, as usual, the soul of kindness.

'I don't get it,' says Owen, holding up his phone. 'My fax parts person has just gone out of business.'

'Is it because faxes are Not a Thing?' enquires Amsan, not as pleasantly as Lish.

'That's weird,' says Owen. 'Because they're how we run this hospital?' He strokes his tiny beard.

273

Amsan looks at his black beaten-up Honda, with heavy metal stickers all over it. 'Do you own that car?' she says.

'Yeah,' says Owen sarcastically. 'It's a sweet ride.'

'Are you single?'

'Amsan!' whispers Janey.

'How's Essie doing?' says Lish as they reach the rotating door.

'Good, I think,' says Janey. 'She's at Lowell's all the time now.'

Lish wrinkles her nose. 'I'm sorry to hear that.'

'Oh, no, it's good for her. And she's still working on the houses – I think if she project manages this successfully they might cut her in on the deal or something.'

'What is the deal?' says Lish. 'I don't understand.'

Janey shrugs. 'I *think* Dwight gives them his money and the properties and they sell them for lots more than he'd get otherwise.'

'Who to, though?'

'Investors.'

'Well, that's no use, is it? Not to the local community.'

'It puts money back into the community?' says Janey, trying to defend Essie. 'Dwight makes money, and the houses might be for rent . . . ?'

Lish sniffs. 'Well, I don't understand business. But I understand we can't find anywhere in town to move to.'

They want to move so Johnson doesn't have to drive everywhere and can get about on foot now his recovery is starting in earnest. It does him good to have an incentive to walk about the place. Also, if she's in town more, Lish can spend even more time with her children and grandchildren than she already does.

'She's heading back to Edinburgh,' says Janey. 'She's got an interview for a part-time job there too. She's hoping to do both.'

'There's no stopping your girl,' says Lish.

'Well, that's true enough,' says Janey.

'At least she's getting on. She's happy,' says Lish. 'You've done your job. You were there when she needed you.'

'I don't think she appreciated it.'

'She doesn't have to. That's the definition of kids.'

'I suppose.'

But Janey can't stop musing on the fights, and the distance, and the misunderstandings, and the heating bill. And her awful feeling of failure. She'd hoped that this would be the time Essie and she would heal, get over the divorce, the blight on their lives, the thing Essie could not blame her dad for. Her dad who hadn't even been over to see her in the past seven weeks. Another reason why her mood must have been so awful, she told herself.

'You suppose right,' says Lish, turning to face her. 'You did your job. Whatever she was like, whatever place she was in. You're still "home", until she can build one of her own. Or build one for some weird hedge fund finance guys, but I don't really understand all that.'

'Thanks,' says Janey. And she means it.

It's almost eight a.m. She heads off to her Portakabin. Lish goes up for another day in the Brand-New Life trenches. Owen descends to the basement somewhere nobody has ever been, where they think he has a small alcove next to the incinerator.

★

And Essie is so excited to be leaving. Packing for Edinburgh, reading up on the company she's interviewing for – she is, she knows, behind, and she knows it's her fault. She is trying nervously to figure out if she can afford to move back if she gets work with Tris's firm. Her dad has not been much use but he has, at least, offered to stump up a deposit on a new room, so that's something too. She's learned a lot from Lowell, she tells Janey. Project management has been very interesting. She doesn't mention Dwight quite so much now. But everyone can see the houses taking shape next door: the window frames going in, carefully; the wood floor laid that looks like parquet but isn't really. It's clever, Janey has to admit. Verity even comes down the day the sofa arrives – one of the houses is going to be dressed before it's sold, which means they've rented furniture and Verity has chosen most of it. The sofa is orange and the rugs are burgundy. Essie was a little doubtful but in fact it turns out to have been a rather excellent choice.

'This is my house,' signs Verity, in a way that is crystal clear to everyone what she means.

*

In Janey's surgery her first patient of the day is speaking slowly, but carefully. She doesn't have any kind of an accent, but that might well come.

Janey smiles sympathetically.

'I know,' she says. 'I forgot to mention in advance. It's amazing how many people think it. It seems obvious now.'

Saanvi was a young woman who'd arrived in the UK to work, and gradually worked her way up the waiting list for a cochlear implant.

'I just thought it would.'

'I know.'

She is far from unusual. It was just not something that occurred to most hearing people: that she had expected the sun to make a noise.

'Just the wind, I'm afraid. And the rain.'

'Snow?'

'No, that's one of the things people like about it. It's completely silent.'

Saanvi thinks this is funny and shakes her head. 'Still. The sun, though,' she adds.

'What sound would it make?' says Janey. 'Humming maybe, or singing?'

'Singing,' says Saanvi decisively. 'I love singing.'

Saanvi's fresh joy in the glories of music has been a wonderful thing, although Janey hopes her music preferences – at the moment, Bonnie Tyler and Meat Loaf – aren't a dreadful inconvenience to her neighbours.

Janey's phone flashes. She had been showing a client who was losing their hearing how to get their phone to show notifications without making a noise, and had forgotten to change it back and just got used to it. She ignores it, and it goes again.

'Someone's trying to get in touch,' says Saanvi, whose phone of course does the same thing. Janey can't believe how improved her speech is.

'They can wait,' says Janey. But the flashing doesn't stop.

'I am going to listen to all the songs about the sun,' says Saanvi, getting up.

'Excellent idea,' says Janey. 'Start with George Harrison. The Beatles,' she adds. 'Ooh, and Katrina and the Waves. And *The Mikado*! And "Sun is Shining and So Are You" . . . Okay, I'm going to make you a playlist. It won't be quite as good as the sun itself singing. But it'll be something.'

She quickly glances at her phone before calling in her next client. And then her heart stops.

It can't be true. It can't be.

But it's there in black and white: breaking news. The BBC. You can only really believe things when they're on the BBC.

★

She has missed calls from everyone. Lish has been in touch. Milton too. Everyone who follows the news and knows her well.

But not Essie. Not Essie. Not again. Bloody financial news. What the hell is happening to this country?

★

A boutique Edinburgh investment fund collapsed at close of business yesterday in what insiders are already suggesting may have been a 'Ponzi scheme'.

★

Janey grabs her glasses, scans the text in a panic, unable to make sense of it in her head.

★

Tristan Morgan, director of the fund known for its huge returns and its hand-picked clientele, was not at home last night as the news began to spread and desperate investors turned up at the office, only to find the doors locked.

★

Janey's heart is in her mouth. She can't let down her patients, who have been waiting for months to see her, but she sleepwalks through till morning break at ten, then, unable to face the canteen, sends an emergency WhatsApp to her friends.

As soon as they enter the consulting room, carrying treats, she knows they all know. And they know she hadn't been sure. It had never felt right. She didn't believe in doing anything with her money that she couldn't touch and feel or live in or eat. Which was why, of course, as Essie kept pointing out, she was always poor.

But Essie had accused her of never being proud of her.

So she hadn't said anything. She'd known deep down something wasn't right about this, and those boys – so young, although she knew they didn't look like that to Essie; she thought they were men. Janey knew they were boys bluffing their way through, showing off, like when Al came home from school at fourteen and said apparently he was the only virgin in the class. That was what little boys did. And sometimes they invented Facebook or rockets. But sometimes they just blew everything up.

Lish hugs her. 'This is Essie's thing?'

She can only nod, the lump in her throat too big, the blood in her veins running freezing cold.

'Have you spoken to her?'

'She already hates me, Lish,' says Janey suddenly, all of it coming out of her without her even wanting it to, without her wanting to say anything at all. 'She thinks I'm stupid and slow and to blame for the divorce and a total idiotic waste of space! And this will just make everything worse! She'll blame me for making her live back here or not giving her advice or not knowing about money or . . . I don't know. It's all my fault somehow. She'll never speak to me again!' She screws up her eyes. 'Oh God, that's before I even find out what the rest of the village thinks.'

'I thought you said it was a town,' says Milton in his gentle way, and they all look up, surprised, as they realise that's Milton's way of trying to make a joke.

'That's even more people,' says Janey, sobbing. She keeps staring at her phone. Nothing.

'What have you got on the rest of the day?' says Lish.

'Community visits.'

'Just say you're not well,' says Lish. 'They'll get done. Half the hospital is off sick anyway. Go and find your daughter.'

'She doesn't want to talk to me. She won't even pick up the phone.'

Lish rolls her eyes. 'She's your *daughter*.'

36

The stupid thing is, at the moment she gets the call, Essie doesn't even realise that she is happy. Undeniably, undoubtedly happy. It is a lovely morning and she is in the garden at Lowell's house, braiding Verity's long dull hair, while the puppies cause trouble at their feet. They have already dug so many holes in the flowerbeds that Lowell has more or less given up on the garden for the summer, but he is being good-natured about it.

Essie is good at braiding and has, at Verity's pointed requests, taken up long chains of daisies and is weaving them in and out of the braids. They have a mirror set up and Verity is undoubtedly approving. The wind remains chilly, but in the pretty garden they are well sheltered from the wind and can sit in full sunshine; like most Scottish gardens, it is not designed to shade but to trap, so it is perfectly comfortable out here in their cardigans.

Lowell brought her coffee, paid her cash – an undeniably comforting thing to have in her pocket – then vanished to do some work, so it is just her and Verity, who doesn't choose to say much to her – they have the iPad, too, which she can write on if needed, but the girl is happy to have her hair braided and Essie is happy to do it. Verity has, it seems, taken a liking to Argyll, Lowell's favourite. She glances at her longingly, nestling her under her hand. There will, Essie thinks, be no dogs left at this rate. She wonders how Dwight is getting on with Smokey, then tells herself not to think about him. Stupid cowboy.

Verity stares very hard at her hair from all angles. The sweep of the braids is transformative, taking the lank locks and giving her head height and grace. It's undeniably pretty, and Essie is proud of her handiwork.

'We could put some streaks in it,' she says to the girl's face. Verity looks excited then shocked.

'Toxic,' she writes down.

'And it's not toxic. We could use a natural colour like henna.'

Verity's face is suddenly full of longing. She hasn't stopped staring at her painted nails either. Essie suddenly wonders about taking her shopping – her clothes are horrible, plain and far too young for her – then realises maybe she's going too far . . . and then, suddenly, the phone starts to buzz, and buzz and buzz, and Verity puts her hands flat down on the earth, because she can feel it.

★

She realises Verity is tugging at her skirts; realises she is frozen to the spot. Her brain cannot compute what she's looking at. It can't be. It just can't . . . Tris's fund . . . there is a picture of him, in the newspapers, his face hangdog. No mention of Connor's name. But.

The moment is endless: the moment when you realise you have hurt yourself, but before the pain reaches you, before it's reached you, that split second, when you know it is coming and nothing, absolutely nothing can stop it. She sits there paralysed, waiting for the blow.

Verity continues to pluck away, wanting to show her that Argyll will give her a paw (if she grabs it vehemently, repeatedly), but Essie can't even see her. Oh, my God. Dwight. The cottages. Everything. Everything. Every single penny.

It's been a week. The money will all have been transferred.

And the deeds to the properties.

Oh, my God. Everything. Of course. It all makes sense. No wonder Tris was willing to let Dwight into his fund. He must have been desperate to stop it all collapsing. And it hadn't been enough.

They are the definition of collateral damage.

Verity goes and fetches her father.

'Essie, what is it?' She has gone white as a sheet, and he is very worried she is about to faint. 'Sit down . . . you're freezing.'

He takes her inside instead. The puppies romp along behind them, but for once he doesn't even notice, as they trail mud from his ruined flowerbeds on to his pristine wooden floors.

'What is it? What's happened? Is it Janey?'

Essie just about unfreezes her head for long enough to shake it, and Lowell lets out a sigh of relief. He fetches her a glass of water and, by the time he gets back, with trembling fingers she has managed to pull up the story and shows it to him. At first, he doesn't quite understand it – he hasn't been following – then he looks at her.

'This is linked to you?'

Panic flares in Essie again.

She nods mutely and breaks down in sobs. Verity creeps forward, reads the story on the phone but doesn't understand it. Nonetheless her little paw pats Essie on the shoulder, which makes Essie sob even harder. Lowell thinks he had better call Janey, double quick, and, just as he is thinking this, Janey bursts through the door, not even bothering to knock. The puppies go nuts.

'Essie!'

Janey is bright pink and she's sweating and her hair has escaped from its bobble but she couldn't care less. Lowell in contrast is rather impressed: she looks like a proud Valkyrie, determined and fierce and, frankly, incredibly sexy.

'Darling. Darling,' she says, unfortunately to Essie, Lowell thinks. It would be quite nice if she were saying it to him.

Verity signs frantically and Janey, anxious to lower the emotional temperature in the room suddenly – Lowell looks rather startled too, Janey can't help but notice – crouches down and rapidly signs to her. 'You know how your dad thinks you're still a baby sometimes?'

Verity nods her head vehemently.

'Well,' she signs, speaking out loud at the same time. 'This is my baby.'

And she sits down and takes Essie in her arms, and she meets no resistance.

37

Janey eventually glances up at Lowell, even as she's helping Essie out to the car.

'Sorry,' she says. 'I'm sure you've had enough drama.'

He shakes his head. 'Don't be ridiculous. Is she going to be alright?'

'Nobody died,' says Janey, loudly. 'Nobody's in hospital.'

Verity's face relaxes as she reads Janey's lips, and Essie feels even worse, for not explaining herself to the little girl.

'Sorry . . . ' she manages, before her entire face crumples once again.

'Ssh,' says Janey. 'Let's get home and get this sorted out.'

As if. As if there is any sorting it out.

This is a community where memories are long. And this is a community that has lived on the breadline for a very long time. The beautiful hills, the green fields, the rich waters conceal some very poor people indeed. When Janey started her career, it was not at all uncommon to visit homes without electricity. People remember bad harvests, hungry nights. People's grandparents were crofters, who lost it all, overnight. The wolf is not always far from the door, even now.

She steels herself. 'Come on.'

She nods gratefully at Lowell, who has his arm around Verity, who isn't resisting him either, and half-drags Essie, who only has the very faintest idea where she is, out to her car, which is parked half on the kerb at the worst angle, and they drive off, Lowell and Verity visible in the rear-view mirror looking highly concerned.

The radio blares on automatically, an oldies '80s and '90s station that normally makes Essie grimace, or keel over laughing, depending on the mood she's in. Today she just sits there, motionless, as Janey shuts it off, looking at her; her heart full, bursting all the way up to the teeth with how much she loves this wayward, ambitious girl of hers, every single inch of her, remembering the little face contorted in a rage as Al had knocked down one of her sandcastles and she had systematically kicked his bike in a fury while he aggrieved her even more by laughing; her set face as she did her maths homework in the kitchen, even as, God, she and Colin had tried to have their fights quietly in the back room. Who had they ever thought they were fooling?

She sees teenage Essie, thin, determined, opening the website to find her exam results; the smile creasing the face; a dam bursting inside Janey of pride and adoration and love and the bittersweet knowledge that it meant her girl would go; her darling baby girl, who used to cling in the night, beg her to stay in bed with her – which she would often do, if it meant not having to go back to her lonely bed – in case she had 'mightmaze'.

The little paw hands, holding on to a lock of her hair.

Had *she* made Essie run so far away? Made her change so much; made her try to be completely different from Janey, in every conceivable way?

She'd voiced this deep, awful fear to Al one night, and he had merely smirked and said, well, in that case she could also take full credit for him turning out terrific; and she had laughed then, but she remembered – of course she did – Al being born and arriving in the world, serene, passingly interested . . . and Essie showing up, fists balled up, shouting at it suspiciously, always spoiling for a fight. She finds herself thinking, ridiculously, of the puppies: Smokey, hopping about from the second he opened his eyes, getting into mischief, establishing his dominance; little chunky Bute, fussing about like a big-bummed busybody, a matron among the dogs; timid Argyll, leaning into Lowell as her protector. Felicity hadn't made them that way, she told herself.

It doesn't change how she feels. She leans over to her stunned, unhappy girl and, as they turn into Seagate, lays a hand on her arm.

Essie clasps it.

'It's a mistake,' she says, her face still very white. 'It's definitely a mistake. They've made a mistake.'

'It's on the BBC,' says Janey, gently. 'They don't . . . I mean, they will have checked it a lot.'

Essie looks up at her mum, her face terrified. 'But that means . . . '

Janey wants to gather her up in her arms but knows that that won't work well at all.

'I would love to say . . . I would love to say I know how it can be fixed,' she says eventually. 'I'm not . . . I don't know, Essie. I'm sorry. I really am.'

Essie's face stiffens even more. 'I can't . . . it can't . . . '

She jumps out of the car, runs, up the stairs.

★

Janey goes to fetch some food for lunch, but she can tell already from the atmosphere in the bakery that word has got around. Jean the hairdresser is in there.

'What's happened?' she fusses. 'Is it true Dwight's lost the cottages? Lost everything?

'I . . . I don't know,' says Janey.

'Was it those boys that were up with your Essie?'

'I think . . . I don't know. Maybe. It's all confused. Essie didn't know anything about it,' she says, quickly and fiercely. 'She's in pieces.'

Jean shakes her head. 'So he handed over everything he had, everything that was invested into this town, into some smart-talking boys from the city and . . . they just made off with it?' Her lip curls, and Janey can't blame her. This is, indeed, exactly the size of it

'What's going to happen?' says a man on the other side, with a doleful beagle who is looking plaintively at the sausage rolls in an atmosphere of eternal hope.

'The bank will take it,' says Jean, as if she knows everything. 'If this Tristan Morgan owes people money, they'll take whatever he's got and give it to whoever is owed the most. Or who was owed it first.'

Janey realises the truth in what Jean is saying while being simultaneously being annoyed at her for framing the problem so succinctly. The hairdresser runs a small business; she knows how all of this works, only too well.

So Dwight will lose everything – and it will probably go to some dodgy Edinburgh bloke who had invested money he could well afford to lose, years back. And if it truly is a Ponzi, to someone who had probably been benefiting all along, making money right from the start.

She closes her eyes. It just gets worse and worse.

'So Essie didn't know,' says Jean.

Janey shakes her head crossly. 'Of course not! She wouldn't do that in a million years!'

There's a pause as, blank-faced, Carrie the baker lets Janey beep her phone to pay. Nobody says anything. But Janey can feel it, hanging in the air, and it's unbearable. Essie still brought those men to Carso.

Alasdair phones as Janey is leaving and she answers the phone, grateful to have something to distract her from all the eyes behind her, watching her go.

'Fuck a duck,' he says, which at least has the bonus of being concise, as well as appropriate.

'I know,' says Janey in a low voice. 'There's nothing good to say about it.'

'These are those stains Essie worked with, aren't they?'

'Yeah.'

'So she . . . '

'Oh, God,' says Janey. 'She didn't know. Nothing about it.'

'Oh, come off it,' says Al. 'They were so obviously *dick-heads*.'

'Yes, but I'm not sure that's unusual when it comes to bankers. It doesn't mean she could know they were crooks.'

'Oh, my God,' Al says. 'You know what it took Dwight to earn that money.'

'I do,' says Janey. 'I know what that family went through.'

Al sighs. 'Oh, God, Essie, the stupid, stupid . . . '

'Al.'

'No, but, Mum . . . '

'She's made a mistake . . . '

'No,' says Al. 'Making a mistake is when you put on the wrong colour of shoes or accidentally knock someone's wing mirror. *That's* a mistake. This is a fucking disaster, and it's not even her disaster. It's Dwight's.'

Janey sits on a wall, holding the cooling bag, talking to Al until she feels herself calming down. But she doesn't know what to do, and Al hasn't a clue. He hasn't heard from Dwight; it doesn't sound as though anyone has.

Oh, God. She's not going to lose her house, is she? No. She can't. Essie has nothing to do with it. Apart from opening the door to Carso: inviting the wolves in.

She drags herself home.

'Essie?' she yells. 'Sweetie? Come on, let's eat.'

But there is no reply. Essie has gone.

38

Lowell answers the banging at the door, and sees Essie has come back again. He's read all the news reports now.

'Essie,' he says. 'You have to go and talk to Dwight.'

'No time,' she says.

'What do you mean.'

'You know about this stuff,' she gasps.

'What do you mean? I don't know anything about finance. I'm an architect.'

'Not about the finances! That's pretty obvious. No. You know about housing.' Essie glances at her watch. 'I have to catch the midday plane,' she says, in a warning voice. 'You have to tell me about the housing office. Also,' she says, in a slightly meeker tone, 'I need to borrow the money for the plane ticket.'

Roused from her iPad, Verity jumps up excitedly, waving, and Essie waves back. Verity beckons her over to show her that she has taught Argyll to raise a paw for a piece of cheese without having to yank her. And Essie, for all her impatience, the headstrong mess she's made of everything . . . she goes over to her. While Lowell is pulling up internet pages that might help, and printing them out, she goes and sits and watches patiently while Verity shows her.

That's her mother, Lowell thinks. That's Janey all over. He sighs internally.

'Have you asked your mother?'

'No,' says Essie. 'She'll lock me in the kitchen. Please, Lowell. Please just answer my questions and then I'll go.'

'Do you promise not to incriminate me to the police?'

Essie doesn't want to think that this might be a police matter, even though it so obviously is. She just has to do something.

'ABSOLUTELY,' she hollers back, while still holding Verity's gaze.

★

Lowell drops her at the airport and she just makes the flight.

She hasn't been able to think straight from the second she was sitting in her mother's car, surrounded by love and sympathy, realising she had everything. But this is her mess and she has to do something. On the flight, her fists clench. And then her fury turns outwards, towards Connor, Tris, the whole frigging arrogant lot of them, the smug, rugby-loving bastards, listening to any old BS. And she'd fallen for it.

Her stewardess friend, Gertie, hasn't heard the news yet, and thinks her tension is due to Essie being a nervous flyer; she comes and says comforting things to her, which Essie barely hears, but feels guilty at more kindness she doesn't deserve.

The little plane judders and hops and comes in to land on the huge international runway in Edinburgh, just behind the vast Airbus coming from Doha; the tiny tin bus they're in bounces down in its slipstream just behind it.

Essie jumps down the steps and tears through the airport hordes towards the tram stop, hopping in just before it glides off, then paces, anxiously. She can't think about everything, can't think about the mess she's left behind her. She has to keep moving.

She jumps out on Princes Street, the castle towering above her, unchanging through history, which normally she finds comforting but today she doesn't give it a second glance. She tears through the crowds enjoying the bright light and cool winds blowing down from the north, charging down Frederick Street into the grey grids of the New Town, the cacophony of traffic, sirens, people, buskers, socialist workers completely overwhelming; it's amazing how quickly she'd forgotten the noise and the chaos of the city, got used to the quieter, easier pace of life. This seems crazy, to try to fit so many people into such a small place. Buggies skirt huge grey cobblestones; bicycles take daring swoops around the statues, trying to quickly make it from one truncated bike lane to another without being run down by irate taxi drivers. It's absolute havoc. Out of breath, desperately enervated, she pounds past the people reconstructing their favourite scenes from *Good Omens*, *One Day*, *Trainspotting*, appears in hundreds of people's photographs of the beautiful city, a fleeting glimpse of a striped T-shirt, blurred, in the background, later removed from some as spoiling the image, kept in some as a view of a living city in motion.

But Essie is heedless, and runs, on and on, towards her goal. He has to be in. Where else would he be? And will the others be there? She will deal with that as and when. She certainly isn't calling ahead. Isn't warning anyone what she's doing.

She is making for the flat. The flat is part of an entire circle, or circus as it's called, on Moray Place: a perfect set of tall houses around a beautiful round park – private, of course, to the lucky people who live there. No traffic is allowed to drive around the circus, which means children can play happily in the streets or jump in and out of the gates, into the rose garden and past the flowerbeds towards the swings. It's heavenly. Looking upwards through the elm trees towards the tall glass windows of the ancient buildings, far away from the noise of the city, it is easy to believe you are in the past, back when these houses were built, and the ladies would stroll to their garden, lifting their long skirts up from the mud and mess of the cobbles; and the noises would be carriages, not the zoom of electric cars and the far-off ding of the trams.

Essie realises as she approaches the flat that she has been terrified there might be police there, or journalists, but there aren't; it is the same as ever. It is going to destroy lives, but it isn't even the worst thing happening that day, which is a sobering thought.

She doesn't ring the big old metal doorbell. She hasn't heard from Connor. Which means he knows and Tris knows and they all know that what has happened is unspeakable. Which means he won't want to see her. People hate, she knows, people who make them feel they are behaving badly. Or make them feel guilty for not being better. She thinks briefly of her mother, then banishes the thought.

One of the downstairs neighbours, an elderly woman who is made up immaculately every day, her hair set, with a tiny dog she takes for slow, meandering walks while it barks furiously at every dog, child, lamppost and blade of grass it encounters, is on her way out and, recognising Essie, gratefully lets her take the weight of the big black entry door. That beautiful big, heavy door, that leads to the black and white tiled entrance; the curling black wrought-iron balustrade that loops the stone steps gracefully up to the three flats; the usual jumble of expensive estate agents' magazines on the marble-topped table next to the huge gold-framed mirror that hangs by the door. Essie does not stop, as she normally does, to check her make-up, but instead hurls herself up the steps, two at a time, to Connor's flat on the third floor.

And now Essie is back at the flat; the place she so coveted and so adored; had always dreamed of.

The circus is still quiet and beautiful; there are still gardeners making the private garden perfect, and the hollyhocks are starting to show. But those glorious shining doors with their brightly polished knockers, the elegant secret back gardens that go down the banks to the Water of Leith . . . this one has something ugly behind all its beauty.

Essie hammers on the front door. She doesn't know what she will do if Tris answers. Surely he'll be busy, or in hiding or something. The reports said he'd been taken in for questioning, she doesn't even know what that means. Presumably he has access to some very expensive lawyers.

She hammers again. No response.

Then it occurs to her that, if Connor is in there, he might think it is the police. She kneels down to the letterbox.

'Connor? Connor. Let me in. Please. It's me. Sweetie, I just want to make sure you're alright.'

There is a feeling in the air; there is a way you can tell that there was someone inside. The air is disturbed, just a tiny amount.

'Sweetie, I'm worried about you. Darling. I just want to see you.'

Essie feels bad, briefly, for lying. But it's small beer compared to what's happening.

'It's just me, darling. I just wanted to give you a cuddle and . . .'

His pale, strained face is visible through the letterbox.

She can tell by his expression that he wants to believe her so much. She doesn't want to say it's going to be alright, in case that's going too far and he'll be able to tell immediately that she's lying. She smiles at him, as sincerely as she can. 'My love.'

'Oh, God, Essie. I've been so . . . I've been so scared . . .'

'It's okay,' says Essie. 'I just want to make sure you're alright.'
And he opens the door.

★

'Give me the office entry code.'

Connor is blinking. He looks awful; he is in his pyjamas, unshaven, and he obviously hasn't slept. All his pink and white clean-cut freshness has gone. Which means he must have known this was coming. None of his sleek suits or Burberry raincoats today.

'What? I can't . . . '

'Okay,' says Essie, ice-cold. She was an idiot. He is an idiot. He is an idiot who worked in the actual criminal office and shared a flat with the criminal, so who even knows how deep in it he was.

'Those first investors of Tris's when you set up this fund – it's his rich uncle, isn't it? Who owns this place. It's all his family?'

Connor stutters, his eyes darting about. He doesn't recognise this Essie, his sweet, quiescent girlfriend. Hasn't recognised her since she moved back north, in fact; her behaviour in Carso was completely out of character too. He doesn't understand anything.

'Uh, yeah – yeah, I think so. They gave him seed money to begin with—'

'So they'll be the first to get their money back,' says Essie, almost to herself. 'And it will be the little guys, the last-minute guys who suffer.' Then she repeats, 'Give me the office entry code.'

'Don't be daft. There's people there,' says Connor miserably. 'It's a crime scene. It'll be crawling with police. And you can't touch anything; you'd be interfering with evidence. You can't do anything, Essie. It's all gone.'

'Fine,' says Essie. 'Well, then, it doesn't matter anyway. Give me the code.'

295

'No way.'

'I'll tell them . . . '

She realises just as she starts saying it that she doesn't know whether this is true or not, is too scared to even let herself think. She finishes the sentence anyway.

'I'll tell them you knew.'

He freezes, and the colour drains from his face.

'I didn't. Essie, you have to believe I didn't.'

'You spent a lot of time saying it was a fund for ultra-high net worth. Then you all let in some two-bit rigger, no bother at all.'

He's white. Essie lets the silence hang.

'Tris told us . . . he told us it was going to be fine. He was going to get sorted. I didn't . . . I thought it was just a bump. Honestly. I promise.'

'Give me the code.'

'You have to believe me.'

'Give me the code.'

'They'll have changed it now probably.'

She waits.

He sighs. 'It's Tris's date of birth.'

'Oh, my God, that is *so lame*. I could have got that from his Facebook. How could you ever think he was a financial genius? I bet the password on his files is password 123.'

Connor looks up at her, blinking. 'Are you . . . '

'Don't worry, I'm going, I'm going,' says Essie. She looks at him, his expensive haircut, his expensive watch. Everything she ever wanted, standing in tears like a little boy who has been caught with his fingers in the honey jar.

'I didn't know,' says Connor. 'You have to believe me.'

She doesn't know if it makes it more pathetic if he did know or if he didn't.

The downstairs doorbell rings suddenly. Essie has a sudden premonition that it is the police.

'I'm going.'

Her voice echoes off the beautiful tiled hallway, the great echoing ceilings with their moulded roses, the expensive bookshelves, the beautiful paintings; the expensive glorious building, all of it, built on the wreckage of people's dreams; on other people's money, earned on the windswept platforms of the North Sea; earned with sweat and graft.

Connor stiffens suddenly, as if annoyed she dares leave.

'You go now,' he says, 'and we're done.'

She just stares at him, jaw dropping that this is even an issue.

'Well, duh,' she says.

39

Essie is absolutely terrified to see them but does her best to look insouciant as she passes the two police officers at the front door on her way out.

She heads away from the flat, slower now, out of puff, the adrenaline still pumping, slowly crossing past the beautiful round park, where nannies rock babies still in beautiful, expensive, high Silver Cross prams; up round Ainslie Place, with a quieter, smaller park, where the less well-behaved dogs are taken to be exercised, the green metal circles on their collars proclaiming that they have the right to enter the private parks in the way most humans do not; and up and across the busy Queensferry Road.

The investment firm is low-key, barely noted outside, except now, because it has a couple of photographers and journalists outside it, and a police officer on the door. Essie's heart beats faster. This is happening. It's terrifying. This is a big, notorious criminal Ponzi scheme imploding and the world is interested.

What would they do if they caught her? she wonders. She could pretend she was looking for a toilet, got lost, say nothing. She's white, middle-class, they would probably just tell her to piss off.

Worth it.

★

She sneaks round the back of the street, to the tiny hidden mews behind. Goes to the little door she knows from back in their wild early days. The door to the next-door house, which also leads to his office, in the maze of old Edinburgh terraces, the little corridors, that hot night . . . she sighs, remembering.

She can't think about that now. She has one shot at this, the very worst thing she has ever done. But the alternative is worse still.

40

Janey goes driving about, desperately searching for her daughter in the town, more worried with every second that passes.

She can see people looking at her, in her familiar red Kia. She is used to being the ear lady, to being liked, stalwart member of the choir and the book group once she'd started picking herself up from the divorce. Part of the town; at the Christmas Fayres, the Easter egg hunts. Now it is unsettling when people look, and wave, or don't. What are they thinking? Are they thinking, there's that Janey with the daughter who thought she's too good . . . you know what she did?

Would Essie be with Dwight? Janey screws up her face. She can't bear it. She will have to see him at some point. There was nobody at the buildings next door to the house, nobody working. She doesn't know where Dwight lives, but she could try the End of the World . . . but what would she say? And would she even get to say it before Shelby punches her in the face?

She goes everywhere else, everywhere she can think of. The harbour, the walks, the forest. Looking for Essie, staring at her phone, calling, calling, calling.

Eventually, almost without realising it, she finds herself right at the very edge of town, outside Lowell's. Essie wouldn't be back here, would she? Hiding out? Of course not.

She's about to turn round, when Lowell sees the car and comes out into the garden.

'It's been a very busy day, with one thing and another,' he says to her.

'Is Essie here?' she says, desperate, and he shakes his head, then, when she bursts into tears, he pulls her towards him and hugs her tightly.

Even in the depths of her misery and pain she takes comfort, so much comfort from his broad presence, his reassuring arms, the pencil-sharpening scent of his sweater. Part of her wants to stay there forever. But she can't.

'I've lost her,' she says, trying not to sob.

Then Lowell says the best thing he possibly could.

'I know where she is.'

★

He leads her inside. Verity looks up and smiles to see her. 'Essie's mum!'

'I'm Janey, too,' says Janey, but she smiles back at her as she signs it. 'Has she been here?'

Verity nods and beams. 'She came to say goodbye and talk to Daddy. When is she coming back?'

Janey looks at Lowell, wiping her eyes, confused. 'She came back here?'

He nods.

'Is she in trouble?' signs Verity.

Janey starts to sign 'no' but then realises she has no idea if that is true or not. This is trouble, alright.

'I don't know,' she manages finally. 'I just want to talk to her.'

'Nobody is allowed to be mean to Essie,' signs Verity. 'She's the best.'

Janey lifts her hands then drops them again. Then she raises them again. 'I believe she is too.'

Lowell shuffles his feet a little. Then he tells her. And then she goes ballistic.

41

Essie is, it turns out, right. Police Scotland are wildly over-stretched. Tris is already in custody, being interviewed by the lead detective, and finding, for possibly the first time in his life, someone he cannot charm with his money, good looks and connections; in fact, quite the opposite. Detective Sergeant Nisha Malik has met a few people like Tris in her time, and she doesn't care how expensive the jacket is that he's wearing; her world is divided into radges, neds and bawbags, and this one is a bawbag.

Tris's expensive lawyer, who looks exactly like him except a lot fuller and redder in the face, keeps trying to get him to shut up while also feeling distinctly queasy, partly because of the amount of port he drank at the Malt Whisky Society last night, and partly because he recommended more than a few people to Tris's incredibly successful wealth fund himself, and they are all going to be out for blood.

There is a uniform on the front door of the office, stopping people from going in, but the other police on the job are still at Moray Place, trying to get Connor to stop crying for long enough to put his shoes on.

There is nobody on the back door.

★

Inside, the office is deserted and there is yellow tape on the office door. Yellow tape stating in absolutely no uncertain terms that this is a crime scene. That, by entering it, Essie will be entering said crime scene. She wonders if there is CCTV anywhere. Then she remembers that Tris has been committing massive fraud for years. The absolute last thing he would want is CCTV around the place.

Okay. She doesn't have long. They'll be back, or she'll make a noise. Or she'll just lose her nerve.

She squats under the tape, and dashes towards the first pile of papers.

★

'What the hell??'

Stupid bloody open-plan house. There is nowhere to go to have a proper argument without Verity being able to lip-read or even tell from their backs that they are having a massive argument. Janey orders him into the laundry, where the dogs go mental.

'She might go to prison!'

'I think there's plausible deniability,' Lowell says as gently as he can. 'Janey, she was going to go anyway. I couldn't have dissuaded her.'

'You should have locked her in this laundry until I could get here! She's out of her mind.'

'I don't . . . she won't get into big trouble!'

'You don't know that!'

'It happens all the time. Look at all those American presidents who take papers home. They won't waste police time on her.'

'YOU DON'T KNOW THAT.'

'Janey, she's an adult. She was going to do it anyway. I just told her what she was looking for.'

Janey bites her lip and folds her arms, breathing heavily. Her face is pink. Lowell suddenly, unexpectedly, finds he is incredibly turned on. He squashes the feeling down. This won't do at all.

'What *is* she looking for?'

And he tells her, and she takes out her phone.

★

There are piles and piles of paperwork, printouts spread every-where. Essie scans a couple. They look like profit and loss accounts, with adjustments, presumably. He must have been paying some people out of fake accounts and . . .

She's pretty sure this must be what Connor was doing: being the sweet, innocent front man, showing off the pretty P&L accounts, keeping the money flowing. That absolute bumhole.

Nearest his desk she finds a pile of post, unopened, wait-ing for him. Her heart races. She goes through, glancing at the postmarks . . . and then, finally, she sees it.

The Land Registry. Lowell showed her what it looked like.

Her phone rings. The noise in the room is shocking, horrify-ing. She fumbles with her phone; how could she have been so stupid? She's clearly not cut out for a life of crime. She pulls it out – OMG, her bloody mother, again. She presses no and tries to turn the phone off, but now her hands are shaking far too much to manage it.

Downstairs, she hears a noise. It's the crackle of a radio. She freezes. There's a muttering, but behind the windows she can't tell what the police officer is saying. She glances around. Everything else is just sheets of paper, investment brochures, marketing leaf-lets. Nothing that makes any sense. The radio crackles again. Her blood is throbbing in her veins. She grabs the envelope, jumps over the tape as quietly as she is able, dives down the stairs, tip-toes down to the back door and out into the mews as quietly as she can, shutting the door millimetre by millimetre.

She wants to run but doesn't dare. She is terrified of hearing, 'Stop! What the hell are you doing?' And at the far end of the mews is where the CCTV will start, if they do suspect someone of being in the building.

She has one chance. She texts Lowell.

And then, once again very quietly, she turns, heart pounding in her chest, to the old black wooden door, which doesn't look as if it has anything to do with the glossy office, which is indeed a relic of a different time . . . and gently slips inside.

★

Janey puts the phone down.

'She's still not answering. She's probably in police custody.'

'I didn't know she hadn't told you.'

Janey is teary with rage. 'Well, she hadn't. You didn't think I'd be worried out of my wits?'

'She seemed . . . resolute. Organised. Janey, she's a grown-up.'

'She's *my* grown-up.'

'I'm sorry,' says Lowell. 'I thought it was best. Janey . . . she's a wonderful girl. She's just . . . she's so amazing with Verity and . . . I mean, it's been lovely having her come in here.'

Janey is speechless. 'Thank you,' she says finally. 'Thanks.'

And then, finally, the phone rings. Not her phone. Lowell's.

42

Janey is completely furious once more as Lowell picks up.
'Where are you?'

'Hiding in a hayloft. Long story.'

'Did you get it?'

Essie fingers the deeds to the cottages. 'I did.'

'Good. Now we need to let the Land Registry know. You've got a cooling-off period. It should just make it. And very, very quickly, before the police start going through the paperwork.'

'You can't call them,' says Janey, staring at the website disconsolately. 'You can't email them either. There's a form. It needs a signature. And then a copy of the deeds, initialled. That's the withdrawal procedure.'

'You need Dwight to sign a form *and* initial the original deeds?'

'That's what it says here.'

There's a pause.

'But we don't have *time!*' says Essie, in agony.

'Can't we get Dwight down there?'

'There isn't another flight today,' says Janey in a low voice.

'Bring the deeds back here,' says Lowell. 'Can you make the return?'

'If I run,' says Essie.

'Well, do that. We'll figure it out from here. It's already good you've got the deeds.'

'Okay,' says Essie, then hears a siren in the distance and abruptly hangs up the phone.

'So if we have the deeds, and withdraw the property transfer instruction from the Land Registry . . . '

'It might work,' says Lowell. 'Unless they realise it's missing from a police point of view first. In which case it will go into the bankruptcy pot . . . '

'And pay the earliest investors back first.'

He makes a noise of agreement.

Janey stares down solemnly. 'Oh, Christ. Come on, Essie.' She looks up at him. 'And you recommended she do this?'

'No!' says Lowell immediately. 'She was absolutely going anyway. Her plan was to punch everyone in the face. I just suggested . . . something that might be more useful.'

Janey searches his kind, shrewd, unapologetic face. 'But won't they track her down?'

'Why would they? Nobody knows the deeds were there except for Tristan, who will be expensively advised not to say a word, and Dwight, who won't if he knows what's good for him. If the withdrawal note is in and we have the deeds, it won't be worth their while to chase it down.'

'I need to get to Dwight.'

Lowell nods. 'He needs to sign the withdrawal letter.'

'And then . . . ' She can't let herself believe what this might mean if Essie doesn't make it. Or even if she does . . .

'We'll see,' says Lowell. 'Don't . . . let's just wait and see for now.'

She can't help it. She hugs him, his big scratchy jumper, the comforting heft of him; the pleasant smell of graphite and flowers from the garden, and just a trace of puppy. He puts his arm around her. It is suddenly alarming to them both how comfortable and comforting this is; not embarrassing, not strange. Not strange at all. And suddenly something shifts in the air between them as she rests against the large bulk of him she has dreamed of, the adrenaline still in their bodies, caught up in the excitement of the moment, and for once she isn't thinking about her wrinkles or her breasts or her to-do list or her family. She isn't thinking about anything apart from how much she wants to kiss this man's soft lips, and she wants to kiss them now.

The laundry door opens without a sound. A small, exasperated person is standing there signing furiously. 'What are you doing?'

They both freeze. Janey disengages herself, as the puppies run up to Verity to rasp at her with their little tongues and bite her shoelaces. Verity's giggle is curious; startlingly loud and deep. It is lovely to hear it.

Janey steps outside and opens up her hands.

'Your dad,' she signs, even as he moves ahead and opens the door and they all tumble out into the garden, the sea in the air, the early afternoon sun with warmth in it, as the meadowsweet blows. 'Your dad did something very brave and kind to help my daughter.'

'Essie?'

'Yes. It was brave and kind and possibly a bit stupid.'

Verity lets out a giggle again, eyeing her dad curiously. Then she pulls Janey down so Lowell can't see them or make out what she's saying.

'Is he a good dad?'

Janey nods. 'I think he is a very good dad,' she signs as emphatically as she can. 'And I think he loves you very much.'

'Mum says . . . '

'Your mum is a very clever person. But also . . . '

This is a lot to sign. She's more used to discussing treatment options, or discussing Frisko the Bear with very small patients.

But somehow, in this other language, she feels freer. Her hands can express so much more, than even saying it. As she says it to Verity, this solemn child caught in the middle of something nobody understands, she wishes she were saying it to Essie – realises she should be.

'Sometimes if people love a child but not each other . . . it can make things very difficult.'

'Like when Daddy gave Felicity away because he was so sad?'

'Exactly like that.'

'Does Mummy hate Daddy?'

Janey thinks back to her own feelings. Well. Yes. Maybe. But children don't need to know that; shouldn't have to inherit it. They should be protected in every way possible.

'She's just sad. Sad that you don't all live together and that it has all happened. Sad. That's what it is.'

Verity nods. 'It makes me sad too.'

'I know.'

'Does it make Daddy sad?'

Janey thinks of him in the bluebells. 'So sad.'

'Does he hate me?'

'Never. You are his best thing in the world.'

Verity looks at her, frowning. 'Should I cuddle him?'

'You don't have to,' says Janey. 'It's up to you. You don't have to cuddle anyone you don't want to. But I should say he would like it.'

Verity nods.

Then she stands up, the imperious little figure, like a tiny queen with her long hair, the noble dog never leaving her side, and walks up to her dad, who is extremely happy to be overwhelmed for the second time that day.

43

Essie's phone rings one more time. She looks at it. It's an incoming Zoom call.

It's her interview. It was today, and she completely forgot.

She looks at it for one long moment, longingly, a little. But then she thinks of the scandals, the greed, the misery of where she's been working. And she thinks of what it has done to Dwight and her community, and remembers the happy days they have had, building the place from nothing; looking after the pups, scraping the wallpaper, helping Verity choose the furniture. She stares at the phone for a long time. Then she closes her eyes very tightly, and presses 'cancel'.

★

After twenty minutes of not hearing a thing outside, the longest twenty minutes of Essie's life, desperately needing to catch the return flight, she creeps downstairs, through the opposite exit of the mews, tries to walk innocently, which is a very difficult thing to do if you haven't had to do it before, and jumps on a tram straight back to the airport. Gertie is surprised to see her on the turnaround.

'Hiya!' she says. 'That was fast!'

'Gertie,' says Essie, 'do you think if anyone asks if they saw me today you could possibly say you didn't?' She has had enough quick thinking for one day. 'I was organising a surprise for Mum. For her birthday.'

'Oh, how lovely!' says Gertie. 'I should do something like that for my mum; she's always complaining she doesn't see enough of me because she only sees me three times a week.'

Essie smiles awkwardly.

'What did you book?'

'I . . . can't . . . remember.'

Gertie frowns, but she is an understanding type of soul, so she leaves Essie be. Essie sits on the left-hand side of the tiny plane, near the back, and, unable to move right at this moment, her hand inside her handbag, holding tightly on to the letter, the adrenaline draining from her body, she instantly falls asleep as a tall man sits down beside her, pulling out his police file. Financial crime is not normally quite as interesting as this.

★

The End of the World pub is shut when Janey pulls up to it in the afternoon light. She can hear the shouting from the outside.

Shelby is comparing Dwight to their idiot dad, which is a terrible comparison. Janey remembers him; he made Colin look like Man of the Year. At least Colin had stayed till the kids left home. Kenny was a drifter, in and out of their lives, always with a guitar on his back, and a sad song. He would make huge promises to his children then never turn up at all. Or turn up out of the blue, arrive at the school with gifts and surprises that completely overwhelmed them. It was an awful thing to witness, Shelby trussing herself up every day with the eyelashes and the make-up, just in case that was the day her daddy came, even years after it was clear he wasn't coming at all. Their mother dragging them to all those dances and competitions, in the hopes of once again catching the eye of the steel guitar player.

Janey feels the utter shame of her family doing this to their family, as if they hadn't been in the same boat.

She knocks quietly at the back door. Shelby answers, her face murderous.

'What the hell are you doing here?' she says. 'I hear Little Miss Princess scuttled back to the city.'

Someone must have seen her at the airport. Janey looks past her. Dwight is sitting at a table, hat in front of him, whisky in front of him, head drooping. His normal cockiness has completely gone; instead, he is pale and shell-shocked by it all. He doesn't even raise his head.

'She didn't even come to say sorry,' spits Shelby. 'Took our money, took our home, and waltzed off fancy as you please.'

'Shelby,' says Dwight. 'This is all my fault. There's no point in trying to pretend it isn't.'

'None of this would have happened if it hadn't been for her!'

'I had a choice,' says Dwight. 'I was greedy. It's my fault. I had my shot, and I missed it.'

'Um . . . ' says Janey. This is obviously a conversation that has gone round and round the houses. ' . . . I've got a message.'

'We don't want to hear it.'

Shelby goes to shut the door in her face.

'Let her talk,' says Dwight, suddenly, pale white, his knuckles clenching the glass, as if she might have brought a tiny bit of hope.

Janey thinks of the bank loan, the mortgage, the deeds. Can this possibly work?

She takes out the piece of paper she managed to get printed.

'There's a small possibility . . . '

Dwight squints. 'What's this?'

'Essie has gone to Edinburgh and "reclaimed" the land deeds. You need to sign this to withdraw them from sale. And the deeds as well.'

He frowns.

'There's a cooling-off period,' says Janey. 'The problem is it expires today. And the office closes in just under three hours.'

'We can't get there,' says Dwight.

'Can you email it?' demands Shelby.

'I'm afraid not.'

Janey had already phoned Morag, the local pilot, to see if there was anything she could do. Morag is sympathetic but says it's not even a question; there isn't a slot for them at Edinburgh airport and even if there were, it would cost more than the price of the houses in the first place. That's not the answer.

'I could drive,' says Dwight.

'You'd die,' says Shelby. 'Stupid idea. It's three hundred miles.'

Janey sighs. 'We'll think of something. Essie will have the deeds back here soon enough.'

Dwight's phone rings. His face creases.

'It's the police,' he says. 'They want to interview me.'

★

The little plane bounces and hops to a stop in Carso on its afternoon run, the sun chasing their tail all the way north. It's one of the most beautiful trips in the world on a good day, the Highlands in all their glory stretching out on all sides. Essie doesn't notice a bit of it. She holds her bag with her fingers on the papers.

Essie gets down the steps just as the policeman is getting his bag. She doesn't notice him.

Her mother is waiting in the draughty tin shed that functions as an airport and runs towards her. Essie discreetly shows her the envelope.

'Oh, my God,' says Janey. 'You're an international criminal.'

'I'm a fricking idiot,' says Essie, ruefully. 'I'm ... Mum, I'm ... '

Janey shakes her head and hugs her. 'You're everything.'

Dwight is waiting outside by his car. 'The policeman's here,' he says. 'I'm meant to meet him.' He glances up in terror.

Then, from Dwight's car, an absolute vision emerges.

It is Shelby. Her bright blonde hair is piled high on her head. Her face is made up perfectly and she is wearing a lacy white top that makes her enormous bosoms look even larger, on top of a denim skirt and pure white pointed cowboy boots. Her eye-watering perfume fills the air.

'Can you get us a couple of minutes?' says Janey urgently.

'Can I?' says Shelby.

And she walks – no, she sashays, in a way that cannot help reminding Essie of Bute – over to the policeman who is already slightly disorientated by the freshness of the air, the great long views out to sea, the sense that the mountains and bens are all behind you and that you have landed at the very tip of the world.

Shelby touches his arm and smiles up at him with her huge spidery eyelashes. He turns to her, like a hypnotised man.

'*Quick!*' hisses Janey to Dwight. 'Sign them! Sign them now.'

Dwight scribbles his name on the page, his hand shaking, and Janey whips them away. Shelby glances back, and Dwight takes a deep breath.

Janey fumbles the papers, drops them as she tries to stuff them in her bag and retreats towards her own car in confusion. Fortunately she looks like any other slightly overworked middle-aged woman who has lost her car keys, and everyone completely ignores her.

'Mr McFlynn? shouts a voice across the car park.

Shelby stands back, satisfied.

'Oh, God,' says Essie. 'Remember, don't mention the houses. Just the money.'

'Damn it all to hell,' says Dwight, straightening up.

Then he grabs Essie, pulls her tightly towards him, kisses her full on the mouth with a force that leaves her limp and breathless, then strides off without a backwards glance to meet the policeman.

44

'What are we going to do with them, though?' says Essie, clambering, rather breathlessly into the car with her mother.

Janey stares at the deeds and the form, both of which she now has. She had, with exceptional but, she believes, forgivable sneakiness, dated it yesterday, and is hoping she might be able to blame the post, but will that be enough? They watch Morag and Gertie leave the terminal; there are no more flights today. It is four p.m. They are too late.

'I can't believe they won't accept email,' says Janey, as Essie morosely scrolls through the Land Registry web pages. Then she stops suddenly.

'Huh,' she says. It's an old, cached page. She shows it to her mother.

'No way.'

They look at each other, then Janey takes off at speed.

★

They gather reinforcements en route. Lish stands there with the expression on her face she employs when she is telling women to either push or not push and requires immediate obedience. Milton is carrying a Tupperware container of his famous chicken stew, a rare delicacy most people would give anything for. Essie smells it and realises she hasn't eaten all day and Dwight nearly made her swoon and she could do with some to revive her, but her work isn't done. Amsan turns up; she has Yasmin in tow, a round, soft, huge-eyed beauty, wearing her usual faintly truculent expression and dragging her heels. Daughters, thinks Janey, smiling faintly.

En masse, they descend into the basement. It is twenty to five.

★

Considering that the rest of them work out of Portakabins, or a dank porter's lodge, Owen's den is quite formidable. It is a windowless corner of the basement, very warm but incredibly spacious. He has two huge screens – how? what for? – which appear to be showing some kind of massive star-based computer game. Piles of tech litter the desk. His seat is a top-of-the-range black leather console chair. They look at each other in disbelief.

Owen spins around dramatically as if he's been waiting for this moment.

'Aha,' he says, pointing his fingers underneath his chin. 'My quizzers. We meet at last.'

'We see you every second Thursday,' points out Lish.

'Ssh,' says Janey, panicking while looking at her watch. 'We need him on-side.'

Milton steps forward with his Tupperware and lays it quietly on Owen's desk.

Owen frowns. 'Has it got vegetables in it?' he asks. 'Because I'm allergic?'

Essie whips the tub away and stores it for later.

'Owen,' she says in her sweetest, most appealing voice. 'Owen. Could we possibly use your fax machine?'

'Is it for official hospital business?' says Owen.

'Not exactly.'

'Well, no, then,' he snorts. 'Okay, next? And maybe next time bring cake.'

'Owen,' says Janey, 'this is important. Really important.'

'To you,' says Owen, still eyeing the Tupperware with disappointment.

'Have you got any cake?' whispers Janey to Lish.

'Johnson's diet!' says Lish. 'Nothing!'

Owen is looking smug. 'Well, nearly clocking-off time. I never work a second after my schedule.'

The others, who regularly work vast amounts of time over their schedule, for no extra money, try not to look furious.

'Please, Owen,' begs Essie.

'For what?' says Owen. 'So you can totally ignore me in a pub again? I'm amazed you remember my name.'

Essie flushes bright red. She was awful that night. Angry and snotty and determined to look down on everything in Carso, even though those very same people were around helping her now.

She clutches the piece of paper, fingers shaking.

A small cough sounds at the back.

'I've got some custard doughnuts,' comes a soft voice from the depths of the gloom. Everyone turns round.

It is Yasmin, Amsan's unfortunate daughter. Her dark hair glows in the soft light as she steps forward, rummaging in her handbag.

Owen stops suddenly.

'He-hello,' he stammers, in a much less assured tone.

'Hello,' says Yasmin in return. 'I like your big computers.'

'I'm management,' says Owen quickly.

'That's amazing.'

She offers him the bag with two custard doughnuts.

'I told you to stop buying those,' mutters Amsan.

'I haven't even shown you the best bit,' says Owen. 'Come here.'

And he stands up, grabs the bag and, ignoring the rest of them, walks Yasmin into the centre of his Starship Enterprise control booth.

'Wow, what's that?' she says, eyes wide.

He smiles in satisfaction at being able to tell someone something they don't know. 'It's . . . a fax.'

'How does it work?'

Amsan beckons urgently for the papers from Essie, who hands it over, panicked. It is five to five.

'Well,' says Owen, but Amsan has already smuggled the papers to Yasmin.

'I mean,' goes on Yasmin, 'can it send anything? Could it send these?'

'You genius,' says Janey under her breath.

They watch as, anxious to show off, doughnut crumbs all over his beard, Owen, as if he is doing something profoundly difficult and sacred, punches the number into the fax machine.

It actually whistles and burrs, a noise familiar to the older generation and quite startling to the younger. Yasmin jumps, and Owen puts a tentative comforting hand on her forearm.

And slowly, ringed in darkness, they all watch the pieces of paper disappear. And then there is nothing to do but wait.

45

Essie runs to the Seagate cottages first thing the next morning. Dwight is there already and they fly into each other's arms.

'What did the police say?'

'I told them about the money,' says Dwight. 'And they wrote that down. But they don't know about the houses.'

His phone beeps. He pulls it out. She is clinging to him, she finds, and she tries to pull away, but he casually grabs her and pulls her in tight with one hand, opening the phone with the other. She finds this incredibly sexy for some reason.

He whistles, and touches his hat with his phone.

'What? What?'

He shows her.

It is the confirmation from the Land Registry that they have received the withdrawal notification.

'Oh, *that* they can email,' says Essie.

The door opens and Essie and Dwight leap apart instantly, which is probably just as well, as it's Shelby. She grimaces.

'Hey, sis,' says Dwight.

'Okay, everyone wants to know what they can do to help,' says Shelby, looking around the place. 'Get it finished, if you can.'

Word has obviously spread quickly. For once Essie doesn't mind.

'I've got the timeline,' she says.

'I don't need to talk to you,' says Shelby. 'The one who made my brother give up everything.'

'I didn't *make* him do anything,' says Essie. 'Although I'm sorry I introduced him to those guys. I didn't know they were crooks.'

'You're sleeping with one of them.'

'Have you never slept with a crook?'

Shelby thinks about this for a moment. 'I think I've only slept with crooks.'

'Lay off, Shelbs,' says Dwight, but she ignores him.

Essie steps forward. 'Shelby – why . . . why were you always so mean to me?'

'*Me*?' says Shelby, turning back, her face completely astonished. 'Me, mean to *you*?'

Essie blinks, slightly taken aback. 'Yes. You know, at school.'

Shelby looks at her, astounded. 'What are you even talking about? You marched around the whole time talking about how Carso sucked, how you couldn't wait to get out . . . and always boohooing in the toilets about your parents fighting, when *you* still had a dad, two parents, a home. You knew where your dad was. You know we had to leave our council house? Move into a bedsit? Because Kenny threatened my mum?'

Essie goes quiet. She had not quite realised this. She knew they had had a divorce too; that was all she'd thought. And she'd thought that Shelby hadn't given a toss.

'You treated us all like idiots. Then and now.'

Essie's hand flies to her mouth. I mean, everyone joked about the tiny town, didn't they? It was hardly a town at all, really, just a village that happened to have a Scot Nor minimarket which gave it ideas above its station.

'I didn't mean to.'

'So you keep saying,' says Shelby.

'I'm sorry,' says Essie. 'You were always so pretty and so popular.'

'Is that what you think?' says Shelby. 'That I had it easy?'

Essie remembers the way people whispered about Dwight and Shelby's family, bad things, half heard, half remembered. Bad stuff. A bad lot. She shakes her head.

'I got . . . I think I got a lot of things wrong.'

There is quite a long pause, and a draught is getting in the house.

'Well, it's good of you to say it.' Shelby draws herself up to her full height, bosoms on full point, checked shirt tied at the waist, eyelashes to put Dolly Parton to shame. 'But if you ever, ever, ever think you are slumming it with my brother . . . you'll have me to answer to.'

'Understood,' says Essie, watching her turn around and head up the little close – an indomitable woman, she realises, from a bloodline, a tradition, an entire musical culture of indomitable women to whom men have done wrong. And she does understand.

Dwight looks at her, grinning.

'What?' she says.

'You think my sister's tough, wait till you meet my ma.'

46

Sure enough, all of Carso suddenly descends on the Seagate cottages, taking direction from Wee Jim, showing up with an unfortunate number of unnecessary carpet oddments and strange cushions and of course – of *course* – everything knitted for a house that can conceivably be knitted for a house. Antimacassars and curtains – curtains! – blankets, cushions, throws, a lampshade which looks point-blank dangerous. Essie's eyes are wide. Verity shows up, armed with a new set of knitting needles and looking ready to get stuck into the fun. Gradually the oil rig boys take over with the hammering, and, as the afternoon creeps on, Essie, utterly exhausted – she barely slept – looks around to see where Dwight has got to.

He's out, on the other side of the street, looking out over the sea.

'Hey,' she says, joining him.

He glances up, nods. He's holding up a stick; Smokey can already jump up past his thighs.

She stands in front of him. 'You okay?'

He shrugs. 'I was an idiot.'

'So was I. I was worse. And you still lost the bank loan.'

'I'd have lost it all if it wasn't for you. I'd have lost everything.'

'My mum said . . . ' begins Essie.

'She's alright, your mum,' says Dwight.

'She really is,' says Essie.

She thinks back to the trip to the hospital in the car, dashing across the hills in the tiny red car she had disdained.

'I'm so sorry . . .' she had begun, and Janey had turned to her.

'You never, ever have to apologise to me. I'm so sorry it was so hard on you.'

Essie had thought of the missed calls; of the fact that her father hadn't come to see her even once.

'No,' she had said. 'I get it. I do. I'm sorry.'

She had watched the little pretty town in the side mirror, vanishing behind them, nestled between the sea and the soft rolling hills. How had she never noticed how beautiful it was, how lovely; that it was home.

'She said . . . it's good to get your mistakes out of your system while you're still young. She said it quite a few times, in fact,' says Essie.

They look out over the bright blue water, the tips just bobbing white in the northern breeze.

'What were you thinking now?' says Dwight, and for the first time since she met him again he seems slightly nervous.

'What are *you* going to do?' she counters. 'With your properties. That are now full of . . . ' Former Essie would have said 'absolute tat,' but new Essie says, ' . . . a lot of eclectic things.'

'Well, I thought . . . I thought I might take one of the cottages myself. And then the other ones . . . well, your mum's friend Lish – her husband needs somewhere he can walk to work . . . '

'That's a good idea,' says Essie neutrally.

He looks at her.

'Maybe . . . I could come and stay for a little?' Essie says.

Dwight shrugs, but suddenly the cocky twinkle is back in his eyes.

'That sure depends,' he says.

He pulls her close, until they are hip to hip. She fits him perfectly. She finds, immediately, that she is trembling. The effect on her is extraordinary. He leans his lips to her ear, and she feels him hard against her. He whispers in her ear.

'A man has needs, you know. Reckon that's something you can handle? Because I am planning on being in the business of not really letting you go.'

'That,' says Essie, 'is probably the only business we should be in for a while.'

And she puts her hands in the back pocket of his tight jeans, and, as the houses are still full of people, they go and take a very long walk, along the great crashing empty beaches, into the wide, glorious white sand dunes, utterly deserted, where they can make as much noise as they like, underneath a sky blown white and clean and new.

47

It is puppy day. Janey has woken up with a heavy heart.

Verity went back to her mum's two weeks ago, at the end of the Easter school holidays, but has insisted Thalia bring her back for this. She is clinging to Lowell and Felicity. Janey and Essie are there because Ahmed is going to give them all their vaccinations and their certificates before they get handed out to the world. Janey cannot help but notice how affectionate father and daughter are, and how much happier Verity is. She's filled out a little and has some pink in her cheeks, and happily runs around through the distinctly careworn garden. Janey pretends with all her might to be very engrossed in combing Freuchie's beautifully lush snow-white coat, as opposed to the terrible wiry bits and bobs the others have got in odd places, when the small car draws up.

Ach, there is no doubt. Thalia is lovely-looking. Shiny hair pinned up; a thin face with high cheekbones that Verity has absolutely inherited. Her mouth is pursed and her eyes cool; she is wearing baggy hippy trousers rather too loose for the weather, Birkenstocks and a variety of feather bangles, and glancing impatiently at her watch, which doesn't really sit well with the hippy aesthetic.

Janey glances at Verity, who looks awkward and torn, then looks at Essie. They share a look of deep understanding.

Verity is signing frantically to her mother, and trying to introduce her to all the puppies at the same time. 'What's she saying?' Essie whispers to her mum.

'She's saying she wants to move here, to be nearer Felicity and Daddy,' says Janey. 'I'm glad she mentioned her dad.'

Thalia raises her eyebrows and signs something back.

'She says . . . she's saying she can't afford to live up here,' says Janey.

Essie looks at her seriously. 'Is that really what she's saying?'

'Yes.'

Essie frowns.

'I mean, if you knew of anywhere . . . ' adds Janey. 'She looks as if she likes handmade things . . . '

'*Mu-um.*'

Verity comes bouncing over and stands in front of Essie, looking up at her.

'Goodbye,' she says, out loud, slowly and carefully. Thalia scowls.

Essie takes two fingers to the side of her nose and signs, 'See you soon.' And then they hug and Janey watches.

As the car drives off, Lowell is by her side. He can't speak. She takes his hand and squeezes it firmly.

'I just miss her so much,' he says.

'I know,' says Janey. 'But I once tried to keep something together that shouldn't have been together. And that didn't really work.'

He squeezes her hand back, and she sees tears glistening in his eyes. 'I know,' he says.

'I think she'll be up a lot more,' says Janey. 'Now she's seen you're not trying to cut her brain open.'

'Oh, no, I did that, that's why she's so cheerful now.'

'*Lowell*!' and Janey is giggling. Although her smile fades a little as Ahmed comes up the path.

'Okay,' she says, 'you're about to get your house back. Are you going to miss them?'

The puppies are all trying to eat the bees that are buzzing around the wildflowers that have sprung up as Lowell has been short of time to work in the garden.

'Am I going to miss sharing my space with seven farting cart-horses? Not really,' says Lowell.

'Are you absolutely sure you're not tempted?'

He shakes his head.

'Really?' Janey is sad. They've told the village that if anyone wants a dog, they should show up at two. There are already quite a few bids in for Freuchie.

'Apart from Argyll, you mean?' says Lowell, with another smile, and bends down. Argyll has her wet nose on his trousers. Janey hadn't even noticed her. She seems to stick two inches away from her master at all times.

'I never even saw her,' says Janey. Lowell picks her up lovingly, even though she is now extremely ungainly, even as the smallest in the litter. She has a grey fringe over her eyes and a snout so long she looks like a cartoon and she gives Lowell several licks. He holds her gently while Ahmed gives the jabs with speedy efficiency, and stills her surprised whimper with soothing words and cuddles, while Felicity pads around the vet, looking confused and slightly irritated.

'And you?' he says in return.

'Mum, you promised,' says Essie.

'Did I nothing promise!' says Janey.

Essie picks up Bute, with her big fat flolloping bum, and brings her over. Bute is wildly excited by this turn of events and scrabbles around excitedly, clawing Essie thoroughly in the process.

'Mu-um,' says Essie in her most wheedling tone. 'Can we have a dog? Can we? Can we?'

Excited, Bute barks loudly.

'Oh, lord,' says Janey. 'I thought my life was supposed to get *quieter.*'

'Great,' says Essie. 'Oh, I have to take Freuchie too.'

'*What?*'

But before she can ask any more, Essie has disappeared with both dogs.

Janey and Lowell look at each other.

'Who's left?' says Lowell. 'Eriskay?'

Eriskay is digging a large hole in the flowerbeds.

'Ah,' says Janey. 'I'm afraid I rather promised him early.'

And sure enough, a car pulls up, before Lish gets out and goes round front side and opens it. Emma is in the back and comes to help. As the dogs start yipping, very, very slowly, they raise Johnson up out of the front seat and help him with his walker. He cracks a half-smile, and inches to the pavement.

'Well, well,' says Janey going forward, smiling.

'You said come early,' says Lish. 'But there are no dogs left apart from the really funny-looking ones'

Johnson has a slightly worried look on his face and Janey looks around for a garden chair. Lowell of course doesn't own anything as vulgar as a garden chair but leads him over to a minimalist bench. Janey starts to wonder. She had thought this was a brilliant idea, and Lish had agreed; something to take Johnson's mind off things – his recovery would be ongoing for a long time – and get him out of the house and exercising again. They had both been rather proud of themselves and Lish had sworn the children to secrecy.

But Johnson is frowning – his usual expression these days, such a change from the friendly face he wore before – as he sits on the uncomfortable bench. The left side of his face is still a little droopy, Janey observes. Emma covers his knees in a blanket and Lish and Janey swap glances, then they lead Eriskay over. Eriskay has found something in the flowerbeds – at first Janey dreads to think, but it turns out to be a small wooden mouse; Verity must have lost it.

Eriskay drops it at Johnson's feet and looks up, his ugly fuzzy face expectant and his pink tongue out. There is a moment of silence. Then, very slowly, Johnson leans out his right hand and scritches the dog on the head. The puppy's tail thumps on the ground.

'What's his name?' says Johnson.

'Eris—' starts Janey.

'Whatever you like,' says Lish, quickly.

'He's the colour of a dustbin,' says Johnson, slowly.

'You can't call him Dustbin,' says Lish. As she says this, Eriskay looks down at the wooden mouse again and picks it up, nearly swallows it, almost starts choking and has to be picked up and patted on the back. He is clearly not the smartest of the beasties.

'Dusty?' says Emma. And they decide, on balance, that Dusty is a very good name for their new grey dog.

There is a commotion on the street. It is a whole line of cars, and nearly two o'clock.

'Oh, crap!' says Janey. 'We've only got Caithness left!'

Her phone pings with a message: *Hi sis. I forgot to say, keep me a dog. Love you!*

'Ah.'

'I didn't think anyone would want one of these dogs,' says Lowell. 'Except for Argyll, and they can't have her.'

He backs away protectively.

'We'll get going,' says Lish, kissing Janey. 'He's a hunk,' she whispers in Janey's ear. 'I mean it. Keep hold of him. Shame his house looks like such a mess. Also you might want to have a word about his trousers.'

Lowell's trousers are covered in dog slobber.

'Uh-huh,' says Janey, as they help Johnson back into the car, where Lish throws open the boot and shows the secret cache of pet supplies all picked up and ready to go, including a seat belt.

'I love you,' says Johnson, haltingly.

'Course you do,' says Lish as they all drive off.

★

The cars are starting to park up the narrow road.

'Oh, no,' says Janey. 'Me and my big mouth.'

'That's village life,' says Lowell. 'Word gets around.'

'What shall we do?' says Janey, watching two families – oh, my God, with children – getting out of their respective cars.

'Let's pretend we're not in,' says Lowell, and he grabs her hand and pulls her round to the back garden, entering through the back door. They put Felicity, Argyll and Bute in the laundry together, where the puppies curl up and go to sleep, circling and clearly a bit confused as to where the others have gone. Janey nearly tears up again, but reminds herself they'll be seeing their siblings around town all the time, and Smokey is with Dwight.

She gets Lowell to give her a pencil and paper and writes 'ALL DOGS GONE. SORRY' and sticks it out of the letterbox just in time to hear some disappointed noises from outside. She winces, but Lowell looks at her and she finds that in fact she can't stop giggling.

Lowell on the other hand is walking around as if he can't believe it.

'I've got my house back,' he says. Then he frowns. 'Well, when I've tidied it up.'

The previously immaculate empty property is no more; on every surface are pictures, friendship bracelets, bottles of nail polish. Janey knows better. She knows him. His innate orderly instincts have been overwhelmed by how much more he enjoys life with his daughter around.

'Don't tell me you gave her your iPad,' says Janey.

'I'm expecting the angry phone call in three, two—'

His phone actually rings and they both jump, and burst out laughing. Then Janey's starts ringing too. They have some very annoyed, frustrated dog-lovers out there. It appears somebody has been crocheting dog jackets, from Janey's messages.

Al calls. 'Did you get a dog for Essie and not for me?'

'I'll call you back,' says Janey, and turns her phone off.

Lowell comes towards her. 'I just wanted to explain . . . what it was. With . . . marrying a younger woman.'

'You don't have to,' says Janey.

'No, I do . . . Janey, it's the optimism. The hope. That everything might be alright. And I am so sad and battered by the wars of love, and midlife, and getting older and everything that means, and I wanted someone who still believes in happy ever after, and the future. And older women can be just so sad. And that makes me sad. Because they've been let down by horrible men. Men just like me. And it makes me feel ashamed and shabby. That's why.'

Janey takes this in for a moment and looks out of the window. A moment of quiet sadness settles on the bonny garden, teasing them in all its brightly coloured young beauty: the first blush of the slowly ripening strawberries; the straggling, laughing daisies; the tentative, unfurling rosebuds, the poppies gradually standing higher, waiting to puff out into their full summer crimson beauty – then fade, then die, like everything else, as everything must. Janey looks around the garden for a long time, and at the hangdog shape of the large man in front of her. She doesn't know how to answer what he's just said. Because it is true. And she doesn't want to be sad any longer.

'Even if they know all the lyrics to that song by Sharpe and Numan?' she asks, finally, tentatively.

At first, he looks confused. Then he glances up and there is a twitch, just the tiniest twitch of a smile at the corner of his mouth.

'Change Your Mind?' he says.

'Well, it's not an instruction,' says Janey. 'I just really love that song.'

'I really love that song too,' he says. 'I thought nobody else remembered that song.'

'Not if they were born in the year they made that song.'

'Yeah, yeah, yeah.'

He looks at her and pulls one of the roses out of the simple vase he keeps on the table. 'Here,' he says quietly.

'Oh, goodness,' says Janey, looking at its perfection and beauty.

'I'm sorry I hurt the rose bush.'

She strokes the velvety soft petals and holds it to her nose. It smells so fresh and sweet and new. She closes her eyes.

'I feel like the Queen Mother,' she says. 'I shall put it on a hat and be eccentric.'

'No, you shouldn't,' he says. 'You don't understand what I'm saying. I'm saying what I used to feel like. Before I met you and realised that was rubbish. And I'll be away a bit but not all the time, and oh, for God's sake, Janey, let's just pretend that getting older doesn't matter.'

And, gently but firmly, he cups her face with his large hand, and kisses her hard on the mouth.

And Janey, who has feared and worried in her deepest, most solitary moments that she might never be kissed again, feels an extraordinary wave of happiness; relief and joy crash over all at once; gives herself a moment to just feel it. And then another, to realise, with joy anew, that the person kissing her is Lowell and that there is no one in the world she'd rather be kissing.

He towers over her, cradling her face with his large hand and, suddenly, he stops.

'What?' says Janey, panicked.

'I can't kiss you if you won't stop smiling,' he says. Then he frowns, that characteristic little line on his brow she has grown so familiar with. 'Unless you're laughing.'

'I'm not laughing,' says Janey. 'It's a happy smile.'

He grins back at her.

'I . . . good,' he says.

'I'm sorry,' she says, terrified she's going to giggle, nervously. 'It's . . . I'm out of practice.'

'We weren't very practised at eighteen either.'

'True.'

'Shall we discover it together?

She has never been to his bedroom, of course. He takes her small hand in his huge one and leads her upstairs. It is on the mezzanine, metal and glass lining the deep, soft wooden steps. The window looks out over the fields behind the house, so they don't have a view of any dog-deprived rioters.

Even his bed is beautiful: simple wood, pale grey sheets. What an interesting man he is, she thinks. What an interesting person he will be to discover. And then she starts to panic again.

'Oh, goodness,' she says. 'Why aren't we drunk?'

'Because we're too old and we have to drive places and it makes us feel really terrible the next day.'

'Oh, yeah,' says Janey. 'Well, is it too much to ask for dim lighting?'

'We don't have to do this, sweetie.'

'No,' says Janey. 'I'm just wittering because I'm nervous. Can you shut me up, please?'

And he absolutely can. Just to kiss him is a delight; she loves the warmth and bulk of his body. She was right: he does have a hairy chest to go with his thick hair, and she runs her fingers through it, inhaling the wonderful scent of him.

And he, she notices, doesn't ask if she minds a hairy chest, or apologise for his large girth which she doesn't mind a bit, finds comfortable, in fact. He is perfectly happy, she can tell, just to be there, in the moment, on a golden afternoon in spring, alive in that moment, with her.

And she tells herself that she can do that too. Step out of her scrubs, her job, her divorce, her worries and work and friends and family and care and concern. Live like a rose. She boldly pulls her shirt off in front of him and he is delighted.

'Look at you,' he says, happily, and sits down on the side of the bed. 'Can you come here, please?'

'You're very polite,' she says, walking towards him.

'Oh, you're about to find out how wrong you are about that,' he says, and pulls her towards him until she is sitting astride him.

She looks up at his face, terrified, excited, turned on, joyous, everything at once cascading through her brain. She smiles. 'We're not too old.'

'I haven't got my glasses on,' says Lowell.

'Me neither,' says Janey.

'But I can tell you I want you as much as . . . Kelly LeBrock in *The Woman in Red*.'

'Really?'

'Absolutely.'

'Well, then, I want you as much as Patrick Swayze in *Ghost* and also *Dirty Dancing* but not *Road House*.'

'Do I have to dance?'

'Not at our age!'

He grins, and then he kisses her, and pulls her abruptly closer to him, then closer still, and everything is bliss.

★

Afterwards, dazed and stupefied, astounded that it is even the same day, astounded that it has taken her until she was fifty-five to have sex like that, Janey sits downstairs, languid, unable to move, like a happy cat, a sleepy puppy under each arm. Lowell has put some Bach on his record player.

'What happened to Gary Numan?' she asks. He is dressed again – in clean trousers – and is making them omelettes, which makes her very happy because she is unbelievably hungry.

'Well, you change as you get older. I like this too now.'

She listens. She doesn't know much about classical music. It is a piano, that's about all she can tell.

'Is this sexy?' she says. 'Because if you were planning on seducing me later, I think that horse has bolted.'

'I am planning on seducing you later,' he says, tossing up the omelette, and the straightforward way he says it makes her shiver. 'But also, this is very sexy! Listen!'

She does.

'Do you hear how one hand picks up the tune and the other repeats it and turns it round? Total equality. Neither partner is dominant. Balance.'

She listens for a while until she can hear it.

'Beautiful, yeah?'

'I thought Bach was all, like, churches and stuff.'

He comes over with the pan and kisses the top of her head. 'He had nineteen children,' he says. 'Sex is all he knew.'

'And this,' says Janey, 'is why you are so very useful on a pub quiz team.'

And she gets up to join him at the kitchen table, wondering where he stands on giving large dogs small titbits.

48

Essie has been back to the fancy gift shop, which has been overwhelmed recently, and bought the biggest, fanciest ribbon she can find. It is pink and covered in diamanté studs. She adds some clip-on hair bows to keep Freuchie's hair out of her eyes. She adds a leopard print leash. Then on a whim she buys the dog a leopard print jacket. And then she walks to the End of the World pub.

Shelby is chalking up the board for that night's specials. It is Mexican night, apparently. Suddenly Essie feels incredibly impressed that somebody is having a go.

'Uh, Shelby?' she says.

'Yeah?'

'If you don't want her, there's loads of other people who do, so don't worry about it but . . . I thought for the bar . . . '

And she brings out the carrier behind her.

Shelby comes forward suspiciously. But when she sees what's inside – Freuchie with her adorable little bow and pink diamanté collar and little leopard print jacket, she can't help herself.

'Oh, mah God!' She looks up. 'Really? For me?'

Essie nods. 'I wanted to say thank you for helping us at the airport.'

'Has she got a name?'

'All yours,' says Essie.

'Wanna come in for a drink and show me how to work this thing?' she says to Essie, almost off-handedly.

'Sure,' says Essie.

Shelby is kissing the dog all over its little black nose. It is the only pretty one of the litter. But Bute is still the best, thinks Essie, stoutly.

'Well, then, I am calling you Peggy-Sue,' says Shelby, and Essie smiles.

'That's a great name for a dog.'

Shelby nods, to indicate she already knows.

'So,' she says, holding the door open, and depositing another kiss on Peggy-Sue's head. 'Seems you're going to be hanging out here for a while.'

'Seems like it,' says Essie.

'You'd better get a pair of knitting needles, then,' says Shelby, nodding towards a circle of women drinking coffee, who hail Essie. 'There's a lot of new dogs out there need winter coats.'

'It's halfway through May.'

'Yeah, don't forget how chilly August can get.'

'Plus you need to tell us all about how long you and Dwight have been carrying on,' says Gertie. 'Most of the money's on since April, and Marion reckons you're pregnant already'.

Essie's mouth gapes open.

'Also, Shelby has a police detective in love with her – he's been flying back to see her.'

Essie turns to look at Shelby, who betrays nothing, but sticks a large cup of tea in her hand.

'Come in yourself; sit down, you're very welcome.'

49

'I didn't know you turned down the job interview,' says Janey. They are walking, the two of them, the heads of spiral curls similar in the beautiful June light. The evenings are endless, and they have decided to walk along the beachfront, shoes off, jeans turned up. Essie shrugs.

'What changed your mind? Apart from me, obviously.'

They both laugh.

'I'm not even going to tell you,' replies Essie.

Janey laughs and shakes her head. 'Wee Dwight McFlynn?' she asks.

'Don't say I told you so.'

'I never ever did! I didn't see that coming in a million achy-breaky years.'

Janey is still slightly nervous, and so happy to see Essie smile.

'I think there's a lot of opportunity here,' says Essie. 'You know, Lowell's firm is doing really great work.'

It's true: Lowell took Essie on – not remotely as a favour – and she is thriving in the busy architectural practice.

'They're talking about sending me on an overseas conference,' she says proudly. 'I mean, mostly taking minutes and stuff, but even so.'

'That's wonderful!' says Janey, beaming with pride. 'Whereabouts?'

Essie shakes her head. 'Zurich.'

And Janey bursts out laughing.

They spy Al on the horizon. He is standing with someone very thin and blonde and aristocratic-looking.

Essie squints. 'Is that the same one as the last one?'

'It doesn't matter,' says Janey. 'She won't talk to us anyway.'

And they both laugh, and link arms.

'I'm seeing Dad on Sunday,' says Essie. 'I said I'd take Logan to the beach. I thought I'd build some sandcastles and let him kick them over.'

Janey smiles. 'That's wonderful,' she says, and means it. 'I'm so glad.'

Bute wiggles her arse happily, and arfs. As they get closer to the village park she has caught the scent on the wind: it is mid-summer and time for the annual village dog show.

'Ringers!' moans Janey in despair as she sees people getting off the bus with expensive-looking dog bags filled with pristine pugs wearing diamanté collars.

'Come on,' says Essie. 'They've got no chance. Shelby's bringing Peggy-Sue.'

But as they approach, they realise they have no chance. The entire town's dogs are there – Dusty, who is monstrous, now up to Johnson's waist, with a sticky-out tongue and a fringe that makes him look completely insane (or else the most beautiful dog that ever lived, according to Lish); Dwight with Smokey, who is trying to kick off with the other dogs and is well on the way to getting disqualified before they even start walking round the makeshift outdoor ring; Peggy-Sue wearing four white dog cowboy boots with her pristine hair styled and bows perched behind her ears, and it can't be, surely . . . is that *mascara?* Al and Caithness, who, it turns out, is completely terrified of deer, despite rapidly approaching foal size. And Lowell is there with wee Argyll – Janey grins at him like a love-struck teen and he looks back equally soppily but they don't hold hands because Verity is there, beaming. Both she and Felicity are in matching knitted tank tops with 'CARSO' in yellow, and pink and yellow socks, courtesy of the knitting circle.

'Well, *that's* not fair,' signs Janey, walking towards the girl, who gives them both a cuddle as the dogs sniff their welcomes.

Verity grins widely.

'Hang on, are you wearing hearing aids?'

'In case,' signs Verity with her trademark glorious fluidity, 'the judges don't realise I'm deaf.'

'Oh, my God, you are naughty.'

And Verity's grin splits her face as Janey waves politely to Thalia, who is standing some distance back, nodding reluctantly. She is signing the lease on the last of the cottages today, next to Lish, next to Janey, next to Essie, who appears to be temporarily staying with Dwight while he looks for his next sensible, slow-growth project. Essie had been quite looking forward to moving near her mother, except her mother appears to be spending all her time at Lowell's.

They parade their dogs around the ring, and Smokey is disqualified first for trying to bite an Afghan hound and then, when removed, a horse that was passing by on the beach. Dusty is out next but Johnson is phlegmatic about it – and walking, Janey cannot believe it – with only a stick. He has lost so much weight, looks so well. Lish on the other hand jumps up and is about to start a steward's enquiry but is persuaded to back down. Argyll and Bute both fail to progress, sparking much protest, and it becomes clear Ahmed is beginning to deeply regret taking on this straightforward adorable-pet-judging task he thought would be fun.

Finally only three are left standing: Verity, beaming broadly – she is short a front tooth, which can't possibly hurt her chances – Shelby, who is batting her eyelashes at Ahmed in a way that would be totally lost on both him and his husband, and an out-of-towner holding a box, who looks oddly familiar.

'Wasn't that guy on the winning team at the quiz night?' whispers Lowell.

'I don't know,' says Janey happily. 'All I noticed that night was you.'

'And how I got all the cathedral building terms right?'

'Architrave is a very sexy word.'

'Buttresses,' says Lowell instantly.

'STOP IT!'

The beach is golden; the sea freezing as usual but a glorious turquoise blue; the little plane is circling in to land; the town is full of happy people; and an ice cream van has shown up. What could be better?

Ahmed looks up from his clipboard. 'And the winner is . . . number thirty-two!'

Verity has stepped forward with Felicity, grinning, only for the smile to drop off her face. Shelby looks furious. The man with the box steps forward proudly.

'That's the most beautiful lizard I've ever seen in my life,' says Ahmed, handing over the trophy. The lizard clambers up the side of the box and peers out, flickering its tongue.

Everyone in Carso looks at each other, and then starts to laugh.

'Ach, Verity,' says Janey.

'It's alright,' says Shelby. 'I have a cake for Peggy-Sue. We can go and eat that.'

'Is it a cake for dogs or a cake for humans?' Lowell wants to know.

And they are a happy band, spread out on the dunes, passing around the cake (in fact there are two, both of which say

Congratulations, Peggy-Sue, the best dog, one iced and one made from peanut butter and cheese, which Verity prefers and sticks her fingers in when nobody is looking), and the knitters take out their knitting and Dwight and Essie sidle off early, and Lowell and Janey interweave their fingers from time to time under the sand when they think there is nobody watching, as the summer sweeps the top of the world, and it feels to everyone that they are, very much, in the right place.

Acknowledgements

Thank you Jo Unwin, Felicity Blunt, Deborah Schneider, Sarah Ballard and Kate Burton. Whew, and thank you all.

Thanks also to Jo Dickinson – hooray! – Katie Espiner, David Shelley, Alainna Hadjigeorgiou, Fiona Brownlee, Rachel Kahan, Kirsty Theocharous, Wendy McLay, Katy Archer, Sofia Hericson, Helena Fouracre, Emily Harrison, Juliette Winter, Linda McQueen, Victoria Denne, Polly Peraza-Brown, Cesar Castañeda Gámez and Sam Downs.

To everyone who came to see me and was so brilliant on my travels – Leenastiina and gang in Finland, Lisa, Amelie and gang in France, Kjersti, Jan-Frode and gang in Norway, Gabriela and gang in Czechia and Felicitas in Germany – it seems ridiculous to make such happy memories at work but I really, really have.

To the Bedford Hospital audiology department, Henry Wickham, Lit Mix, Loz King and every reader who reaches out to say hello.

Lyrics from 'Tyrannic Man's Dominion' used with kind permission of Karine Polwart and Mark Whiley Management. The quotation from *Sandwich* used with kind permission of Catherine Newman and Penguin Random House.

Dedicated to my husband. I love you, and I promise to always say it to your face and never to call you from another room.